HOW
not to
LET GO

Also by Emily Foster

How Not to Fall

Published by Kensington Publishing Corp.

HOW
not to
LET GO

A Belhaven Novel

EMILY FOSTER

KENSINGTON BOOKS
www.kensingtonbooks.com

KENSINGTON BOOKS are published by

Kensington Publishing Corp.
119 West 40th Street
New York, NY 10018

All Kensington titles, imprints, and distributed lines are available at special quantity discounts for bulk purchases for sales promotion, premiums, fund-raising, educational, or institutional use.

Special book excerpts or customized printings can also be created to fit specific needs. For details, write or phone the office of the Kensington Sales Manager: Kensington Publishing Corp., 119 West 40th Street, New York, NY 10018. Attn. Sales Department. Phone: 1-800-221-2647.

Kensington and the K logo Reg. U.S. Pat. & TM Off.

eISBN-13: 978-1-4967-0421-4
eISBN-10: 1-4967-0421-5
First Kensington Electronic Edition: January 2017

ISBN-13: 978-1-4967-0420-7
ISBN-10: 1-4967-0420-7
First Kensington Trade Paperback Printing: January 2017

10 9 8 7 6 5 4 3 2 1

Printed in the United States of America

HOW *not to* LET GO

Chapter 1

Everybody's Got to
Learn Sometime

I've never driven a moving truck before, but I drive this one for twelve hours, Indiana to New York, sobbing off and on the whole way. I listen to Beck's version of "Everybody's Got to Learn Sometime" on repeat. The sky is gray and it spits rain all day, like there's a raincloud following me east.

By the time I pull up in front of my parents' building on Fifth Avenue, opposite the park, the sky is thundery and dark, too dark for an evening in June. My parents meet me under the green awning and hug me in happy greeting. If they notice my blotchy, tear-stained face, they don't mention it. If they wonder why, when I say I'm so glad to be home, I instantly burst into tears, they don't ask.

Maybe they think it's because of the rain.

I was nine years old and living a little over a mile from Ground Zero on 9/11. Mostly what I remember is the way a bright sunny day was transformed into the uniform, infinite gray of my parents' fear, the smell of burning, and the taste of ash. It felt like the whole world was covered in ash and debris. It was Charles who pointed out to me that this is probably why sometimes when it rains I get this swamping dread that the sun might never come out again, that the universe is a fundamentally unreliable place and the laws of physics could simply stop functioning at any time.

It's maybe also why I had a thing about heights until Charles took me rock climbing and I learned to trust the harness and the rope and my partner.

Charles, I should explain, was the postdoc in my research lab—or anyway, that's what he was for almost two years: my research supervisor, my mentor, my tutor, my climbing partner, and, not least, my hot crush.

Then at the end of my last semester, we spent four weeks having sex, because I was like, "Dude, we have A Thing," and he was like, "Yes, we do, but it's not appropriate," and I was like, "Once I graduate, it's appropriate," and he was like, "We'll talk about it when the semester ends." And when the semester ended, I went over to his apartment and . . . I spent almost every night there until I left Indiana for good. Until last night.

And I—ugh, god, it seems so inevitable in retrospect—I fell in love with him. How could I not? Brilliant, compassionate, beautiful, funny, I mean how could anyone *not* fall in love with Charles?

He, I think, may have fallen in love with me, but he never said it and he told me that he was broken, that love didn't happen for him. He explained it with science, so I believed him—but I didn't believe him when he said it wasn't fixable. Everything is fixable. Except he didn't want to be fixed.

And so this morning, at the end of our month, I left before dawn, sneaking out of his bed and out of his apartment while he was still asleep, because I was too much of a coward to say good-bye.

And I drove home.

And here I am.

The super found a couple guys to move my stuff into the library, so Mom and Dad and I have dinner while the guys bring it all in. I take a shower and wash away last night's sex, and then my parents and I sit on the living room couch and celebrate my homecoming by binge-watching *Gilmore Girls,* which was one of my favorite shows when I was little.

And then I go to bed alone. I lie there, wondering what Charles is doing, how he feels, how he felt when he woke up and I wasn't there.

The swamping shame of sneaking out like that is too much. I curl up in a ball, teeth gritted, and try to soothe myself by making lists in my head of the many valuable things I've learned recently:

- How you feel about a person doesn't necessarily match the kind of relationship you can have with them.
- When you and your partner laugh during sex, you can feel the laughter inside your body.
- If a baby monkey's mother starts abusively rejecting the baby, it will abandon all its friends and obsessively try to make its mother love it again.

Bonus lesson: The best way not to fall is not to mind falling, and the way not to mind falling is to fall a lot.

That one is about rock climbing.

I cry myself to sleep.

I wake up, cry a little more, go for a run, take a nap, eat dinner with my parents and watch a movie with them, and then cry myself to sleep again.

This is most of how I spend my month at home before I leave for medical school.

At my parents' suggestion, I start attending the drop-in ballet classes for adults at Joffrey a few times a week. They think the discipline and the community will do me good. They're right. I rip the shanks out of some old, dead pointe shoes, stop eating sugar, and kick my own ass three nights a week, and it keeps my bleeding heart tethered to the rest of my body. I enjoy being in a group of "adults." Which is apparently what I am now.

And every night for a month, I lie in bed staring at my Alan

Turing poster—"We can only see a short distance ahead, but we can see plenty there that needs to be done"—and I make lists in my head to remind myself of all the important things I'm learning:

- The death of hope is like the death of a parent, the permanent loss of the place you would return to when life is at its worst.
- When you sob until you can't breathe, you don't die, even though it feels like you might. All that happens is you stop sobbing and you start breathing.
- The universe is not, despite my dread and my despair, a fundamentally unreliable place; it behaves with perfect consistency. However, my expectations of it have been warped and confused. Now that my expectations are more realistic, it's easier for me to trust that the universe will catch me if I fall.
- My mom is really, really, really smart.

I knew that last one already, but about ten days into my cry/run/nap/ballet/dinner/cry/sleep routine, she follows me into my room after we watch *Groundhog Day*, sits on the bed, and pats the spot next to her.

"Tell me what's going on, girl."

"Nothing."

"Yeah," she says, rolling her eyes, and she pats the bed again.

So I sit beside her and bunch my lips together against the trembling they've learned to associate with lying in this bed: If on bed, then cry until asleep. Ugh.

"Charles," I say, suppressing my tears. I stare at my hands.

"What did he do?"

"Nothing."

"I repeat: Yeah."

"He didn't—" I stop and hold my breath, and then whimper, "He just didn't love me." I curl up in a ball with my forehead against my knees and let myself cry in front of my mom. I feel like a six-year-old confessing that another kid at school didn't want to be my friend.

She sighs heavily and brushes her hand softly over my hair. "Annabelle Frances Coffey." She only uses my whole name when she's about to say something she feels self-conscious about saying. My mom isn't demonstrative the way my dad is.

"Yeah," I sniff.

"Are you listening?"

"Yeah."

"I'm only going to say this once. Are you really listening?"

"Yeah," I huff into my knees.

"Your heart. Is too wise. To love someone. Who doesn't deserve it. So either: He's a superb human being who has earned your friendship. Or else you will stop loving him altogether, and soon. I don't know which it is, but I know it's one or the other. This thing you're experiencing right now is the chaos as your heart decides whether to let go of the love or . . . hold on to it in a new way."

I wipe my nose on my sleeve and try to breathe. I ask, "How do you know?"

"How do I know what?"

"How do you know my heart will figure out what to do?"

"That's what hearts do, when you let them."

I sigh and sniff again, and I believe her. "Okay."

And she's right. That's what my heart does.

Slowly, painfully, like a hand uncurling from a fist to an open palm, my heart opens up, exploring ways to hold Charles differently.

But.

I'm not out of the chaos yet when Margaret calls me, barely three weeks after I left Indiana, and says in an urgent voice, "I know the answer is probably no, but you're my best friend and I have to ask: Can you fly to Indiana *tomorrow* to attend my wedding?"

"What?!"

"The district court overturned the same-sex marriage ban today. We want to go get a license right away because you *know* that shit is going to be stopped within a matter of days."

"Oh my god, yes! Oh my god!"

I ask my parents for the thousand dollars it costs to book the next flight to Indianapolis, explaining about both the personal and the historical importance of this moment, and they agree that I should be there if I can.

Margaret and Reshma pick me up at the airport the next morning and take me to Reshma's moms' house, and we clean and decorate and cook and hug and laugh. I go out and mow the lawn while Margaret and Reshma weed the flowerbeds, which seems to be mostly an excuse to roll around in the dirt, tickling each other. The moms are inside moving furniture around to create space and "flow." They're getting married, too—a double wedding in the backyard—and I feel so, so lucky to be here with these amazing people on this amazing day.

I also feel like I'm a one-hour drive away from Charles. I don't know if he's coming and I can't bring myself to ask. I just do what I'm instructed to do, being as helpful as I can until it's my turn to take a shower and put on a dress, and then I start meeting guests at the back fence. My job is to let people in without letting the dog out. (The dog has no interest in getting out. He's a twelve-year-old bulldog with an underbite and a casual attitude about licking his penis in public.)

I don't know any of the people who start streaming in with potluck dishes and folding chairs—the planning was so last-minute that the e-mail invitation literally asked people to bring their own chairs—but every one of them is beaming with joy in the midst of the makeshift, overnight wedding.

Eventually Margaret's and my research supervisor, Professor Smith—"*Diana*," she insists—arrives with her husband. I hug her hello. She's so pregnant I worry she might pop like a balloon if I squeeze her, but I hug her as hard as I dare.

"Hey, is Charles coming?" I ask casually. The impression I want to give is that this isn't something I've been obsessing about more or less nonstop since Margaret called.

Professor Smith—Diana—looks at me suspiciously but only says, "He's here—we drove up together."

"Oh." Something cold drops into my stomach, even as my heart starts fluttering.

All of our heads turn back to the driveway, and there he is.

Chapter 2

Tell Me What to Do

I've hardly ever seen her in a dress. Mostly it's skinny jeans and novelty T-shirts; you'd mistake her for an awkward fourteen-year-old boy, if it weren't for the way she moves—not awkward, not a boy. But she stands at the fence now in the same red silk thing she wore under her academic regalia at commencement and to dinner in Montreal. At commencement, she looked pretty and happy. In Montreal, she looked fucking gorgeous, tousled and pink-cheeked from sex. Now, though, she looks pale and sick and much too thin, with exhaustion in her eyes.

That's my fault.

There's a look of dread on her face as her eyes find mine.

That's my fault, too.

I wouldn't have come if I had known. When the e-mail from Margaret came yesterday, and Diana asked if I would drive her and her husband up, I said yes easily, thinking there was no chance Annie would fly back at one day's notice. No chance.

But she is a better friend than I gave her credit for, and now I am imposing myself on her, at her best friend's wedding. Fuck. I am a waste of skin and oxygen, and she—god. Brilliant. Strong. Dazzling. Sane, so sane, when I was with her I felt like an escaped convict with his face turned toward raw winter sunlight. Clear. Vivid. Luminescent and illuminating.

I made her cry. I made her hurt. I am the lowest thing on Earth.

I tuck the crate of wine bottles and presents under my arm, put on my sunglasses, and go to the fence.

"Hey," she says, not quite looking at me.

"Hey," I answer, as blandly as I can.

"Need help with that?" she asks, squinting against the sun.

"Just point me to the food table."

"In the house." She closes the gate behind us and waves us to the back door. "Living room. It's easy to find."

I head for the house, planning tactics for staying out of Annie's way for the next couple of hours.

Reshma and Margaret are married in the backyard, right after Reshma's parents. Annie cries becomingly through both ceremonies, standing beside Margaret and handing over the rings when it's her turn. I watch her the whole time; I can't take my eyes off her. She looks so obviously unwell—can anyone see her and not see the grief, the loss of appetite, the disrupted sleep? They're all my fault.

And at the same time . . . her feet are bare, her bare toes in the grass. Can anyone see Annie's long, bony bare feet in the grass and not imagine the dirty, cool soles pressing into the backs of their thighs as she laughs and wriggles under them? I want to make love with Annie outside. I've never done that.

I never will do that.

Just stay out of her way, you arse, I chide myself.

Margaret's family hasn't come, so the only guests I know are Diana, her husband, and Annie. During the reception, mostly I occupy myself with noticing when Annie comes into the room, so that I can leave it—trying to give her space, trying to do what she asked. The third time this happens, Diana comes over and asks me what the hell is going on, and I look at the floor and the wall and the furniture as I confess, "Er, it's awkward. Annie told you that she and I had, as she put it, 'A Thing,' but it ended rather messily when she left Indiana, and she asked for space."

In fact, what the note said was *You're the best man I know. Please don't call or write for a while*, and I haven't called or written, so *technically* I'm not violating her request, but—"I'm trying to give her that space," I conclude.

Diana pats my arm and gives me a sympathetic smile.

"We'll go," she says. "We don't need to stay for presents. I'm hot and tired and my feet are swelling anyway. Let me just say good-bye to Margaret."

I nod—then I notice Annie watching us, and I walk out the front door. I put on my sunglasses and sit on the porch swing to wait for Diana.

After just a minute the door opens and I look up, expecting Diana, but instead there's Annie.

"Hey," she says.

"Hey." I look out at the garden. "I'm really sorry. I thought you wouldn't be here or I wouldn't have come. We're leaving as soon as Diana's ready."

"Oh," she says, and the hurt in her voice stabs at my heart. "I didn't realize you wouldn't want to see me."

At first I'm too stunned by the irony of that to say anything at all, but finally I babble, "You asked me not to contact you. I didn't. I wouldn't. I won't, not until you say. I'm not avoiding you—I mean, I was, but it's to give you the space you asked for. Not because I don't want to see you." I stare at her with my mouth open for a few desperate seconds, and then I add, just to be clear, "I do want to see you."

"Oh," she says, and she looks tired and gaunt. She must feel it, too, because she says, "Okay. Um. I'm gonna sit down for a second."

"Okay."

When she sinks onto the other end of the swing, I feel my weight counterbalance hers. Our bodies automatically find a shared rhythm, a slow, steady rocking that moves us back and forth together. We're connected this way, through the swing, as we sit in a long silence. I feel all the things I want to say stack up inside me as I try to think of which thing I should say, but everything I can't say jams up my thoughts and so I just sit there, bottlenecked, silent. This is probably my only chance to fix our ending, to give us something besides "You're the best man I know. Please don't contact me."

I look down at Annie's bare feet, the dirty soles turned toward each other on the wooden porch. I glance at the front door. I don't know how long we've got before Diana comes. I take a deep breath and say, "Thank you for the note."

It comes out at the same time she says, "I'm sorry I left without saying good-bye."

"The note?" she says, turning to look at me, while I say, "You did say good-bye."

I say, "With the key," as she says, "I didn't, I snuck out like a coward."

"The note was your good-bye," I say, folding our two conversations into one. I add, formally, "And it meant a very great deal to me."

We sit and rock in silence, connected still through the swing, even as we each struggle with all the things we haven't said, the things that have to be said now, when we have this last, unexpected chance.

"I'll follow your lead," I tell her, staring straight ahead. "When you're ready, write to me."

I feel her nod, but she says, "How will I know when I'm ready?"

Which makes me laugh a little. I tell her the truth: "Fucked if I know."

She frowns at me. "Well, how long will it take?"

I laugh a lot this time and turn to look at her, grinning as I drape my elbow over the back of the swing. "Young Coffey, I know even less about this than you do. You're leading us."

She stares at me, dumbfounded, before she says, "Then we are screwed, because I have no idea what the hell I'm doing."

And so I tell her the truth again. "I trust you."

"I—" she starts.

And then Diana comes through the door, followed by her husband, and I can't tell if I feel more relieved or frustrated. I join them at the steps.

"Ready?" Diana says to me.

No, I think.

"Yep," I say.

"Gimmee a hug," she says to Annie. They hug and then I watch as, with her hands on Annie's shoulders and her eyes watching Annie's face very carefully, Diana announces, "It's none of my business. But let me know if you need anything."

"Okay. Thanks." Annie nods, her eyes tearful and bleak. "Bye."

Diana's husband supports her unsteady bulk down the three steps, and they walk toward the car.

Annie turns to me.

I put my hands in my pockets and say, "Bye, Annie."

She crashes her body against mine, her face pressed against my chest, her arms around my waist. Reflexively, my arms go around her shoulders and I hold her against me, tight, close. She feels bony and fragile. It's terrifying. And it's my fault. I touch my lips to the top of her head and say, "Take care of yourself."

She takes a deep, slow breath, and as she exhales, her arms relax. She lets me go. She takes a step back. We stand there looking at each other. Her face is so thin and tired, it breaks my heart. *Food and sleep*, I think. *The world needs you.*

"Bye, Charles," she says, her eyes exploring my face. "I'm glad we got to say good-bye for real."

There's something about those words—"good-bye for real"— something conclusive, something intolerable. I haven't fixed anything, I haven't undone any of the damage. Oh god, I am crap at good-byes. I glance at Diana near the car, and back at Annie.

I say, "I don't want 'good-bye for real' to mean good-bye forever."

She shakes her head without taking her eyes from mine.

"Tell me what to do," I say, still watching her wide, sad eyes. "Tell me what you need."

"Kiss me good-bye?" she says, and the words are hardly out of her mouth before my lips are on hers, my fingers laced in her hair, even as I know it's the wrong thing to do.

"CHARLES!" Diana's yell breaks through, and I pull away, feeling like I've been slapped. Annie and I stand there, breathing hard, watching each other, and I know, I *know*, this will not be the last good-bye. I do not fail often, and this matters too much—*she* matters too much—for me to allow it to end this way.

"I'm sorry," I say.

"I'm not," she answers.

"Termagant." I grab her and, with her throat braced between my palms, I press my cheek to hers, press my lips against her ear, and I make a promise.

"When you're ready, I will be where you need me to be. I will be there."

"Where? How will I know?" she says desperately. She touches a hand to my sleeve, and I know she's looking for strength in me, and I hate myself for not having it to give.

"You'll know," I say. "If you trust yourself half as much as I trust you, you'll know. Bye, Annie." I kiss her earlobe and walk off the porch.

I look back once, see her watching me.

I get in the car.

I drive my boss and her husband back to Bloomington.

"We're not going to talk about it," she says. Fair enough.

And then I go back to my flat, change my gear, and run seven miles in the June heat, with "The Scientist" on repeat on my headphones.

An hour later, I'm standing under a stone cold shower, and I've got a plan.

Chapter 3

The E-mails I Don't Send . . .
and the One I Do

He looks back once, and I can't quite see his expression behind his sunglasses. It's not excited or affectionate or pleased. He looks the way he used to look at the beginning of a difficult climbing route.

He gets in the car.

They drive away.

I sink down onto the steps, brace my hands over my mouth, and sob for five minutes, with not a thought in my head but the sound of his voice, the sensation of his breath against my ear, as he said, "I will be there" . . . and the smile in his eyes, half-hidden behind his sunglasses, as he said, "I trust you."

I don't know what it means. I don't know what I feel. But I know Charles believes I'll find my way to . . . wherever it is we're going next. He believes there's somewhere worthwhile on the other side of the chaos, and he believes I will find my way there.

So, okay.

When I go inside, they're opening the small collection of presents. I sit in the corner and watch.

"Who are these from?" Reshma asks. She's holding up a pair of kitschy vintage salt and pepper shakers, in the shape of two ducks that are hugging, eyes closed, smiles on their faces. It's adorable and exactly the kind of thing Margaret loves. And Margaret was a duckling to Charles's Momma Duck and Professor Smith's Poppa Duck.

I was a duckling, too. I was Head Duckling.

"I bet they're from Charles," Margaret says.

I'm sure they are. I get out my phone and take a picture of the ducks.

I sit on my own for the rest of the day, watching everyone's joy. I had assumed it would be months or even years before Margaret and Reshma could be legally married, but here we are. It's amazing. I feel proud and happy and grateful I could be here.

And . . .

Today is the day I learn to let go. Mom said the choices were to let go completely or to reshape how I held Charles in my heart, and I can't imagine letting go completely of anyone who would give a friend these hugging-duck salt and pepper shakers. So, reshaping it is.

It feels like a roulette ball settling into a niche on the wheel. The chaos disperses as the choice settles inside me. I sit by myself and close my eyes against tears.

When the guests have left and it's just me, Margaret, Reshma, and Reshma's moms, I explain about the reshaping thing. The four women nod at the wisdom of this.

Reshma's mom Judy says, "Did you have braces when you were a kid?"

"Yeah."

"Do you remember how your teeth ached sometimes?"

"Yeah."

"Reshaping hurts, honey, and it's a gradual, ongoing process. That's normal."

I nod and I try not to cry.

"Do you think he's thinking about me?" I ask, ashamed of myself for saying it out loud.

"Does it make any difference, if he is or he isn't?"

I shake my head and I try not to cry some more, ashamed to be talking about myself on this day, ashamed to be sad when Margaret and Reshma and Reshma's parents are so full of joy. I resist the temptation to tell them the whole story of what happened this afternoon, to talk about myself even more, on a day that is really all about them.

Still I moan, half joking, "Maybe it would be easier if I were a lesbian." All four women shake their heads and roll their eyes, with varying levels of tolerance and patience.

"Your parents would attend your *divorce*, never mind your wedding," Margaret reminds me, squeezing my hand.

I nod again, and then I hug her. "I am so, *so* happy for you. I'm so glad I could be here." I step back and put my hands on her shoulders.

She says, "I didn't get how bad it was between you, or I wouldn't have invited him. Am I a horrible person?"

"You're a fantastic person and you know it. I'm glad he was here. I love you a lot."

"Love you, too." She squeezes me before she lets me go. "Go to bed."

I try to remember how lucky I am, how easy I have it. I try and try. I hug my friends and put myself to bed and rewrite the list of all the things I'm learning, including how lucky I am, how easy I have it. An embarrassment of riches.

I fly home in the morning, and then I start . . . getting ready. Letting him go. Getting myself to the place where Charles will meet me.

A week after the wedding, my parents help me move into the house in Boston that I'm sharing with two other students in my program, and then they drive off after giving me a sandwich hug, in which I am the cheese. I stand on the curb, watching until their car turns and is gone.

And then I start building a life.

I get to know my housemates. I get to know my cohort, my Society, my professors. I attend all the guest lectures. I start rock climbing, too, when it turns out one of my housemates, Sylvia, also climbs. There is a group that climbs on alternate Wednesdays and Saturdays, and we both join. I buy my own harness and climbing shoes and a chalk bag, and I become a climber.

It's actually pretty okay for the first few weeks. I start my first lab rotation and the molecular biology course, which has always been a strength for me. We have to pair up to lead sessions, and mine goes really well—I collaborate with my other housemate, a gigantically nerdy Jamaican guy named Linton who laughs with a silent shoulder shake that cracks me up every time. We have an awesome time reading the paper together, meeting with the professor to discuss it, and preparing our session. I catch the flaw in the study design, and Linton instantly starts redesigning it to fix the flaw. We high-five, because: science.

The Charles stuff feels okay—that's not true, it hurts like I'm dying every day, but it also feels like at least there's some purpose to the suffering. There's somewhere I'm going, someplace Charles will meet me. I have no idea where it is or how to get there, but Charles trusts me to figure it out, so . . . I'll figure it out.

I begin to stumble when the neurobiology paper we're assigned is one coauthored by Charles. I'm surprised Professor Feany selected this paper, since her research is on neurodegenerative disease, not trauma, but I'm even more surprised by the date of publication. This is a paper Charles coauthored while he was still in *undergrad*.

At home that night, I tell Syl and Linton, "You guys, that paper? Charles Douglas was my lab supervisor in undergrad."

"Oh my god, you know Douglas?" Syl says.

That's who he is to them—Douglas. An author in a list of authors on a journal article—and in a way, that's who he really is. Douglas, et al. Douglas and Compston. Agarwal, Oyuela, Compston, and Douglas.

I am, of course, already aware of his stature in his field. I already know he's a genius and a prodigy and all the rest of it. I already know he's a leader in his field and that he's worked with the very best trauma specialists alive. But I'm struck by this: An assigned reading in my first course in medical school is work Charles did when he was younger than I am now.

Somehow, when it was just him and me naked in bed or eating in the kitchen or climbing at the rock gym, I felt as if we were peers, as if he and I could just love each other, like normal people. But he's not normal. He's a genius and a prodigy and a leader in his field at the age of twenty-six. I'm about to turn twenty-three and I'm just in the first year of med school.

When we were in the bed, skin to skin, I *knew* I had a right to love him and I deserved to be loved by him. But now . . .

Then we get to the cancer genetics paper.

I haven't had any substantial genetics since high school, and I barely make it through the abstract of this paper before I'm out of my depth. Glad this isn't the discussion I have to lead, I hole up in my room alone with the paper and try to Google Scholar my way through it. During the discussion the next day I sit in the corner, silent, nodding wisely and writing down everything everyone says. Then I spend the entire weekend with Google Scholar and YouTube tutorials trying to figure out what the hell they were talking about.

It doesn't get better from there. When the fall semester begins, we are inundated, flooded, drowned in work. I enjoy working hard, but this is not like anything I've experienced before. Usually working extra-hard puts me ahead of other students— ahead of *all* the other students. Now I'm working on overdrive just to stay caught up with everyone else. The hit to my sleep and the hit to my ego are about equally devastating.

In October I start writing e-mails to Charles, but never sending them.

> *October 12*
> *Dear Charles,*
> *   Hey, sorry to bother you, but it turns out med*

school is way harder than I thought, and I'm so scared
I might not be able to do it that I just sit staring at my
textbooks feeling like there's no point in even starting
because I already know I'll fail.

Can you help? Like you did when I was an under-
grad? Point me in a direction? Show me what I
missed?

I know how much more important pretty much
everything in your life is compared to me, but there
you were for two years, and I didn't even realize how
much you helped me.

Shit, I'm not gonna complain about this stuff to
you

Months of this. Every time I feel the urge to call or e-mail
Charles—and I feel it pretty much every day—I tell myself,
"Whatever 'ready' is, that is not what you currently are," and in-
stead I write an e-mail I'll never send.

November 8

You know what I'd really like right now, Charles,
as I sit here in the library at ten p.m. on a Friday?
I'd like to get home tonight and find you in my bed,
ready and willing to spend the whole night fucking my
brains out, letting me fuck your brains out. I want to
get lost in sensation and raunchy raw lascivious
naked, skin against skin, gripping my hair to tilt my
head, pinning my wrists behind my back, fucking hard
and fast and long, putting our bodies together and
against each other in every way we can think of, in-
venting new ways no one has ever done it, in the bed,
on the couch, against the wall, in the shower, on the
kitchen floor, on the kitchen counter, in the hall, in the
park, in the library, I want you to fuck me and lick

me and I want to fuck you and lick you and I am
never going to send this e-mail.

Months, too, of obsessive phone conversations and online chat-
ting with Margaret about what I should do, whether I should call
him, e-mail him, how I'll know when I'm "ready."

I try explaining the sex to Margaret, since there's literally no
one else I can talk to about that kind of thing—I don't care how
smart my mom is or how nice my dad is, *no way* am I telling them
about Charles making me come until I couldn't come anymore,
until I could barely move, and then fucking me while I was all
limp and exhausted.

But even Margaret kind of freaks out about this.

"Oh, that's not cool," she says over the phone, with a grimace
I can hear.

"I liked it," I say, defensive.

"I mean . . . it's fine I guess . . . it just sounds like he was, like,
using you. I mean it's kind of creepy, him having sex with you
when you can't move."

"It is? It didn't feel creepy, it felt amazing."

"I don't know, I don't even like the idea of a penis, don't ask
me. Let's talk about something else."

So now I feel weird and worried about having liked a thing
that sounds creepy to my best friend. Why did I like it, being all,
I guess, helpless? Why did *he* like it, this self-identified feminist
who clearly enjoyed my intelligence and my persistence and my
autonomy?

What's worse is my fantasies get . . . I don't know. Weirder. I
fantasize about rock climbing with him. Then I start fantasizing
about him tutoring me. I will literally lock my door, get out my
vibrator, and imagine sitting side by side at a table with Charles
while he talks to me about telomere maintenance. I miss him so
much, even the thought of hearing him talk about genetics turns
me on desperately.

I try fantasizing about other people.
Meh.

November 28
Hey, Charles,
I talked to my mom and dad over Thanksgiving,
and they helped me with school stuff, but it's not the
same as with you. They want me to ask people here,
they think I should ask my professors, but how can I
do that? I'm the only one who feels overwhelmed,
everybody else is all, "It's cool." I should be able to do
it myself. I want to be able to do it myself.
Charles, I'm tired all the time and I don't have you
to sit down on the couch with me and calmly guide me
through it all, like you used to.
God fucking damn it, why did I have to fall in love
with you? If we had just stayed friends I could call
you and you'd tell me what to do next and I'd know
I'll be okay.
But god fucking damn it, why didn't you fall in
love with me? Why?! I fucking hate you for that.
I'm never going to tell you any of this, am I?

As time passes, my missing him becomes less and less about missing him romantically or sexually and more and more an overwhelming sense of how much more he was in my life, that I hadn't even realized. For years he prodded and shepherded and cajoled me into working harder, learning more, understanding more deeply. Margaret was the friend I came home to; Charles was the friend I went to for direction when I was lost. And I'm so lost now.

December 3
Dear Charles,
Tyuyhu6

That was my forehead on the keyboard.
Why am I doing this to myself?

I try to explain to Margaret what it was like between Charles and me, how he was my tutor and my friend and my mentor, as well as my lover, and how I miss all those things, but what I miss most, what I need most right now, is the friend, the voice in my ear saying, "Of course you can do this," the voice of someone who has done it already and knows what it's like and knows me and knows I can do it, too.

And Margaret says, "I know you. You can do it!"

"Thanks," I say. And it feels good. But it's not the same. Not because Charles is so extraordinary and special—though he is—but because Charles knows me *and* he knows this insane life I'm leading, in a way that Margaret can't.

> *January 3*
> *Seven months today. I had no idea "ready" would take so long.*
> *I miss you. And I hate you.*
> *I miss you coaching me through the concepts I can't understand, challenging me to think more deeply, pointing me where I need to go. I'm exhausted and overwhelmed, and all I want is to lie in the dark and hear your voice in my ear, hear you tell me that I'll be okay, that I'm amazing. I know I'm amazing. I don't need you to tell me. But I miss it. I miss you. I have this rudderless feeling without you.*
> *I don't know what name this feeling has. Do I love you, still? Are you my teacher? My ex? My climbing buddy, my boss, my brain scaffolding, my heartbeat and pulse, the dilation of my pupils and the slowing of my gut, my intellectual mentor, my sexual tutor, the man who holds my hand and looks into my eyes and*

says yes? The man I would choose, if I got to choose—
except YOU DIDN'T CHOOSE ME. You just RE-
FUSED to recognize what there was between us. It
was RIGHT THERE and you wouldn't even admit
it was there, much less take the tiniest step toward it or
make any space in your life for it.
    And that makes you a coward. You're a coward
and I hate you, and I miss you, and I do not, I do
not, I do not understand why you couldn't just let me
love you.
    One of these day I'm going to hit send.
    Not today.

In the end, the decision of when to hit send gets made for me.
In January, my proposal is accepted to the World Congress on
Psychophysiology. Charles has attended this conference every
year for ten years, and I'm sure he'll go this year—it's in London.
As far as I know, he hasn't been home since he started at Indiana
almost four years ago.

With my heart thumping in my throat, I forward the acceptance e-mail to Charles, adding only the comment, *See you there?*

He replies within minutes, *I'll be there.*

And something inside me softens, just seeing his name in my
in-box.

My friend, I think, *I could have my friend back.* The thought
rushes in like hot water over ice.

And so I reply, *I'll be ready.*

I'm not there yet, but I have the spring semester to . . . get
"ready."

And this is when I find Harry.

Harry Belafonte.

Linton is dating this girl Angelina, and he comes home one
day singing a song called, it turns out, "Angelina." And there's
just something about it. At first I attribute it to Linton's bouncy

jubilance; he is *ridiculously* in love, which is awesome to see, even if it breaks my heart a little. But then I search YouTube . . . and a whole world opens up to me.

You guys, Harry Belafonte is, like, the *opposite* of rage, despair, and loss. Harry Belafonte is the opposite of "Everybody's Got to Learn Sometime."

And "Turn the World Around." Do you know this song? This song will change your life. Especially if, like me, you have every intention of actually changing the world, you know? But also you have feelings and are a person with a heart that gets broken? And you're like, "How can a plain, ordinary human with a heart that gets broken and a body that gets tired, possibly do anything big enough to change the world?"

Harry Belafonte has the answer, and the answer is in asymmetric meter.

So, Harry and his stable of raucous women—Matilda, Dolly Dawn, Senora, Angelina—inspire me, remind me what hope feels like. I continue listening to Harry Belafonte, I continue running, I continue climbing rocks, and I continue going to class and doing my work.

And I continue writing e-mails to Charles that I don't send . . . but the e-mails change.

> *February 17*
> *Dear Charles,*
> *I met a faculty member from the School of Public Health who's doing research on motivational interviewing with sex workers in New England, to increase harm reduction behaviors. I approached her after her talk and she ended up inviting me to help with outcome evaluation over the summer. So that's really exciting.*

I only had the courage to approach her because I heard Charles in my head, going all Socratic, asking me why I shouldn't go talk to her, what was the worst that could happen. That's been happening more and more lately. The Charles in my head coaches me through stuff, so it's like he's with me, even though he's not.

> *March 2*
> *I've been having all these fantasies of dropping out*
> *of school because it's so exhausting and I'm so tired*
> *and seriously what is the point? My parents listen to*
> *my complaints with calm smiles and say, "It's a*
> *marathon, Annie girl, the point is to finish. And the*
> *only thing you have to do to finish is just not stop until*
> *you get to the end."*
> *What do you think I should do?*

The Charles in my head says, "It's not a rhetorical question: What, young Coffey, *is* the point?"

And I tell him that the point is to become a doctor, so that I can change the fucking world.

"Well done," says the Charles in my head. "Full marks."

I don't even know what "full marks" are but I know I've heard him say that, and I know if I could tell him all the things I'm learning, he'd give them to me.

> *March 12*
> *Happy birthday.*
> *I've stopped needing to know why you didn't love*
> *me. I only wanted to know why so I could change it,*
> *and in the end what I had to do was accept that I*
> *can't change it. And that hurt. Oh man, did that hurt.*
> *Letting go of the hope hurt worse than anything else in*
> *my life.*
> *I was so mad before, as if you were deliberately,*
> *obstinately just refusing to love me. Refusing to let me*
> *"fix you." Now I'm amazed you didn't hate me for*

*that, for trying to make you something you aren't and
don't want or need to be.*

*That was what you meant last year by "The
Acceptance Deal," huh? That I accept all of you, including the parts of you that made it impossible for
you to be what I wanted you to be? That I welcome
you into my life as you are, and not try to jam you
into a space where you just didn't fit?*

I didn't get it. I'm sorry.

By the end of that semester, there's nothing I want more than to
hang out with Charles and spend hours telling him all the things
I'm learning:

- Medical school is hard because being a doctor is hard and
changing the world is hard, and this is the time when I'm
learning how to keep doing things even though they're so
hard I don't even know if I can do them.
- Comparing yourself with other people only gives you justi-
fication to resent your peers, to celebrate their failures, and
to congratulate yourself for mediocrity as long as it's "better than most." And fuck that.
- You can learn a lot from every single human, if you listen
well. The way to listen well is to pay attention to all the
things they're saying, all the things they're not saying, *and*
the context in which they're saying it, all at the same time.
This is extremely difficult to do.

And, as a bonus, I've learned what "ready" is. In June, two
days before I get on a plane to London, I write an e-mail that I
actually send:

Hey, Charles,
"Ready" is when you anticipate something because

it will bring you pleasure, rather than because it will
relieve suffering.
    I'm ready.
    See you in London,
    Annie

He writes back right away:

    Which makes the answer to your second question,
"About a year."
    Let me buy you a drink?
    Cxx

Chapter 4

Remember the Ducklings

MUSHROOMS WTF IS WRONG WITH YOU PEOPLE

Annie alerts me to her arrival in the home of my fathers via text, with a photo of her breakfast accompanied by this opprobrious remark.

I'm on the plane when I receive it. I respond with an image of my own breakfast and a note—

Submitted without comment from somewhere over the Atlantic, on *US* Airways

She doesn't respond, so I don't text again. This is my strategy: Follow her lead. Follow her lead, and do what feels good—which is different from doing what relieves suffering.

The plane lands, an hour on the Tube, and then I'm in London. I get off five stops early and walk the last mile or two.

London was never home for me—Cambridge was home—but after four years of nearly unrelenting American Midwestness, this city feels like a favorite pair of pants I thought I'd lost in the wash and then discovered this morning behind the dresser, where they fell when I carelessly tossed them one night before bed. I savor the sense of rediscovery, of fitting easily into something for once.

Simon texts me as I'm arriving at the hotel—

Mums spending the weekend with me how about dinner Sat 7

Standing in line at the hotel desk, I respond—

Hells to the yes—which is American for with knobs on

I don't see Annie at the conference registration desk or at the opening plenary. I'm not looking for her, per se, and it is a moderate-sized conference, a thousand people or so, so not seeing her should come as no surprise—especially as I'm not looking for her.

She texts me at last, half an hour after the plenary ends—

whoops, well I missed that session. working, lost track of time. Omw back to hotel now

I'm just leaving for drinks with some people—see you tomorrow?

What you mean is you have my talk circled and starred in your schedule.

I do indeed. We'll go out after to celebrate?

Sure!
Have fun tonight

The drinks are with my future colleagues, some of the team with whom I'll be working when my fellowship starts in August. They're a nice lot, but I excuse myself early, pleading jet lag.

In the middle of the night, I wake up out of a dream that she's in the bed. As my eyes open, I'm reaching for her, craving her, and when I realize she's not there, it's like it's happening all over again. She's gone and we never said good-bye, and the dirt under her feet is worth more than I am. I scrub my hands over my face and swear at the ceiling. It takes a long time to fall back asleep.

I don't see her all day. With a dozen concurrent sessions, it's hardly remarkable that we don't seem to attend the same ones, and if I don't see her at lunch, that too is to be expected. Especially as I'm not looking for her.

Her session at four o'clock fills past capacity, because another of the three speakers is a rock star of psychophysiology. I'm sure she's nervous to be presenting in the same session—indeed, immediately before him—and I had every intention of being a supportive presence in the room, but there's a knot of people at the door.

I text her from the hallway outside.

Can't get a seat, you're too famous. Meet you in the lobby after?

She answers immediately, and I have to stifle a laugh.

GET IN HERE YOU FUCKING TRAITOR WHAT IF I FORGET HOW TO SCIENCE

You'll do brilliantly with or without me—remember the ducklings— but I'll try.

At the lab, I'm Momma Duck and Diana is Poppa Duck and the students are ducklings. Diana called us that because Patrice, the postdoc who preceded me in the lab, told her about a documentary she saw about ducks. It turns out ducklings are hatched high in a tree, and the first thing they have to do when they leave the nest is jump out of a tree (this is long before they can fly), thump onto the leafy ground, and then waddle their unsteady

way to the water, where Momma Duck and Poppa Duck are calling for them.

Annie doesn't feel ready.

She is ready.

She should just jump.

But I squeeze into the standing room at the back. I lean against
the wall, cross my arms over my chest, and raise an eyebrow at her.
A huge grin spreads across her face. I grin right back.

She looks amazing. Different glasses, different hair—shorter
and sort of fluffy around her face—and much healthier than the
last time I saw her. Still a little tired, which is only natural, as
she's a medical student, but she's dressed like a grown-up, in the
black trousers she apparently reserves for conferences and a shirt
that doesn't have screen printing on it.

Her talk is fantastic. Unlike me, Annie is a born public speaker.
I love seeing her present her research. Last year in Montreal, I sat
in her session and, like the Neanderthal I am, I thought, *Mine*. I
knew that afterward she would come up to our room and I'd have
her naked and panting and writhing under me. I allowed myself,
in fantasy, to feel that I was sharing her with the others in the session, that the scarf round her neck was a collar and I'd let her off
her lead, to play—confident that she'd come when I called.

Today, of course, she is not mine. I know that afterward we
will sit over beers and she will tell me that she has a partner. I'm
longing to hear it, so that I can finally break this unholy grip she's
had on me for years now. The Thing, she calls it—this overwhelming craving for her that began when she was still a student
in the lab, when there was nothing I could or would do about it. I
let myself enjoy the wanting, then. I let myself imagine all the
things I could never, would never, do. I let myself imagine her
face at orgasm. I let myself, because it was harmless and totally
under control.

That was before she asked me to take her to bed. Before she
told me she was a virgin and she wanted me. God, Christ, the

moment she told me that, The Thing exploded to monstrous proportions, it roared inside me like a bonfire. And for that one month, she *was* mine, her body belonged to me and I could make her come as many times as I wanted, could fuck her any way I wanted, and I was the first, the only one.

I knew she would have other partners after me, and I knew The Thing would die a natural death when that happened. That's how it was always going to be. It's how it ought to be. But The Thing has not gone yet. I watch her click through slides of P values and effect sizes and it seems to me that The Thing has only gotten a stronger hold on me.

I need her to tell me she has a partner, so that my body can let go of this absurd, obscene, intractable medieval fantasy that she is my property. I need that, because as overwhelming as The Thing is, her body is not what I've missed most this past year. When my headshrinker asked me, "What makes you want to deserve her respect?" I surprised myself with how easily the answer came:

"The clarity of her," I said. "When she is angry, she is simply angry; it is this pristine thing, unpolluted by shame or manipulation. And the clarity, too, of her thinking. She recognizes when she's wrong—which she isn't, very often—and she dives into learning from mistakes. There is no cloud in her, no conceit or fear. She doesn't fear losing control."

It is that clarity, more than anything, that I have missed.

So I stand at the back and watch her talk and tell my body to sit the fuck down. Fingers crossed she's in love and having brain-melting sex with someone who deserves her, so that I can let go of the medieval fantasy once and for all, and just be near her, bask in the sunlight of her, without wanting to pin her to the wall by her hair and listen to her moan.

Lots of people come up to talk to her afterward—so many that I text her in the middle of the melee.

*Well done you—meet me in the lobby when you've autographed every-
one's programs*

Twenty minutes later, when my phone rings and I see her
name, I answer with a cheerful, "Where the fuck are you?"

"Where the fuck am *I?*" she laughs. "Where the fuck are *you?*"

I scan the hallway, searching for the girl with a phone to her
ear—and I hear a click.

Chapter 5

Ye Olde Mitre

He doesn't see me; I'm looking at his back, at his blue oxford shirt and khaki pants and his pale gold hair. It's shorter than last year around his ears and neck, but still all floppy on top. He's standing with his shoulder against a column, a dark blue jacket draped over his arm and his phone against his ear, searching the hallway I'm not coming from. With my heart pounding and my hands shaking, I step toward him in silence and hang up my phone.

"You there, young Coffey?" he says into his phone.

"I'm here," I say, as I step forward and put my hand on his sleeve.

His head turns.

He opens his mouth but no words come, just a little breath, and he takes one step back.

"Hey," I say, smiling like a goon.

"Hey," he says. He stuffs his phone in his pocket and then goons right back, and it's Charles, right here with me.

We just look at each other for a moment, taking each other in.

"I want to hug you," I announce, bouncing a little on my heels. "I feel like that's the normal thing to do."

His eyes dart around the room, as if he's worried someone he knows might come along and hear him talking about hugging.

"Go on, then," he says at last.

I step forward and put my arms around his waist, my head against his shoulder.

I feel one of his arms go around my shoulder. And then a few seconds later, when I don't let go, the other one comes around me, too, and then a few seconds after that, he actually hugs me for real, tightening his arms around me and exhaling into my hair. And it's just *right*. It's just good and warm and comfortable and real that the two of us should be standing with our bodies held close together like this.

"Hey," I say into his shoulder.

"Hey," he says into my hair.

Then I pull away and, because it feels like the normal thing to do, I kiss him on the cheek.

He raises both his eyebrows, takes a deep breath, and says, "Shall we go and have a drink, then? Get out of this hotel?"

I nod. "Lead the way. Where are we going?"

"Not far. About a mile."

He leads me out of the hotel, and we both simultaneously take deep breaths of city air, then turn to smile at each other.

"Lead on," I say, with a gesture in the direction I expect we're going.

"Right," he says, and he goes the other way.

The pace of London feels faster than Boston but slower than New York. Charles drops into the rhythm instantly and I sync myself to him, keeping my shoulder beside his as we walk along wide streets—taller than Boston, shorter than New York.

As we walk in silence, I try to adjust to being in the same space with him, walking by his side. He's tall, I forgot how tall, and his body is strong in the way it moves. How could I have forgotten how his physical presence feels? From the first moment, he has done this to me, made me feel . . . conscious of him. Sensitive to the movements and moods of his body and brain. I grin uncontrollably as we walk.

For the whole walk, most of fifteen minutes, we don't say anything. Charles barely looks at me, even, just glances at me with a quiet smile before he turns a corner, to make sure I follow. And it's good. It's . . . amazing. It's Charles and the way our bodies behave beside each other. This is as much a mutual greeting as any conversation could be. This is us reconnecting, settling into each other's physical presence.

Our destination is down a Dickensian alley, complete with beer barrels and gas lamps, though neither seems to be in active use, apart from a pair of barrels with flowers blooming in them. The grungy yellow brick of the alley ends with a familiar sight. There are a lot of bars in Cambridge that resemble this one, with windowpane fronts and glazed timber. But when we go in, it's all British, all the time, tiny, dark, and squat. There are beer bottles lining the walls and beer steins hanging from the ceiling.

It's early yet, so there are plenty of tables. Charles waves me to one and goes to get us drinks. I sit on the booth side and leave him the chair. He comes back with two pints of dark brown beer and a tray of sandwiches.

"What's a mitre?" I ask, thinking of the sign over the pub's door, as Charles sits down.

He holds his fingertips together over his head. "Big funny hat for god."

"Arritey. Ye Oldee Big Funny Hat for God bar. I'm in London."

"Cheers," he says, raising his beer and grinning.

"Mud in your eye," I answer, and take a drink. Beer isn't my favorite, but this is pretty tasty. Encouraged, I pick up a sandwich while Charles watches me with curiosity.

I take a bite.

It's like someone put chopped bits of onion and rubber in mayonnaise between two pieces of thinly sliced particle board. I chew disconsolately in Charles's direction. After I'm finally able to swallow, I say, trying to be conciliatory, "I like the beer."

He shakes his head, grinning. "I forget sometimes how American you are," he says. "Stick to the cheesy ones. That's pickled egg."

"Oh." I take a heavy swig of beer, returning the "sandwich" to its plate.

"So what's new?" he asks, taking the "sandwich" for himself.

"Uh . . ." I blow air through my lips and sift through the last year of my life. "Well, I survived my first year of medical school. Barely."

"Rough?"

"Oh my god." I lean back and slump dramatically. "It was that, or else I was dragged underwater in the tentacles of a giant octopus for three months, escaped, just barely broke through the surface to get some air, and then got dragged back under. Twice."

Charles laughs and I feel a smile spread across my face at the sound.

He says, "There's good shit down there, though, if you can stay down long enough to explore. You need an oxygen tank—or else learn to breathe underwater."

"That's great advice, thanks Charles," I say, knitting my eyebrows as if I'm considering this seriously.

"It's a metaphor, Coffey. You learn to love being down there. You find purpose and meaning in the struggle. You bring what you need, skill or resources, with you, so that you can survive."

I narrow my eyes at him. "Actually, that is good advice. All my parents keep saying is it's a marathon, and the point is just to finish."

"They're not wrong. I'm just describing *how* to finish—they probably assume you're clever enough to work that out on your own."

"Whereas you assume I need coaching!" I grin.

"Well, that's my job, isn't it." He's grinning back again—still.

"No, it isn't. But I appreciate it and I really, really missed it," I say. Our eyes meet over the little table.

"Me too," Charles says softly.

"Aww!" I lean forward with my elbow on the table and prop my chin in my hand. I grin at him.

He inhales and watches his finger travel over the rim of his glass.

"You're still dancing?" he asks.

"No, god, there's no time. But I'm climbing, actually, every week. There's a group of us."

He tilts his head at me. "I'm glad."

"Me too. It's the most satisfying thing I do all week, the one place where I feel like I actually *accomplish* something."

He crosses his knees, his smile softening, and I'm reminded strongly of the day in Indiana when he looked at me just like that and said I had a big brain—a big, puppyish, coltish brain that I was only beginning to grow into. This time he says, "Are you happy there?"

I look into my beer and shrug. "Sure. I mean, it's where I want to be."

"But . . . ?"

"Not 'but,' just 'and.' It's where I want to be, *and* . . . it's really hard." I roll my eyes and wave the question away. "It's amazing and horrible and I love it and if you let me whine about how hard it is, I'll just get sucked into the abyss."

He accepts this and changes the subject. "We could go climbing next semester if you like."

"Okay," I say—and then I look at him blankly. "We could?"

"We could. That's my news, actually. I got the psychosomatic medicine fellowship at Boston University. I'll be there for a year."

I sit up, mouth open, eyes wide. "You're coming to Boston?"

He grins crookedly and nods.

"No fucking way!"

"Way," he answers, his grin widening.

"Oh my god that's—" I stand up and wave at him to stand too. "Let me hug you, asshole, why isn't this the first thing we talked about?"

He gets to his feet and I throw my arms around his neck.

"That's so amazing, Charles," I say into his neck, noticing the smell of him, noticing that he's hugging me back without hesitation this time. I hear and feel him laugh, and I laugh, too.

I let go and only look at him for a quick moment before I sit down again, and he follows me.

"Okay," I declare. "We will go climbing."

"I'd like that," he answers. "We could go out to the Gunks, if you like."

"The whats?"

"The Shawangunk Ridge, a few hours away. I've been there a couple of times since I moved to the States. Beautiful. And there's nothing like climbing actual rocks for feeling like you've accomplished something. Are you lead climbing at all?"

"What's lead climbing?"

"That's a no. Well, go back to your rock gym and ask your group to teach you to lead." He drains his beer and says, "Another?"

"Okay." I finish off my pint and sit back.

He raises an eyebrow at me as he takes my glass and stands. "When did you last eat, young Coffey?"

"Uh . . ." I try to remember.

"Right," he says. "You can have another pint if you eat two toasties."

"Two whats?"

"The cheesy ones." His eyes indicate the sandwiches. "Eat." And he goes to get us another round.

The cheesy ones are pretty good. I eat while I watch Charles lean his elbows on the bar. With the mild disinhibition that comes with a single beer, I think to myself, *That beautiful man would sleep with me tonight if I asked nicely*. I suck melted cheese off my fingers and think about whether that would be a good idea. Yes. The fucking would be *excellent*. That beautiful man would kiss me and make me come and tell me I'm amazing. The next day, though . . . I might—probably would—have all kinds of feelings, which would create drama, and since he's anti-feelings the drama would poison our friendship, maybe kill it dead this time, and that would crush me into emotional dust, and it would be a disaster.

He's coming to Boston. We're going to go rock climbing. Everything I've missed . . . well, *most* of the things I've missed.

So no, I should not ask this beautiful man to go to bed with me tonight.

I'm proud of myself for considering the consequences before I jump in.

"Oh, well done," Charles says. He's back at the table with two more pints, and he's looking at the tray. I have eaten all the cheesy ones.

"Turns out I was hungry," I say in apology. "They were good. Thanks." I take my second beer.

"So we'll go climbing," he resumes.

"It's so amazing that you'll be there! Why Boston?"

"It's where I got a job," he shrugs, but his eyes are on the table.

I lean forward, my arms on the table, and regard him skeptically. "I feel like you could probably have gotten a job, like, anywhere in the world you wanted. I'm sure everyone wants you. You would get all the grants, you could do all the science, you could do anything you wanted."

"Ah, well, there's the rub, eh? What is it that I want to do?"

I am totally baffled by this. "Haven't you spent the last ten years basically preparing to be faculty at a medical school? Teaching, research, clinical work?"

"Indeed I have. Ten years. The whole of my adult life." He raises his eyebrows and quirks up one corner of his mouth—this is a new thought for him.

"So . . . ?"

"So . . . I like being a *doctor*. I don't dislike the rest of it, but I want to work with patients. I'm not terribly interested in pushing constantly against the edge of knowledge, and I'm certainly not interested in the whole publish-or-perish hamster wheel."

"You're not?"

He shakes his head and his bottom lip tugs downward apologetically.

"I am," I say.

"I know," he smiles. "It's seeing how much you love it that made it obvious to me how little my heart is in it."

I try something new: I don't say anything. We learned in our Patient/Doctor seminar that listening is crucial, and sometimes silence is the best way to facilitate communication. So I try it. I nod silently. I wait. I bite my lips between my teeth to keep in the things I want to say, and I wait some more.

It's easily ten whole seconds of silence, but I struggle through.

And my reward is rich. With his eyes on his finger as he traces the rim of his glass, he says, "I've always been given the role of golden boy, head of everything. I can play the game. But I don't have what you have, that raw curiosity, the insatiable urge to understand. I thought I did—and then I met you, and I saw how much of my drive was not curiosity, but fear of falling short.

"But it's more than that, too. It's that Spider-Man thing: With great power comes great responsibility. I was born with nearly every advantage a human can have, and I've felt an obligation to use that advantage to do good things. But what counts as a 'good thing'? When I was young, I thought it meant accumulating honors, and then I thought it meant simply working *more*, 'doing all the things,' as you might put it. But the more I did, the smaller my efforts felt, in the infinite, sucking vortex of the world's needs. I've thrown everything I have into that vortex, and it was like a handful of sand tossed into the ocean.

"And so here are the variables." He holds out his hands, palms up. "There is what I am best suited to doing—by temperament and training and identity and resources. And there is the infinite sucking vortex." He brings his hands together in front of him. "So the question is: Is it enough, practicing medicine, helping one patient at a time? Or do I owe it to the infinite sucking vortex to write grant proposals and churn out twelve journal articles a year?"

He crosses his legs and drops his hands to his lap, giving me a little smile with a self-deprecating shake of his head. "I don't mean to go on about it."

I am stunned by what he has just handed me—a degree of self-disclosure he has never come close to sharing with me. Charles the genius, Charles the übercompetent, Charles the calm, the omniscient, the generous . . . Charles is afraid of falling short. He feels inadequate.

I say, "I never knew you felt that way. All these years, I never knew any of that."

"It's only in the last six or eight months that it's been obvious to me. I haven't talked about it, not with anyone. Except you." He glances at his watch. "Do you have other plans for tonight? A time we should get you home?"

I slump back in my seat. "Just more work to do. I found this twenty-four-hour diner where they let me take up a booth for hours at a time. It's called the VQ. I don't know why it's called that."

"*Vingt-quatre*," he says with a tilt of his head. "If I tell you *vingt* means twenty, what do you suppose *quatre* means?"

"Oh, I see. Twenty-four. Well, I was there until two last night. I'll probably do the same tonight. And tomorrow night." I sigh mightily and drink some beer. "I have a ton of theory to wrap my brain around between now and the sex workers."

"The . . . I beg your pardon?"

"The—oh right, I didn't actually tell you! I've written you all these imaginary and unsent e-mails, so I forgot you didn't know." I recite: "I'll be interviewing sex workers in and around Boston about whether and how they've implemented harm reduction strategies they were taught in a brief motivational intervention."

"That's fantastic," he says.

I nod. "It turns out I love public health policy, like *whoa*."

"Of course you do," he grins.

"What, 'of course'? It came as a total surprise to me!"

"Well, you're prevention-oriented, at your core, you won't be satisfied treating one patient at a time. You want to change the entire world."

"Yes, I do."

"So no wonder you look tired."

"Thanks a lot, and fuck you, too!" I laugh.

"Of course what I meant to say is that you look charmingly bedraggled." He toasts me with his pint and a laughing smile.

Chapter 6

You're the Sun

By the time we leave the bar, the sun is beginning to set, the temperature has dropped, and Annie is very slightly drunk. We walk slowly in companionable silence as I guide us back toward the hotel. She bumps my shoulder with hers, and we smile at each other.

"This is Russell Square? Are we back?"

"Mh," I nod.

She crosses her arms against the evening chill and says, "Wanna hang out here a little while before we go in?"

"Sure," I say.

Maybe if we sit out here she'll tell me about her love life. Maybe I'll bring myself to ask. Maybe. But it's pulling off a bandage—no matter how gently you go, no matter how gradually you do it, there's no getting away from the fact that it's going to hurt. And I am a coward.

She inhales deeply, looks up at the sky, exhales hugely, and smiles at the trees. She tucks her fists into her armpits and moves her smile to me.

I shake my head at her in mock sadness. "You're hopeless, you are." I take off my jacket.

She protests, "No no, you don't have to—oh. Thanks," as I drop it onto her shoulders. My hands grasp the lapels a little too long. My eyes hold hers a little too long.

I should say something. We should talk about it.

But I don't. I pull myself together and drop my hands away as I put on a smile. I guide us to a bench and we sit together in silence for a moment.

She asks, "Are there more people you're seeing while you're here? Family? Friends? Anybody?"

"I'm having dinner with my mother and my brother tomorrow," I say.

"Simon," she says.

I look at her, surprised to hear his name from her lips. "I forgot I told you about him."

"You didn't, much, just that he's my age."

"He is. He lives here now, in London. Works for the government." I look at my hands. "Last time I saw him he was at university, a scrawny, spotty, anxiety-ridden little swot. Much as I was at twenty."

She says, "And how's your mom?"

"She's okay," I answer. "She comes and stays with Simon a lot. It's good."

"And Elizabeth?"

"Massachusetts, at school. Summer research project."

"Boston?"

I shake my head. "Little town out in the middle of nowhere."

She says, "And your dad's still a douche bag?"

"Still utterly a douche bag." I grin a little, and my eyes go to hers—and suddenly I'm caught in an onslaught of physical memories. The night in Montreal, after I had told her more about my father than I'd ever told anyone and we made love in the dark, celebrated our bodies and sensation, and I said into the darkness, "You're not wrong," and she answered, "I love you, too."

But the next day she told me I didn't care enough, that I wasn't trying, that I had to fight harder . . . when I had been fighting so hard for her that my heart was on its knees, covered in blood and mud and scar tissue. I was failing her. In a matter of weeks, I had lost the respect I had earned from her over two years.

She pushed me, I remember, physically shoved me, trying to make me fight harder. My whole body reacted with the defensive rage it learned a quarter of a century ago, as a survival strategy. I didn't touch her, though. I bolted. I stood in a cold shower for fifteen minutes, with my hands fisted against the tiles. I let the water spray on my neck and my scalp and my face and my throat.

And then, after I washed away the rage and the shame, I took her to bed and held her body against mine, skin to skin. I kissed her as I fucked her and she whimpered and gasped as she came, her body taut and flexing under my palms.

My attention clicks back into the present, where Annie's eyes are on mine, and I realize I've been silent and staring. She's breathing too fast—so am I.

The Thing. My body feels hot with it. This beautiful woman would go to bed with me tonight if I asked her. Even if she's seeing someone, even if she's not mine anymore, she would say yes. I can feel it. She would come to my bed and look into my eyes, her breath caught in her throat, as I drowned her in pleasure.

And tomorrow morning she'd get on a plane and go home to . . . whomever. And I'd go home to my headshrinker, who will ask me if I've earned Annie's respect.

I look away, into the trees and darkening shadows.

"I've been seeing this woman," I say. "Clarissa. She's, erm . . ." —I gesture at the back of my head—"got this long braid down to her waist and she wears these dresses . . . these dresses that can only be described as upcycled from an elephant's saddle blanket."

Annie laughs and says, "Charles Douglas knows the word 'upcycled.'"

I smile at my hands. "Learned it from a patient. She would

buy these secondhand children's sweaters at the Goodwill and make them into all kinds of art projects."

"Neat," Annie says.

"Mh. She was an incest survivor. It was her way of turning her childhood into something new," I say.

"Whoa, jeez," Annie breathes.

I shake my head a little, still looking at my hands. "People are astonishing, eh? I can hardly—" I stop myself. "Anyway. I told Clarissa of the elephant's saddle blanket that I was coming here and that I'd likely see you for the first time since . . . well, since the last time."

"What did she say?" Annie asks.

"She said . . . it's a slightly complicated and extremely boring story, but in short she told me to do what felt good."

And I had suggested the compromise: Follow Annie's lead, and do what feels good.

"That's an impressively evolved thing for a girlfriend to say," Annie says.

"Girlfriend?" I blink at her.

"Clarissa? The woman you're seeing?"

"No no, sorry, she's—er . . ." Well, I've fucked this up utterly, haven't I? "I'm not seeing her romantically. Sorry. I'm—she's my therapist. In fact."

"Ohhhhhhhh," Annie says.

"Sorry. I didn't mean to be unclear. Just, I'm not quite used to talking about it."

"Yeah," she nods. "Is it helpful?"

"It is," I say, with my eyes on the ground, but smiling. "She was trained in what she calls 'the naked massage on an orange shag carpet' school of psychotherapy, which makes her more or less my precise opposite."

"You like her."

"I do," I grin.

"And so what have you learned? I mean—sorry, can I ask?"

"Sure, yes, ask whatever you like. I brought it up, actually, because I told her that I'd probably be seeing you again and she said—"

"Do what feels good."

"Yes, which—"

"Wait, you talk about me in therapy?" she says, as if this is a surprise.

Talk about her? When Clarissa asked me last July what my "goals" were, I said, "I'd very much like to deserve the respect of a woman I badly hurt, and I've finally realized that if that were something I could do on my own, I'd have done it by now."

And she hadn't said anything, just radiated warmth and compassion.

So I told her, "Er, some history: I'm a psychiatrist, in fact. Er, alcoholic father, avoidant attachment, lifelong depression . . ." I watched her face and bit my lip, reining in the dread at having said even this much to a stranger.

At last, she said, "You've been carrying a lot of heavy stuff around for a long time."

My face went cold. All I could say was "Yeah."

"Which has made you really strong, but it's also really exhausting."

My hands went cold. "Yeah."

"So basically you're looking for somebody to just . . . hold one of your bags of groceries while you find your keys."

I smiled at the image, but my lungs went cold. "Yeah."

"And one question is: How are you going to trust anyone to hold that bag for you? Because once you put it in their hands, they could do anything to it."

"Yeah."

"Like, what could they do?"

My heart beat faster, just to think of it. "Run off with it. Drop it and break everything. Have it stolen from them. Throw it all at me. All I need them to do is hold it, just stand still and hold this thing for me, just for a second, but they can't even do that much—and I know that's arrogance and conceit, the idea I'm the only one good enough to do even simple things, I know—"

"It's not arrogance and conceit," she corrected, "it's avoidant attachment, like you said."

"Oh," I said, and my stomach went cold. "Right."

"And then a whole other question is: If you're looking for a key, where are you trying to get into, and how did you get locked out?"

It's been nearly a year and I'm still trying to reckon with where I am, never mind where I'm trying to go.

Where I am now is in a park in the middle of London, sitting on a bench beside the woman whose respect I would very much like to deserve, who wants to know if I talk about her in therapy.

"You're in the big metaphor and everything," I tell her. I wince up at the trees.

"Metaphor?"

"Er, yes . . ." I glance at her. "You can't possibly want to sit here and listen to me talk about therapy. Jesus and Moses, is there anything more self-indulgent?"

"Dude, there is literally nothing I want more right now than to sit here and do exactly that," she says, with complete sincerity. "Wouldn't you be interested to hear about my therapy, if I were in therapy?"

"I would, yes," I grin. "I'd be totally fascinated."

"So, go," she gestures. "Therapy metaphor."

I clear my throat and lean back on the bench, unsure how much to tell and already in deeper than I meant to go. "Well. You remember, I'm sure, the gist of my early life."

"Your father is a monster, and because you couldn't save your mother from him you believe you've got a monster inside you that you've trapped in a pit of despair so that you don't hurt anyone."

"Er, in a nutshell." I shift in my seat and rub a hand on my forehead. "Jesus."

"Sorry."

"Well." I clear my throat again. "The metaphor is about the . . . sort of . . . nested protective structures I've built to separate myself from other people, as a result of . . . all that. There's the external, protective wall of perfectionism."

She nods.

"Then there's the defensive mountain of rage. The swamp of self-criticism. And finally, the pit of despair at the center of it all." I gesture with each layer, then fold my arms across my chest. "Four layers of defenses. And I was in the pit."

"I thought the monster was in the pit."

"It turns out, as far as the metaphor is concerned, I *am* the monster, though apparently I'm *all* the things—the pit and the swamp and the mountain and all the rest, as well as the monster, and I'd be better off if I identified with all of them. But it took two months just to get as far as working out what the layers are, because I kept talking about the neurophysiological analogues of the metaphor. Clarissa said I wasn't so much talking about that as I was avoiding the metaphor itself and that was fine, some people are just slow and it's okay if I'm one of the slow ones." I smile, thinking of the way she knits her eyebrows seriously as she asks me if I'm aware of how full of shit I am. "She mocks me a lot.

"Anyway. Eventually I acknowledged that my job is to move through the layers of defense."

"Okay. And did you? Move through them, I mean?"

I tip my head side to side. "I've made it out of the pit. I am currently in the swamp."

"Am I in the swamp?" she asks eagerly.

"No no—or sort of. The people in my life are all sorts of different things. My mum is—it really feels absurd to say these things out loud."

"It's not, keep going." Annie turns her whole body to me, sitting with her legs crossed on the bench. She props her elbows on her knees and her chin on her palms, listening, rapt, like a child at story time.

"Well. Er. My mum is this swan with a broken wing, and Simon and my sister are these two baby birds that I carry with me. My job is to keep them safe as I go through the layers."

"Awww!"

I make a "wait for it" face and add, "My father is a dragon at the top of the mountain."

"The rage mountain."

"Yeah." I lean forward, elbows on my knees, and drop my eyes to my feet.

"Yikes."

"Yeah."

"Am I a bird?" she asks.

I take a breath, hesitate for one more second, then say quietly to my feet, "You're the sun."

"I—" she says. "That's . . . good?"

"Yeah," I say. I close my eyes, turning my face away from her a little.

We sit in silence awhile. The Thing has a grip on me, pulling me toward Annie. What is it about this girl—this woman—with her fluffy hair and her casual genius, her eyes so clear and penetrating behind those tortoiseshell glasses? I want her clarity. I want her brilliance. But god, god, right now I want her body in the dark, helpless and bowed with pleasure.

When I can, I say, "Which brings us back to why I brought up Clarissa in the first place."

"Do what feels good," Annie repeats, sounding dazed.

"Yes. I . . ." I bring my eyes to hers at last. I tell her, "I never meant to hurt you."

"I know."

Our eyes hold, and it's there, the tension, the question, the wanting. The Thing.

"I never want to hurt you again, if I can avoid it."

She nods. "I know."

"So what do we do now?" I ask softly.

"About what?" she asks, matching my tone.

"We have A Thing," I say. "Am I wrong? Has it gone?"

"You're not wrong," she says instantly.

"So what do we do?"

We look at each other in wonder, in longing.

Without looking away from her, I take a deep breath and, very, very quietly, say the thing I've been avoiding for hours now. "You're probably seeing someone."

She huffs a laugh and says, "Like I've got time to date."

My body receives her words like a punch in the gut. I groan, "God, Annie," as I turn my eyes away and rub my hand over my mouth. Every muscle in my body tenses. My heart thuds in my chest. I grip a hand in my hair, jaw tight, and glance back at her. She's watching me, thoughtful and silent. She looks calm. How can she look so calm, when I feel like a lion about to pounce on his prey?

With her elbows still on her knees, her chin on her fists, she sighs, "I don't know. I mean obviously I'd like to . . . you know. But at the same time it seems like a really bad idea. And then I ask myself, 'Why is it a bad idea?' and the only answer I get is this big feeling of disaster"—she sits back and makes a feeling-of-disaster gesture in the space between us—"with no rational anything to go with it. Just like, if we do anything about The Thing, then, you know . . . bad things. Disaster."

"Fair enough," I say, holding myself utterly still.

"How about you?" she asks, glancing back up at me. "Do you want to?"

"Not if it's followed by disaster, no. Disaster is not what feels good." I jam The Thing into a tiny box in my brain.

She nods and bunches her lips over to one side. "And if it weren't followed by disaster?"

"Then yes, immediately please, yes thanks, yes," I nod playfully. Clamping the box shut and locking it.

"Me too," she says sadly, and adds, "Sorry."

My smile fades and I shake my head, accepting this. "Nothing to be sorry about."

There's a long silence, and we just look at each other, allowing the bridge between us to finish repairing itself. My remorse and hers. Her gratitude and mine.

"I really missed you," she says, her voice not much more than a whisper. She looks down at the bench between us. "I mean there you were, almost every day, and then all of a sudden you were gone and I didn't even realize how big a gap that would leave."

"Me too," I say.

"Really?" she says, as if it never occurred to her that I might have missed something other than The Thing, as if all she ever was to me is what she was in that last month.

"Yeah. Annie."

Her eyes come to mine and I look for a way to tell her what she was before that month, how she made me feel hopeful, joyful, and how lonely I was after she left. But I can't. There aren't words.

"Best go in," I whisper at last.

"Yeah," she whispers back.

We stand up together.

We walk side by side, not touching, into the hotel, onto the lift.

I say, "What floor?"

"Six."

"Me too." I push the six button.

"Seriously?"

"I would not joke about such a thing." I keep my eyes on the display, watching the numbers change. I stuff my hands in my pockets.

We step off the lift on the sixth floor.

"Well," she says, "I'm going this way." She points in the direction of my room.

"Me too," I say on a sigh, and I follow her down the hall.

She stops at the door immediately across from mine and says, "This is me."

I laugh, a tense chuckle. "And this is me. Ye gods."

Our eyes meet.

And then she says, "Oh!" and takes off my jacket. She hands it to me. I take it and step away.

"Night, then," I say.

"Night." Her eyes stay on mine for a suspended question of a moment. And then she turns and lets herself into her room. I stand in the hallway staring at her door for a moment, thinking of all the things I didn't say.

That night I wake up out of another dream that she's in bed with me. My hand is searching for her, futilely, as I come to wakefulness.

It's so much worse, knowing she's not with someone, and knowing she feels The Thing. She could be mine again, just for a little while. I glance at the clock—past three—and wonder what would happen if I just walked across the hall and pounded on her door until she opened it, all rumpled and warm from sleep. I could step into her room and pull her to the bed. I could have her naked and be inside her before she had come awake enough to react, and by then she'd be halfway to orgasm and she wouldn't stop me. She'd let me.

Fantasizing about fucking a woman who's only half-aware that you're there. Classy.

But I don't stop. I imagine making her come, how she'd make those little noises, how she'd press me closer with her hands and feet, how I could kiss her and kiss her, even as she slipped back into sleep. I could fuck her all night like that, as she drifted in and out of sleep, rising to consciousness as she turns her face to my throat, kissing me when she finds I'm inside her still. I'd make her come again, and again she'd fall back into sleep, and even as she slept, I'd kiss her with my tongue in her mouth, fuck her all the harder. And then, maybe not for hours, she'd wake again and still I'd be inside her. I'd roll onto my back with her, watch her ride me in the pink of the rising dawn, come on me again, sleep again. I'd never leave her, all night. I'd never come, not until the morning, when I'd roll her to her back and see how the sun illuminates her skin as I press her into the mattress. Then I'd fuck her until she screamed. I'd fuck her until she begged to come just one more time. I'd fuck her—

She's right across the hall, not twenty feet away, and I'm lying
here in a sticky mess, like a pubescent boy.

I don't see her at all the next day.

No surprise, given the size of the conference.

And it's not as if I'm looking for her.

Chapter 7

Massively Complex Dynamical Systems

I walk the long way to Simon's house on Saturday night, past the gardens and low terraced houses of the mews off Gray's Inn Road, and then the comfortable muddle of Rosebery Avenue and Coldbath Square. When I'm near, I look at my phone for Simon's directions.

> *Google Maps can't get you there—another dog and pony show of security—but come down St John St. On the west side just south of Aylesbury there's a red brick archway. I'll ask Stig to meet you there and take you through to the house. There are cameras and a sniper on the roof and things but they know you're coming and this isn't America so I expect they'll only shoot at you a very little bit, strictly for form's sake, and then Stig will let you into the house.*

I chuckle again, still reading as I approach the red brick archway in question. He's told me he works in government intelligence—"Oxymoron Division," he wrote—and he mocks the secretiveness of it, while also, I notice, genuinely not telling me anything.

"Dr. Douglas?" says a woman's voice with a faint Hindi accent, and I look up from my phone to see a woman in a black suit and a hat.

"Yes."

"I'm Mr. Douglas's driver. I'm to—"

I laugh. "You're Stig."

"Yes sir, that's what he calls me," she smiles back. "Please walk behind me, if you would."

She leads me through the alley into a square paved in yellow brick. Three sides of it are glass high-rises, and the fourth side is—

"Blimey," I breathe.

It's lovely for what it is, but it is distinctly odd, this squat red brick Victorian with a clock tower at the top, surrounded by the concrete and glass that have grown up around it.

Stig punches something into a keypad on the wide doors and lets us into the bright entryway of mosaic floor and white walls and pale marble stairs. Thundering from upstairs, I hear the piano piece that in my mind will always be John Cleese's "Oliver Cromwell" but I know is actually Chopin or similar.

"Er," Stig says over the racket, her hand on the doorknob. "Don't go out without him."

"Why?"

She shrugs. "Just . . . don't go out without him."

I don't want to describe this as ominous . . . but it is. It is decidedly ominous.

"Right. Thanks."

She leaves me alone in the entry, and I go quietly up the curving stairs, following the music to the long, narrow room to the left of the stairway. Simon is at the piano, his back to me. I lean against the doorframe and watch him play.

Four years. It's been nearly four years since I was in the same room with my brother. He's a little less narrow than the last time I saw him—which isn't saying much. A skinny, swotty twenty-year-old boy could slip through a crack in the floorboard.

He gets through the last thumping chords, concluding with a

triumphant little bounce on the bench, and then, without warning, he collapses, banging his forehead over and over on the keys with a clang of notes and a frustrated groan. But he sits up and, with a great sigh, closes the lid over the keys and puts his elbows on it, rubbing his face with both hands, under his glasses.

To announce myself, I say, " 'The most interesting thing about King Charles I—' " and Simon turns to me, grinning, but then turns back and opens the piano again to start playing, so I continue reciting the interesting fact of Charles being ten inches shorter by the end of his reign than he was at the beginning of it.

" 'Because of . . . ' " Simon declares, and he sings the whole thing, in a spot-on imitation of John Cleese. I take Eric Idle's part and do the sound effects, using the marching of the New Model Army and the hoofbeats of the Battle of Naseby to canter into the room, then drop myself onto the couch near the piano, contributing further facetious narration of the history of the English Civil War.

This is Simon as I remember him best: behind a piano as I lie on the couch. I was usually reading as he played, and the piano was our mother's blond Broadwood in Cornwall or the black Steinway at the London house. His own piano is a glossy redbrown, with ornately carved columnar legs, but the Simon behind it appears mostly the same—focused, unsociable, and odd, behind the pink-tinted lenses of his glasses, yet still handsomer than any of the rest of us.

He mimics the screechy falsetto at the end, and concludes the song with the flourish of scales and the punctuating chords. Then he grins at me, wide and relaxed. "Thanks, I nnneeded that," he says, and his voice is soft and light, with hardly any of the stutter left.

I sit up on the couch and, because I can't say, "I'm sorry I haven't been much of a brother to you," or "I feel profoundly moved to find myself in your house and singing with you, as if the last ten years hadn't happened," or "Please tell me what I can do to earn your forgiveness, after being such an unutterable shit for so long," I say instead, "That is a bloody enormous piano."

"It's in-insensitive to comment on the sssize of a man's piano," he admonishes benignly, and I laugh and feel the bridge between us begin to repair. He adds, with a self-deprecating wince, "It *is* the largest of the four."

"Four?"

"Well, there's this one," he says, and he plays a bit as he talks, "and then there's the baby grand—"

"The one you had when I left for the States."

"Yes, I'm afffraid they've accumulated at rather an alarming rate since then. Er, there's the Clementi sssquare on the ground floor, and the Mmmanxman upstairs."

I recognize the song now. It's Dire Straits, "Brothers in Arms."

To cover the rush of emotion, I ask, "What's a Manxman?"

"Oh," he says, with raised eyebrows, and he stops playing. He stands and gestures for me to follow. We go up another flight of stairs, and there, on the right, is an asymmetrical white-walled room with no seating but a piano stool and some heavy pillows on the floor. There are windows on the east- and west-facing walls, and between two closets along the south wall is what appears to be a cabinet. But Simon opens the doors to show me the slightly yellowed keys and the interior panels painted with peacocks. Simon sits at it and plays a quick burst of "Yes, We Have No Bananas," accompanying himself as he toots the tune, making a noise out of the side of his mouth like a horn, rather than singing the words.

When he finishes, he turns to me with a very, very serious expression indeed.

Biting away a smile, I say, "Simon?"

"Mh."

"Why have you got four pianos?"

He scratches the back of his head and winces. "It's ridiculous, I know. I c-can only play three at a time."

When I laugh, he adds, noodling on the keyboard with one hand, "Well, I've got to spend the b-blood pump money on something, haven't I, and it's this or the world's largest antique pants collection, really, so . . ." He makes a "yikes" face, plays "Shave and a haircut," without the "five bob," and says, "Drink?"

"Sure."

Down we tromp to the ground floor and into the kitchen, which is an extravagant display of wood, stone, and appliances that would be unobtrusive if they weren't so remarkable for their unobtrusiveness. Where Americans fill their kitchens with monstrous, shining, stainless steel edifices, Simon has fitted his with matte retro things, small in scale—apart from the six-foot range that fills the space where the fireplace used to be—and the whole thing is so tidy it looks like a magazine photo.

Simon pulls a bottle of wine from a wine fridge and three glasses from the cupboard.

"Mum'll be back soon. Shhhe's food shopping," he explains, as we sit opposite each other at the large farm table under the windows. He uncorks and pours for us both, then holds up his glass.

"Welcome home," he says, meeting my eye.

I smile through a tightness in my chest and throat, and raise my glass to his. "Cheers."

As we drink, I hear the front door, and Mum calls, "Hello, dear!"

Simon and I rise simultaneously and go to help her as she comes bustling in under a load of Waitrose bags.

"Darling," she says, kissing Simon on the cheek, "there's a gunman on next door's roof, did you know? Charles, dear, how lovely." She kisses me on the cheek as well. "You've had your hair cut."

Simon huffs like a bored teenager and moans, "Yes, don't ask."

"What?!" I interject, as I start unpacking the food. My bag is all vegetables. "A gunman? That wasn't a joke, in your e-mail?"

"Well the b-bit about shooting at you was a joke," Simon says.

I laugh, thinking this is an elaborate prank. But Simon just looks at me with a lopsided, apologetic moue.

I stand there with carrots in my hands, stunned and baffled.

"What?!" I say again.

He just rolls his eyes and waves his hand like he's shooing a fly. "If I think about it I'll only get cross again and have to go beat on another piano. Come on, make yourself useful, lad," and he wields a chef's knife at me before turning to the stereo.

He turns on Blondie and Mum says, "Charles, dear, would you set the table, please?" and all of a sudden it might as well be fifteen years ago. There is cooking and dancing to loud pop music from the seventies. And the food—I'm a competent cook, capable of feeding myself and, when necessary, Annie, but—

"Bloody hell, Simon," I say around the first bite of fish.

He wrinkles his nose on one side and says, "I know."

"When did you get good at this?"

His Blackberry buzzes. He makes a frustrated noise, then gets up from the table, answering it with, "Guh-good evening, sir."

"Oh dear," Mum says.

I look at her in question.

"Well." She stops and looks a bit guilty. "He's set up his mobile to buzz differently for different people, you know, so he can recognize callers by sound rather than sight."

"Sure."

"Well, I've heard them often enough that I've come to recognize a few of them, you know, and that was . . ." She looks over her shoulder to where Simon is talking on the phone while miming stabbing himself in the head. She looks back at me and whispers, "That was the prime minister's buzz."

"*What?!*"

Simon comes back to the table just then.

"Right," he says. "I've got to go g-give the government a bollocking. I expect the dishes will fffind their own way to the dn-dishwasher, so feel free to leave them here, Charles, honestly, do go eat bonbons with Mum while I make the world safe for democracy. I'll b-be back up in half an hour."

And he leaves, taking his dinner with him, plate, cutlery, and all.

"Where's he gone?" I ask Mum.

"Down to the cellar. He calls it his bat cave, you know, but it's his home office, really."

After we've eaten—and put the dishes in the dishwasher—Mum suggests I bother Simon in his bat cave.

"Will any alarms go off or target lasers float over my chest?"

"It's just an office, dear. Well, there's the piano, but apart from that."

So I descend the stairway to the cellar and find myself in an alcove with three doors. I poke my head through the open one and see weights and mats and balls and things. Then I hear the sound of typing coming from the next door, and I knock.

"Will I find glowing formaldehyde vats with floating heads in there?" I ask through it.

"Not today, alas. C-come in, I'm just finishing."

I open the door and peer in. It's another asymmetrical room, this time windowless with purple walls. He's sitting on a stool between a desk and a piano. The desk has two enormous screens, with the type so large I can read it from across the room—or could do, if it were in a language I recognized. It looks like a combination of logic symbols and calculus, so I decide it's none of my business anyway.

"It's Willy Wonka's chocolate factory, this house," I say, sitting on the black chesterfield sofa. Hanging on the opposite wall is a large black-and-white photo . . . of a black chesterfield sofa.

"So you've been into the conservatory," he answers, eyes on his monitor.

"You've got a *conservatory?*"

"It's where I keep the chocolate waterfall, and of course, my enslaved foreigners." This last he says in his Leslie-Howard-as-Henry-Higgins voice.

"You are a twisted individual," I say.

"It's the only way to get through the day," he sighs.

"May I know what's going on?" I ask, expecting him simply to say no.

"Baaaaaad things," he says. Then he swivels on his stool and looks at me. "I can say that I build computational models of mmmmassively complex dynamical systems that the government uses to make decisions."

"Oh. Well, shit."

"Yes. I can say that because only about six people know what it means. Anyway. The model is telling them to do something, and they're not doing it, and so the model is saying, 'Well, if you don't, then these things will happen, and you'll have to do this other thing instead,' and they don't want to do that, either, and so the model is saying, 'Then you are fucked.' That's the technical term, you understand, apologies for the jargon. Anyway, they don't like it and they're telling me to make the model say something else." He swivels back and resumes typing. "If all goes *well* . . . you'll never know what's going on. If not . . . well, at minimum you may be somewhat inconvenienced tomorrow."

"And at maximum?"

"Oh, you know. Death and destruction, war, et cetera. The *usual*." He's not joking. And yet he takes a deep breath and lets it out through his lips, making a noise like a motor as he exhales, exactly the way he did when he was eleven.

"Simon," I say.

"Mh." He's still focused.

"Please tell me the fate of the free world doesn't rest in the hands of a half-blind toff with more pianos than he can play at a time and a way with haddock."

"God, if only it did!" he moans. "We wouldn't be having these difficulties."

He's joking—only he isn't.

I snort a laugh and say, "No, we'd have an entirely different set of difficulties."

We sit together as he finishes, and then he turns to me again and says, "So: 'However entrancing it is to wander through a garden of bright images, are we not enticing your mind from another subject of almost equal importance?' Who, may I ask, is Annie, and why have you mentioned her twice, when you have previously never mentioned any girl, ever?"

"God, is that true?"

"I have a rather good memory," he says simply. He leans back and puts his stockinged feet on his desk. He's wearing yellow socks.

"Er." I lie back on the sofa, propping my crossed ankles on the arm. "We got together briefly last year, I was a total bastard to her, and then she moved away. We had drinks last night."

"And?"

"And . . . I dunno. She's . . . I don't know what you find attractive in girls—come to that, I don't even know if it's girls you're attracted to—"

"I lllike the ones who dn-don't treat me like a freak." He says it so blandly I almost miss the pain under it. Then he adds, "If they're intelligent on top of that . . . phwar."

"Well. If you think intelligence is hot, Annie would burn you alive. And she's a dancer, for god's sake. She's bloody gorgeous and brilliant and funny and deeply, agonizingly *sane*. When she laughs I just . . . I look at her and think, 'That. That's what I want.' And then I look at myself and think, 'No way, lad. No way you're getting anywhere near that.'"

Simon winces and nods.

"I hurt her badly last year. Very badly," I say. "She's forgiven me, of course, because she's . . . well, because she's Annie. But she deserves . . . someone whole."

Simon nods again.

And then his Blackberry buzzes again and he rolls his eyes, moaning, "Glutton for punishment, this one."

"I'd better leave you to it," I say, rising. "I'll go keep Mum out of trouble."

"Mh," he says. And before I walk out, I do a daring thing: I put my hand on my brother's shoulder. I don't try anything as reckless as squeezing it, I just rest it there for a couple seconds, and then I go.

I feel inordinately proud of this miniscule gesture in the direction of being a human being with my family.

Chapter 8

The Edge of My Own Terrain

After I say good night and Stig leads me back through the arch, I don't feel ready to go back to the hotel. The pavement is wet and there's a smell of dampness and of impending rain—*petrichor*, I think, remembering how Annie inhaled the scent in Indiana like it was a drug; I gave her the word, and she said it was her favorite fact ever.

For somewhere to go, I wander to the VQ, not really expecting her to be there, but there she is, deep in a health policy textbook, with her elbow on the page, her hand in her hair as she scribbles notes and mutters to herself. I approach her table, watching as she takes a sip of coffee and a bite of pie, then dribbles cherry filling all over her notes.

"Balls," she mumbles. She wipes at the page with her hand, then sucks her fingers.

"Hey," I say.

With her fingers in her mouth, she looks up at me. She takes her fingers out of her mouth.

"Hey," she says. "How was family?"

"It was . . . yeah. Good. Dunno yet. Still processing. Are you here for a while? May I join you?"

She gestures expansively over the mess, says, *"Mi mesa es su mesa,"* and then stacks up several books and packs others away, while I slide into the opposite seat and pull my laptop from my satchel.

An hour of near silence passes, broken mostly by the waiter asking me if I want anything and I say yes, I'd like as large a cup of black coffee as possible and a slice of that cherry pie please, and Annie calls me Agent Cooper. When I look at her blankly, her eyes widen and she says, "You've never seen *Twin Peaks?"* in the same tone she'd say, "You've never *voted?"*

Mostly, though, we work. It's my favorite way to work: in silence, in the middle of a crowd, with a mate.

Sometime after one, she pulls eyedrops out of her bag.

"Your eyes bother you?" I ask. I'm thinking about Simon when I glance up and see her with the eyedrops, but then I notice the way her lashes clump together and it triggers a chain reaction of physical memories—that moment when she came to the lab, soaked with rain, and I first felt the pull that has drawn me to her ever since; the night she laughed in the bathtub, while I sat and read P. G. Wodehouse to her; the day she came to my flat after her recital, damp with rain, and told me she loved me; the night she cried in Montreal, when she fell asleep in my arms, the tears still wet on her face.

"Just a little," she says. "What? Is something wrong?" She puts a hand over her mouth and nose, like she's worried about crumbs.

I shift my attention back to the present. "No, just . . . I haven't seen you without your glasses for a while."

And then her eyes meet mine and I'm drowning again in memory—the last time I saw her without her glasses, that last night, the good-bye sex when she came like a volcano, vast, slow, thunderous, and she said, "It hurts," and I said, "Hurt me, Annie," and she did. Hit me and bit me as I fucked her. And then, she wrapped her arms around me and kissed the teeth marks she had made in my shoulder. She told me she loved me and I said, "I can't." But I kissed her face and lips and held her close, only letting go when we fell asleep.

And in the morning, she was gone.

The whole memory, the whole look, lasts less than a second, and then my eyes are back on my laptop. I'm flushed and breathing too hard.

Disaster, I tell myself.

After a long silence, Annie says, "Could I ask a personal question?"

"Sure." I don't look up from my typing.

"It's about sex."

"Er." Still not looking up. Still typing.

She says, "So . . . you know how one of the things we did a couple times was how you made me come until I couldn't move?"

I don't look up, but my fingers go still.

"Except the last time we . . . you know . . . kinda the opposite was true. And I wondered—"

"You want to talk about this here? Now?" I whisper, as I glance around the half-empty diner.

She rolls her eyes. "Dude, nobody gives a shit what we're talking about."

I shift in my seat. "If it's all right with you, I'd prefer to talk about it some other time, somewhere less full of people."

"Okay." She shrugs and returns to her textbook.

And I sit there arguing with myself.

Where else are we going to talk about it, if not in a mostly empty diner in the middle of the night? Am I going to invite her into my room, for god's sake, for a cozy chat about the different ways my body has wanted to possess and control hers?

And does she not have a right to ask? Though she isn't with someone now, presumably she's had experiences in the last year that have created some context for what we did, and isn't it perfectly reasonable that she would question it? And was I not always the person she came to with questions? Do I not want to be that person still?

I have no idea where the boundaries are. I'm following her lead. She says sex equals disaster, so sex is out of bounds. Fine. But she wants to *talk* about sex, so . . .

I say, "Annie."

She looks up.

"That last night was—" I stop, abashed. I start again, but so quietly that she leans forward to hear me. "That night I wanted more than anything to give you what you wanted, and I couldn't, and I knew I was hurting you. Somehow that turned into . . . wanting you to hurt me back, I suppose."

She nods. "That part makes some sense to me. I mean, you beat yourself up enough for three people, so of course you would want me to beat the shit out of you. That's just me doing to you what you do to yourself all day, every day."

"Er," I say.

She seems utterly unaware that she has just flayed me open.

She continues, "It's the passivity that confuses me. Why would you like me not to be able to move, and stuff? I thought one of the things you liked about me was that I'm, like . . . the opposite of passive. Isn't that a contradiction?"

I clear my throat and glance around the diner again, then say very slowly, and still very quietly, "It is your strength that made your . . . your acquiescence so, erm . . . For you to hand me your body, trust me that far . . ." I stop, look down, biting my lip, remembering too vividly the feel of her body pliant and yielding under me. I say, "I did worry that I was subsuming you."

She uses her fork to gather the crumbs left from her pie. "Yeah. I've been worried that I turned myself into an object."

"Is that how you felt?" I'm appalled. It's my absolute worst fear. I lean forward and say in an even lower voice, "Less than your entire self? Less than . . . less than me?"

She makes a scoffing noise. "I always feel less than *you*."

I laugh—but then I see her face. "You're not joking."

She shrugs, still collecting crumbs into a little pile in the center of her plate. "Look at you: dozens of publications, you invented the blood pump—we had an entire lecture in my policy class about how that thing has saved lives—plus, you're about to start an amazing fellowship, and you're not even thirty. I'll never be what you are. But when we . . . at the time, when we were . . ." She pauses, pressing the heap of crumbs with the back of her fork. "I felt the opposite of all that. I felt . . . worshipped. Like you worshipped me."

"I did."

She looks up then and finds me watching her. Her eyes return to her fork. She says, "What did I do to deserve that, though? Just what you told me to do? Just have a body that could do what you wanted it to do? Or . . . I don't know. It was like a monthlong seminar in sex, and I got an A, not because I really understood anything, but because I memorized what you taught me. Like, did I like what we were doing . . . or did I like being praised for doing what you liked?" She trails off and her eyes lift to mine briefly before she looks back down at her fork and concludes, "I don't know what I mean."

"The question is: Did you like it because you authentically liked what we did, or did you like it because you liked meeting my standard? Intrinsic reward versus extrinsic reward. Have I got that right?"

She stares at me, then says, "Yes."

"There is a third possibility."

"There is?"

"That . . ." I stop and look around, then say more quietly still, "That what I worshipped was not a standard that I held and you met, like a teacher and student. What if the thing I worshipped in you was as brand-new to me as it was to you?" I keep my eyes on her fork as I say it.

"Was it?"

I nod and say softly, seriously, "I didn't spend that month coaching you in the things I knew. I was at the edge of my own erotic terrain. You—and all the things we did together—were and are without precedent in my life."

Our eyes meet and hold over the table, and her lips part. My jaw tightens as I remember how it felt when I told her to look at me and she did, and she came and came and couldn't stop coming, suspended and gasping and out of control and I thought it was the most erotic moment of my life, to look into this woman's eyes as I made her come—and then she said, "It hurts."

And in the morning she was gone.

Disaster.

I sit back, raising my eyebrows, and say, "Well. This has been a fascinating discussion, but I believe I'll go back to the hotel, take a cold shower, and go to bed. . . . Unless you want to tie me up and torture me with pleasure?"

I grin at her, to make it a tease, rather than an invitation.

She sighs and blinks at her books. "What time is it?"

I check my watch. "After two."

"Dude. I gotta go to bed. My flight is at eleven tomorrow. I'm leaving here at seven."

"Come on, then. Get your stuff and I'll walk you back." I put things away and stand up, buttoning my jacket discreetly.

She crams her stuff into her bag and follows me to the door . . . where we find it's pissing down with rain.

Glumly, she watches it fall. "Aren't you people supposed to always have an umbrella?"

I grin at her. "I've lived in America too long. Come on, it's only a few blocks, you won't melt."

Chapter 9

Give Me a Fucking Hug

Charles leads me briskly through the rain back to the hotel, but by the time we get inside we're drenched and dripping. We ride the elevator in silence. When I notice I can't read the number panel through the rain on my glasses, I take them off and stuff them in the side pocket of my backpack. I'm chilly in the air-conditioning. I push my wet hair back from my wet face, then rub my wet hands on my wet jeans.

The elevator dings. We step off.

As we walk toward our doors, I say, "When are you going back to Indiana?"

"Tomorrow. My flight's at half two."

I sniff and fold my arms across my chest, against the cold of the air-conditioning on my wet skin. "We could have breakfast."

He shakes his head. "I have plans."

"Oh, okay." I'm starting to shiver now.

We arrive at our doors and face each other. Rainwater is dripping from his bangs, and his pants are plastered to his legs and his jacket is soggy. Where his shirt is open, his clavicles and throat show little streamlets of water.

Then I register the expression on his face, and I remember:

Charles likes me wet. It was seeing me wet from the rain that made The Thing start.

Our eyes meet and hold for a long moment, and for an instant it seems like a really good idea to take those two steps across the hall and just kiss him, put my arms around him, do it, just do it, and he'd pull me into his room and into a hot shower and he'd fuck me under the spray and then fuck me again in the bed or on the floor and I'd come and he'd say I'm amazing and we'd fall asleep together and then in the morning . . . a few hours from now . . . I'd wake up and fly back to Boston. Alone.

So I say, "It would be totally amazing, at the time." I watch his jaw tense and his nostrils flare at this. I continue, "I mean the 'during' part would be amazing, right? It's the 'after' part that would potentially be, ya know . . ."

"A disaster," he says through his teeth.

"Yeah." I look down again. I tighten my arms across my chest, against a shiver that makes my teeth chatter. "So maybe we *could* have—" Down the hall the elevator dings and three people get off. We wait for them to go to their rooms before I continue more quietly. "Maybe we could have, like, a nice fuck for an hour or two and then I'd get on a plane and go home tomorrow and we'd stay as we are, e-mailing and stuff. But maybe I'd end up as"—I shake my head and close my eyes, remembering how it was— "ugh, as vulnerable and torn to pieces as I was a year ago."

He says seriously, "I don't want to tear you to pieces, Annie."

I take a deep breath and shiver some more. "Okay, so I'm gonna say this thing, and I want you to think carefully before you respond."

He crosses his arms over his chest and leans back against his door. He's shivering too now. "Okay."

I look at him and announce solemnly, "I think you're probably my best friend."

I wait.

He watches me wait.

I wait some more. My lips are numb with cold and my hands are stiff.

I say, "Are you thinking carefully about how to respond?"

"Is that it?"

"Yes, that's it. You're my best friend. I don't want to screw that up just to get laid."

"Annie, you'll have—" Again the elevator dings and this time the people come our way. We wait in silence until they've gone into their room.

He takes a single step toward me, halfway across the hall, and, more quietly still, he continues, "You'll have my friendship as long as you want it. Without condition."

He holds my gaze until I nod, accepting this. I whisper, "Me too."

He nods, too.

Then I turn and open my door.

As I step through into my dark room, he says, "Can I . . . say something, too, and you'll think carefully before you respond?"

I drop my bag and lean against the doorframe. He stays in the hall. There's rainwater trickling from his hairline at his temple, down to his jaw.

He says, "In fact, you don't have to respond at all. I'd just like to say this thing."

"Okay."

"You remember—" Again the elevator dings. Saturday night in a London hotel.

"God," I groan at the interruption, and I open the door wider and step back to let him in. I lean against the closet wall, and I see him lean against the bathroom wall as the door closes, and then we're left in total darkness, three feet apart from each other.

This was a mistake. I shouldn't have let him in. I shouldn't be standing here in the dark with him. My heart starts racing. I fist my hands and cross my arms again, shoulders raised, shivering.

"I wanted to say . . ." He stops. In the dark, I hear the tremor in his voice and I wonder if he's as cold as I am. I hear him take a deep, unsteady breath before he continues, "Do you remember what I said at Margaret's wedding?"

"You trust me," I say through cold lips.

"Yes. And that when you were ready, I'd be where you needed me to be. And I am. I got out of that fucking pit. 'Friends and colleagues,' we said, and I want that, Annie. To have—to *deserve* your respect means more than I can say. That's what I wanted to say: that I've endeavored, in the last year, to be worthy of your respect."

"You always were," I say.

"No, I wasn't," he answers instantly. "But I might be now. I'm learning how to be." He makes a frustrated little noise then and blows out a breath. "I hadn't . . . quite . . . taken The Thing into account, though."

I hear him move and then feel him—not his body, but the heat of him. He's leaning his elbows on the wall next to my shoulders. He isn't touching me anywhere, except with his breath, almost as unsteady as mine, on my temple. I feel my own breath ricochet from his throat back onto my lips.

I'm trembling still. And when, after a long, still silence, his lips just graze my temple, I feel that he is trembling, too.

"We have A Thing," he whispers against the corner of my eyebrow, a tense shudder in his throat.

I nod.

"I've never known anything like it." He sounds helpless, puzzled. "There's nothing I can do and nothing I can ask for that won't hurt both of us, now or later, and yet there is this . . . Thing."

I shake my head slowly, back and forth, lifting my head so that his lips brush my eyelid. When I'm still again, he kisses along the crest of my cheek—not even kisses, just the barest touch of his parted, trembling lips, and the rush of his shaky breath on my skin. I lift my chin to put the corner of my mouth close to the corner of his mouth.

A suspended moment. We're both trembling, our breath shallow.

I wait for him to move.

He doesn't.

"What do we do?" he breathes. "Tell me what to do." I don't know if it counts as a kiss, but my open mouth is barely touching his open mouth and now we're both breathing in hot, desperate gusts. His nose is against the side of mine. Our glasses tap.

"I guess . . . think about what it would be like tomorrow?" I whisper. And if he kisses me now, I'm his.

But he doesn't. Silently, he pushes away from me, the palms of his hands flat on the wall, his head bowed before me.

I put my cheek against his wet hair.

We stand there that way for I don't know how long, until at last he says from between his teeth, "Bye, Annie."

The air in front of me cools as he moves away.

As I stand there shivering, the door opens, I see his silhouette move through it, and then it closes again.

When I can move again, I turn on all the lights and take a hot shower, scrubbing my body under the stinging spray. Then I change into my pajamas and lie in bed, shivering still.

I sleep off and on for four hours, unable to stop playing and re-playing his words in my mind. That he is literally across the hall from me, that I could knock on the door and he would let me in and I could lie down and have him inside me tonight, right now, or not even lie down but lean against the door and wrap my arms and legs around him, is agony.

The possibility that he too is in his bed alone but thinking of me, fantasizing about me, stroking his cock and imagining that it's my hand on him, it makes me desperate. The knowledge that this might be the very last time we ever have this opportunity . . . both tantalizes and sobers me.

Why am I not over there? Because if I go over there, I will fuck him. And then maybe nothing, maybe it would be fine . . . but maybe it would be a disaster. What if I lose him for real this time? In just three days with him near me, I feel nourished in a way I haven't in ages. It makes me want to jump up and down and scream, throw myself on my floor and sob, dance and run and stay utterly still and just let this feeling happen inside me. Above all, it makes me want never, ever to be without him in my life.

He's coming to Boston. I will have my friend back—if I don't fuck it up just because we have A Thing. I'm not sure I could survive the loss of him again.

But now I wonder if I can survive this intensity of wanting.

My alarm goes off at six. My eyes feel pasty and gritty, and my bones ache with exhaustion. I do not want to get out of this bed and get on a plane. I'm swamped with dread at the thought.

At six thirty, my phone rings. I answer it without looking. I know who it is.

"Hey," I say, through my mop of hair.

"Hey. Did I wake you?" he says, his voice gravelly with fatigue.

"No. Not sure I ever fell asleep."

"Jesus. Sorry. I called to ask if we might try saying good-bye properly, without my fucking it up. I've ordered some coffee. Would you come over?"

"Okay," I sigh, "I'll be there in a couple minutes." With a weary groan, I drag my body out of bed and haul it to verticality. I pack my pajamas in my suitcase, so I'm all ready to leave, and I put on my travel clothes.

The room service guy is leaving right as I step into the hallway, so I just catch the door and let myself in.

Charles has a suite. I'm standing in a living room three times the size of my entire room.

"Dude," I say, looking around. "All that time in the diner, I could have just worked in here."

"Do you really think that if you'd come here to work last night, you'd have gotten anything done?" Charles is pulling chairs up to either side of the table where the coffee tray sits. He's freshly shaved, wet hair combed off his forehead, but with bags under his eyes and exhaustion in every line of his face. He pours us each a cup of coffee and then drapes himself in one of the chairs, legs straight out, ankles crossed. He gestures me toward the other. I sit—or rather, drape—mirroring him. We stare at the table.

"What are your plans for this morning?" I ask through a yawn.

He yawns, too, and says, "I'm meeting Melissa."

An unpleasant jolt of adrenaline sours my mood even further. What I needed to hear right before I leave is that the last thing he's doing before he leaves the country is having breakfast with his ex-girlfriend. Good. That's awesome. I mean it's fine.

He pushes his hands through his hair and sighs. I wait for him to figure out what he wants to say.

Apparently, he doesn't know, either.

"I'm crap at good-byes," he says, rubbing his forehead against his palm. "You're good at them. Teach me how."

"I don't know," I groan. "You just say shit like, 'It was great to see you!' and 'I really enjoyed blah blah blah,' and 'I'll see you again at thus and such!' and 'Thanks for the whatevers!'"

"It was great to see you," he says obediently, but genuinely.

"I really enjoyed hearing about your existential crisis," I say, taking my turn.

He laughs on a quiet breath and then says, "I'll see you again in August."

Then I grin. "Thanks for all the sandwiches."

"And you'll write to me when you can," he adds extemporaneously. "And hit send."

"Yeah."

We look at each other across the table in silence for a long, bleary-eyed moment.

He says, "Is that it? That's a good-bye?"

I shrug.

"So it's not that I'm crap at them, it's that they're awful. Well, that's a sort of relief, I suppose. *Par la souffrance, la vertu,*" he says bleakly.

His family motto. His family has a motto. "Virtue through suffering."

We sit in silence for another moment. Twice, he takes a breath as if he's about to say something, and then he stops himself.

At last, with his eyes on his fist, which he's bouncing on the arm of his chair, he says, "I've been dreaming about you." I watch him swallow. "I wake up in the middle of the night, convinced you're in the bed, and then . . ." He stops and presses his fist against his mouth for a moment. Then, flattening out his hand and rubbing his eyes under his glasses, he finishes, "And then it's exactly like the last time I woke up and you weren't there. So it feels like I've been saying good-bye to you over and over."

I don't know what to say, so when he lifts his weary eyes to meet mine, I just say, "I'm sorry."

He laughs with a harsh suddenness, like he's had the wind knocked out of him. Then he leans back his head and closes his eyes. "Darling girl, it is I who am sorry. I am sorry, Annie. I am sorry."

Again I don't know what to say, so I just say, "It's okay. There's nothing to be sorry for."

More silence, more exhausted looks across a table.

I pull out my phone and check the time. "I should probably go."

Looking at his watch, he says, "Yep. Okay." He stands up and leads me to the door, but he stops with his hand on the knob, and we stand there looking at each other. He says, "Is this . . . are we okay? Have we sorted this? Is it just a terrible, hopeless mess?"

I pull half a smile from my weary brain and say, "Of all the things you've said in the last twenty-four hours, for me the most important was 'You'll have my friendship as long as you want it, without condition.' If that's true . . . then I think the rest of it will work itself out somehow. Now give me a fucking hug," I say. I raise my arms and stand on my toes, and he puts his arms around my waist. He hugs me for real, without hesitation.

Still holding me, he says into my ear, "I keep wanting to apologize."

"There's nothing to apologize for."

And he hugs me a little closer.

When he pulls away, he puts a hand on the back of my neck and kisses my cheek. I hear him inhale through his nose. I smell him—soap? aftershave? what would make a man's neck smell so good?—a scent so familiar and beautiful that my breath catches. There is a tiny cool spot on my cheek where he kissed me, and it takes a great effort not to put my hand there, to hold on to it.

He steps away and opens the door. I look up at him and see the anxiety still in his eyes.

"Bye, Charles."

"Bye, Annie."

With a deep breath, I look away from him, turn, and walk out the door.

I go to my room and collect my stuff.

I walk to the Tube stop.

I get on a train and go to the airport, four hours ahead of Charles.

And that's when things really go wrong.

Chapter 10

I Was Never Unsafe

Annie, give me a bell. You're about to get an alert that all flights are being canceled.

Are you all right? May I call you?

I'm on my way.

I'll be there soon. You okay?

I can't call from the train. How are you?

FInr

I'll be there soon. Which terminal?

5

Nearly there
Tell me where you are and I'll come get you.

I don't know.

Can you look around tell me what you see?

I don't know it's the airport.

And then he's there beside me. He's squatting beside my chair with a hand on my arm.

"Hey," he says.

I turn my face to his, my lips numb and cold, and search his kind, calm, earnest blue eyes. I ask, "Is anybody dead?"

"Nobody's dead," he answers easily. He stands up, guiding me to my feet. "Let's go somewhere quieter, what do you think?" He's already steering me back to the entrance by the time I nod.

"I should call my parents. Where are we going?"

"To my brother's. There aren't any taxis, we'll take the Tube. How does that sound to you?"

"Can I call my parents when we get there?"

"Yep."

And then somehow we're on the train with my bags at our feet. It's crowded and hot and noisy but Charles is sitting next to me and he's really calm. I feel like there's no blood anywhere in my body except my stomach. I turn to look at his calm face. He smiles at me a little. It's genuine.

I smile a little back, and begin to shake minutely.

Four stops later, I say in a quavering whisper, "Charles?"

"Annie."

"Could you maybe put your arm around me?"

"Sure."

Two stops later I'm shivering with my face against his shirt.

"Next one's us," he says into my hair. "Ready?"

I shake my head no, but gather my things and stand up. Charles leads me by the hand off the train, through the station, out onto the street, which is wide open and looks much too normal to make any sense.

"How far are we going?" I ask.

"About a mile," he says, "unless we—ah!" I startle when he

throws his hand up at a cab. He touches my arm and looks at me, questioning, as the black cab pulls up.

I nod, and we pile my stuff into the taxi. Charles gives the address and I sit there swallowing and shaking, with Charles's hand on my arm. We pass the alarmingly named Slaughtered Lamb, make a left, and the cab stops at a dead-end.

Charles carries my stuff as he leads me, saying, "It's the brick one there on the left."

I follow him, shaking like it's freezing out, but it's June. The house looks old to my eyes, worn red brick and yellow stone decoration around the windows and door, but it's surrounded by ominous glassy high-rises on every side. Charles lets himself into the house not with a key but with a passcode typed into a number pad.

"Where are we?" I say through chattering teeth.

"This is my brother Simon's house."

"Where's he?"

Ushering me in, Charles says, "At work. Let's go into the conservatory."

"Your kid brother has a 'conservatory,'" I clarify numbly.

Charles rolls his eyes and grins. "I know. Wanker."

He rests his hand between my shoulder blades and guides me through to a sunny room at the back of the house. He escorts me to a soft beige chair with an enormous matching ottoman, and he hands me my phone. Did he take it from me? Did I give it to him?

"Thanks," I mutter, incurious.

I curl up in the chair and, hands shaking, call my dad.

"Hi, honey!"

"Hi, Dad." And at the sound of his voice, the dam breaks. I sob into the phone, "I can't come home. I wanna come home." And I start gusting out the story incoherently.

"Honey, slow down. Take a deep breath. Tell me what's happening."

I explain, gasping to hyperventilation, "They shut down the airport. I was there and they canceled all the flights and told everybody to leave and—and—"

Dad already knows I'm not a great flier. When the announce-ment was made at the airport, I was already wallowing in dread, and then I went into a little bubble of denial. I thought, *No, they're not canceling all the flights out of this gigantic international air-port! That's ridiculous!* And then I thought, *Well, okay, so they're can-celing all the flights, but that doesn't mean there's anything particularly bad happening.* And then I realized that they wouldn't shut down an airport unless it was something bad. Like, *really* bad.

Which is when my brain went into lockdown.

I sat in the airport, smelling burning and tasting ash and feel-ing sure that people were dying all around me. It seemed unreal to me that the airport looked so ordinary—all that glass and steel and the people, frustrated, worried, but healthy, sharing cabs and calling people for rides and stuff.

And then Charles was there.

Dad doesn't need to know all that. Still struggling to breathe, I conclude, "And I'm . . . I don't know. I'm with Charles. He came and got me and brought me to his brother's house."

"Charles? *Charles* Charles?"

"Yeah. It's okay, that all got worked out," I say vaguely, and I glance around to find that Charles is gone and that there's a soft blanket over me. I tangle my fists in it, pull it up to my chin, and curl up in a tight ball on the chair, eyes closed. I start crying again and can barely talk. "God, I'm too old to feel this way. Why do I feel this way? Why am I panicking like this?"

"There's no why to feelings, Anniebear, it's just what you feel."

"I was never unsafe," I say, wrapping an arm around my head and curling myself up as tight as I can. "Why is this happening?"

"We were all unsafe, honey, and you're sensitive. Kleenex commercials make you cry, sweetie. A national tragedy is gonna leave a mark."

"Right," I sniff, still curled up tight, and laugh a little. "That sounds like total bullshit but I'll take it."

"We miss you at home, kiddo, but we're so proud of you. I know you'll come back safe to us and we'll—"

I grab on to this. "How do you know? I mean, how can you *know?*"

"Sweetie, I don't know."

"You don't know? Or, you don't know how you know?"

"I mean I don't know. How could anybody know for sure that something terrible won't happen? But I think it's gonna be okay, Annie Bee. And you're safe right now, right?"

I sniff into the phone. "Yeah."

"Yeah. And your mom and dad love you just as much now as when you're sitting between us on the living room couch."

"I know."

"And you and me and your mom will be sitting together on that couch very, very soon."

"Okay," I sniff. "Okay."

"So what are you going to do to take care of yourself, honey?"

"Well, calling you guys was the first thing."

"Good plan, that's good. What's next?"

"I think . . . maybe I can take a bath?"

"Okay. Sounds good. What else?"

The answer clicks into place, and it feels inevitable: I want to sleep with Charles. I don't just want him, I need him, need the feel of his skin against my skin, his sweat against my sweat, and then I need to fall asleep in his arms. There is no potential aftermath of that comfort that wouldn't be worth it. Just the thought of him holding me, kissing me, letting me wrap my whole body around him, loosens a knot somewhere inside me and I take a deep, deep breath and let out a long, slow sigh. My muscles relax.

I don't say anything about any of this to my father, of course. To him I say, "We'll probably get something to eat."

"And maybe go to bed early? Get some sleep?"

"Definitely."

"Maybe even take a nap?"

"Yeah."

Somewhat calmer now, I let Dad say good-bye, and look up to see that Charles is back, sitting in the chair opposite mine, texting diligently. I keep my eyes on him as I stretch my body and yawn. I'm not shaking now, but I feel uncomfortable. Jittery.

Chapter 11

Welcome Back to the Present

My phone buzzes—Simon is texting me.

Much ministers. Very farce. Have complained to mgmt.
Home by 6 with lemon soaked paper napkins

Mum plans to truss a chicken to Abba.

Dig it

I hear Annie take the deep, deep breath, with the long, slow exhale, still unsteady, but her breath grows softer after that, and I know she's nearly returned to the present.

Her father must be asking her what she'll do next because she's saying, "We'll probably get something to eat."

She agrees to a few more things and says a painstaking good-bye—"Bye. I love you. Bye."—and when she hangs up, she stretches in her chair, flexing her spine and shoulders, arching her neck, and then allowing it all to collapse, limp. Her body is much softer now, and she's not trembling. Her face has color.

"Hey," she says.

"Hey," I say with a grin. "Mum's on her way now—she was just out doing the shopping—and Simon'll be home around six."

"Okay." She sits up, taking a giant breath, and then groans her exhale, slumping down, not stopping until her whole upper body folds down, her torso draped over her thighs, her head between her shins, backs of her hands relaxed against the floor.

"Ugh," she says.

"Everything okay at home?" I ask.

"Yeah. I mean, I knew it was, but . . ." She turns her head to look at me, without sitting up. "Ya know."

I do know.

She sits up, then stands up. Then squats, then jumps, then begins swaying side to side, shaking her hands like they're coated in sticky dough. All the while she's looking around the room, noticing the space she's in. Most of my patients need to be taught this skill. I had to be taught this skill. But for her, it's all automatic, intuitive.

She looks at me and says, "I didn't even realize this room was, like, a greenhouse until I stood up."

"Welcome back to the present."

"Huh?" She's still swaying, more slowly and subtly, and her hands are just rotating at the elbow like she's coaxing blood into them after holding them over her head too long. She asks, "Is this annoying? Should I sit down?"

"On the contrary—"

Her phone rings. She holds up a finger and answers it.

"Hey, Mom." She sits cross-legged on the ottoman. "I'm at Charles's brother's house. . . . It's okay. I'm okay, I was kind of freaked out, but Charles came and got me. . . . Um." She glances over at me, holding the phone away from her ear. She says, "She wants to talk to you."

So I hold out my hand. She gives me the phone.

"Dr. Coffey," I say.

And Dr. Frances Coffey proceeds to give me the bollocking of a lifetime, explaining to me precisely how heartbroken Annie was when she came home from Indiana, how hard she worked to heal, and that if I take advantage of her, she—Dr. Coffey—will kick me in the teeth. I agree with everything and return the phone to Annie when she's finished.

"What the hell was that? Were you mean to him?" Annie says into the phone, looking at me suspiciously, and then she asks me, "Was she mean to you?"

"Not at all," I say.

"Well, quit it," she says to her mother. She flops back onto the chair and puts a hand on her forehead. "I'd be curled up in a ball, shaking in some corner of the airport right now if he hadn't come to get me."

I hear the front door and go to meet Mum at the entry.

"Annie's in the conservatory," I say, accepting my kiss on the cheek as I take her bags. I set all of it in the kitchen and lead Mum to the conservatory.

Annie looks up when we come in and says, "I will. I gotta go now. . . . Okay. Bye, Mom. I love you. Bye."

I say, "Annie, I'd like you to meet my mother, Carol Douglas. Mum, this is Annie Coffey, the friend I was telling you about."

Mum goes to Annie, who's getting to her feet again, and presses Annie's hand between her two. "What a pleasure to meet you, Annie," she says. "You're just as I imagined."

"Hi," Annie says, basking in Mum's warm glow.

"Mum, we come seeking refuge," I say. "Heathrow is closed because the universe is a fundamentally unreliable place."

"I'm sure Simon will be very pleased to have you both," she says cheerfully. "What would you like, dear? Drink? Snack? What'll it be, miss?"

"Can I take a bath? And then a nap, if possible?" Annie asks, and then she adds with a groan, "And then I really should get some work done. I have to read half a public health theory textbook today."

"Right," I say, taking over. "Follow me."

I guide her with a hand on her shoulder through the maze of the house. We go up the stairs and through the asymmetrical rooms until I deposit her in the pretty first-floor bathroom, with its claw-foot tub under a large window.

"Towels are in the cupboard. Text if you need anything," I say, putting her phone on the edge of the sink—she keeps leaving it behind—and I leave her to it.

When I check on her an hour later, she's out of the tub and dead to the world, deeply asleep on the guest bed, wrapped in an enormous towel. I fetch the blanket from the conservatory and drape it over her, and then I sit by her feet and watch her sleep.

The text from Simon this morning rescued me from the awkward breakfast with Melissa. There I was, allowing her to explain my many defects to me, nodding sincerely as she told me she forgave me, when my phone bleeped. Simon.

Outcome: inconvenience for you. Heathrow airport about to be shut down.

Sorry about your flight

Thank god for Simon.

"Er, sorry, hang on," I said to Melissa. "I think a friend of mine might be . . ."

I text—

Annie's flight too?

All international flights out of Heathrow

Thanks for the advance notice. May I bring Annie to yours?

I'll alert the sniper

"Er." I glanced up at Melissa, who was waiting without much patience to hear that this friend of mine had died, which is surely the only thing that would justify the interruption. I disappointed her by saying, "I'm so sorry, this friend of mine from the conference is stranded at the airport. I've got to go."

And I went.

And now here this friend of mine is, curled up in a warm, pink ball, sound asleep in a guest room in my brother's house.

I've worked hard this last year to earn what she brings to my life. If she's willing to have me in her life, there is nothing I want more. I think I might deserve her as a friend now. I know, without a doubt, that I *want* her friendship. I may even need it. I went without it for a year, and I never want to do it again.

Chapter 12

Waterloo

I wake up under the blanket that seems to be following me around the house. My face feels stiff with dried tears, swollen and tender. My eyes burn a little.

My suitcase has found its way into this room, so, bleary and feeling jet-lagged, I put on clean clothes and then I wander until I find Charles in a book-lined room, where a grand piano takes up about a quarter of the space. He's asleep on the couch. His glasses are off, folded on top of his nearby laptop, and his shoes are lying haphazardly under the coffee table.

I sit down on the couch by his feet and watch his face as he sleeps. He has a straight, bony nose, like the nose on Michelangelo's *David*. My nose is aquiline, which my mom tells me is a nice way of saying large and a little bit hook-shaped. I got it from her. It was one of my worst attributes as a dancer, actually, this big schnoz of mine, not at all the petite, graceful lines of a dancer. My ears are big, too. And my feet. But Charles is handsome, with his gracefully arching light brown eyebrows and his gold-tipped eyelashes and his heart-tugging smile full of slightly imperfect teeth.

I think about how he smiled at me on the train, warm and

calm, totally sure that everything would be okay. The memory makes me a little wobbly, and my eyes cloud. I bite my lips between my teeth and sniff against the sting in my nose.

This guy. This man. There is such kindness in him . . . and such fear. I didn't understand the fear last year. I'm not sure I understand it now, but I can feel acceptance of it in my body, an easy welcoming of everything he is. Everything. Right now, in this moment, if he told me that at his breakfast with Melissa he remembered how much he loved her and they decided to get back together, most of what I would feel is glad for him that he'd found someone he could feel safe with, someone who felt like home. I would give him a hug and tell him "congratulations" and hope against hope that his finding someone he could love wouldn't mean I'd lose his friendship.

Above all, I do not want to lose his friendship. I tried living without it, and I never want to do it again.

But if he'll have me, if he can say yes to me without breaking his word to someone else, then tonight I want to press my naked skin against his naked skin. I want to put my tongue in his mouth and receive his body into mine and breathe with him in the dark.

And tomorrow will be fine. My sense of disaster from last night has vanished, as if the bigger disaster of the airport has blown away every other paltry little fear.

"Hey," he says.

I hadn't noticed that he'd woken up. "Hey."

"Feel okay?"

I nod and shrug and, despite my best efforts, lose control of my lower lip as a tear falls down my cheek.

"Sweetheart. Come here." He opens his arms and I tuck my body between him and the couch, resting my head on his shoulder. His arms go around me and it feels so good it almost hurts. With a hand gripped in his shirt, I let myself cry in his arms, let the warmth of his body and his heart thaw the remnants of my frozen panic, let it evaporate out of me until I'm left with a tender sort of bruised feeling that needs only time and kindness to heal. I sniff and sigh myself toward calmness and then lift my head to rub my nose on my sleeve.

"I'll get snot on your shirt," I say.

"Doesn't matter," he says easily.

"Maybe not to you. Let me get a tissue or something." I sit up and look around.

"On the desk under the window."

I bring the whole box back with me and sit myself at his feet while I tidy up my face. "Sorry I'm such a mess," I say at last. It crosses my mind to bring up the subject of sex, but I decide to wait until I'm less blotchy and swollen and his shirt doesn't have a wet spot on it from my tears and possibly also my snot. "Thanks for being so nice."

"Least I could do." He smiles gently and sits up in the corner of the couch. He puts on his glasses.

"No," I say. "The least you could do is nothing. Instead, you came and got me when I was having a massive meltdown."

"How are you now?"

I sigh and relax a bit inside my body. "Good. Better. A little . . . raw."

"Perfectly normal."

"Why was I um . . . do you know why I couldn't stop shaking? On the train?"

"Self-paced termination," he says, folding his hands behind his head. "You went into freeze. The shaking was part of coming back out."

"Oh," I say. "Dude."

"Being a mammal is a bitch sometimes," he says, and he grins over at me. I smile over at him. Our eyes meet.

My smile fades but my eyes stay on his, and his grin transforms into the warm, affectionate look that always took my breath away. It takes my breath away now.

I should say something. We should talk about it.

But I don't. Instead, I look away, while I fiddle with a button in the couch cushion and bite my lip.

"Where's your mom?" I ask.

"Kitchen," Charles says, and he leans an elbow on the back of the couch, his head propped on his fist. He crosses his legs toward me. "Simon'll be home soon. He and Mum cook together when she visits. She's setting the *mise en place,* she told me." He says it with a grin, like it's a joke, but I don't get it.

"So there will be food eventually?" I'm suddenly aware that I haven't eaten since that cherry pie around midnight.

"There will," he affirms, "and it will not contain pickled anything."

"And I get to meet your brother. That'll be fun. His house is *ridiculous.*" I gesture at the room.

"And there are two more floors you haven't seen yet. Er." Charles leans forward conspiratorially. "You should know before you meet him, Simon's the really clever one in the family. Some people find him disconcerting at first."

I lean forward, too. "Did you find him disconcerting last night?" (Holy moly, was it just last night?)

Charles nods but says, "Not at first. At first he was just my wee brother, all grown up. But then it turned out he's Mycroft bloody Holmes."

"Who's Mycroft Holmes?"

He turns his eyes heavenward on a sigh. "Who's Mycroft Holmes, she asks."

Just then I hear sounds in the hall downstairs. I ask Charles, "That him?"

He nods again. He's smiling now. "I think you'll like him. I do."

There are voices—Simon and Carol talking—and then a quick step on the stairs, accompanied by a soft call of "Charles." And then Simon comes through the door, barely glancing at me as he takes off his sunglasses and his—are you fucking kidding me— *bowler hat*, revealing hair so blond it looks white. He blinks against the light as he switches glasses. Charles rises to meet him.

"Annie, my brother, Simon. Simon, this is my friend and colleague, Annie Coffey."

"A-aaaannie," Simon nods, and I think, *Of course he stutters.* With an anxious smile, he meets my eyes from behind pink-lensed glasses. Nystagmus—tick tock tick tock tick tock of his eyes. His hair doesn't look white, it *is* white. So are his eyebrows and eyelashes.

And what Charles felt he has to prepare me for is his intelligence.

Well, shit, he must have one hell of a brain.

I resist the urge to barrage him with questions. Dudes with albinism probably have to cope with nosy jerks all the time.

"Thanks for letting me crash," I say.

"N-nuh-n sure thing," he says, and he flushes to his hairline. He turns to Charles and says, "I-I've only got the one sssspare bed at the moment. Why is your shirt wet?"

"It's nothing." Charles waves this away and then gestures toward the couch. "I'll sleep here."

"No, sleep with me," I burst out.

They both look at me, Simon pink, Charles openmouthed.

I look at Charles and say shyly, "I don't want to be alone."

"Right," he says with a businesslike nod. He turns to Simon. "I'll go and get our stuff out of your way."

When Charles leaves, Simon turns toward me with a puzzled grin, his eyes on the floor. "Hhhis accent!" he says. "He sssounds almost American."

"Does he?" I say. "He sounds really, really English to me."

"It mmmight be his ssssyntax more than his accent, I sah-sssuppose. Ya-you shhhould've heard him tah-t-ten years ago. N-ngh-now he sah-sssounds like John Wayne, tahhh-to my ear." And then he says, with no sign of a stutter and in a startlingly accurate imitation of John Wayne, 'I'll get our stuff out of your way.' "

I laugh out loud, and Simon shakes his head, grinning at his feet. He adds quietly, "He ngh-never used to flap his *t*'s that way."

"You remember how he pronounced his *t*'s ten years ago?" I ask, not believing it.

"Oh yes," he says, twirling his hat on his finger. "I was fffourteen when he cah-c-came home for the lllast tah-t-time and he was sssso duh-dismissive of Fahhh-f-father, and Fah-fuh-father so b-b-baffled by him, I was stah-st-staggered. *Staggered*," he repeats emphatically. Just then, Charles appears at the top of the stairs with his luggage and turns into the other side of the house toward the room where I napped. Simon's whole body goes still as he watches his big brother. With his eyes on Charles, he says very softly, "I remember everything about him then."

A-bite. He remembers everything *a-bite* him. I can hear how his accent is different from Charles's, now that he's pointed it out.

"I'm sah-sssorry ab-about the flights," Simon says, leaning against the arm of the couch in a posture that reminds me of his brother.

"It's not your fault."

"Well, it is, ab-a bit." he says. "I wrrrote the a-a-algorithm that says whether the p-planes should go or stah-ssstay."

"Oh," I say. "That's a job a person can have?"

He nods like a six-year-old affirming that he found a frog in the backyard, but what he says is, "I build cuh-computational models of mmmassively complex d-dynamical systems, and the gnh-government mmmakes decisions b-based on them."

"Oh. Well, shit," I say.

And then Charles comes back in. He's changed his shirt—it's the windowpane-check one now. I love the windowpane-check one.

"I was just ap-pologizing for the inconvenience."

"Fitting. God's Final Message to His Creation," Charles says. "Right. Bags sorted. Mum's in the kitchen. Drink?" He says this to Simon, without looking at me, but then when Simon says, "Sure," and heads downstairs ahead of us, Charles's eyes come to mine. He puts a hand on my shoulder and holds my gaze. "All right?" he says with a quiet smile.

I nod and think, *I should say something. We should talk about it.* But I don't.

Then I think about kissing him. But I don't do that, either.

Then the disco strains of "Dancing Queen" come floating up from the kitchen. And then Charles's smile transforms into a giggling grin.

He brushes a hand over my hair and says, "Ready?" and I nod.

He leads me down the stairs to the kitchen, where Simon is opening a bottle of wine and Carol is doing something to a raw whole chicken. I can smell rosemary and lemon, and I suddenly feel sure that the food tonight will not suck.

But that's not what's most salient about this room. What's most salient is ABBA's greatest hits, playing at eleven, and the fact that Carol and Simon are both singing along. Carol's singing the melody, Simon is singing harmony. They're both smiling.

And dancing. As Carol wrestles delicately with the chicken, she wiggles her hips and her shoulders. Simon—who has taken off his suit jacket, revealing the pink satin back of his vest, gaudy against the dark blue of the rest—tips his head from side to side as he pours the wine into four massive glasses.

And Charles begins singing along as soon as we get into the kitchen!

Charles! *Singing!* ABBA!

I saw *Mamma Mia!* on Broadway and have the soundtrack and everything, so I'm not ignorant of ABBA, but I'm nothing next to these people. All three Douglases know *all* the words.

Singing the whole time, Charles takes two glasses from Simon and gives me one, then guides me to the kitchen table, where a tray of vegetables, olives, pickles, crackers, and cheese greets me cheerfully. I start eating.

Charles sits beside me and puts an olive into his mouth. He says into my ear, under the music, "This is what we did when we were kids—it was probably the closest thing to 'normal' we had. Mum would cook and we'd help, setting the table, chopping vegetables, that sort of thing, and sing along to pop music from the seventies. Last night was Blondie. I couldn't believe it."

Between "Super Trouper" and "I Have a Dream," Carol calls, "Charles, would you please set the table, dear?"

"Yes, Mum," he says promptly, and he stands.

I watch as he collects plates and silverware and arranges them on the table and Simon scrubs tiny, pale gold potatoes. I compare the brothers—Charles, solid and graceful, confident; and Simon, who looks like a strong wind would blow him off his feet. Charles, with his calm eyes behind gold wire glasses; Simon's anxious eyes behind pink-tinted glasses that wouldn't be out of place on a 1960s science teacher. Charles is handsome. Simon, I realize, is frankly beautiful. When he finishes with the vegetables and turns to approach Charles, the haze of his anxiety and his awkwardness diminishes, and I see a profoundly beautiful face.

But then he tugs on Charles's sleeve like a little boy and lowers his eyes and says under the music, "Er, Ch-Charles, I huh-hhhhate to-tuh-t-to bng-be the one t-tah-to t-t-t-tell ya-you tha-tha-this, b-but—"

He stops, unable to struggle through another syllable. He looks at Charles with a plea in his eyes.

I watch Charles search his brother's face. At last he says, "Oh god. You're joking."

Simon shakes his head no.

"How did he know?" Charles asks, running a hand through his hair.

"What?" I ask, lost. "How did who know what?"

"Ah-I-I-I—" Simon says, but his eyes dart to his mother and back to Charles.

"Never mind," Charles says gently. He puts his hand on his brother's arm but looks at the window and winces. "Fuck."

"I-if yah-y-you aren't *heee*—"

Charles turns to face his brother, "No, I'll be here. I wouldn't put you and Mum in that position."

"What position? What's going on?" I feel like they're speaking a foreign language that sounds tantalizingly like English, but isn't at all.

"My father knows I'm here. He's . . ." He looks at Simon. "Coming to dinner?"

Simon nods.

"Right. Okay." He sighs and glances at his mother before he says, "I'll give him an hour. Any more than that and I'll probably punch him in the jaw."

"Chance'd be a fine thing," Simon says smoothly, and both men laugh. Carol looks over and smiles to see her two sons laughing together, and I conclude that she can't have heard what they're laughing about.

Charles sets another place at the table. The chicken goes into the oven during the flute and drum introduction to "Fernando." Carol washes her hands, and, as the chorus starts, before she has time to put down her dish towel, Simon grabs hold of his mother and starts dancing with her.

"Do you hustle?" Charles asks from behind me, with his lips against my ear.

"Do I what?"

"That's a no. Come on. Best thing for you, after the airport." He holds out a hand. I take it.

Holding both my hands in his, he says, "Right. Mirror me." And he teaches me to hustle, there in his brother's kitchen.

It takes me all of "Fernando" and half of "Voulez-Vous" to figure out how to combine the easy rock-step-step-step footwork with the unaccustomed practice of following a leader who, as far as I can tell, is improvising.

"Just follow," Charles calls over the music.

"Follow you where?" I call back.

"Like this." He stops and holds out his arms, bent at a ninety-degree angle, elbows at his sides. "A little tense, like you're pushing a trolley. A cart."

"Okay. Um."

And I try it. It works—mostly. Sort of. Then he shows me how to lay my left forearm against the back of his upper arm, with my hand not on the front of his shoulder, but curled over the back. That changes everything. I get vastly more information from his body this way. Concentrating hard, with my tongue sticking out, I keep my eyes on his sternum, which seems to be where he telegraphs what he's going to ask of me.

Just as I think I'm getting the hang of it, "Gimmee! Gimmee! Gimmee!" comes on and Charles passes me, mid-turn, to his brother, who is much easier to follow. Simon's body language is utterly clear, his arms flexible but unambiguous.

"Ohhhhhh!" I exclaim as I follow him through a series of turns—I have no idea what's going on, I'm just following, but it is fun as hell. Out of the corner of my eye, I see that Charles is dancing with his mom, both of them laughing, but I'm concentrating too hard to look away from the buttons of Simon's shirt.

And then for the length of "Does Your Mother Know" Simon teaches me another basic—rock-step-triple-step, rock-step-triple-step, around in a circle. He doesn't talk me through it, the way Charles talked me through the hustle; he just does the steps in half time until he feels me getting it.

Now that I get the idea of following and I'm learning how to read what the leader is trying to do, it's easy to add the new basic step. His lead is so clear that even when the footwork is unclear, I just go where he puts me and it's fine—it's not just fine, it's easy! It's fun!

When the song ends he clicks the remote control to skip ahead to "Waterloo." He takes my right hand, bounces his head from side to side to show me the eight-count—as if it's not thrummingly obvious—and then he stops teaching and just dances with me. I look wide-eyed, openmouthed at Simon, who is smiling at the floor as he leads me. It's maybe the most fun thing I've ever done.

When the girls are singing, "*I feel like I win when I loooooooose,*" Simon sends me into a turn and I find myself in Charles's arms.

Charles pulls me out of the turn and spins me around in a circle, sending me out and pulling me back in. His lead isn't as straightforward as Simon's, but it doesn't matter. His shoulder is so much more substantial under my hand, his chest so strong, his eyes so warm on mine, and, when I look up from his sternum into his eyes, his smile so affectionate and happy, as he mouths the lyrics, his face so utterly relaxed, I laugh out loud.

At the end of the song, he turns me three times, wrapping my arm around my back and his arm around me, and dipping me to the floor.

When he brings me up from the dip, he bows over my hand and says, "Thank you," before I pull my hand away to jump up and down and clap and say, "Do it again!" I glance around the room—Simon is sitting with his feet propped on Charles's seat, drinking his wine, while Carol pours herself a second glass—which she is destined never to drink. I stand, panting with exertion, beside Charles as he fiddles with the remote to try to play "Waterloo" again. The whole kitchen smells of roasting rosemary chicken and garlicky potatoes, and I feel more content, more peaceful than I could have imagined twelve hours earlier.

"This is fun!" I say, and Charles gives me a grin.

Then the doorbell rings.

Charles's face just shuts down. He clicks off the stereo and turns blank eyes to Simon. With an audible sigh and a roll of his eyes toward Charles, Simon goes to let their father in.

Chapter 13

Rage Over a Lost Penny

He goes after Annie. God, how had I not anticipated that? He walks into the kitchen and the first thing he says is, "Who's this little bitch?" and with every cell in my body I want to grab him by the throat, slam him against the wall, and hit him until he's unconscious and bleeding.

Mum is saying, "This is Charles's young friend Annie."

He looks at Annie—not at her face, but at her chest—and then looks at me, and he says, "Got no tits on her."

And then the cold descends on me. I knew it would. I knew that when it came to the point, the adrenaline would turn my blood to stinging cold and I would crust over with ice. A frozen, impenetrable barrier grows around me. From behind this wall, I'm utterly disconnected. Numb.

Annie laughs, shocked. She has no idea what's happening—I see her look from me to Mum to Simon and back at me, trying to understand. I feel her standing beside me, but there's a million miles between us.

From behind the wall, I say to him, "Not compared to you, you fat fuck."

"Now Charles," Mum says to the table, and I can't tell which of us she means, him or me.

But he laughs. He thinks it's funny.

"Shall we sit down to dinner?" Mum says, and if I weren't crusted over with ice, the unsparing gentleness in her voice would tear me apart.

"Yes," I say immediately, and I take a seat at the table. Simon follows suit, then Annie.

And then it might as well be fifteen years ago. Everything is exactly the same. Mum serves dinner—literally serves it, will hardly sit down until he folds his knife and fork together. He'll drink a bottle of wine in the next fifty-eight minutes. Simon is silent, will stay silent.

And then there's Annie. She's looking around like she's landed at a table of aliens. I think vaguely of meeting her parents—her *sane* parents. She has no context for understanding this. In a corner of my mind I'm aware that she must be depleted from the day and now I'm inflicting this on her. I could have told her to go upstairs, I should have, as soon Simon told me he was coming. I've never let any woman within fifty miles of my father. Why didn't I tell her to get out, to go?

Because I'm a self-centered little shit, that's why. Because I wasn't thinking about her at all, only about myself, about shoring up my own defenses.

Somewhere deep in my chest, a small part of me thaws, painful and aching, as I realize what she is about to witness.

We've only been at the table a few minutes when Simon's Blackberry vibrates. I recognize the rhythm. He rolls his eyes at it and says to us, "P-p-pardon me, I've g-got—" He answers it as he rises and walks out the kitchen door, "Gug-good evening, sir."

"That boy—" He glares at Mum.

"It was the prime minister," I interrupt dully.

"I don't care if it was the fucking Queen, he can't—"

If I weren't frozen to numbness, I'd feel proud of my brother and I'd feel rage at our father for his contemptuous neglect of the better man among his sons. But as it is, I don't feel anything when I say, "I'm sure he'd take her call, too. They'll want to put his name on the New Year's list—again—for his work today, you stupid fuck. And he'll ask to have it withdrawn—again—"

"Everything all right, dear?" Mum calls, interrupting me. Simon is coming back in, Blackberry still in hand, texting rapidly.

"Yes, Pah-p-Peel is having kittens of course, but fffair enough."

Lacking any opening for professional criticism, he decides that this is a good time to explain to us that it's Simon's fault that Mum has to cook and serve dinner because Simon won't hire a fucking—

"You're the only one who gives a shit," I say, bored. "None of the rest of us are such arrogant tossers we can't get off our arses to get a fucking spoon."

He laughs again, like this is just some lads' humor between us. He says, "Showing off for the flat-chested feminist, eh? She must be more horizontal than she is vertical."

He came close on that one. I feel a hairline crack in the ice.

"Wouldn't you like to know," I say.

He leers at Annie and pokes his elbow toward me, saying, "You offering?"

Bang. First blood to him.

Bleeding under the ice, I say, as lightly as I can, "Over my dead body."

He laughs again. He slaps me on the shoulder—the first time he's touched me at all in I don't know how long—and all I can think is that I want to jam my knife into his heart. I sit there imagining it. With a knife this small, I'd have to aim for the third or fourth intercostal space. If I had a cleaver, I could just go straight through the bone of the sternum. I let my body feel the swing of my arm, the weight of a cleaver in my hand, the sound and feel of bone cracking under the blade, the spurt of blood through his shirt. His surprised, dead face.

I become aware that he's telling the Pansy story. Apparently, he's been reminded of it because, like Annie, she had no tits, either. Pansy had a hard time keeping track of things, he's telling Annie, possibly because she wasn't very bright, and possibly because she was high pretty much all the time. And one of the things she couldn't keep track of was her tampons. Sitting at the dinner table with his wife, his two sons, and a stranger, he explains to us how he found a month-old tampon in Pansy's vagina one night.

"And the smell—" he exclaims, and the clatter of Mum's cutlery brings me a little bit more back to the present.

He doesn't stop. "This little girl of yours, though, I'm surprised you can get it in her! All the Douglas men are as thick as that bloody tree of yours."

He wins. I lose. I can't answer, and that's what he wanted. I feel sick.

Eventually, he leaves the table to go to the loo. As soon he's gone, I look at my watch. Forty minutes. Twenty to go. I put my elbow on the table and rub my palm over my forehead.

"He's been ill," Carol explains to Annie.

"He's drunk," I correct.

"He'll be dead within twenty months," Simon says cheerfully, no stutter in sight, eyes on his plate.

We all look at him, astonished.

He looks up at us, genuine remorse on his face, "I b-b-beg your pah-pardon."

But I laugh. I can't help it. Thank god for Simon. He's always right about everything, and every time he makes me laugh I am reminded that somewhere inside this mess, I am a human being. I know he pays a price for it. He has no armor—little good though mine seems to be doing any of us, I'm so out of practice. But Simon? He is omniscience wrapped in music wrapped in purple candy floss. I don't know how he survives. I should ask him one day.

Mum says, "Please, dear."

"Sssorry, Mum, sorry," Simon says.

"I am so sorry, Annie, for how rude he was to you," Mum says, fussing with her fork, still not eating.

Annie waves a hand. "Oh please, it's not your fault." She looks at me then. I sit right next to her and watch from a million miles away as she tries to find me. *I'm not here*, I want to tell her.

And then he comes back and it all starts again.

I don't know how I get through the last fifteen minutes. When I look at my watch and see that my hour is up, I rise and say, "Excuse me." I don't even try to be polite.

Annie follows me out. The little bitch with no tits. The flat-chested feminist. Oh god. As soon as I'm a human being again, I'll repair that. Try to.

"Go upstairs," I tell her when we're at the bottom of the main stairs. I head toward the cellar stairs.

"Where are you going?" she calls.

"Cellar," I answer, without looking back. "Go upstairs."

The key is to work to the point of failure. Strength is built in a muscle the way skill is developed in *Tetris:* there is no "win," really. There is only the increasingly long delay of failure—if you keep going until you can't, and keep going just a little beyond that, then next time, failure will be just that little bit further away. Squats, pull-ups, lunges, dips. After about thirty minutes, I lie on my back, shirtless, sweating, panting, and drained at last.

Just as I'm considering climbing all those stairs, I hear the piano in the other room.

Simon.

I haul myself to my feet, pull on my shirt, and stand at his office door. I have no idea what he's playing—it's swift and light—and I can't tell if he knows I'm there. His face is concentrated, with his chin taut and his eyebrows raised. As the music gets quiet, he leans over the keyboard, as if he needs to move closer to hear, then he plays louder and louder, sitting up gradually, culminating in one giant forte chord . . . and then one tiny, pianissimo chord.

I laugh out loud, and he smiles at the keyboard and folds his hands in his lap.

"What was that?"

"Rage Over a Lost Penny," he says. "Not *very* good, I know, but quite good considering the composer was deaf." He ends the sentence in the kind of confidential whisper people use when they talk about disabilities. He adds, "Actually, he wasn't deaf at the time he composed it—but!"—he holds up one finger at me—"Never let the truth get in the way of a good story."

I drop my fatigued body onto Simon's chesterfield and ask, "How do you do it? How do you . . ." I don't know how to finish that sentence.

Simon does. "Sussstain a relationship with the ap-appalling creature who sired us, who t-t-terrifies me still, yet retain a-any sense of reason and peace?"

I lay my head against the back of the sofa and close my eyes. "Exactly."

" 'B-boil me some more,' said the chickpea to the cook. 'Hit me with your spoon.' In Ministry of Love speak, 'Thy rod and thy staff, they comfort me,' but I prefer Rumi's goofier analogy. We are all food for god, and the ways we suffer are . . . tenderizing us, essentially. Dissolving us."

"Rumi does love a colloid."

"Well, quite." Then he asks with evident curiosity, "How do *you* do it? I'm a chickpea, what are you?"

"I'm an abominable snowman," I moan. "Shields of ice and useless snowballs of rage. I've lost the knack, though."

"He g-got to you?"

I raise an eyebrow, jaw clenched. "Annie. He—"

Simon nods.

"They're gone, by the way," he says after a silent moment. "Mum took him back to the London house."

In a flash of panic, I ask, "He's not driving her, is she?"

"Stig," he explains.

After a minute or two of silence, each of us pondering our survival, such as it is, Simon closes the piano and says, "Well, I've g-got to compose an e-mail to the Queen and a few other things, so kindly b-bugger off if you would, there's a good fellow."

He's joking—but he's not.

I stand. "Right. Get on with it then. I've got to go grovel to Annie."

"E-mail to the Queen, grovel to Annie," Simon says. "Six of one."

Chapter 14

Look at Me

I shower first, then go to our room with a towel around my waist and another on my head. I drop my clothes on the floor and put my glasses on the desk. All at once I feel my exhaustion—no sleep last night, and then dinner tonight, and a year, really, of feeling lonelier than I've dared to realize.

Annie's lying on the bed, reading. Dressed all in black, with her new glasses, she looks as European as I've ever seen her, but her shoes and socks are on the floor by the bed, her bare feet flat on the mattress.

I shut the door behind me and lock it.

I want her. I am abominable, a fuckshow, and I want her to kiss my cheek and forehead and nose and whisper to me and giggle in the dark. I want to drop all my weapons and let her touch me, undefended. I want to make love with her, feel those bare feet cool on the backs of my legs, and then fall asleep with her body pressed against mine, and then I want to wake up and do it all again. I want it so much my breath stops in my throat.

But: Disaster. Torn to pieces.

I rub the towel against my hair and then drop it beside the pile of clothes as I try to breathe.

"Hey," she says, and she sets her book aside.

"Hey." I sink onto the bed, lying next to her, and scrub my face with both hands.

"What's in the cellar?" Annie asks.

"Simon's bat cave. Gym, office, command center," I answer without opening my eyes.

"Ah."

"I had to beat the shit out of something. Better myself than you, I thought." I look at her then, see her exhaustion, and I feel all the horror that I couldn't feel before. "Oh god, I'm sorry, Annie. I am so sorry. I wouldn't have brought you here if I had known this would happen. I can't begin to tell you—"

She turns to her side and props her head on her hand. "It's not your fault he's so awful. And he is. I mean, he is really, really awful."

I nod, wincing, and grip my skull in both hands, looking at the ceiling. "I had to stay. If he had come and I hadn't been here, he would have taken it out on them."

"I get that," she says lightly. "What's weird is how he never targeted you. Everyone else, even me, a total stranger, but never you."

"Not directly," I say to the ceiling. In disgust I add, "He was using you to get to me, just as he uses them."

"Dude, that is fucked up."

"It puts me in a hopeless . . . in an invidious position, because there's nothing I can do or say to protect them. I've tried drawing his fire, I've tried putting myself between him and them, I've tried simply attacking him. Nothing works, not really. And I wind up . . . just . . . being a wanker."

"Yeah, you were a douche bag there for a minute."

I close my eyes against the wave of shame. "I hate that you saw that. I hate that I am that, I hate that that exists inside me and that I allow him to draw it out of me. God, what a fuckup I am. What a total wanker." I rub my hands hard over my face again.

"You want a hair shirt to go with that flagellation, swamp boy?" I laugh under my palms. "Oh, for fuck's sake. Fuck my self-indulgent self-pity. I'm such a fuckshow—"

"Hey," she interrupts. "That's my friend you're talking about."

I drop my hands to my chest and look at her again. But I can't think what to say. There are too many things to say—and nothing to say, since words can't change anything.

Softly, gently, she says, "I didn't get it, when you told me last year. It took seeing it in real life to understand."

I say, "That wasn't even particularly bad. That was him behaving himself. All the same, I wish you hadn't seen it. Especially today." I reach out a hand and touch her face with my fingertips. I say, "They've gone now. Mum took him home. So I can sleep in the other room." I search her eyes, wanting so badly to stay with her, wanting so badly to leave, now, before . . . Disaster. Capitalized. I add, "If you want."

She just returns my gaze. She looks calm. Tired, but calm.

"How was Melissa?" she asks.

Oh god. I drop my hand, letting my arm drape over my belly, but I don't look away from her. "She's excellent. She's getting married."

"That's nice."

I sigh, remembering the awkwardness of breakfast. "She wanted to meet so she could tell me she'd forgiven me."

"That's nice, too."

"She asked if I was seeing someone."

"You told her you were seeing Clarissa," Annie jokes.

I blink and bite my lip. She doesn't look away.

I say, "I'm a fuckshow, Annie."

"You were my knight in shining armor today."

I close my eyes and shake my head through another wave of shame.

"Hey," she says again.

I open my eyes again, despairing, hoping, so lonely I can hardly stand it.

"I want to come over there," she says. "I want to lie there with you."

I open my arms and she comes to me, tucks her long, strong body against me, and I pull her to my chest. Her head fits neatly in the crook of my shoulder. Except—

"Hey," I say.

"Hm?" She lifts her head and looks at me.

I pull her glasses from her face and put them on the night-stand.

"They were poking me," I say, grinning, and guide her head back to my shoulder.

She settles against me and drapes an arm across my body. I feel her sigh and soften, and my body relaxes with hers—and then I feel her lips on my chest. She kisses the bare, damp skin, and then inhales . . . holds the breath in her tensed, flexed body . . . then releases a huge, muscle-softening sigh. Her body relaxes fully in my arms. She kisses my chest again and nuzzles against me.

So I sigh, too, coaxing my muscles to relax. I put both my arms around her and we lie quietly, breathing together. And if this is what we do all night, I think, it will do nicely.

But then she kisses my chest again, lightly.

And then again.

Then her palm begins to travel over my skin. I tell myself she's only making contact, she's just reconnecting, but my heart begins to thrum anyway. I kiss her hair—only to make contact, only to reconnect.

She turns her lips to my skin again and places another soft, silent kiss over my heart.

And then another one, right next to it, her mouth open this time.

And then another one right next to that one, her lips and tongue warm on my skin.

She kisses me this way, slowly and softly, across the whole breadth of my chest. Each lingering kiss is its own event. Each one could be the last. After each one, I wait, taut, to see if she decides to rest her head against my shoulder again . . . or to put another kiss next to the last one.

Her palm drifts over my stomach and chest, brushes my nipple in a slow, soft circle, and her touch becomes more decided— though still calm and unhurried. More contemplative than erotic. Painstakingly, systematically, she kisses every inch of my chest and shoulders.

I touch her hair, brushing it away from her face. I touch her face, trying to be delicate even as my breathing accelerates and the muscles in my neck and jaw tighten. When she bites at my nipples softly, I make an involuntary noise through my nose.

Her lips follow a line up my chest and then my throat, and I know she's going to put her mouth on mine. I know that's coming. I wait, anticipating, even as I savor each touch, as her lips brush lightly over my larynx. She touches her fingertips to my throat as she kisses a slow, deliberate path, one kiss at a time, up to the corner of my jaw . . . and then along my hairline . . . kisses on my forehead and I put my palms on her back; kisses on my cheek and I caress my hands up her scapulae and down to her waist; kisses along my jaw, in no hurry, one kiss at a time, bringing her mouth closer to mine.

She kisses her way to my chin, and it's too much. With another small noise, I lower my chin the little bit that it takes, and I find her mouth with mine. I kiss her mouth.

And then I open my lips and kiss her again.

Then I pull away a fraction of an inch. I push her hair away from her face and search her eyes.

"I'll tear you to pieces," I say. I meant to say it confidently, to put a substantial barrier between us, but it comes out as a whisper.

She shakes her head slowly, her eyes never leaving mine.

She whispers back, "You'll put me back together."

The words shoot through my heart like a bullet, and I'm done for. With my hands in her hair and my eyes on hers, I tell her, "It's the other way round."

And I kiss her. I kiss her and kiss her, as if kissing her is all I ever intend to do for the rest of my unworthy life. I put my hand on the back of her neck to hold her there, and I put my tongue in her mouth—she answers with hers. With a growl, I pull her over me. I run my hands over her body, feel the shape of her as her clothes slide between my hands and her skin. I follow the shape of her with my hands, I coax and caress and hold her as she kisses me. She aligns our bodies so that the heat between my legs presses and rubs at the heat between hers. Still I'm kissing her, my tongue in her mouth. She has one hand around the back of my neck, the other in my hair. With my hands everywhere on her, I offer my body to her like a scratching post to a kitten. I push and pull at her body, helping her, urging her, until she comes with high, soft, urgent sounds, kissing me the whole time, as her body softens over me.

As she pants and kisses my neck, I reach out to the nightstand and turn off the light.

"Charles, I need—"

"I know what you need."

It's what I need, too. Contact. Reconnection. Our breath in the dark. One body.

I turn her to her back and pull off her clothes, push off my towel, and lay my body over hers, all of my skin touching all of her skin, and we both gasp with it, her hands gripping my shoulders. I kiss her everywhere, as she kissed me, every inch of skin I can reach from her forehead to her waist. My mouth and hands never leave her body. In the dark, there's only the feel of our bodies and the sounds of our breath. I kiss her shoulders and throat and ear as I put my cock against her entrance. I touch her face and kiss her lips as I begin to push into her, and her arms come around me in a desperate grip.

"Is this all right?" I whisper against her lips.

"Yeah," she says, just a high whisper.

So I hold her close, push into her gradually, a little deeper with every small, slow thrust, kissing her tenderly all the while. I remember this so well, every angle of penetration, every pulse of pressure. I know the way her breathing changes, the way her belly tenses under me.

Her back curls, her legs wrap round my waist, and her arms tighten around my neck, and I feel her want, feel her need. I push deeper and deeper into her in small, slow, focused thrusts.

"Don't let go," she whispers.

"I won't let go," I tell her, and I push deeper still into her.

Gradually, I move in longer and longer strokes, pressing my body more and more firmly against hers. Little by little, she tightens around me. She doesn't move with me, she just lets me in, her whole body wrapped around my whole body, my lips kissing her lips and her cheeks and her jaw.

She's breathing in heavy gusts when I move my hand to her forehead and touch my lips softly to hers and whisper, "Look at me."

Her eyes flutter open and find mine in the darkness. She watches me while I kiss her softly and fuck her hard. We watch each other, with my tongue in her mouth and my cock finding a way to go even deeper inside her.

As the tension in her body builds and layers, mine builds with it, until my jaw is taut and my hands are fisting in her hair. I put my forehead against hers, eyes still trained on hers.

I watch the pleasure and tension in her face grow, see her slowly nearing the edge.

Her eyes flutter closed, and I beg her, "Annie, please."

Her eyes open again. I keep my eyes on hers, my breath suspended in my throat, as hers is suspended in her throat. Right at the edge, not wanting it to end, wanting to drown in pleasure and her eyes and this, this, now.

"Charles?" she breathes.

"Yeah."

"Charles, don't—"

"I won't let go, Annie, I'll never let go."

In silence, she erupts around me. I drink in the sight of her as she comes almost silently. I go still as her hands grip and slap at my back, her feet press my hips hard, as her body pulses around mine. I brace her head between my palms and put kisses on her wide-open mouth, watching her eyes as she comes and comes, writhing and pushing under me. She's still coming as her eyes mist with tears, as one falls down her temple into her hair, and still I'm watching her. I watch her as she quietly pours herself out, rolling and melting under me into softness and a half-hidden glow, until her eyelids drift down at last.

As her limbs soften around me, I kiss her cheek and her nose and her chin, kiss the tear clinging at the corner of her eye. I kiss her and hold her, still hard inside her, until her breathing steadies and slows.

"I won't let go," I whisper with my lips near her ear. "I won't let go."

Little by little, her body relaxes, until every bit of tension drops away, at long, long last, in a deep, shuddering sigh.

I pull out of her then, gently and slowly, turn her to her side, and spoon myself behind her. I hold her close, both arms wrapped around her.

"Sleep, sweetheart," I say. "Everything's okay."

Chapter 15

So I Let Him

I wake in total darkness and feel him wrapped around me.

I turn in his arms and I put my nose to the corner of his jaw and inhale quietly, deeply, the familiar scent of this man asleep beside me. I smile and watch his face, soft in sleep.

And then I disentangle myself and get up to go pee.

And then I feel inconveniently awake.

Well.

I put on my underwear and Charles's shirt, and wander across the hall to the living room with my phone. I check my texts and my e-mail—Simon has e-mailed Charles and me in the middle of the night, telling us that "it's all sorted now" and we'll be hearing from our airlines within twelve hours. Okay. I still don't understand why or how he knows these things, but it is extremely convenient.

I fiddle with my phone, checking various social media, checking my e-mail, just . . . checking. When I run out of things to check, I turn on a light and browse Simon's bookshelf. I pick a book and lie down on the couch to read, but I can't focus. I'm exhausted and wrung out, yet fidgety and unsettled, like there's an itch somewhere in my mind that I can't reach. So I stare at the pages of the book and think about Charles, and that seems to help.

I lie here on the couch in his brother's absurdly nice house, remembering the relief I felt when I saw Charles. It fills my eyes with tears. He really was my hero. He got me out of there and put me somewhere safe, and by the time his douche bag of a father showed up, I felt normal.

I did a new thing during that dinner, a new, grown-up thing. I thought, *Okay, so Charles can't give me anything that I need right now. But what can I give him? How can I help him?* I don't know why it was a new thought, except that I was always the young, inexperienced one, and he was the one who had done everything. But here was a moment—maybe the first in all the time I'd known him—when his need was greater than mine.

I think maybe there was nothing I could have done to make that dinner easier. I think sitting and observing—witnessing— was maybe all that was available to me.

And I hope that afterward, when he came into the bedroom with his towels and his self-contempt, maybe I helped him. He helped me, I know that much. Maybe under other circumstances I would have been torn to pieces, as I had feared, by going to bed with Charles.

Or maybe the year I spent reshaping the way I hold Charles in my heart really did change how I feel about him, so that even the sweet way he touched me and held me couldn't make me afraid of losing him again. I don't know why I'm okay, but I know for sure that I am. I know for sure that Charles isn't going anywhere. He wants—and needs—our connection, whatever it is, as much as I do.

I'm half asleep, lying here with the book open on my chest, so I startle and look up when I hear, "Annie."

Charles walks toward me in pajama pants, his face tense and wrinkled with sleep.

"Hey," I say, smiling at his rumpled frown.

"Are you all right?" He sits near my feet, his hand on my ankle.

"Of course."

"Thought you'd gone," he says, and he rubs his hands against his face. Then, with a groan as if he's surrendering to something, he lies beside me on the couch and puts his arms around me, tight, pulling me to my side. I wrap my arms around him.

"You thought I'd gone? Where would I go?"

"Last time I fell asleep with you, when I woke up you were gone," he says, his lips in my hair. His arms tighten around me.

"Oh."

"I thought it was happening again. I thought I'd hurt you and you'd left. I thought—" He kisses my neck.

"I didn't leave," I whisper.

"I'm sorry."

"You didn't hurt me."

He turns us together so that I'm lying over him and his arms are wrapped hard and close around me. He's breathing into my hair, "I'm sorry. I never meant to hurt you. I'm such a fuckshow. I should never have—god. I'm sorry. I'm such a fucking nightmare."

I kiss his chin. "You didn't hurt me," I tell him. "You're not a nightmare. You're the best man I know."

His eyes close and his jaw tenses. He shakes his head minutely.

"Believe me when I say it," I say.

He swallows and doesn't answer.

"I'll just say it again, if you don't believe me," I say, trying to tease him.

His lips tighten. He swallows again.

"Charles."

"Mh."

"Look at me."

He does.

I hold his gaze steadily and say, "You're the best man I know."

He struggles for a moment, like he can't breathe. Then, when he manages to open his mouth, he says, "Stop."

"Make me," I whisper.

He actually laughs a little, even as tears grow in his eyes. "I can't."

"Oh, honey," I say, and I put my arms around his neck. With my mouth against his ear, I say, "You're the best man I know."

"Termagant," he says through gritted teeth, and he wraps his arms tight around me. Tight.

"Do you believe me?" I ask.

He shakes his head. Just once.

"Am I a liar?"

He shakes his head.

"Am I crazy?"

"No," he whispers.

"Am I stupid?"

"Christ, no."

"So why not believe me?"

He shakes his head again and kisses my temple, kisses my eyebrow, kisses the corner of my parted lips. He whispers, "Come back to bed, Annie."

We don't make it back to bed. We don't make it off the couch. He kisses me softly, while his hands travel all over my body, over my shirt—his shirt—and then under it, and he keeps murmuring, "We should go back to bed." But then he pushes my panties aside and undoes his pants enough to give me his cock. He slides into me. And then I fuck him. I set the pace; I move how I want to. I rub my tired, hungry body against his until I come with small, gasping noises into his kiss, with both his palms on the backs of my thighs.

And then I soften incrementally over him, and he moves gently into me while he grips my ass. I'm sleepy and relaxed and it would be okay with me if he fucked me like this for the next day and a half.

"I want to make you come again," he grinds between his teeth. "I want more. Do you want me to stop?"

"No," I breathe.

With a grunt, he pulls out of me and I start to protest—but he moves from under me, leaving me on my stomach, tugs my panties down to my knees, and slides back into me from behind. He tucks my hands between my legs with his hands, all four of our hands sandwiched together so that I can feel our fingers on my clit, can feel how he's moving inside me.

Lying fully over me, he bites hard into my trapezius, and I gasp and thrust my pelvis back against his hips. He bites me again, a sting that makes me cry out, and he fucks me deeper still, long thrusts that seem to reach somewhere untouched inside me. I rock my body between his cock and our hands, pressing my clit against his palm, seeking orgasm, craving it.

"Do you want me to stop?" he whispers into my ear.

"No!" I lift my hips and he fucks me even deeper, and our fingers slide over my clit, and I grunt into the cushion, "I want to come."

"Come for me, Annie."

"Oh god." As if my body had been waiting for this permission, the tension and pleasure inside me peak and I come hard, and he pulls a hand from between my legs, pressing over my mouth to muffle my cry.

I lick and bite and suck at his fingers, tasting myself, and I push my hips back against his, thrusting and rolling my body as I come.

Exhausted then, every limb heavy and soft, I sink toward sleep, but he's guiding me onto my back as he tucks himself beside me on the couch. I feel him unbutton the shirt, sliding his hand over my newly bared skin. His mouth goes to my breasts, kissing and sucking in sweet, affectionate touches that make me sigh. I watch him lazily before my eyes drift closed again.

And then his hand is on my vulva. And a finger is inside me. And then another, pressing into me and palming my clit.

Then another.

With three fingers inside me and his whole palm pressing on my clit, he growls into my ear, "Don't sleep yet. One more, my Annie. Give me one more."

"I don't know if I can," I mumble.

"You don't have to do anything, sweetheart," he whispers, his lips against my ear. He touches me, deep pressure on my clit, as he talks to me. "I'll do everything. Just be still for me, darling. Just let me. I'll make you come just once more, and then I'll fuck you, all right? I'll come inside you. I want to come inside you, Annie. Just be still for me, sweetheart, be still and let me. Just one more. Oh god, you're amazing. You are amazing."

I lift my eyelids and find him watching my face. It dawns on me, even as I see the first pink light of dawn reflected in Charles's hair, *why* I'm amazing when I'm still and why he needs that from me now: If I'm still—if I'm so totally exhausted from the plea- sure he gives me that I literally just can't lift my limbs—then I can't leave him. Nor can I hold on to him, I can't stop him from going. But I can't leave him. I can't get up in the middle of the night and leave without saying good-bye.

So I let him, just like he wants me to.

My arms tremble. My belly trembles. My thighs tremble. His fingers move in me, hard and deep and slow, flexing my whole pelvic floor. He kisses and sucks and licks my breasts.

I think of how he'll fuck me after this, how my body will ac- cept him, how he'll feel safe because he knows I won't leave, that I won't hold him down and I won't leave him. And all I have to do is give him everything, empty myself of my will and my reason. I can do that. He can have it. I want him to have it.

Reflexively, I grab his wrist with one hand and flex my body against his palm. I come, feeling the pulsing of my body around his fingers. My trembling muscles convulse and flex and my hand grips hard into his wrist, and then my whole body softens to a panting puddle on the couch. My hand drops away from his. He brushes my hair back and I drift closer to sleep, but he kisses my mouth and I make a small noise of pleasure, though I can't muster the energy to kiss him back.

"You're amazing," he whispers urgently. He braces my jaw in his damp hand and kisses my mouth, pushing his tongue between my teeth, with a growl in his throat. When he pulls away, he begins to move over me as he says against my lips, "Let me fuck you, my termagant. May I?"

I inhale and sigh with the slightest smile.

"Annie," he says, his voice serious. "You must answer me."

Summoning my last reserves, I breathe, "Yeah."

With a groan, he comes into me, my leg slipping off the couch. It's hard and deep and fast and short; in a scant dozen thrusts, he comes. With those three final thrusts, half-forgotten but so familiar, he breathes, "Oh god. Sweetheart."

He collapses on me, wraps his arms tight around me, panting. He holds me this way, kissing my neck and shoulder. But then he's starting again, still hard, with his arms now wrapped fully around me, moving in the wetness between us.

"Oh my god," he groans. "Oh my fucking god."

He kisses my neck, then growls against my shoulder. I feel the wet of his sweat on my neck, and he bites and kisses my shoulder. He presses his face to my neck, gasping and panting as he mutters incoherently against my skin, fucking me in deep, solid strokes that shift my whole body on the couch. His fingers grip me hard, almost painfully. My arm drops off the edge of the couch. With one leg and one arm dangling off the couch, I let him have me, all of me. I surrender my body to him. I'm half asleep and wide awake, ready to stop but I never want to stop. I'm his. I am his. And he is mine.

And then he changes his angle of penetration so that his pubic bone is pressing against my clit, and he's whispering in my ear. I can't hear the words, only the pleasure and desire and coaxing in his voice. He bites my earlobe and my internal muscles pulse once around his cock and he fucks me deeper, so that even though I don't have the will to put my arms around him or kiss him or

open myself more to him, he's coaxing rough little moans of pleasure from me, and every time I moan, he whispers, "Yeah." One
thrust at a time, one bite of my earlobe or my lip at a time, he
drags me, yielding and acquiescent, to another orgasm—or not
quite an orgasm, but the reflexive, rhythmic contractions of my
pelvic floor muscle. When he feels the pulsing, his body freezes
over mine, his cock as deep inside me as it can go. He makes a
sound, muffled in my hair, like he's in pain, and then I feel those
three thrusts, hard and slow, and he whispers, "Annie. Oh god.
Oh god."

His muscles soften then, little by little, by shuddering, trembling degrees. He presses his face to my neck and I feel his breath,
rapid and ragged, on my skin. I'm drifting into sleep when I feel
his lips move to mine, feel his hand brush over my forehead, hear
him murmuring words I can't understand against my lips.

I feel a lifting sensation, then a gentle lowering, and a soft welcome of the pillow under my head, and the warmth of a familiar
male body in the bed beside me.

Chapter 16

Because You Hate Me
So Much?

I dream about him, about the two of us alone on a beach at sunset, him on his knees and—then I wake up.

He's spooned behind me when I open my eyes, his arm heavy across my waist. Even in his sleep, he hasn't let go. I smile into my pillow and then turn in his arms. I can't tell if he actually wakes up, but he rolls to his back and adjusts his arms around me. We lie there, peacefully immobile, with our arms around each other, for a long, long time.

He must wake up at some point, because I feel him kiss the top of my head and then feel his chest rise and fall as he sighs.

When he starts chuckling lightly under me, I make a small interrogative sound, and he says, in a grumbly, sleepy voice, "Your mum specifically told me not to sleep with you."

"That doesn't sound like her," I mumble into his chest.

"What she actually said was, 'If you take advantage of her, I'll kick you in the teeth.'"

"Okay that sounds like her." I grin and listen to his heart beating under my ear.

We lie silently for another long while. Eventually, he kisses my forehead and whispers, "Have I taken advantage of you? How's your vulnerable and torn to pieces?"

I can hear the genuine worry in his voice, so I lift my head enough to look at his face. I say, "I do not feel the least bit vulnerable or torn to pieces. How's your monster?"

He smiles crookedly at me and runs a hand over my hair. "Very sleepy at the moment."

I bite my lip and watch his face as he watches mine. We're searching for each other in the sunlight of this unexpected day.

With his eyes still on mine, his bottom lip tugs downward and he says, "I did not ask about contraception. I should have."

I roll my eyes at him, "Duh, I have the thing in my arm."

He nods and swallows. "And . . ." His jaw tightens for a moment. "Nor did I ask about condoms and . . . other partners and things."

I shake my head. "Just you."

"I," Charles says in a light voice, but his face changes to a dark, almost angry look, "am a medieval troglodyte."

"Oh?"

"I . . ." He's breathing more heavily all of a sudden, and as he speaks he covers his face in his hands. "I fucking love that I'm the only one. Oh god, it turns me on so much. What an arse I am."

I laugh at him—cackle, really—and he says, "Don't laugh, Christ, that only makes it worse! I'm sure I'll get over it when the time comes, but in the meantime I—oh god, I—Annie, I—" His coherence dissolves, because now my mouth is on his fully erect cock. I'm kissing and licking and sucking his cock with a slow, easy, contemplative pace, tasting my own body on his skin.

And then a quicker pace.

Steadier.

More pressure. Feeling how easy it is to arouse him.

I lift my head and meet his eye as I stroke him with my hand. With a wicked grin I tell him, "Yours is the only cock I've ever had in my mouth." And then I suck him again, my eyes still turned to his.

"Annie, I—you don't—oh god I'm—" He comes in my mouth, panting, "Oh god I'm sorry I'm sorry, oh god yes. Yes."

In a flash of inspiration, I move over him, lie on top of him, and kiss him with my mouth full of his come. He groans and licks and sucks my tongue, swallows greedily, his hands coming up to hold my face and my hair.

"You're a dirty fucking bitch," he says approvingly, his breath still labored.

"And you're easy," I answer.

"A slut," he assures me. "For you." Then he keeps kissing me, biting at my lips and my jaw and my throat, groaning. He kisses my mouth again and growls into the kiss and I giggle—and that's when he moves fast, off the bed, yanking me down on the bed so that my knees are over the edge. Leaving his shirt on me, he spreads my thighs wide.

"Go ahead and laugh, termagant," he says into my vulva. "Laugh, my dirty-minded harpy, while I make you come, over and over."

"Oh," I say.

With my eyes closed, my whole world is his hands on my thighs and his mouth on my vulva and quick, firm movement of his tongue on my clitoris. He slips a finger into me as he licks— just one finger, just a little bit—and my muscles pulse around it. He wants to make me come. I feel the intention in him. My belly goes taut. I grip the sheets over my head and breathe, "Holy moly," and he laughs as he licks me, and his laughter makes me laugh, reminding of his vulnerability.

"You're the only one who's done this, too," I say with a grin at the ceiling, and I spread my legs wider.

The sound he makes isn't a laugh. He rests a palm over my mons as he licks me. His fingertip is still inside me, pressing up gently. I drape my thighs over his shoulders and cross my ankles against his back as I tangle my fingers of one hand in his hair. With the other I'm still gripping the sheets.

"You worship me," I say, grinning as I echo his words from the diner.

"Yes," he says against my body, and I come in a sharp, sudden burst that makes me push my body down to take his finger deeper, feel his mouth more firmly. I grunt, *"Ohgodyes,"* with each pulse, until the grunting gives way to giggling. He doesn't move his mouth or his hand. I don't move my legs from his back, but he presses a hand to my belly as I giggle.

When the giggling fades and my legs soften over him, I sigh, "This is fun."

He moves again, this time to lie over me. He's looking into my eyes—I'm smiling, but he's not. He slides into me as he pins my wrists above my head, twining our fingers together.

"I do worship you," he says. And he kisses me. His mouth tastes of me and him and I sigh and lick his tongue, and he fucks me deep.

"Say it," he says, so softly I can barely hear him, though his lips are right against mine. "Tell me I'm the only one."

With my lips brushing against his, I whisper just as softly, "You're the only one."

He growls and fucks me even deeper.

"You're mine?" he prompts gently.

"Yes. Yes, I'm yours," I tell him, my mouth against his.

For a long time, he moves slow and deep inside me. He fucks me and bites my earlobe and my throat, breathes against my neck, lets my arousal grow gradually, until I'm panting again.

"You're mine," he whispers into my ear.

"I'm yours. You're the only one." I'm pushing and pressing my body against his in rhythm with his movements.

"Yes," he breathes. He moves his mouth to mine again. With his lips brushing mine, he whispers, "Look at me, Annie." And when I do, he says, "You're mine."

"Yes."

"I worship you."

"Yes."

He puts his mouth on mine, kisses me with his tongue in my mouth as we watch each other. I don't know what this feeling is. The orgasm that's growing in me feels slow and massive, like I'm a ship rolling on a sea swell. My hips are rolling against his body in an oceanic movement. My legs are trembling, my arms feel helplessly weak. I feel saturated by him, filled, disconnected from everything—there is nothing in the world but his body and this moment and all the ways we fit together.

He's moving faster now; he whispers against my mouth, "Say it again."

"I'm yours. You're the only one."

"Mine." The line between his eyebrows deepens.

"Oh god."

"No, don't close your eyes, Annie, look at me, look at me when you come, look at—oh god love I'm—"

His eyes are on mine. His lips are touching mine, parted, with his jaw tense and his brow furrowed ferociously. He releases my hands to cradle my skull in his palms as he kisses me, eyes open.

"Charles?" I whisper as I tremble the threshold into orgasm.

He whispers, "Mine."

"Yes."

He looks baffled by my pleasure. "I can already feel it. I can feel you coming"—and then I wail into the kiss a long, gravelly cry, breathy and burnt, wrapping my arms around him as I come and come and come around him, my whole body bowing and arching between the bed and his body. I keep my eyes open, and he watches me come. It takes a long time to crest. I keep getting hit by jolts of pleasure, and he keeps kissing me, watching me and changing how he moves inside me, and my orgasm sustains, a floating balloon that he taps and it rises again, he taps and it rises. I stay there so long, I'm almost afraid it will never end, I'm almost afraid I've lost all control over my body.

"What is this?" I whisper against his lips as my body pushes and pushes for more.

"I'm inside you, my Annie," he answers, and I know he means more than his body. "I'm inside you," he says again, and he means we're connected to each other, through gaze and kiss and fuck, and when his eyes widen and he presses into me with those three, sharp, final thrusts, I'm sure his orgasm becomes a part of mine, and mine becomes a part of his, and it's not just that we're coming at the same time, it's that we're having the same orgasm, that the physiology of his body isn't just matched with mine, it is the same. We're joined, not just in the obvious physical way, but in our breath and our heartbeat and our attention and our pleasure.

As the peak fades, still we're watching each other, gasping and softening.

"You," he says, touching my face, "are quite literally breathtaking."

He pronounces it "Litchra-ly." Litchra-ly breathtaking. I am.

His eyes close and he wraps his arms around me, his face buried in my neck as his breathing returns to normal. We lie together, silent and still, for long minutes.

And then everything changes.

He mutters, "The Thing, god, this fucking Thing."

He pulls out of me abruptly, moves off me, but doesn't go far. He lies beside me, his hand on my sternum. He watches his fingers playing with the open placket of his shirt, which I've slept in. He says, "Yesterday—it was just yesterday—we stood in that hallway and said . . . you said last time tore you to pieces and so we decided not to—we weren't going to . . . god, Annie, I'd rather tear *myself* to pieces than hurt you again. I can't—"

"But I'm fine," I say, and I brush my hand over his hair. He won't look at me; he's still watching his hand. "Everything's fine."

"Annie, you can't know—your forgiveness, your *respect* . . . if I lost—if . . . that would tear me to pieces." He grips the fabric of his shirt in his fist. "I would rather never touch you again than risk . . ."

He stops, jaw tense, and closes his eyes. I don't understand how all this worry can follow all that pleasure. Minutes ago, we were as close as two humans can get, and now this.

Then he lifts his eyes to mine and I read his expression—the fear and the warmth and the connection and the . . .

My jaw drops a little as his expression registers. "I . . ."

This is not just The Thing.

I'm his secure base.

I'm the sun.

Charles is *in love* with me.

Wait. What? No. That's not what he means, that's absurd.

But then what the hell does he mean? With that look on his face?

In my mind, I dub it The Something.

I'm trembling suddenly and I don't know why. He's moving away from me, getting out of the bed, putting on clothes, and I don't understand how we got from, "I'm inside you, my Annie," to this. He's half-dressed already, looking around for his shirt, and then he looks at me and remembers I'm wearing it.

I don't understand, so I do what my instincts always tell me to do when I don't understand: I ask Charles.

I sit up. "Dude, can I ask a question?"

"Yeah," he says, barely voiced.

"What do you mean by 'torn to pieces'?"

"Annie—" He presses his hand over his eyes.

"When I say I was 'torn to pieces' last year, I mean something like, 'My heart was broken because I'd been so in love with you.' Is that what you mean?"

He doesn't answer, but paces in silence from one side of the room to the other, his hand over his mouth.

"I just want to understand what's happening in there," I say, as I gesture around my head. "Because a couple minutes ago we were having, like, the most amazing orgasm in the history of the universe, and now you're over there putting on clothes and pacing like you've got somewhere you need to be."

He stops, with his eyes on the floor and both fists gripped in his hair. Painstakingly, he says, without looking at me, "What's happening. Okay. Intellectually, I am in awe of you. Physically, I want you in ways I didn't know existed." He clears his throat and says, "Emotionally . . . when I believe you consider me a friend, that is as great a source of pride as anything in my life." He takes two steps and puts his hands against the wall. He keeps his eyes on the floor as he says in a different, choked voice, "And when I think I might hurt you again as I did before . . . I am terrified . . . terrified that . . ." He closes his eyes and swallows hard, fisting his hands against the wall.

I try to help him. "When I was hurt before, it was because I couldn't have what I wanted. That wasn't your fault."

"You left." Without opening his eyes, he rests his forehead on his fists, still pressed to the wall. "You had to, for your own sake, I don't blame you. But I'm terrified . . ." He stops again.

"Terrified . . . that I'll go away again?"

He nods stiffly, his eyes still closed.

"Because you hate me so much?" I say, trying for a joke, and he does laugh a little, a sad, tense pulse of breath.

But his jaw tightens. He's breathing so hard his nostrils are flaring. I watch his rib cage expand and contract much too fast.

And then I say, "Because you love me so much?"

His jaw clenches ferociously. "Because I can't," he says from between his teeth.

He takes a deep breath, raising his face to the ceiling.

He exhales and flattens his palms on the wall.

After a quick step back and a fast breath in, he looks at the wall, then makes a fist and punches a hole in it.

Chapter 17

I Felt Trapped

At first, time slows down and the world seems to glow with serenity. I turn and lean my back on the wall, glancing all around the room until my eyes find Annie. She's looking at me with her mouth open, her eyes wide. Bedhead and my shirt, wrinkled and baggy on her, and the freckles across her nose and that expression on her face like I've just teleported in from another planet.

I look at her and I think, *Yes, it's because I love you so much.*

And time stops.

It's so clear. Though my lungs contract like I've been punched in the chest, my mind is quiet and calm. I love her. I'm in love with her. That's what this strangeness in my heart and mind is. That's why I'm so terrified of hurting her, of losing her, of somehow pushing her away.

And then time starts up again and the pain makes its way to my consciousness, burning and insistent. I cradle my hand against my chest, holding my wrist with my good hand, never looking away from Annie's face.

She figures out what to say first. She hitches up one side of her mouth and says, "Welcome to rage mountain!"

I start to laugh, softly. I close my eyes and raise my eyebrows and inform her gently, "I've broken my hand."

"Oh, shit." I hear her get out of bed and approach me. She touches my forearm and says, "Dude, that looks bad."

"Hurts a bit, too—which is a shame because otherwise I feel remarkably well," I say, and I can feel the blood draining from my face.

She sighs dramatically and says, "Well, there go my hopes for more sex this morning. Can I take a shower before we go to the emergency room, or does it hurt so much I should just leave the house covered in semen?"

I laugh again, silently now. I haven't opened my eyes. "I'll put ice on it. No rush."

The corners of my mouth go down. I can't stop them. The pain is getting worse. My hand feels enormous, like it's about to burst through my skin. I slide carefully down the wall, all the way to the floor.

"I'll bring you ice," she says.

"I can get it."

"Oh, for the love of god," she groans, already on her way out the door. "Doctors are the worst patients."

It's a transverse fracture of the extra-articular neck of the fifth metacarpal—bog standard boxer's break, in other words, though impressively angulated. I've also sprained my wrist and various finger ligaments.

And I am not the worst patient. I am polite and apologetic, self-effacing when the A&E nurse, seeing my hand, laughs sympathetically, and says, "Hit a wall, mate?" and stoic when he maneuvers my fingers into a boxer splint, as a temporary solution to the newly-broken-bone-about-to-go-on-a-plane problem. They give me a prescription for narcotics and tell me to see a doctor when I get back to the States.

And that's that. I'm fine.

At different times during the afternoon our respective airlines have called Annie and me, and we've both got flights home tomorrow.

Simon gets home around six, taking off his jacket as he walks into the library, where he finds Annie and me in our pajamas, on his couch, her with her next public health theory book, me just staring at the ceiling, stoned on painkillers, my splinted hand resting over my sternum.

"Wh-wh—?" Simon says.

"'Lo, Simon," I slur. "I got to Rage Mountain."

Simon questions me with a look.

"He punched a hole in your wall because: feelings," Annie explains. "Fortunately for your wall, the hole is really just a dent. Unfortunately for Charles, it's a dent because he hit the stud."

We worked this out on the way to A&E.

"I'm a fucking idiot," I moan at the ceiling.

"A mmmoron," Simon says.

"Thick as two short planks," I add.

"Thick as that bloody tree of yours," Simon says in an impression of our father so true to life that I feel a little nauseated at first, but then I laugh hilariously, and Simon joins me.

"Bluch, what tree?" Annie asks.

"Oh god," I sigh. I hate this story. "They planted a tree at the house in Cornwall when I was born. Mum thought it would be sweet and he was pleased to have an heir, so they had one planted. And of course Mum wanted a tree for each of us, but he couldn't be arsed, so there's just the one tree, the Charles tree."

"Wh-er . . ." Simon sits on the table by the couch. "Wwwhat was it like? Her-hitting it?"

"It was like . . . god, it was like heroin," I tell the ceiling. "Time dilated and everything was just a bit brighter and more beautiful, just enough to make you think that's how life actually is, or how it's supposed to be. Just enough to fool you into thinking this is how being alive is supposed to feel."

After a short silence, Annie snorts. "Like you've done heroin."

"I have, you know," I say, turning my eyes to her briefly before looking back at the ceiling. "Pretty much everything at least once. When you've got a monster to subdue and a well-padded bank account, you can and will try anything. I was bad, before, you know? Sex, drugs, and . . . well. Coldplay, anyway."

I've surprised her. Probably appalled her.

Simon, though, he giggles. And then he starts making a weird noise—it takes me a second to realize he's singing—"Nungnung-nungnungnungnugnungnungnung *ningningningning* nungnungnung-nungnugnungnungnung . . ."

You wanker, I think, *how did you know?* But I grin as I think it, and then I'm singing along to Simon's guitar imitation. He moves to the piano and plays instead, singing the harmony. I'm not a musician. I don't really know how to sing. I can match pitches, but Simon . . . I drop out at the end and let him sing the ending. I chuckle when he gets to *"And ignite your bones."*

Eyes still on the ceiling, I say, "Yes, exactly. Fuck you, you wanker. How did you know?"

Simon doesn't answer—or rather he does, but not with words. He starts playing "The Scientist."

And I think, *How can he know me, when I've done my best not to be known?* I laugh silently at the ceiling and whisper, "Wanker." The corners of my mouth won't stop down again and my nose stings. I grit my teeth to stop it.

When I have it under control, I call, "How did you know?"

Without stopping, Simon sings, as if these are the lyrics of the song, in a dead-on Chris Martin imitation, "First was the title/and major seconds/and there's some deee-scending major thirds." He transitions to a light, easy falsetto, to add, "Charles is a sucker for pop tunes. Oh, it's such a shame his taste in music is so . . . much worse than his taste in girls."

"Fuck off," I shoot back, and I listen to the rest with the remnant of a grin lingering on my face.

At the end of the song, Simon says, "How lllong did it lll . . . er . . . ?"

I chuckle again. "How long did it last? 'Bout fifteen seconds? Twenty? After that, it just hurt a lot. I feel okay now, though— I'm surprised they gave me a narcotic." I stop and swallow, then give a little vocalized sigh. "I haven't given so little of a shit in a very, very long time." I scratch my itchy face.

Simon starts playing the Beatles song "Fixing a Hole," and I laugh out loud. At the end, he transitions right into "With a Little Help from My Friends."

I turn to look at Annie, who's watching me with an expression of astonishment. Confusion. Like she has no idea who I am. Well. Neither do I. I feel like someone's broken me open and dumped all the pieces of me out onto the floor, a puzzle with no edges and no pattern, just an undifferentiated mess.

The pain wakes me in the middle of the night. Annie is fast asleep.

I go down to the kitchen for water and meds, and hear music, a piano, coming from the bat cave, so I take my drugs and follow the sound down to find Simon playing in his office.

"What was that?" I ask, when he gets to the end.

"Bach's 'Little' Fugue," he says, not looking up. He closes the lid over the keys and rests his elbows on it, rubbing his forehead against his hands. "Even I get tired of chaos."

I lay myself down, bleary and hurting, on the black chesterfield. My eyelids are heavy, but my body is restless.

"Will there be fallout from Heathrow?" I ask.

He turns to me and tips his head from side to side. "The of-official consequences will certainly inclllude an investigation by the defense committee."

"And the unofficial consequences?"

"Oh, there's no percentage in prevention. I'll be sacked," he says, unconcerned. "Not for months, mh-mmmaybe years, but I'm finished."

We share a long silence.

"Worth it?" I ask.

"My career in exchange for, ooh, anything between five hundred and fifty thousand lives?" he asks, pretending to calculate in his head, like he's setting up a joke. But then he says, "It's worth it for even one life."

I look at him steadily. "Was one of them Annie's?"

He nods without speaking.

My heart clenches in my chest and I close my eyes.

"Thank you," I whisper.

When I open my eyes again, he says, "She's . . ." He trails off, searching for an adjective he can't find.

"I know," I sigh, and sink a little further in my exhaustion.

Into the silence, Simon asks, "Whhhy did you hit the wall?"

I clear my throat against the instantaneous physical memory. "Because I felt trapped."

He nods and waits. I see him imagining me as a wild animal, bleeding in a snare.

"Not by her," I say through the tightness in my throat. "By my whole life, my whole identity. I've worked so hard. I've never stopped working. I'm exhausted from it. But still I'm throwing myself against these walls, as if I'll ever get free. Hopeless."

He opens the piano and plays three slow notes, each higher than the last, and then another series of three . . . and then a third series . . . and then the unmistakable riff of "Take On Me."

I grin and imagine myself as the crosshatched cartoon of a man from the video, slamming himself against the cartoon walls to get to the real-life girl, while she watches in sympathetic agony, until at last he breaks free of the cartoon box and into the real world.

I'm stunned speechless by the simplicity of it. The obviousness. And it clutches me by the throat. I take off my glasses and put my intact hand over my eyes.

I'm not trapped. There is a way out. But oh god it will hurt.

As I lie there, swallowing and silent, he begins playing "Brothers in Arms" again.

I press the heel of my hand and the wrist of the brace against my eyes when he finishes.

"I'm going in early, ssso I won't see you in the morning," he says lightly. "Safe flight, et cetera."

I feel his hand on my shoulder. And then he's gone.

I don't know how long I lie there. I don't know what emotion makes my diaphragm convulse and shake, makes my jaw lock, teeth gritted. I don't know how to take the next step forward. All I know is that my body is wracked and wild. The only thing to do is to allow this thing to roll over and through me, like a riptide.

When my body quiets to stillness, wrung out and limp under the influence of the trembling and the drugs, when I can breathe again, I haul myself upright and climb the stairs out of the cellar.

And find Annie sitting on the main stairs.

"Hey," she says. "I woke up and you weren't there. I was waiting for you. Where'd you go?"

I'm muzzy-headed from the drugs and the persistent, low-level throb of pain, but I feel like I'm seeing her clearly at last, without the haze of fear and denial and posturing.

I could tell her, I think. But I'm too drugged, too exhausted, too wrung out.

I sit beside her on the stairs. "Cellar with Simon." I take her hand in my intact one. "Come to bed."

We go up the stairs together, hand in hand, and get into bed. I pull her against me, her back to my front, and hold her.

"Charles," she murmurs.

"Mh," I say into her hair.

"We have to talk about The Thing."

"Yeah."

"And Boston."

"Yeah."

"You broke a bone, dude."

I don't answer.

She turns in my arms and gently pushes me to my back. She looks into my eyes as I touch her hair with my intact hand.

She says, "I think the whole Rage Mountain thing is, like, so amazing and important, and I want to help if I can. But I think The Thing is like . . ." She rests her cheek on my chest. "I don't know. You tell me. Where does The Thing fit in the metaphor?"

I take the question seriously, thinking carefully for a long time. The Thing seems almost beside the point now—and that's the problem, really. The Thing is a way I can feel closer to her, without actually *being* any closer. I feel the lower half of my body try to convince me that The Thing could dynamite my way through the mountain, but the upper half of me knows I'd only be crushed in a rockslide—and it might be a pretty good way to go, all things considered, if only there weren't the risk of crushing Annie as well.

No. If I want to make my way to her, The Thing will not get me there; only reckoning with my own internal shit will do that. I've got to climb this bloody mountain.

Part of me wants to tell her that. Another part of me knows that if I tell her, she'll take me seriously and not sleep with me again until I've dealt with the dragon—and even though I know that would be the wisest choice, I can't bring myself to say it.

And then it turns out I don't have to. She sits up, pushing away from me. She crosses her legs under her and says very seriously, "You know that Disaster thing I talked about?"

I nod.

"I think the Disaster isn't mine; it's yours. We do things about The Thing, and *you're* the one who's torn to pieces."

I don't answer.

"You broke. A *bone*."

Again, I don't answer. I watch her face. I feel the space between us widen, feel her creating distance. I'm panicked by it. I'm ashamed of making her responsible for saving me from The Thing. I feel rescued and abandoned at the same time.

She sits in silence, brow furrowed with that look of intense processing. And then her face changes, brightens, softens with insight—a shift in expression familiar to me, familiar and beloved. It makes me smile, even in the midst of the maelstrom inside me.

What I want to say is *I love you, Annie. I love you.* But instead—

"Can I—" I begin. "I'm not changing the subject. I just want to say . . . do you remember lab meetings at IU?"

"Of course."

"You'd sit there silently for the first half hour, with your eyebrows crinkled together, a thoughtful moue on your face. And then, about halfway through the meeting, you'd say something like, 'Sorry, I know I might be wrong about this, but the problem might be x' and then you'd articulate precisely what everyone else has been trying to get at all along. As the semesters passed, that introductory apology disappeared and you'd just say, 'Are you saying x?' and then, in that last semester, you started to say, 'I think you're saying x.' The shedding of the apology told me you were gaining confidence, but it was those silences that first made me think, *This girl has a brain.* And eventually I realized it was one of the most astonishing, curious, insightful brains I will ever encounter."

Her face changes again, crumples into a tearful smile. She folds herself back into my arms.

"You have no idea how much I needed to hear that," she says, her face against my neck.

I put my arms around her, careful with my broken hand. I kiss the top of her head and ask, "May I offer a bit of unsolicited advice?"

"Of course."

"You never need to worry about what you hear; no one listens as intently and integrates as quickly and connects ideas as broadly as you. And you need never apologize for it. You'll grow fastest if you focus instead on what you give back—make it about what the patient most needs to hear, rather than what's most salient to you."

I feel her nod. She sniffs and says, "That makes sense."

As her body relaxes against mine, I consider the possibility that I've just told her how to help me with the mountain. I consider the possibility that, with her help, I might have nothing to fear from the dragon. For a long time, I consider the possibility that I can accept her help with the same easy confidence with which I have always offered help to her.

I say, "Annie, I've missed you so much."

She's asleep.

I don't sleep at all. I touch my lips to her head and smell her hair.

Three days. Three days, a short-circuited terrorist attack, my appalling father, and a broken bone. That's what it took to make a large enough break in the wall for me to glimpse what's on the other side.

If I tried to beat my way through it, I'd kill myself. So I'll have to climb it.

And then there's the dragon at the top.

But there's Annie on the other side. If she'll have me. And even if she won't—like medieval knights in courtly love, the dragon's got to be slain either way, so it might as well be done in a lady's name, even if the lady is married to the king.

My lady is not married. My lady has only ever been mine. Perhaps . . . perhaps, if I'm very lucky, she may only ever be mine.

Mine.

As I am hers.

I think about the six months it took to get out of the pit, the four months in the swamp. I'm more afraid of the mountain than I was of either of those . . . but if I can just get past the dragon—hopefully with nothing worse than a broken bone and maybe a few scorches—then I might spend all my nights with Annie's hair tickling my nose and her breath on my chest. Then I'll be free to love her and, if I'm very, *very* lucky, to receive her love.

And all I have to do is climb a mountain, battle a dragon, and break through a wall of my own construction.

So, okay.

Chapter 18

Only a Flesh Wound

Two months later, I shortcut across the campus of Northeastern University in the muggy heat of August. When I cross onto his block of Mass Ave, I get off and walk my bike up the sidewalk, looking at house numbers—but then I see him. He's sitting on his front steps, waiting for me. He smiles when he sees me and waves with a splinted hand as he gets to his feet.

"What time do you call this?" he calls. He walks toward me with his hands in his pockets, grinning madly as I walk faster to him, taking off my helmet. When I reach him, he puts an arm around my shoulders to hug me.

"Sorry I'm late," I say, hugging him with the arm that isn't holding my bike. He's bearded—I feel it against my cheek—and I smile up at him. "Mountain man."

"Let's go climb some rocks," he says, and leads me back to his steps, where his bike waits. We ride to the rock gym, and it's as easy and comfortable as if we'd been doing it since forever.

"Annie Coffey!" Linton calls across the rock gym, putting on the American-white-girl voice he uses to tease me.

"Linton Adams," I call back. As he walks over to me, I point behind me with my thumb. "I brought the guy I was telling you about."

"At long last!" cries Linton, extending a hand to shake. "She's been promising me someone who'll talk cricket with me!"

"If you loathe Australia, we'll get on like a house on fire," Charles says, and he takes Linton's hand in his splinted one.

"And my job here is done," I announce, and I leave them to it.

For half an hour I climb with Sylvia, glancing periodically toward Charles and Linton. Linton climbs first with Charles on belay, then they switch. I watch Charles's first few moves, marveling as always at the ease and grace of his body when he climbs—then I realize I should be watching the climber I'm belaying and I turn my attention to Syl. She's climbing a really difficult route. I try to help her from the ground, and I'm so focused that I miss the minor ruckus happening behind me. It's only when Sylvia's back on the ground and we're switching ropes that I turn and see that Linton is being belayed by another guy.

When he's lowered back down, I call, "Dude, where's Charles?"

"Oh man," Linton answers, untying his knot. "He fell off the overhang and his hand broke again. It was sick."

"Oh my god!"

"I had to untie his knot for him."

"Where is he?"

"Emergency."

"Alone? He didn't come and get me—or at least *tell* me?"

Linton just shrugs.

Men. Honestly.

So there goes my plan. I wanted Charles and me to go climbing and then get coffee and talk about The Thing, about which no explicit decision has been made. See, I've been thinking about everything that happened and everything Charles said, and I've concluded, tentatively, that The Thing is a risk factor for Disaster and he must avoid it for his own well-being. And that would be fine. We avoided it for a year in Indiana; we can avoid it some more. We'll be friends, like before.

Except now it seems like Disaster will happen even if I'm just in the room.

So, do I leave him alone with his broken hand at the ER, safe from me and Disaster?

Or do I go take care of him, like I would any other friend?

I decide to compromise. I text him.

That does not go very well.

Dude let me know if you're okay.

Also let me know if you're NOT okay.

Y U NO TEXT U MAD BRO?

Basically just let me know you're not dead.

Or whoever finds this phone on Charles's mangled corpse, please let me know.

I'M GOING TO SIT ON YOUR FRONT STEPS UNTIL YOU GET HOME.

I'm not kidding. I'm sitting on your steps.

Awesome, you're dead and your mom is going to come collect your body and find your phone full of crazy texts from that American chick she met that one time.

I might order a pizza. Let me know if you want anything.

It's past sunset by the time a taxi drops Charles off at his front step, where I'm sitting, reading by the light of my phone's flash. I look up at the sound of the car—then stand up.

"Oh my god! What the hell happened?" Charles is gingerly getting out of the car, his arm in a sling. He limps toward me. The look on his face says he's in nine kinds of pain.

"How long have you been here?" he asks.

"A couple hours. You didn't get my texts? What happened?"

"My phone died." He climbs the steps carefully.

"Dude," I insist, "what *happened?* Where are your glasses?"

"Still in hospital." He fumbles one-handed to unlock his front door.

"Here, let me," I say, and I take the key from him. I let us both in. "Where's your apartment?"

"Fourth floor," he says. "You don't have to go all that way."

"Of course I will!" and I march up the stairs ahead of him, saying, "You look like you got hit by a bus."

"Nearly," he answers, following me slowly. "Car hit my bike while I was walking it in a crosswalk. Mild concussion, whiplash, slightly broken arm. On top of the re broken hand. Various scrapes and bruises. My glasses and bike were totaled. I'm fine." There is only one apartment on the fourth floor. I unlock it and wait for Charles to hobble up behind me, then I follow him in and switch on the light as he cautiously drops his gear to the floor.

"Holy shit!" In the full light, I see the purple lump on his temple. I reach out and touch a couple of fingers to it.

"I'm fine, domina," he says, his voice croaky with exhaustion and pain. Then he says, "Your eyes are pretty."

I smirk. "You're stoned?"

"No, just concussed," he says. "But I ought to lie down."

I follow him to his bedroom, where he sits on the bed to undress. As I watch from the doorway, he takes off the sling, then pulls his shitty old climbing T-shirt slowly and painfully over his head and drops it on the floor. He looks down sorrowfully at his shoes.

"Need help?" I ask.

"No, no," he responds automatically, but I come in and sit on the floor by his feet. I pull off his shoes, one at a time, and tuck them under the bed. Then I put my palms on his insteps and look up at him.

"You seem really sad," I say. His feet are warm and smooth under my calloused hands.

He shakes his head. "Feeling stupid."

"How can I help?"

"Can you rewind time to about twelve hours ago?" he asks. He sounds sleepy.

"I'll work on it," I answer with a grin.

"Meantime, you could get my phone for me."

"You got it."

I trot out to the living room, and by the time I rummage through his stuff, find his phone, and get back to his bedroom, Charles is sitting with his pants around his ankles, trying to kick them off his feet. Stifling a laugh, I plug his phone in and leave it on the nightstand. And then—

"Holy shit!"

Along his right leg, a swollen, purple bruise extends from his knee halfway up his quadriceps.

"Nice," he says blearily. He watches as I untangle his feet from his clothes. "That explains why the stairs hurt."

"I'll get ice," I say.

"Okay," he agrees. He lies back carefully and drags his legs up onto the bed, and I head for the kitchen. He only has two ice packs. I bring both, along with a couple of dish towels. When I get back, I find him reading on his phone, holding the screen right up to his nose.

"Did you order a pizza?" he mumbles.

"No, but I can. You want pizza? Here, stay still."

"Mmmmh . . . circulatory turnover," he says, like he's Homer Simpson with a doughnut, as I tuck a wrapped ice pack under his neck.

"Do you have spare glasses?"

"In a box somewhere," he sighs. He's only half unpacked.

I wrap the other ice pack in a tea towel and strap it to his knee, then sit beside him on the edge of the bed.

"My own stupid fault," he says. "I'm a plonker. Showing off. Competing—as if climbing that difficult overhang would . . ." He delicately turns his head in my direction and says, "You might have told me about you and Linton."

"Told you what?"

"He indicated, via wink and smile, that you and he . . . have A Thing."

I snort. "Linton's pretty sure every woman he meets is secretly in lust with him."

"Aren't you?" He watches me for a moment, then closes his eyes. "You could tell me, you know. If you had A Thing with someone."

"I know," I say.

We sit in silence together for a few minutes. Finally, I say, "It's a relief, in a way, that you got hit by a car."

"My bike got hit," he corrects without opening his eyes.

"Right. That. The important thing is that I wasn't there when it happened. So I'm not necessarily a curse."

He shifts his intact hand so that his fingers just touch my leg. "You're not a curse."

"But if I'm not," I persist, "it'd be nice to know what I can do to help while you—"

"Just this," he says. He stops and swallows, brushing his fingers against my leg. He opens his eyes and swallows again, and I'm astonished to see him fight tears before he says, "I need you near me, domina, accepting me as I am—broken and afraid—and where I am in the pit and on the mountain and all the rest of it."

"I do," I say, and I put my hand in his.

He closes his eyes again.

And that settles that.

We sit together in another long silence. I watch the pain in his face. I brush my hand over his forehead and hair, the way my dad does when I'm sick. Charles sighs and the tension in his faces eases a fraction.

"You're gonna need like eight ice packs to cope with the demand here," I say. "I'll go out and get some, and then I'll see if I can find your glasses. What else do you need?"

"Nothing, young Coffey, I'm fine," he mutters. "It's only a flesh wound."

"It's not!" I say.

"I'm going to tie you down and force-feed you Monty Python one day."

And then he's asleep.

Well, now.

I wait ten minutes and return the ice packs to the freezer without waking him. Then I grab his keys and race home on my bike to get some books and stuff—hurriedly explaining to Syl and Linton that I'll be staying with Charles because he totally got hit by a motherfucking car on his way to the emergency room, I KNOW, ISN'T THAT CRAZY?—and stop at the drugstore for ice packs.

When I get back, he's still fast asleep, his phone under his palm on his sternum, mouth slightly open. He doesn't wake when I re-ice his neck and knee. Lying there in nothing but his underwear and his cast and his bruises and his beard, he looks like a boxer after a hard loss. A very handsome, very intelligent boxer. And a very hard loss.

I order a pizza and work in the living room. I keep rotating the ice packs on Charles's neck and knee, twenty minutes on, twenty minutes off. I sit on the edge of the bed and hold an ice pack to the bump on his head, too, as I watch him sleep. When I need to take a break from studying, I search his place for boxes in which I might find his spare glasses. His apartment is super nice, with two bedrooms, a kitchen full of granite and stainless steel, and shiny old wood floors. But the main thing you notice is that the entire front wall of the apartment is windows, five of them, floor to ceiling, so that the kitchen and living room overlook Boston in a wide-open expanse. There's a spiral staircase, too, that leads up to a roof deck that's got two Adirondack chairs and a little table between them. Uh, his glasses aren't up there.

I find them easily enough, in the boxful of nightstand detritus. I leave them on his nightstand.

Four hours after he fell asleep, I turn on a light and wake him as I'm tying a fresh ice pack to his knee.

"Chaaaruuuuuls," I sing. "Wake uuuu-uuup. You have a con-cuuuuu-siooooon."

"Annie?" he mumbles, his eyelids barely lifting. "Time is it?"

"After one."

"What are you doing here?" And his eyelids drift closed again.

"First aid."

"Mh."

"What's the date?" I ask.

"Fuck knows. Look at a calendar."

"I'm checking if your brain is broken, dumbass," I laugh.

"'Course my brain is broken, got a bloody concussion, don't I?"

I try again. "What's two plus two?"

"Five," he says with a sleepy smile. "Two and two make five. Freedom is slavery. Ignorance is strength."

"Arrite, Winston." Even I know *1984*. "Any numbness? Look at me for a sec." I lift his eyelids with my thumbs and check his pupils. They're fine. He's fine. I just like feeling like I'm taking care of him.

He sighs deeply and says, "No numbness. No nausea. No memory loss—as far as I know. Who are you?"

"Ha-ha." I press an ice pack to his temple and he sighs again.

"'S'nice," he says, eyes closed. After a little silence he says, "It was fun being a patient. There were these students shadowing Clemente. Clemente's the psychiatric medical director in Emergency. She's brilliant, just fantastic. Anyway, I got to teach these adorable little students about defensive responses and self-paced termination."

"Like my shaking thing after the airport?"

"Mh-hm." He sighs heavily. "You were 'mazing that day. Your body just knew what to do. What's it like, just knowing, innately, how to live inside your body and feel safe?"

"I don't know," I say. "I don't know what it's like not to feel that way."

"You were beautiful," he says, so softly I almost can't hear him. And then he's quiet for so long I think he's fallen asleep again.

"Charles?"

He answers, "Mh?"

"I'm gonna stay tonight, okay?"

"'Kay."

"And I'm gonna take off the ice now."

"'Kay."

"How's your pain? Did they give you a script?"

"I'll just take some paracetamol."

"I'll get it."

I take off the ice packs and return them to the freezer. I bring him the bottle of Tylenol and a glass of water, but he's asleep again.

So I turn off the lights and get under the covers, fully dressed, on my side of the bed, where I'm surrounded by the smell of him.

My alarm goes off five hours later and we do it all again. With the sun brightening the room in pink and gold, I sit beside him again and press an ice pack to his temple. He wakes slowly and his eyes drift up to mine.

"Hey," he says.

Eschewing the usual questions, I say, "Name for me, please, Dr. Douglas, the cranial nerves. In order."

"CN one . . ." he says with a lazy smile, "CN two . . ."

"Smart-ass. Touch your nose with your left hand."

Slowly and carefully, he touches *my* nose with his left hand.

"Did I do it right?" he grins.

"Yes, you're very smart. Here, take these."

He drags himself, wincing, upright enough to swallow water and pills. He scrubs a hand over his face and, with an uninhibited groan, says, "God, I feel about a hundred and eight."

"Is it too early for coffee? I can make coffee."

"Bless your cotton socks," he says.

So I make coffee and carry two mugs back to the bedroom. He takes a sip of his, closes his eyes, and sighs. I watch his face. I watch him breathe. I wonder how his pain is. I wonder what he's thinking. I aim for silence. It's hard.

Then he opens his eyes, brimming with The Something, and he says, "Thanks for staying."

I smile. "I have my study group at noon, but I'll stay until then, if you don't mind."

"I don't mind," he whispers, closing his eyes again.

Chapter 19

The Relationship Is
the Medicine

Thus Charles becomes a part of my climbing group. After giving his arm and hand a month to heal, he begins belaying and climbing with great caution. He fits in easily, everyone likes him, and there's a not insignificant amount of jockeying among the women climbers (following an inquiry to me about his sexual orientation and romantic status) to get his attention.

He doesn't give anyone his attention—or rather, he gives everyone his attention, shining his radiance equally on everyone who comes in his path. Yes, he'd be glad to belay you. No, he hasn't tried that bouldering route yet, he's still supposed to go easy on his hand. Yes, he'd love to join everyone for a drink after. No, he's afraid he can't have dinner with you, he has work early the next day.

At the end of September, he shaves his beard and stops wearing the brace when he climbs. He spends more time doing finger exercises and strength training than actually climbing, but apart from that everything feels really normal—including the familiar moments when I look at him and all I can think is *I want to lick your throat and bite your ropy forearms.* But not once does he do anything to indicate the least bit of Thing. Still, I've lived with

The Thing for so long that letting it go is second nature to me now. It fills my brain, I take a breath, it moves through me.

He becomes friends with Linton—I knew he would. While I'm practicing lead climbing, Charles teaches Linton to boulder—low climbing on very difficult, usually overhanging routes, without ropes and harnesses. If you fall, you free-fall, but you're never more than ten feet off the ground. They lie on their backs on the mat, under the lower of the gym's two overhanging walls, and Charles points out holds and describes moves. And he teaches him to do circular pull-ups and negative pull-ups and one-arm pull-ups, and by October their biceps, triceps, and deltoids are, frankly, mouthwatering. If we see Charles and Linton approaching the hangboard, the women in the gym will stop what we're doing and watch them. Linton starts taking off his shirt and flexing for us, as we laugh and catcall.

Charles never flexes for us, never takes off his shirt, but he wolf-whistles at Linton.

At home, Linton talks about what a great guy Charles is, what a good teacher, what a good listener, what a good friend.

"I know," I say. "I don't know what I'd do without him."

I don't see Charles that often, compared to Indiana, where I saw him almost every day. We climb once a week, either Wednesday or Saturday. We work together every Monday at seven at a local coffee place. But the change these two days make in my life . . . I feel so much stronger, so much more competent with him here. I'm not doing any better in school—I was already doing fine—but my state of mind is vastly different.

He goes away periodically, flies all the time. If he's climbing Rage Mountain or confronting his dragon, I don't see it. Or rather, I don't see it until I finally ask him if I can walk home with him from the rock gym one pretty October evening.

"I want to talk to you about something," I say.

"Sure."

It takes me about half the walk to make myself finally ask what I've been wanting to ask:

"Are you interviewing for jobs? Is that why you travel so much?"

"Hm? No, no."

Okay, phew. So he's not leaving instantly.

"Are you going to conferences?"

"No, nothing like that. It's nothing."

"Are you visiting your mom, since you're a thousand miles closer than you were last year?"

"Annie, it's nothing."

"Nothing, as in you just like going on planes a lot so you fly places and then fly right back, just for the pleasure of drinking Bloody Marys at thirty-five thousand feet?"

"You're a pest," he says with a grin.

"I know," I say. "So where do you go?"

"If I said I didn't want to tell you, would you stop asking?"

I open my mouth to say, "Of course," but instead what comes out is "You have a girlfriend somewhere but you don't want to tell me because you think it might be awkward?"

He sighs mightily. "You're a pain the arse, young Coffey."

"It wouldn't be awkward, you can tell me."

"A virago," he says. "A harridan."

"I know." We've arrived at his building. I follow him up his front steps, and as he opens his door I bargain, "Or, instead of telling me where you go, you could just tell me why you won't tell me where you go."

"Come inside," he says, and what it sounds like is "Let's get this over with."

"No no, that's okay." After all, I don't want to impose.

"I put that badly," he says, holding the door open. "What I meant to say is, get your little monkey arse inside because you bloody asked for it."

"You mad, bro?" I ask, climbing the last step to his front door.

"No." Then he closes his eyes, leaning his head back against the door, and says as if it surprises him, "Yes, a bit. Now will you *please* go up, you curstest shrew."

I do, meekly.

In his apartment, Charles dumps his climbing gear and jacket by the door and goes to the kitchen. "I'm making coffee. Do you want any?" he asks.

"Okay," I say, and the grinder goes on. I drop my stuff next to his and sit myself on my end of the couch, where I watch Charles make coffee in silence. He's finally unpacked, but he still doesn't have any pictures on his walls, no art, no photos of family. Just lots of books.

He brings two cups, hands me one, and sits on his end of the couch.

I wait.

He drinks his coffee. I drink mine.

I wait some more.

"I fly to Indiana to see Clarissa," he says at last.

I blink and have to remember who Clarissa is. Then I open my mouth to ask if she's never heard of Skype or even the telephone, but he preempts the question.

"The relationship is the medicine, and she and I both find that technology interferes."

"The relationship is the medicine," I repeat.

"I'd fly to see a renowned specialist or receive treatment if I had any serious illness." He's trying to justify it. I don't need him to justify it. I get it.

"Is our relationship medicine?"

He's silent for so long, I think he's not going to answer—but then he does, by asking me a question. "You know how you can watch someone climb a route once, and your body knows how to do it?"

"Yeah," I say.

"Well, no one else does," he says. "You think that's normal, to watch someone and feel their movement in your body, so that you just know how to do it."

"Don't—"

"You think it's normal that when I taught you to hustle in Simon's kitchen, you just learned how to follow in a matter of minutes."

"But—"

"You think it's normal to be able to name your emotions, to speak your feelings aloud, to feel safe and alive in your body."

I just stare at him, feeling scolded for doing the right thing.

"It's a delight to watch, and it's infuriating to see you take it for granted. So many gifts. You have so many gifts, termagant. When you're pleased, your joy fills the room. When you're frustrated or angry, it's a pure, pristine thing, without shame or fear. Yes, domina," he concludes grumpily. "Yes, our relationship is medicine."

"Because I'm . . ."

"Because you're you, termagant. Have you met you? And I'm angry—not at you, at me, because I don't know where the boundaries ought to be. When I was your boss, the boundaries were clear. When we were lovers, the boundaries were clear. When you left, I knew where the boundary was. And now . . . I don't know anymore. Should I tell you about seeing Clarissa? Should I tell you about the phone calls with Mum about how ill my father is? Should I tell you I've been thinking about getting a cat? I don't know.

"And tonight you push me for more and I feel like I'm doing it wrong, but I also resent that you want more than I'm inclined to offer, and I'm frustrated because I don't know which is right or wrong. I don't even know if I should be telling you any of this."

We sit in silence for a long time. I drink some coffee. Charles sits with his cup on the coffee table, his elbows on his knees, his fingers laced together, his mouth against the backs of his fingers.

He gets up and disappears into his room, but comes back with his brace. He sits on the edge of the couch and puts it on with a snap of elastic and a rip of Velcro. His right wrist is still noticeably smaller than his left.

"Your dad is sick?" I say, watching him adjust the brace.

"Yeah." Charles throws himself back on the couch, takes off his glasses, and rubs his good hand over his face. "Serves him right, the tosser. *And* he's making Mum's life a misery."

We sit in silence with this until I say, "I don't know which is right or wrong, either. I don't know where the boundaries are."

"Well, I'm glad I'm not the only one," he says.

More silence.

"Hey," I say eventually.

"Mh," he says back.

"Were you just mad while I was in the room?"

He looks at me. "I suppose I was."

"That's the first time you haven't kicked me out when you were angry."

"I suppose it was."

"Well. I don't want to be a know-it-all, but: boundaries schmoundaries. It seems to me that letting me be around you when you're annoyed is more important than any specific thing you tell me or don't tell me."

He half smiles at me from his end of the couch. "I'll bear that in mind."

Chapter 20

Doctor Scientist

The first time I walked back into Clarissa's office after moving, I was in a cast, with a bad limp and a bruise going green on my temple, and she said peacefully, "You look like you've been in a war."

And I just sank onto the couch and sobbed for most of the two hours. Gradually, I explained how, at the first merest suggestion that I had lost Annie, that I was too late, I had, like a fool, climbed a 10b route with a tricky overhang, when I knew for sure that I ought to stick to easy climbing and spend more time doing physio. I told her how Annie had met me on my steps. How she had touched me with such tenderness, so that I wondered if this is why men get into fights—so they can go home and be cared for by tenderhearted women with cool, gentle fingertips and pretty eyes. How she had stayed with me all night. How she left for her study group with a cheerful kiss on my unbruised eyebrow and a promise to come back the next day.

And Clarissa said placidly, "Okay. We've got a lot to work with here."

And work we have.

It's been three months now—three months of climbing together each week, and working across a café table from each other every Monday at seven.

Three months, too, of watching Linton, who has every virtue I might dare to claim, and all the virtues I know very well I lack. And if I've had more fantasies than I can count of dragging him into the street by his shirt and beating him to a pulp, I've never once lost sight of the fact that it's not really him I want to destroy. It is my funhouse mirror image, reflecting back my every shortcoming, my every failure, all my guilt, my shame. It is that image that I want to smash. It just happens to look like a Jamaican-Canadian son of a playwright, a poet scientist with big brown eyes and an ego the size of a small nation-state.

"Annie and I have been negotiating boundaries," I tell Clarissa in November. "The question is whether we keep or share the things that could be potentially uncomfortable or hurtful to the other."

Clarissa says, "What could she tell you that you're too fragile to bear, or what could you tell Annie that she's too fragile to bear?"

"It's me who's fragile," I say, realizing it at last. "I thought I was afraid of hurting her, but really I'm afraid of her turning away from me . . . and she might do that even if I don't hurt her."

"And she might not turn away, even if you do."

I frown at my hands. "I hadn't thought about it that way."

"That's why they pay me the big bucks, Charlie," she says. "You've got a plane to catch, hot shot."

On a Saturday afternoon in mid-December, I'm walking back from the rock gym with Annie.

"Bring climbing gear," she tells me. "We don't have to miss a Wednesday climb just because we're in a different city."

"Sure. And what's the gift protocol?" I ask.

She's taking me home for Christmas.

"Oh. Uh, we don't really do gifts—not like stuff we bought and wrapping paper and stuff. We pick a nonprofit and give money and time to it, and then on Christmas Eve we write our gift letters, and we read them on Christmas morning."

I blink at her and wait for her to explain.

"I think it started because I wanted to write to Santa Claus when I was a kid, you know, asking for what I wanted for Christmas, but Mom and Dad were like, 'How about you write what you're grateful you already have?' And they did it, too, and that evolved into the gift letters. We write down something we're grateful for about one another, from the past year, and something we hope for the other people, for the coming year," she says.

"Right," I say. "I can't tell if that's deeply charming or insufferably twee."

"What does your family do?" she asks.

"Dunno anymore. Haven't spent Christmas with them for five years." She knows this. It appalled her when she realized. It's why she's dragging me off to New York. "But when I was at school, it was mostly an exchange of socks and cash."

"Oh." She raises her eyebrows and shakes her head. Even having met them, she can't grow accustomed to the idea of what it was like.

"And would I, as a guest, be either expected or welcome to participate in this letter ritual?" I ask dubiously.

"When Margaret came home with me, we just added her to our letters, and she did one, too."

"Margaret went to yours for Christmas?"

She nods. "Our junior year. She came out to her parents that Thanksgiving and they didn't want her to come home anymore, so she came with me instead."

"Bloody hell."

"Yeah, her parents suck," she says without heat. "Anyway, you don't have to do the letter thing, but you're welcome to if you want. And you can be there for it, even if you don't do one."

"I do have plans for—"

But we're approaching my door and there is a girl sitting on my front step, thumbing at her phone, barricaded by two giant suitcases and a shoulder bag. She has curling reddish brown hair hanging in a huge mop over her head and shoulders and arms. When she sees us, she puts her phone away. She looks . . . fantastic. Healthy, at long last.

"Hello!" she calls with a wide grin. "You *said* I should come for a visit."

"Crikey," I breathe.

"Come *on*, Doctor Scientist, aren't you pleased to see me?" she gestures with her whole arm.

As we get closer to the front steps, she stands and grins, "You *are* pleased to see me, you just *don't. Know.* How to show it." She flicks at my nose, smiling the whole time. And then she turns to Annie without waiting for me to respond.

"You're *Annie*," she informs her, in the odd, emphatic rhythm that she's built into her accent since the last time I saw her. "I'm Biz, Charles's sister."

She was Bits as a little girl. Then Elizabeth. Now she's Biz.

"How great to meet you!" Annie says, hugging my sister, who looks nonplussed by this attention. "Let's get all your stuff inside. How long are you here for?" And somehow we're all climbing the stairs, with Elizabeth's—Biz's—belongings distributed among us.

"Just two days," she answers breezily. "My flight isn't until Monday but I had to get the *fuck. Out* of there. But look," she announces as we drag everything into the apartment. "I have a job for you both."

From her shoulder bag she pulls a plastic bag of gnarly green herbs, which she drops on the kitchen table.

"I can't take this with me. We've *got* to smoke it." She looks from us to the bag and back to us before she adds with a crooked smile, "I hope you didn't have any plans."

* * *

"I've never done this before," Annie says as we gather around the living room, while the curry I've made us simmers in the kitchen.

"What, never?" says Biz.

Annie shakes her head. "Busy doing other things."

"*Don't* worry," Biz answers, flicking the lighter. "We'll go easy on you." And she takes a toke on the pipe, then she passes it to me. Annie watches, fascinated, as I inhale and hold the smoke in my lungs. I pass the pipe and lighter to her, and exhale.

"I don't know what I'm doing," she says to us both, gesturing with the pipe in one hand and the lighter in the other.

Biz coaches her in how to smoke marijuana from a pipe. Annie watches her do it one more time, and then tries it herself—and ends up in a coughing fit. Biz laughs and I hand her a glass of water with a smile. "You're all right." She passes the pipe back to me.

Stoned Biz is slow-motion Biz. Slow motion and with the volume turned way, way down. She hasn't told Annie that marijuana is what works for her anxiety, or that it stabilizes her appetite. She seems to be working very hard to appear hip. At first, I thought the show was for Annie, but it occurs to me now that she might be trying to prove how well she is to her big brother, the "doctor scientist" as she's taken to calling me. Which, if true, would be rather sweet.

It's possible, too, that the doctor scientist is smoking for the first time in nearly a decade to prove to his baby sister how totally not prudish or boring he is.

Her voice takes on a fried aspect when she says, "*Oooh!* I know! Let's play the dream game."

"Okay," Annie says amiably, clearly having no idea what the dream game is.

"What's the dream game?" I ask, more suspicious.

"You'll see. It's fun. You use your *imagination*, Doctor Scientist. Okay, so you're dreaming, all right? All of this is a dream. You dream that you're walking along a path, and on this path, there is a cup. So now just imagine that cup and what it looks like and how you feel about it and what you'd do about this cup on the path."

She pauses and waits for us to spend a few seconds imagining our cups.

Annie opens her mouth to tell us about her cup, but Biz raises her hand to stop her. Then she passes her the pipe, to give her something to do as she listens.

She continues, "And in your dream you continue along the path, and you find you're in some woods, and you come to a clearing in the woods, and in the middle of the clearing is a building, all right? So just imagine that, this building in the clearing. What does it look like, what do you do there, how does it make you feel?

"And as you continue beyond the building and deeper into the woods, you see a bear. What does the bear *do*, and what do *you* do about the bear?

"And then you finish walking through the rest of the wood and then suddenly in front of you there appears a wall, *too* high to climb over and *too* long to walk around. What. Do you do. *Next?*

"And that's it. All right. So we begin at the cup. What are your cups like?"

Annie launches herself into the game. "I love my cup. It's a trophy cup. It's huge, like, bigger than my head"—she holds up her arms to show us how big—"and it's gold and it's got my name engraved on it, and it's full of fruit." She grins at us. I grin back.

"Fruit?" Biz says.

"Fruit. Like apples and pears and oranges."

"Okay, and what do you do with it?"

"I pick it up and take it with me," Annie says, clearly surprised at the possibility that there could be a different answer. "I can eat the fruit along the way whenever I get hungry."

"Isn't it heavy?" Biz asks.

"No, it's really easy to carry."

"Okay. Charles?"

"Er," I scratch my head. "It's one of those brown-enameled tin mugs, you know the ones I mean? Army issue, First World War? Sort of dirty and chipped and battered. But that kind of thing is indestructible. It's a cup. Like an army coffee cup." I hold up a hand like I'm holding a coffee cup. I can tell how stoned I am by how much it feels like I actually am holding one.

Biz bites away a smile and says, "Is there anything in it at the moment?"

"There wasn't until you asked, but it magically filled with water."

"What kind of water?"

I shrug. "Drinking water."

"And what do you do with it?"

"Drink it. Not all of it. I save some for later."

"You don't believe it'll just fill up on its own again, like it did just now?"

"Dunno." I blink at her.

"Okay." Biz turns to Annie and explains, "The cup is your idea of love. Whatever's in the cup shows how you've experienced love so far. So Annie, yours is a gigantic prize with your name on it, filled with fruit that nourishes you as you travel through life. Charles . . ." She stops and bunches her lips together again, even as she smiles. "You see, isn't this just the sort of thing we'd never talk about? Your cup is chipped and shitty and, I think not least, a fucking First World War military-issue mug. But it's indestructible and it's magical. It fills with drinking water as soon as you ask it to, but even though it's magical, you don't *quite* trust it, do you, because you feel you've got to save some for later. It's *indestructible*, you said, Charles, and it's *magical*. But it's military-issue. What the fuck?"

"Crikey," I say from my burnt throat, and I take another hit off her pipe.

"What's your cup?" Annie asks Biz.

"Oh, it's a teacup, of course, one of Mum's, *you* know the ones, Charles, the big ugly flowery ones. It's old and chipped, unlike Mum's, but it's not broken; and it's got tea in it, obviously."

"Not indestructible," Annie clarifies, taking the pipe I offer.

"Quite fragile, in point of fact," Biz says primly. "I've been *rather* careless with it, I suppose, which is how it got so grotty. When Mum gave it to me it was lovely and pristine. If I'm not careful I'll ruin it utterly. But I pick it up off the path and carry it gently with me. I *like* it. I want it, and I want to protect it. Also, tea tastes better somehow from a real teacup."

"Ve'y British," I say.

"Okay, so the building in the clearing," Biz directs.

I jump right in this time. "It's a church. I go in."

"And what's it like in there?"

"Cool and quiet. It smells old, in a nice way. There's no one else. It's very peaceful and lovely and I'd be glad to stay awhile if I didn't have other things I needed to do."

"What things do you need to do?"

"Er . . . ooh, fuck knows. My job, I s'pose?"

"Right. And Annie?"

"Oh, uh . . ." She makes a face. "I don't know, it's this giant, manmade ugly thing, like, concrete and industrial-looking. It's a warehouse full of people's stored old shit. The fact that people cut down trees in order to build it just pisses me off. People should have just gotten rid of all that crap instead of building this monstrosity in the middle of the pretty woods."

"So what do you do?"

"I just keep walking. I want to get away from it."

"Well!" Biz declares. "The building is your idea of god."

"That sounds about right," Annie affirms.

Biz continues, "Annie, for you it's a hideous concrete facility for people to store their useless old crap; it pisses you off that people destroyed perfectly good nature, rather than purging the crap.

"But for you," she turns to me, "it's lovely and quiet and you'd stay there if it didn't interfere with the things you need to do."

"What's yours?" I ask Biz, hearing the burn in my voice.

"It's a little cottage, stone and wood, with a thatched roof. Very charming. I take a picture and post it on Instagram, and then I just walk by it because it's not my house."

Annie offers her palm for a high-five and says, "Right on," and they both collapse in hysterics when Biz tries to slap her hand and entirely misses. Biz laughs silently with her mouth wide open, eyes closed, patting her hand on the arm of her chair. She gasps and laughs some more, gasps again, laughs some more, and covers her mouth with her hand.

"It's not funny," she squeaks. "I know it's not that funny."

And all three of us laugh at her helpless, silent, contagious laughter. Even as I laugh, though, I'm trying to remember the last time I saw her laugh. Not since she was little.

"So," she says, trying to clear her throat and breathe more deeply. "The bear."

"Oh!" Annie volunteers. "My bear is attacking someone. I want to protect the person but the bear is just protecting her cubs, so I can't kill her. So instead I lure the bear away with fruit from the trophy cup."

"Well done, you," Biz says, like she's proud of her. "Charles?"

"Oh gawd." I slump down on the couch and rub a hand over my face. "I turn into a bear and fight it."

They both laugh hysterically at this.

"Of course you do!" Biz laughs. Giggling so hard she can barely talk, she says, "And my bear just eats me! I toss"—she gasps, wiping tears of laughter from her face—"I toss the tea in its face, but it just thinks I'm a tasty snack to go with tea!"

When Biz sighs herself into the ability to speak in complete sentences, she says, "The bear is your troubles in life. Annie, apparently your troubles aren't even *your* troubles, you're just a walking, talking, fruit-throwing solution. You lure them away with love. And Charles, you *are* the trouble."

"I'm the fucking dragon, too," I mumble.

"Wha'?"

"Nothing. The wall," I direct.

"Okay, the wall," she says, easily guided.

Annie says, "My wall is a brick wall. I walk and walk but never get to an end. I beat on it for a while until I just give up and sink down next to it and cry." She looks halfway to tears just thinking about it. I try to imagine what it might feel like for her to confront a barrier she can't knock down, what it would take for her finally to give up.

"Okay." Biz turns her gaze to me with eyebrows raised expectantly.

I say, "It's a rock wall, the face of a cliff. I think it's just about the most beautiful thing I've ever seen. Maybe I can't climb *over* it, but that doesn't mean I can't climb *up* it. There's got to be a top, and something at it; and even if there isn't, either I climb or I go back where I was. Obvious choice. I put down my stuff and start climbing."

Biz is staring at me with her mouth open.

"What?" I ask, and I hold out my hand for the pipe.

She answers, "The wall is death."

"Holy shit," Annie says.

"Sounds about right," I say, and I ask Biz, "What's yours?"

"Seriously?" Biz asks.

"There is a lot to be said for confronting death," I say. "I've seen people thrive, live their most joyful lives in their last months. I really enjoy end-of-life care."

They both look at me with their mouths open. Annie looks close to tears.

"I've seen families healed, I've seen people return to god and to compassion, I've seen unimaginable forgiveness and the deepest love humans can experience, all facilitated by the knowledge that death is coming. What's yours?" I prompt Biz again.

But Annie says, "Isn't it sad, though? Isn't it just so sad? I don't know how I'd ever be able to do it."

"It's all right," Biz soothes before I can answer, and she actually moves to sit next to Annie, puts her arm around her. "You're just a bit too high to be thinking about death, eh?"

"What's your wall?" Annie asks her mournfully.

"I've never been able to imagine a wall," she answers, her voice slow and lazy. "It's always a chain-link fence with barbed wire over the top, and I just stand there with my fingers in it, watching everyone on the other side."

"What's on the other side?" I ask, crossing my ankles on the coffee table.

"Tonight? A graveyard. I'm watching the ghosts dance."

"It changes?" Annie says. "Like, you've played the game more than once, and your imagination gives you different answers?"

"Oh yes, in the past it's been a playground and a mental hospital and a nature sanctuary and all sorts. Are you Charles's *girlfriend?*" Biz asks, in a voice that tells me she's been trying not to ask this whole time.

I choke and cough, in the middle of using the pipe.

"No, no," Annie assures her, and then she adds, "We do kind of have a history. But we're just friends."

"Okay." She doesn't sound like she believes her.

"He is very hot, though," Annie says.

I break down coughing again.

Biz looks askance at me, in the middle of my eye-watering cough, and her bottom lip tugs downward. Then she looks at Annie and shakes her head mournfully, "He doesn't trust his cup."

And then she bursts into wild giggles, sliding off the couch almost to the floor.

"Bollocks to you," I tell her with a benignant smile, "and your teacup."

"Bollocks to *you*," she counters through her giggles, "*and* your bloody tree." And she bursts into even more raucous laughter.

"I'm *hungry*," Annie says.

"Me too!" Biz says. "*Gawd*, the food smells *so* good!"

So I feed them.

Biz eats.

And I think about how to trust an indestructible, magical cup.

The first thing you have to do is believe in magic, Doctor Scientist.

Chapter 21

Debbie, Coco, Bananas, Peanut, Parfait, and Éclair

"She's a nightmare," he says affectionately as we board the train two days later. He didn't shave this morning and he's looking adorably scruffy.

"I like her, too," I say. "How come I never met her before?"

"That's the first time *I've* seen her in five years."

I raise my eyebrows, astonished as I think of their greeting—Biz flicked his nose, he didn't say anything. "But she's been in school in the US since . . ." I try to calculate.

"2013," he says. "I invited her to visit Indiana, but why would she travel all that way to see a brother she barely knew? She writes a sort of blog, and I read that. She's been through a lot—struggled with anorexia since she was sixteen. Last time I saw her she was under a hundred pounds and full of rage. It was killing her, quite literally. She looks much better now, though she was in hospital a year and a half ago. The school sent her home."

I wince. "I knew a lot of girls who were going through that. Dancers."

"How did you avoid it?"

I shrug. "My parents taught me that strength and health are the most beautiful things a body can be, and how that looks is different on each person's body."

"Also," he says as the train leaves the station, "you don't have anxiety, depression, and no skill set for coping with the distress of the people around you."

"That too."

Charles watches the landscape go by and I ponder the luggage rack.

I put my head on his shoulder. "Charles?"

"Hm?"

"Can I ask a personal question?"

"Sure."

I take a deep breath and say, "What the hell is that big thing you put on the luggage rack?"

"That thing, young Coffey," he says with a grin, "is a crash pad, for bouldering. Today. Tomorrow. Climbing actual rocks, outside, in the middle of Manhattan."

I lift my head and look at him. "You can do that?"

"Google it," he says, and I do. Phone in hand, I spend the train ride watching videos of people climbing rocks I must have seen dozens of times in my life.

"Cool! We can go as soon as we drop shit off at home," I say as the train goes underground and I lose signal.

"You'll like it. It'll help you learn to see holds and routes in natural settings. Great preparation for the Gunks."

We're going climbing in May, when my semester ends. I'm already terrified.

After taking the subway uptown and walking across the park, I wave a hand to indicate the building for Charles. "Here we are. Hey, Frank, Merry Christmas," I say to the doorman as we approach.

"Merry Christmas, Miss Annie," he says, and then, "This must be Dr. Douglas. Welcome to New York, sir."

"Thank you, Frank," Charles says, and I beam at him. He raises an eyebrow at me, like he's suspicious of something.

We take the elevator up and I lead Charles into the vestibule.

"We take off our shoes," I instruct, and then I lead him into the gallery, and he laughs out loud.

I mean, it is really nice. It's big. It has a lot of windows.

He drops his bag and the crash pad and his shitty old duffle coat the color of baby puke and walks to the windows, overlooking the park.

I stand next to him and watch New York in December.

"Annie," Charles says in a strange voice.

"Yeah."

"In Montreal?"

"Yeah?"

"When you were worried about me having money?"

"Yeah," I say, remembering the fancy dinner.

He turns to me and says, "It wasn't the *money*, was it."

I worry my eyebrows. "You speak French and know how to order wine and eat asparagus without dripping sauce on your clothes," I say.

"I'm a pretentious wanker, you mean," he grins.

"But you're not," I insist. "Most of the people I know with money are stupid, boring jerks, basically. All they care about is being interesting to look at and knowing people who know famous people. They don't do anything *real*. My parents do real work. I want to do real work. What you do is *real*. You help people, for real, every day."

He narrows his eyes. "You have a trust fund, don't you."

I huff. "So?"

"You don't live like a person with a trust fund." He looks amused now.

"Neither do you," I accuse.

"I haven't got one," he counters.

I roll my eyes. "My parents and I decided to set my allowance at the median household income so I could fit in. You know. Be friends with people who aren't rich."

"And then you end up mates with me!" he laughs. "Oh, this is too brilliant. Annie Coffey is a trust fund baby. Finally, a flaw!

Thank *god*." He hugs me with one arm and looks out at the park. Then he looks down at me with excitement. "Shall we boulder in the park, then?"

"Yes, please!" I burst, glad to change the subject. I lead him back down the hall to my rooms, so we can change into climbing clothes. "This one's yours," I say, opening the door to the guest room. "And this is your bathroom—just a shower, not a tub. I hope that's okay."

"Somehow I'll struggle through," he says.

"This is my room," I say shyly, leading him in.

Charles stares at my Turing poster.

"You *are* a swot," he says, sounding impressed.

"That means nerd?" I ask.

"More or less," he says.

"Then yes," I say. "Yes, I am."

"Right. Rock shoes. Chalk bag. Warm clothes for spotting in. Get going."

We get.

We start nearest home, at Cat Rock, then move to Rat Rock. At each, there are chalk marks along the face of the rock, where climbers before us have been.

It works. I learn to see the route without manmade, color-coded holds. I learn to fall off a bouldering problem safely to the crash pad, and to spot Charles as he climbs. I learn to traverse across the rock, seeing moves along the horizontal, as well as the vertical. I learn to feel what a rock can afford my fingers, even when the rock is cold and my fingers not much warmer.

I send a V2 and feel very proud of myself—it's as difficult a bouldering problem as I've ever done. Then Charles does it without using his feet for the whole top half of the climb, his feet dangling in the air.

"Asshole," I praise. "You and your ropy forearms."

I spot him as he works on a V6 problem. It's so hard, I can't even do the first move of this route, but he makes it look easy, as-sembling it bit by bit. First he does just the first move, then begins again, adding the second move, his hand searching for the best hold. Then he begins again and does three moves. The entire problem is five moves, ending with a heel hook that would be easy for me—you just put your knee in your ear, as Charles would say, and then shift all your weight onto that foot—but his groin tendons aren't that flexible. With an "Oof, bugger!" he falls eight feet to the crash pad as I lean in to break his fall.

It's maybe forty-five degrees out, but he's down to a T-shirt and there's sweat down the center of it. He lies there, panting, with his wrists over his head and a dopey grin on his face.

"This is fun," he says.

"It *is* fun," I agree, eyeing the veins in his forearms. "How's your hand?"

"Fine." He flexes it unconsciously, then sits up and turns to the rock. He tries again. Grunting with effort, he pulls through the fourth move, digs his fingers in hard, and tries to get his weight onto his left foot.

"Bugger!" he calls, falling. I break the fall again, and he lies there breathing hard, with that sweaty, smug grin. But he says, "I'm not gonna get it today. That's it. Oh, the lactic acid."

More relaxed than I've seen him maybe ever, he hauls himself, grinning, to his feet. We carry our stuff home, dump our crap in the vestibule, and go to our separate rooms to de-funk.

I stand under the shower, dazzled. This is my city, my home, and I've just spent an afternoon learning things I never knew there were to learn about it. How does he do this to me?

It's the way he sees the whole world as a puzzle he'll never quite solve, but he loves the process of trying and trying again. It's the way he can sit patiently, affectionately, as I work my way toward finding a path that works for me, along a problem he solved long ago. It's his body, too—the way he moves, the way his arm muscles flex as he climbs, the way his fingers press into the rock. The way his hips pivot to shift his body closer to the rock.

And I bet he's naked right now.

Why am I not in there?

I wonder if being able to be mad while I'm in the room has doused The Thing for him, like The Thing was a bubble that popped up when he pushed down the angry, and now that he's allowed to be mad around me . . . no Thing.

It's the opposite for me. I feel it every time I see him, as intense in the coffee shop, when he's helping me study, as at the rock wall, when he's competing with Linton to see who can do more one-armed pull-ups. I love when he gets frustrated or impatient and doesn't kick me out.

I put my hands between my legs and lean a shoulder against the shower wall and remember the night on Simon's couch when he fucked me until I couldn't move, fucked me until I was help-less with it, then just kept fucking me. And the next morning when he told me to say I was his, my body belonged to him . . . and it does belong to him. I want him. I haven't stopped wanting him for a single moment for four years.

With hot water streaming over my scalp and face, I tug at my clit and I mouth the words he made me say. *I'm yours.* I imagine him walking in right now, right now, when I'm this close to com-ing, and pushing me up against the wall to fuck me. Fuck me. I'm yours. You're the only one. The way he'd kiss me. The way he'd come in me.

After my shower, I put on my pajamas and head to the kitchen for food. Charles finds me in the lounge with a trayful of sand-wiches. His hair is damp across his forehead and he looks flushed and happy. He sits on the couch with me. I let him eat for a minute. He inhales his sandwich, then starts a second one.

We sit in another long silence. At last I say, "Hey, so how's your mountain?" my attention studiously anywhere but on him and this very minor question.

"Fine," he says.

"You got to the top? You slayed the dragon?"

"I can't slay the dragon; I am the dragon."

I ask, "Is it a friendly dragon? Like Puff, the magic dragon?"

"Annie?"

I look at him innocently, eyebrows raised, and blink.

He smothers a smile. "If I told you I didn't want to talk about it, would you stop asking?"

I open my mouth to say, "Of course," but instead what comes out is "Does he frolic in the autumn mists?"

"No," he says with a reluctant smile. He sighs massively, leans back, and says lightly, "It's more like Smaug. You know. 'I am fire. I am death,' et cetera."

"Ohhhhh. So it's protecting treasure," I say. "And you have to slay the dragon to get the treasure. No, wait, you can't slay the dragon, you are the dragon. You are fire, you are death. Plus, you're the mountain. And . . . you must also be the treasure."

He turns his face to me, his expression unreadable. "I never thought about it that way."

"What way?"

"Protecting treasure."

"That's what dragons do," I declare. "Harry Potter's dragon was guarding her eggs, along with a golden egg with a clue in it. Maybe that's what your dragon is doing."

"Maybe," he says, and I see that he's had enough, he's about to change the subject, so I say, "In *Shrek*, the dragon's guarding treasure and a princess, and Donkey flirts with her—with the dragon, I mean, not the princess—and by *Shrek the Third* they've had six little baby Dronkeys."

He purses his lips against a smile and says, "Six, eh."

"Debbie, Coco, Bananas, Peanut, Parfait, and Éclair," I recite seriously.

That does it. He snorts a laugh.

"Right. That's enough of that, miss." Raising one eyebrow, he says, "Behave, termagant, or I'll tickle you to death."

Striving to look contrite, I say, "I'm sorry."

"Sorry for what?" he prompts like a patient teacher.

"In *How to Train Your Dragon*—" I start, and he moves fast, launching himself to my side of the couch, to hold me down by my wrists. He tickles me, and I shriek. Through giggles and squirming attempts to get away, I gasp and splutter, "Hiccup—gah!—injures a dragon—stop, don't!—and so he makes it—wait!—he makes a prosthetic fin—" I roll onto my stomach and almost manage to wriggle away from him, but he twists my wrist behind my back and, with the other hand, keeps tickling me. Between cackles and gasping laughter as I try to escape, I say, "Maybe your dragon—wait!—maybe your dragon—gah! stop!—maybe your dragon just needs a new wing so it can fly!"

I manage to get possession of my wrist and I roll onto my back again, then I try to slide sideways off the couch, but he blocks me with his knee, saying, "Oh no you don't!" and pins my wrists above my head with one hand and tickles my waist with the other, so that I wriggle and shriek under him, and gasp to breathe with his weight compressing me into the cushions.

And then I'm not laughing, because he's not tickling me. He's caressing my waist, under my shirt, touching my skin with his rough palm traveling along my side, from my pelvic bone to the side of my breast, my shirt riding up with his hand. He's breathing as hard as I am. I feel it on my neck, feel his unshaven cheek.

His hand slides back down to my hip, then back up, this time palming over my breast briefly and I shudder and moan under him, and his hand travels back down over my belly to the waistband of my pajama pants.

He stops, his body completely still over me, but for his labored breath.

"Sorry," he murmurs into my neck. "I'll stop."

But his hand travels back up. And over my breast. And back down. And it is really hard to remember why we shouldn't do this.

And he's kissing my neck now, and little noises are escaping me. With him pinning me down, I can't move my arms, and he's straddling my legs. So I make the only movement I can—I push my pelvis upward to invite him. I feel his erection against my pubic bone and I press against it. My shirt is bunched up around my armpits now and he's kissing my breasts, his hands laced with mine over my head.

But then, "Sorry," he says again. "This isn't—we're not—"

"We have A Thing," I protest. "Neither of us knows where the boundaries should be."

He's silent and still for what feels like a very, very long time, while I breathe hard, hoping. Then with a growl he bites my nipple and moves his hand to pull down my pants.

"Domina," he whispers urgently. "Let me taste you."

"Yes," I whisper back.

And from somewhere in the distance, I hear the elevator ding.

"Shit," Charles says. He tugs down my shirt and bolts to the far end of the sofa.

"Hello?" calls Dad from the gallery.

"We're in the lounge," I call back, pressing my hands to my cheeks and trying to persuade my blood flow to change directions.

Dad appears in the hallway and I call as I watch him come toward us, "We went rock climbing in the park."

He gets as far as the doorway, then leans against the jamb. "Hey, Anniebear, Mommy had an emergency surgery, so she'll be late. How 'bout we make her something nice for when she gets home? Christmas Eve," he adds with a giddy smile. Then he turns his smile to Charles and says, "You much of a chef, Dr. Douglas?"

"He's a *really* good cook," I affirm, and I begin to usher us all into the kitchen. On the way, I mouth silently at Charles, *Sorry*, and *We'll talk later*.

We make the traditional Coffey Family Christmas Eve Dinner—pizza, with dough from scratch—leaving the dough to rise for an hour while we decorate the apartment.

In an effort to make Charles feel at home, Dad has brought home "crackers"—which I'm disappointed to find are not snacks, but paper-wrapped little firecrackers that you tug on with a partner and they pop open with little paper crowns and toys and candy and jokes. Once I adjust to the idea that they're not food, I love them. I open a dozen, whapping Dad on the arm with the paper end until he takes it and pulls with me. I layer three paper crowns of different colors on my head and wear them all night. I make Dad and Charles wear theirs, too.

When Mom gets home, she disappears into her room for half an hour of alone time, as usual, and then appears, saying, "Oooh, crowns! How do I get a crown?" I try to give her mine but she says, "I want us both to have crowns!" so I pull a cracker with her and, delighted, she unfolds the crown and puts it on her head. We eat dinner that way, royalty all.

At bedtime, we disperse.

"Christmas Eve, Anniebee!" Dad says again, and he means to remind me to write my letter. That's what they're going to do now, write their letter to me and Charles.

"I know!" I enthuse back. I've been thinking about what I'll say in my letter for weeks, but I always end up surprised by what comes out of my pen.

I follow Charles to his room and stand at the door.

"Hey, so, Christmas Eve," I say, echoing my dad. "I have to go write my letter."

"Yeah," he says, sitting on the edge of his bed with his brace in his hands.

"Do you wanna maybe talk about this afternoon, though?"

He makes a reluctant noise and runs a hand through his hair. "There's not much to say. I shouldn't have done it. I apologize."

"I liked it."

"Nevertheless."

"Neither of us knows where the boundaries should be."

He shakes his head at that. He gestures me to the desk chair, rather than to the bed next to him.

"Annie," he begins, but I interrupt him.

"I had an idea about why the boundary feels so complicated."

"Apart from The Thing?" he asks.

"Yeah. It's . . . I mean, even saying it out loud feels like it might be outside the boundaries. But it's what you told me to do—saying what the other person needs to hear, instead of what's most salient to me."

"Oh lord, I'm in for it now," he says with a teasing smile. "Go on, then."

I look down and say, "I realized—god, I can't believe it took me so long—I realized *you're* the survivor you're trying to save. It's not your mom or your siblings or the incest survivor with the upcycled sweaters. I mean, it is all of them, but it's *you*. When you were a little kid, your grown-ups couldn't do the things grown-ups are supposed to do, so you had to be the one who . . . like . . . bandaged your own knee when you fell off your bike. You had to be the one who told you everything would be okay when you felt lonely or sad. You're a superhero now, because little-kid-you needed a hero, and you were all you had.

"And you got stronger each time, right? Each time, you looked around for help and saw there was no one to help you, so you found a way to do it yourself. But that means every bit of strength you have, you paid for in loneliness. Not ordinary 'I wish Person X were here' loneliness, but a bone-deep certainty that when you needed help, no one would come. I think that's what Rage Mountain is made of, just layers and layers of, 'There's no one to help. There's no one to help.' Because there's *supposed* to be someone to help.

"But I think it might even be worse than that. I think little-kid-you maybe decided the reason no one helped you was that you had this monster in you and so you didn't deserve help. Grown-up-you probably knows that's wrong, but little-kid-you is like, 'There's no one to help, because you're not worth helping.'

"And then here's me, totally believing you deserve help, totally seeing that you *need* help, and totally wanting to help, and I think grown-up-you knows you can trust me, but little-kid-you is like, 'Sure, dude, just like you could trust all your grown-ups.' And why give the world yet another opportunity to remind you that you're alone and unworthy of anything else?"

I look up at him at last. He's staring at me. His lips are pale.

I conclude, "No wonder it's hard to know where the boundaries are."

We just look at each other for a minute, and then he says with a tired smile, "Your dad calls you Anniebear. And Anniebee, and Anniebelly."

"When I was a baby, he called me Annieboobers," I admit.

Charles throws back his head and laughs as loud as I've ever heard him laugh. Just watching him makes me smile. Then he shoves me on the shoulder and, with a grin, says, "Get out, you. Go write your twee letter."

So I do.

Chapter 22

Stony Limits

Only when the door closes behind her do I let it go. Elbows on my knees, hands fisted in my hair, I grit my teeth as my eyes burn.

Why give the world an opportunity to remind me how alone and unworthy I am?

Fuck you, Annie. I'm half-enraged at the intrusive intimacy of what she said, and half-disabled by the pain of her pressing mercilessly into an old injury I hadn't realized I was still protecting. There is something delicious in the pain, though. If she had taken a blade and cut a line down the center of my chest, made me bleed, and then kissed away the blood, pressed her tongue to it, I couldn't hurt more, couldn't feel more helplessly in love.

God, this afternoon, the first time I'd touched her that way since London. Every night I've imagined her in my bed, imagined the taste of her, the touch of her skin, her mouth, but no fantasy can match the reality of her body responding to my touch.

You had to be the one who bandaged your own knee, she said; you had to be the one who told you everything would be okay when you felt lonely or sad. And I remember her pressing an ice pack to my bruised temple, asking me silly questions to make me laugh, me giving silly answers to make her laugh.

"Is our relationship medicine?" she asked in October.
Yes. But the medicine isn't always easy to take.
Par la souffrance, la vertu. I think. Thy rod and thy staff, they
comfort me.
It takes me all night to write five mediocre sentences.

*George and Frances, Annie keeps on climbing higher. Thank you for
being the safety net she falls into.*
Annie, thank you for bandaging my knee when I fall off my bike.
*George and Frances, my hope for you, if I may presume to have one,
is that you'll witness Annie's growth with pride and awe at what you
have wrought.*
*Annie, my hope for you is the embarrassingly bog standard but sin-
cerely felt Christmas wish: comfort and joy.*

In the morning, I read them, the paper fluttering in my fingers
I'm shaking so hard, and Frances offers me a kind smile.
"That was good," she says. "You did good."
George says, "Your knee? I thought you broke your arm."
And Annie says, "It's a metaphorical knee, Daddy," and she
looks at me with such tenderness, I start bleeding again.
And then they read their letters to one other. And to me.

"Wow," Clarissa says when I tell her about Christmas. "That's
a lot."
I'm sitting with my elbows on my knees, my face in my palms,
feeling again the way my body had flooded with shame for all the
ways I had fucked up with Annie, as those three people said
those kind things to me.
Primate researchers in the 1970s experimented with social isolation, locking monkeys in a "pit of despair"—a vertical cage
with solid metal walls—isolating them utterly from all social contact for days, weeks, months at a time. Their food and water came
to them through slots, without any contact with another living
creature.

I described the pit of despair research to Clarissa early on. I told her how I imagined that every bite of food those monkeys ate must have been a cruel combination of nourishment necessary for survival . . . and a reinforcement of their profound isolation. Eat your food; you are alone. Drink your water; you are alone. Stay alive. Stay alone.

On Christmas morning, George and Frances said, "As a friend of Annie's heart, you are our son and this is your home."

Annie said, "Thank you for teaching me how not to take my life for granted. You're the best man I know."

Eat. Drink. Remember you are trapped and alone.

"They meant it to feel good," I say to Clarissa now. "I'm sure they meant to—"

I stop. I can't bring myself to verbalize it.

So Clarissa does. "They meant to share their banquet with you," she says. "Annie took you home with her to feed you."

I nod, unable to find my voice.

"What did you do?" Clarissa asks.

I took their offerings into my heart and hoarded them, even as each stabbed at me, a reminder of my ultimate aloneness. Then they hugged one another and hugged me, each of them, and I cleared my throat and excused myself for a shower, tightening the knot of my dressing gown.

"I stood under a shower as cold as I could tolerate for about ten minutes," I confess. The water had stung against the heat of my face. But then—"Annie was waiting for me in my room when I came out. She hugged me and said she was proud of me, then we went bouldering again and she did her first V3."

And then we lay side by side on the crash pad and talked until we were shivering with cold. And I didn't feel trapped. I felt safe. Free. In the light of her smile, I felt held and released at the same time. I felt in love, and I wanted to tell her so.

I didn't.

"So, let's take stock," Clarissa says. She counts off on her fingers. "In the last four months, you've experienced being angry without hurting anyone, including yourself. You've experienced letting go of comparing yourself with others. You've experienced play for its own sake. You've experienced receiving affection without feeling trapped and isolated. That's pretty good, right?"

"Yes," I admit.

"Now, what would happen—just for argument's sake—if Annie, the sun, shone on you and said, 'You've come so far, Charles, I think you're ready.' "

My heart contracts in my chest. My jaw tightens. My eyes close.

"I'd—I might—"

I might lock her in my bedroom and fuck her for three days. I might fall to my knees and beg her to love me. I might—I *might*—consider the possibility that she shows up every Monday at seven because those nights are as important to her well-being as they are to mine.

I shake my head, denying the hope.

"Charles," Clarissa says gently, "I think it's time for you to ask."

In the end, I don't have to ask.

Annie calls me on my birthday. She doesn't say hello, she just starts singing "Happy Birthday" to me, and it feels like all the sunlight in the world. I laugh out loud at the way she breaks up my name as if it had two syllables—"*Happy birthday, dear Chahruuuls.*"

"How has your day been?" she asks at the end of the song.

"Oh, I spent an hour on the phone with Mum, talking about my father and his health and the difficulty of keeping on carers when he abuses them—my word, not hers."

"God, I'm sorry."

"Yeah. So. How 'bout you?"

"Well . . . I have this thing to tell you, and it's awkward now that I know you've had a shitty day."

"Go on then." I brace myself, dreading the worst as a matter of habit.

But she says, "I'm . . . uh. I'm on your street. Look out your window."

"What?" My heart pounds as I go to the window and push aside the curtain. There she is, on the sidewalk, her head craned up to me. She's here. She came. On a Saturday night, on my birthday, she came. God, have I ever been so glad to see anyone in my life?

I smile down at her. " 'How camest thou hither, tell me, and wherefore?' "

"I rode my bike, dumbass," she says, "because it's your birthday. Open the door!"

But it's too good, seeing her there. She's *here*. I grin down at her and say, " 'The orchard walls are high and hard to climb, and the place death, considering who thou art, if any of my kinsmen find thee here.' "

"Huh?"

"It's your line," I prompt. " 'With love's light wings did I o'erperch these walls; For stony limits cannot hold love out, and what love can do that dares love attempt; therefore thy kinsmen are no let to me.' "

"*Romeo and Juliet*," she says, cottoning on. " 'What light through yonder window breaks?' Is it pathetic that I've never actually read it? I'm more familiar with the ballet."

" 'Let me be ta'en,' " I answer, pressing my fingertips against the cold glass, watching her watch me. " 'Let me be put to death; Come, death, and welcome! Juliet wills it so.' "

"Can I come up first, before you hand yourself over to death?" she says. "It's cold and I have a present for you."

I say, "Oh, well, if you got a present, that's different. I'll be right there," and I gesture her up before I go to the buzzer.

"Hand it over," I instruct, raising an imperious eyebrow at her when she comes in, breathless from running up the stairs.

She grins at me and digs around in her bag, to produce a package wrapped in paper clearly intended for a four-year-old. Handing it to me, she says, "Okay, so, as you know, we don't really do presents in my family, so I'm not very good at them."

I ignore this and take the package to the sofa. She sits beside me and I say, "May I open it?"

She worries her eyebrows but nods, and then watches me in trepidation as I lift the sticky tape and open the leaves of paper.

Inside, I find a picture frame. I turn it over and stare at the photos. There are three of them.

"Do you like it?" Annie says.

"How did you do this?" I ask, and I scarcely recognize my own voice.

"They're just pictures from my phone. I had prints made, is all. Is it okay?"

I cover my mouth with a hand.

On the left is a photo of Simon and me, him at the piano, me on his sofa—our customary positions. We're both laughing. In the middle is Mum and me, dancing in the kitchen. And on the right is Biz and me, side by side on my couch, covering our mouths in identical gestures as we laugh.

"Do you like it?" Annie asks again. "I'm not very good at presents."

Looking at the photos I say, "This year has been the first time I've seen either of them in years. It's—" I stop and swallow. Gripping the frame in both hands, I add, "You're good at presents, Annie."

I turn my eyes to hers.

"Yay," she says, lifting her shoulders to her ears.

Did I think I was in love with her before? Did I think that strangeness in my body was love? *This* is love, the swollen, clenched feeling in my heart and the stinging flush of my face.

"I'm . . ." I gesture my hand near my heart. "It's . . . almost uncomfortable to be seen so clearly and . . . known so well."

"I feel that way, too," she says, smiling into my eyes.

"I'm . . ." I look back at the photos. I'm a fool and a coward. "I don't know what I'm trying to say. A lot of things all at once. But the thing that matters is, thank you." I look at her, not hiding anything, but not brave enough to say more. "Thank you for this."

And we sit there looking at each other.

My lower lip tugs downward briefly, then I bite it as I let my gaze travel over her face, exploring her cheeks and eyebrows and, at last, her eyes. She's looking at me like I'm a puzzle she's trying to solve.

I inhale to say the words . . . but the walls are high and hard to climb, and love's light wings are about effective as a kakapo's, so what I say is, "Annie, if I have it to give, it is yours. My trust. My loyalty. The truth in my heart and the reason in my brain. The money in my bank account if you want it." I stop and laugh a little. "The shirt off my back—it looks far better on you anyway."

I reach across the sofa and rest the backs of my fingertips on the back of her palm. With my eyes on our hands, I say, "My whole rebarbative, mountebank self, much good may it do you." I watch as she takes my hand in hers, then I lift my eyes to find her watching me.

Stay tonight. The words are in my mouth, on my tongue. I can't get my lips to say them.

"Charles, I think we might be dating," she says.

I stare at her, not recognizing the tang of adrenaline until several seconds after my heart starts to pound.

She says, "I mean, here we are in your apartment on a Saturday night, right? On your birthday. I'm surprising you with presents, you're quoting *Romeo and Juliet,* we're holding hands. Those are dating things. I never even did those things with Margaret, and she's like my *bestie* best."

"Er." I clear my throat.

She waits. She has gotten so good at silence, so good at waiting for me to unlock.

At last I say, "I've been scared."

"Scared of what?"

"Of pushing too hard or asking too much . . ." I close my eyes and breathe through my nose until the tightness in my throat eases. "It feels fragile, what we have."

"Charles."

I open my eyes, jaw tense, and meet her calm, steady gaze.

"You'll lose me when *you* walk away from *me*. Then and only then."

She watches my eyes until I accept this with a nod. I can't move my eyes from hers. I don't know how to believe her. I don't know how to breathe. She's saying . . . that can't be what she's saying.

But she is. She's saying she would—

"Tell me what to do," I say on a strangled breath. "Tell me what you need."

"You're the best man I know," she says, and when I shake my head, she says, "That. That is what I need. I need you to believe me when I say it. Make friends with your dragon, dude."

"Working on it," I say.

"Okay then," she says, suddenly brisk. "Keep me posted. I'm gonna go before I do anything stupid. I have all this work to do. Degrees to earn. World to save."

She kisses me on the cheek and is gone, while I'm still sitting there on the sofa, gobsmacked.

When I can move, I go into my bedroom and, for the first time in my life, I hyperventilate. I put my head between my knees.

She just took the key from me and opened the door.

I'd be a fool and a coward not to walk through it.

I am a fool and a coward—but a happy one.

The following Monday, I suggest we climb twice a week, in preparation for our trip to the Gunks. I suggest it as if all I'm suggesting is an extra climbing day each week.

"Sure!" she says, as if all she's agreeing to is an extra climbing day each week. But she meets my eyes and I feel a glow of joy.

For the next two months, twice a week, all we do at the rock gym is lead climb together, until Annie's confidence is rock solid.

Everyone at the gym is in awe of the speed with which her strength and skill grow, just from climbing more often, with more focus, and with no fear. She tries her first 5.12a and takes some big, bad falls.

And all spring, she walks home with me from the rock gym and hugs me good-bye—until one day I hug *her* good-bye.

And the hugs get longer.

And then I kiss her neck and she sighs, so next time I kiss her neck and her ear. And the time after that, I kiss her neck and all the skin between there and her ear, and she has to wrap her arms tighter around my neck, to keep herself on her feet.

Three weeks before our trip, she takes a messy fall, banging her knee pretty hard. She tries to ignore it, but it swells and I make her quit. I run home and get my car, so I can drive her back to her place. I help her into her kitchen, where she pulls an ice pack from the freezer and a dish towel from a drawer. I take them from her and lift her onto the worktop, where she sits, watching me silently, as I delicately pull her torn leggings up over her knee and gently explore the red bruise with my fingertips.

"Not too bad." I smile, my eyes on the wound. I tie the ice pack around it and look up at her.

"My hero," she whispers, her face serious.

I hold her jaw in my hands and she tilts her face up to mine, an invitation. I brush my thumb over her bottom lip. Her eyes never leave mine as she opens her mouth and takes the tip of my thumb between her teeth. There's no one in the house—Linton and Sylvia are both back at the rock gym. There's no rush. I push my thumb between her lips and she sucks it as I withdraw it slowly. Her eyes stay on mine as I brush my wet thumb over her parted lips, as I thrust my thumb between her teeth again, my palm on her jaw. She sucks it. Her breathing changes and she makes a little noise through her nose. When her eyelids flutter closed and her mouth opens to take my thumb deeper into her mouth, I push my hands around the back of her skull and I kiss her mouth for the first time since London. She moans against my mouth, puts her hands on my face, presses her body close to mine.

Then I pull away, and we look at each other, breathing hard. Her eyes are on mine, her lips parted and pink. She looks worried.

"Don't be scared," she says.

Until she names it, I don't even notice how scared I feel, how my heart is pounding not just from wanting her, but from how terrified I am by that wanting.

I turn my mouth to kiss her palm and I close my eyes. "Can't help it," I say.

"Charles, look at me," she says, her voice serious. When my eyes meet hers, she says, "I was wrong just now. Be as scared as you want. Just don't run."

"Working on it," I tell her. I close my eyes and rest my forehead against hers, and I wish for a way to tell her how happy I am when I'm with her. I wish for words I'm not afraid of.

Chapter 23

The Money Pitch

My hands are shaking and the only reason I'm not sobbing is that I can't breathe, but that doesn't stop tears from filling my eyes and then escaping down my cheeks as I grit my teeth and jam my cam into a crack.

"How are you doing?" Charles calls up.

"Scared out of my fucking mind, asshole," I answer.

"D'you trust yourself?"

"No," I call with a dark laugh, and I then add begrudgingly, "But you trust me and I trust you, so I guess that's close enough."

The first two pitches were terrifying and amazing. I seconded Charles's lead and felt exhilarated to turn and see the trees. And then on the second belay ledge, we rested for a while to let a group of three climbers go ahead of us. We watched each of them as they traversed under the roof and then took the crux in a breathtaking swing into the wide-open exposure that gives the route its name. It's called "The Money Pitch," Charles told me, because it's what makes this climb the money, the one everyone stands in line for.

Charles talked the whole time, telling me about the decision-making that went with each cam placement, the location of each piton. When all three climbers were up, he looked at me and said, "You lead it."

And I laughed.

And he just looked at me through his sunglasses.

And I realized he was serious and said, "Hell, no."

And he smiled and said, "Scared?"

And I said, "Uh, *yes*."

"You've seen three people do it."

I made a scoffing noise.

"I watched you watch them. The crux is in your muscles already."

I frowned at him then. I knew he was right, but . . . "We're already like two hundred feet off the ground," I informed him—because apparently he had forgotten that small fact.

"You don't have to," he said gently. "I could lead it. We could skip it and go back down. It's your choice."

Manipulative dickhead.

"You fucking suck, you know that?" I said. But of course I started racking up.

As I tied in, he said, "The moves aren't the hard part. You could climb this in oven mitts and bunny slippers. The decision is the hard part."

"Dude, I don't know what you're talking about."

He nodded. "You will."

I began the climb with a slight variation on the usual ritual:

"Check my fucking knot, you asshole," I said as I checked the belay line. "On belay?"

"Belay on."

"I fucking hate you," I said as I turned to face the wall.

"Noted," he answered blandly.

"Climbing."

"Climb on."

"Asshole."

And so here we are. I'm shaking, half-petrified, so flooded with adrenaline I can hardly see. This is not hypothetical or practice. This is me standing on an actual rock, cool against my hands, a hundred miles above the ground, with Charles tethered far below me. If this same route were in a climbing gym, I'd flash it easily, even lead climbing, even with The Move, the famous crux of the climb. But hundreds of feet—literally, hundreds—above the ground, with Charles's life—his actual, literal, not exaggerating *life*—at stake, I'm swamped with fear.

I set the protection deep in the crack, clip in the quickdraw and a sling, and yank hard, angrily, at the cam until I'm finally satisfied with the placement, and I clip the rope into the sling. And now I know why we spent a bunch of yesterday going from crack to crack, practicing setting protection.

"You had this planned all along, you jerk," I call down to Charles.

I tuck my sweaty hands, one at a time, into my chalk bag. I search the rock above me, see the obvious mark where climber after climber has rested their chalky hand and successfully avoided dying. Those three climbers just did this, all of them moving easily. They all lived. It looked fun when they did it. But me, I'm about to die and take Charles with me.

No.

"Okay," I breathe to myself, my heart pounding in my ears, and then I blow out a breath. "Okay."

I've been flashing 5.11a's lately, so this 5.6 should be nothing. I flashed a 5.6 the first day I ever went climbing, two years ago in Indiana, and I'm much stronger now, more skilled, more confident. I can see the move in my head. I can feel it in my body. It's an undercling with the left hand, a sidecling in a vertical crack with the right, get your feet up, and then a big, fat bucket. The move is not the problem. The problem is doing the move while hanging off a rock face several hundred feet above the ground. Safe in the gym, the only cost of falling was looking dumb and maybe skinning my knee. Here, you're like an astronaut holding on to her ship when she goes outside to repair it. Under your

hands is safety. Everywhere else around you . . . an infinite, sucking void.

I am not in space. What are the consequences if I fall with this
next move? A big, ugly swing into wide-open space . . . and then?

And then Charles would catch me.

And then I'd try again.

And I'd keep trying until I did it.

"You know what?" I grumble to myself. "Fuck it. Fuck him,
fuck this rock, fuck this whole thing, just fuck it. If I'm gonna
die, I'm gonna die. Let's just fucking finish this."

I test the vertical crack above me, gripping its cold and gritty
surface against my palm, shifting my hand, trying to make it feel
slippery or shallow . . . and something inside me shifts as I recognize how bombproof it is. It's a layback—a horizontal layback
into an infinite void, yes, but an easy, solid layback.

The move isn't the hard part. The decision is the hard part.

I wrap both my hands around the crack, get my feet up under
me, and swing my body into the void. Another step up, another
jug of a handhold, and I'm standing solidly on the nose over the
crux.

"*Ha!*" I bellow, and I hear my voice echo behind me and
around me.

"Nice," Charles calls.

The piton is right there, solid, waiting for me. With one more
move, I clip into it, draw and rope.

The rest of the climb disappears into an endorphin-soaked
flow. It's almost unbearable to feel so comfortable and confident,
standing on the face of a cliff, with nothing but air between you
and the ground, hundreds of feet below. I feel focused and
strong, connected to Charles through the rope, connected to the
world through the air on my skin.

One last move and I reach up again and I haul myself over the
ledge and stand up at the top. Without stopping to look around
me, I loop a sling around the tree there, a few feet from the edge,
to set up the belay as Charles instructed. Breathing hard, I some-

how manage to communicate with Charles as he follows me up and onto the top. I can't see him; I feel his movements through the rope, feel him pause to pull the cams I placed and then climb on. He appears, first his grimy hands and then his grinning face and then the rest of him, mantling over the ledge.

He stands there, smiling at me, and says, "Off belay."

"Oh my god, we did it." I throw myself on the ground, arms and legs splayed, and give myself over to the trembling, laughing sobs that pull at me like gremlins, pinning me to the ground. I shut my eyes against the sun and lose myself to my physiology.

"Oh my god," I say when I can speak. "I am a-fucking-mazing."

"Yeah, you are," Charles says.

"I didn't die!" I rejoice. "I didn't kill you!"

"Not even a little bit," he says.

I turn my head to find him sitting with his back against the rock, his arms draped over his knees, sunglasses on. He's been watching me, not touching me, not saying anything, just letting me be. He has a little smile on his lips.

"Thank you for making me lead," I pant.

He nods and says nothing.

We stay there like that until my pulse lowers—not to my resting heart rate, but under a hundred beats per minute—and at last Charles says, "When you're ready, we'll go back down."

I groan and sit up. "Let's get it over with."

I rappel down the third pitch and then lower Charles. He rappels down the second pitch and then lowers me. I rappel down the first pitch and then lower Charles. That all sounds really simple, but it's terrifying, and when my feet are on the ground, I untie the rope with shaky fingers, strip off my harness, and pull off my climbing shoes. With my heart still pounding and my bare toes in the dirt and grass and gravel among the boulders, I go to Charles, who's already tidily looping the rope in preparation for hiking out with it.

"Charles." It's no use trying to keep my voice from shaking.

"Yep?" His eyes are on the rope, snaking off the tarp onto the loop on his arm.

I put my hand on his sleeve and he looks at me. When his eyes meet mine, he sees my need. He drops the rope and folds me, trembling, against him. I clutch my arms around him, hold him tight, tight, tight.

"Thank you," I whisper into his shoulder. "Thank you."

"If I were half as brave as you, I'd consider myself a bloody superhero," he says, and I feel him kiss the top of my head. "You are astonishing, termagant, you are breathtaking."

With a few big sighs, I gradually release him. I look up into his face, into his eyes through his sunglasses, and I am dazzled all over again. It's the way he sees the world as a curious puzzle, the way he waits patiently for me, the way his body moves through the world.

Before I can decide not to kiss him, he gives me a peck on the cheek and picks up the rope to continue looping it carefully around his forearm.

"You hungry? I'll make dinner when we get back," he says, his eyes on the rope again, and I shove my feet into my approach shoes.

"Yeah."

Charles and I pack up our gear and hike everything back to the campground, where our tent is waiting, beckoning to me.

"Go on," Charles says. "Have a quick kip."

I nod without speaking, dump my pack to the ground, and crawl into the tent. I don't even take off my shoes.

I had a plan. The plan was to sit under the stars and tell her I love her. I've been practicing. In the shower, on the way to work, while I cook, lying in bed, I've been saying the words out loud. "I love you, Annie."

I'm still not there, I'm not where she's asked me to be. But I have to tell her. I feel the unfairness of holding back. I want her to know what I feel, even if she doesn't feel quite the same. If I can say it out loud to her, that's one more step toward earning her trust.

Now. Tonight. After a day of climbing.

Under the stars.

That was the plan, anyway.

Unfortunately, it has begun to rain.

I carry the pot back to the tent from the cooking pavilion. Annie wakes up as I zip the tent shut.

"Mpfh?" she grumbles.

"Starting to rain, that's all," I say. "Go back to sleep."

"Mpfh, I'm awake now." She sits up stiffly, looking sweetly disheveled. She stretches and yawns and inhales. "Dude, you made curry?"

"Interested?"

She is.

We sit with the pot between our sleeping bags and I hand her a bowlful of rice and curried chicken. She shovels it gracelessly into her mouth as I laugh silently. She spoons herself a second bowlful, which she eats more moderately.

I put a Nalgene full of water in front of her. She chugs half of it, then lies back on her sleeping bag with a groan and, rubbing her belly, says, "I'm never moving again."

"I cooked. You do the washing up," I say, teasing her.

She groans again, but in half an hour, despite my protest that I was only joking, she carries our dishes through the rain to the sink at the pavilion. She locks everything in the bear box, through an abundance of caution, and zips herself back into the tent, where she drips rainwater on everything. I give her a towel.

There's a long, comfortable silence as we lie side by side, listening to the rain.

This is it.

I don't have the stars to help me. I don't have any courage of my own to rally. All I have is the decision, and the bone-deep certainty that Annie will be kind and clear and gentle with me. She won't say she loves me too, but she will know what it means to me that I've said it. She'll be proud of me.

I search for a way to start, and grab the first hold I find.

"Annie, do you believe in god?"

"Of course not," she answers. "Do you?"

"No. No, not really."

She looks at me. "But a little bit?"

"It's not that I believe in god," I say, struggling to find the next hold. I speak quietly, not letting the words carry beyond our two bodies. "It's that I wanted to. I grew up in the benignant arms of the Church of England, but it wasn't the bland ritual that tempted me ever, it was the notion that there was something beyond humanity, a purpose and a meaning greater than . . ." I stop, embarrassed by this bit of arrogance from my adolescent self.

"Greater than?" she prompts.

"Greater than my father, at first, then greater than the masters, then eventually, when it turned out I saw things the beaks didn't . . . something greater than my own power, I suppose. Something permanent. Some essential purpose and meaning. Something beyond biology and evolution and the universe. There is a . . ." I stop again. "There is a surrender that I have longed for. A 'surrender to the emptiness' is how Rumi puts it. Swimming in the deep."

I can feel her looking at me. At last I bring myself to look back. She searches my eyes, trying to understand what I'm saying. She looks away.

She says, "I think the universe and biology are amazing enough to surrender to. I don't feel like I need more."

I smile at this. "Spoken like the daughter of George and Frances Coffey, termagant. You surrender knowing that you'll fall into a safety net."

"I dunno, man," she says, and then she names the real obstacle to her understanding. "What I've felt is the destructive force of fundamentalists. The whole irrational faith thing is just scary."

"I know. Sorry. I was—" I stop again, shaking my head.

We lie there in silence for long minutes, listening to the rain on the tent. Annie sighs contentedly. I look for a different way in.

Just say it, I think. *Just say, Annie, I'm in love with you and I'm aware of how ironic that is, but I had to say it because I feel it, and it's true. That's how you said it—without fear, without shame, without—*

"Do you do this often?" she asks, saving me. "Go to the woods to live deliberately?"

"Not often. Once a year or so."

"I don't remember you going while I was in Indiana."

"I mostly went during the summer, between sessions. And twice after you left. The climbing group came out to the Gunks in August, then I hiked about a hundred miles on my own that January."

She turns her head at that. "Jesus, in *January?*"

"Mh."

"Not to state the obvious, but, ya know, wasn't it cold?"

"Mh." I nod at the tent roof, feeling on treacherous ground. "It—this could be outside the boundaries."

"It's dark," she gestures. "We're in the middle of nowhere. We're celebrating. There are no boundaries."

"Yeah," I say. I look at her. "I feel like in the dark we can say anything."

"So tell me."

I do. Quietly, just loud enough to fill the space between us, I say, "It externalized the pain. Plain, ordinary hunger, frostbite on your toes . . . that kind of pain is so much easier to tolerate than the pain of wanting to die."

"What?"

I sigh and say, "I was . . ." I lift a palm, like I'm offering something, but I have nothing to offer. I drop my hand to my sternum. "Match day was January seven—for fellowships, you know. The day I found out about Boston. I was already exhausted—I'd been running the lab while Diana was on family leave and then sabbatical, at the same time as finishing my residency, and here's the promise of another fucking year of doing exactly what I've chosen to do, when I've lost all sense of why I'm doing it and what it's all in aid of." I turn my head and look at her. "I went to the woods, to get out of the pit."

"So you got frostbite by hiking a hundred miles in the middle of January?"

"My toes healed. The nail only fell off one of them, and it's fine now. And the day after I got back, you e-mailed me." Very softly then, I add, "I had told you, last summer, that I would be where you needed me to be. I had promised you. And there you were in my in-box, reminding me I had a promise to keep." I offer a cockeyed smile, but she doesn't smile back.

"If . . ." She swallows. "If you felt that way again, would you tell me?"

"Would you want me to?"

"Yes. Oh my god, Charles. No matter what, you *tell* me."

"No matter what," I agree, and I turn toward her, rolling to my side, and put a hand on her face. "I will."

"Are you glad you're alive now?" she asks, looking worried and lost.

Glad I'm alive? I think. *God, woman, I've found my way to you.* What I say is, "Yes. Yes, I am."

"I don't want you to die," she says morosely.

I push my fingers into her hair. "I won't. Not for decades, if I can help it."

She turns her whole body toward mine and puts a hand on my wrist. "Is that what you were trying to say when you were talking about god just now? Were you thinking about dying?"

"No," I protest. "I was trying to talk about *hope*. Look, in almost every way, I've had the easiest life a human can have. If a wonky limbic system is the worst of my problems—"

"Don't do that. Don't diminish what you've survived."

"What I've survived is a weekend in the country compared to a lot of people—" She tries to interrupt, but I keep talking. "I had a patient last year—terminal cancer, he was in terrible pain at the end. Hopeless, unbearable pain. Quite literally screaming pain, no meds could touch it, and this astonishing man—listen to me—this man could find *meaning* in his torment, he found hope that his suffering would mean something, that it wasn't all for nothing, that it would help us prevent another person from suffering that way. We needn't exaggerate what I've survived." I find I've talked myself into a sense of perspective. I think, *Fuck it. Just jump.* "Annie. You know what you are to me."

"I'm the sun?" she says with adorable despondence.

"Yeah, you are." I bite my lip and watch her face, trying to find courage as unconquerable as hers inside myself.

Before I do, she's moving off her narrow pad, across the little gap we left between them, onto mine. She pushes me onto my back and curls her body against me, her head on my chest, her ear over my heart. Her touch, her affection, comes so easily. She doesn't know how rare that is, doesn't know what it means to me that she'll just touch me when she wants to feel closer.

"God, Annie." I wrap my arms around her.

"Tell me how to help. Tell me how to make it better."

"Domina, there's nothing wrong."

"In the future! Or to prevent it!"

"Annie, there's—" I stop. We just lay there under the rain. I hold her, unable to find the next move.

"You're my best friend," she says into my chest.

"And you're mine," I whisper.

She must notice that I'm shaking. I don't know when it started, this subtle tremor of tension, but I know she feels it when she says, "Are you cold?"

"Scared," I admit.

She lifts her head and looks at me. "Scared of what?"

"Not sure," I whisper—and it's true. I raise my eyebrows, considering. "You, maybe." My hands are shaking as I move them to her face. "Me."

"What is it?" she says. She's watching me, puzzled, curious, worried.

I take a deep breath, unsteady, and stand at the edge. "I'm . . ."

And pike.

I bite my lip.

I try again, watching her eyes as I say very slowly, "Annie, listen. What I've been trying to say is . . . that vast and eternal something, full of purpose and meaning that I wanted? That surrender to the emptiness, the trust? I'm trying to say that . . . I've found that with you. With you I've experienced the first unfettered joy of my adult life."

She's just looking at me blankly.

That's okay. This is how it was always going to be. I'm not saying it so that she'll say it back. I'm saying it because I feel it and it's true.

"And I suppose I'm scared of losing that," I say, trying for a smile to reassure her. "I'm afraid of the end."

"It won't end," she says.

"It'll change. You'll have a partner and things will change." I shrug. "That's okay. That's how it was always going to be."

She watches my face as I look at her, letting myself look and look, now, while I have her. Her eyebrows knit.

"Charles?"

"Yeah."

"Which scares you more: knowing that you could lose me eventually, or knowing that you could have to put up with me forever?"

I exhale hard, a laugh, but like she hit me in the diaphragm. I close my eyes and tighten my jaw against the sting.

She whispers, "Charles."

And I whisper back, "Yeah."

"Look at me."

I open my eyes.

She takes a breath in. Pauses. Then says, "We have A Thing."

"Yeah."

"And The Thing is a Love Thing."

Fear and hope flare inside me, both.

"I'm not wrong," she says, confident. Unafraid, unashamed. Pure, beautiful, easy.

"Annie." I push my trembling hands into her hair. I touch her lips with my trembling thumb. In a strangled voice, I say, "You're not wrong."

Chapter 24

The Boyfriendy-Girlfriendy Romance Thing

She moves closer, and when her lips touch mine I close my eyes and my whole attention narrows to the few centimeters of her mouth on mine, her lips, her breath, this woman. She kisses me softly, so softly, introducing her tongue into my mouth. I make a little noise in my throat and she echoes it back.

The kiss stays light, soft, delicate . . . but her hands do not. Even as she kisses me tenderly, with sweet, soft whimpers in her throat, her hands are gripping my hair and yanking at my clothes, finding my skin and scraping her nails, marking me. She's pulling off clothes, mine and hers. She kisses my face, the bridge of my nose, the crests of my cheeks, the curve of my eyebrow, the tender place above my temple, whispery kisses as she brushes her breasts against my skin so softly—and yanks at our clothes.

"Charles." She brushes her lips against mine in the lightest of kisses as she kicks off the last of her clothes, rubs her vulva against my erection.

"You can't be ready yet," I say.

"I've had two months of foreplay," she says, her mouth against my ear.

"Right," I laugh. I put a hand between us to move to her entrance. I whisper, "There?" and I feel the way her wetness draws me in.

"Yeah," she groans, and she pushes slowly, little by little, down onto me. "God. Oh god, I missed this."

"Every night," I tell her, letting my hands rove over her body. "Every night, domina."

She bites into my pectoral muscle, pushes hard against me, I'm deep inside her, she's pulling us both so far, so fast. But I need time.

I hold her face in my hands. "Let it be slow. Please, sweetheart."

She lets her body soften—but then she groans and lays her body over mine, her face tucked into my neck. She murmurs, "As soon as I slow down my whole body wants now, now, now." She jams her hips back on mine with each "now."

"Please, Annie."

"Yeah. I'll try."

She lifts herself a little and, with her forehead against mine, her breath careful and slow, she moves minutely, barely perceptibly, just a tensing of her muscles . . . and a relaxation. Her eyes are watching mine, her lips parted.

"Perfect," I whisper. "You're perfect."

A tiny smile flashes over her face, chased away by serious concentration. We stay there for a long time, inching toward ecstasy by fractions until the tension in her crests, in that familiar, pulsing way. She tells me softly, "I'm really close."

I stroke a hand down her back. "Not yet, sweetheart."

She whimpers and softens her body over mine, going perfectly still, laying her head in the crook of my neck, and I wrap my arms around her, one hand holding her waist, the other holding her skull, and I lift my hips to move with slow, shallow thrusts. I feel her struggling to breathe slowly; I feel her muscles pulse involuntarily around me as she breathes into her abdomen, trying, trying to stay below the threshold. I give her a little more—a little faster, a little deeper, a layer of intensity that makes us both tremble.

"Charles," she breathes.

"D'you like it?"

"Yeah."

"I could do this forever."

"Okay."

We both laugh tremulously.

I hold her face between my unsteady hands, kiss her eyebrows, and she whimpers.

"Not yet," I plead.

She breathes through a shuddering sigh and tries to soften her body again. Her hands flex in the effort. She thinks I'm torturing her—and I am, both of us. But I can feel the words on my tongue, feel the last fears letting go, freeing me. If she only gives me time—

"Be really still for me, domina."

"Okay," she whispers, her lips against mine, and she breathes softly, stays very still. We're both shaking now, hard. I kiss her with desperate, trembling tenderness. We hover at the peak, trembling together, panting together.

"Oh, my Annie," I murmur against her mouth, my breath shuddery and harsh. "You are amazing." I hold her skull with trembling hands, meet her eyes. "Annie."

"Yeah." She's shaking in every muscle—we both are.

I say, "I want—I'm—"

"Anything, anything you want. I'm yours," she says.

I give a strangled groan and my trembling hands grip her skull as my heart releases. With a smile that surprises me, and a blur in my eyes, I feel the words take shape, here in the dark, in the rain, as I move inside her, as we hold each other; with my eyes watching hers, at last I say what my heart has been saying with every beat since the day I met her.

"Annie, I love you."

She comes, silently. She throws her head back, mouth wide open, but I pull her face down so that I can see her, see her eyes, even as her body convulses over mine and she pulls me with her, over the edge. Mouths open, foreheads together, eyes locked, we come together, silent except for our rasping breath. Fucking into her, I grip her neck in my hand and watch her come, while she watches me fall apart under her, bursting heat and joy.

And then she begins to laugh, a delicious, wicked cackle, triumphant with joy. I grip her laughing, jubilant body, holding her as close as I can. I cling to her—this girl, my salvation, my heart, my breath. I hold onto her and clench my jaw against the wracking, shuddering weeping that wants to claim me. I breathe against it, hold her as my anchor against it. She lays her body over mine, her face against my neck, kissing my neck, and sighs herself into quiet as I hold her body against me. My arms begin to shake with the pressure, but I can't bring myself to let go.

"Charles, you're squishing me a little," she murmurs into my ear. I try to gentle my hold—try and fail, and she laughs again as, with a growl, I pull her closer still. She lets me do it. Always, she hands her body over to me fully, lets me have what I want.

"How ya doin' there?" she whispers.

I shake my head once, without access to voice or words, and try to relax my trembling, aching arms. With a few deep breaths, I manage it, but still I touch her, touch her compulsively, not wanting to let go.

"I'm scared out of my fucking mind," I tell her.

I feel her nod.

"Do you trust me?" she asks.

"With my life," I answer instantly, and my arms relax a little more.

"Do you trust yourself?"

I laugh into the terror. "Not one inch." And then I say, "But you trust me and I trust you, so maybe that's close enough."

I feel the expansion of her ribs and then the slow contraction as she sighs. Then she pulls away just slightly, to put her hand over my heart, tucked between us. She says, "Thank you."

My heart cracks open under the tender pressure of her palm. I put my hand over hers, put my fingers between hers. I search out her mouth; my lips wobble pathetically, but I press them against hers, then say, "I don't know what good it does either of us."

"What good it does?" I hear the bafflement in her voice. Sitting up, straddling me, she says, "Love . . . I think . . . love doesn't do good—*people* do good, you know? Love just *is* good. Don't you think?"

I nod, gazing up at her, and the corners of my mouth won't stop going down. "I don't know. Feels dangerous to me."

"Well, yeah," she confirms gently. "All feelings feel dangerous to you. Love feels dangerous and anger feels dangerous and—"

"Fear doesn't," I put in. "I'm not afraid of fear." My throat is tight. I press my lips together hard, fighting the sting in my nose and the clouding in my eyes.

"Well, you go right ahead and feel all the fear you like."

I lose the fight. Sitting up, I wrap my arms around her hips and press my face against her chest and whisper her name.

She won't let me hide. She pulls back, holds my face between her hands, looks right at me as I try to breathe. I pant, "Christ, I'm a coward."

"You are?"

"I'm trying to ask . . . Please don't say anything yet. Not yet. Please just—"

"Okay," she agrees.

"I think I must have been in love with you all the time, from the very beginning. When I look back, I can't find a time when I didn't. But I only knew it that day I broke my hand. But there's Rage Mountain, and then I thought you were with Linton, and then . . . I'm still not where you need me to be. I know that. But

I wanted to say it, because that's how you said it to me. Because you felt it. Because it was true and you wanted to share it." I laugh suddenly, loving her, loving my memories of her, with a bubbling joy I can't contain. I say, "Like bread."

She laughs, too. And that sound gives me what I needed.

I take a deep breath. "Right. Okay. If you can lead the Money Pitch, I can ask a simple question, surely. So. Miss Coffey: I don't suppose there's the least chance—no. Hang on. I'll do it properly." I take another breath, hold her hand between my two, and look at her directly. I say, "Annie, you know my deficiencies; you know I've got this fucking dragon still . . . like a mean-tempered dog I inherited from a disliked relative and I have to keep my friends away until I can bring it to heel." I stop and look down, shaking my head. "That's not what I want to say." Adjusting her in my lap, I return my eyes to hers and try again. "Annie, you are my heart. I love you so much I can hardly breathe. I know I've hurt you, and if you can't bring yourself to trust me, I'll understand. But I ask . . ." I stop. Swallow. Take another big breath. "I ask that you let me try to be the partner you deserve. Let me love you and . . . and let me try to deserve your love."

I can't bear to watch her eyes. I look down. I bring her hand, clasped between mine, to my lips.

"Charles."

"Yeah," I whisper against her fingers.

"Charles, look at me."

I raise my chin and look into her eyes, feeling like I'm looking into the eyes of my executioner.

She takes her hand from mine and puts it on my face. As the rain patters on the tent, she tilts her head, watching my expression.

She says, "You're asking for us to, like, be a couple?"

"Yeah," I answer.

"You want us to do the boyfriendy-girlfriendy romance thing?"

I chuckle tensely and swallow. "Yeah. The boyfriendy-girlfriendy romance thing."

"Okay," she says lightly, but her eyes cloud and her nose turns red and her smile is tense.

It can't be true.

"Okay?" My hands clench on her hips.

"Of course," she whispers, and a tear slips from her eye. "You're stuck with me, asshole." She leans forward and presses her lips to my temple and I close my eyes to feel her. Then she pulls away again. Looks at me with contentment radiating from her very core. She widens her eyes and says, "Because guess what?"

"What?" I say, grinning.

She touches her lips to mine and whispers, "I love you, too."

"Termagant," I say through the clutch of my heart. I grab her head and kiss her hard, then hold her against me, hold our bodies skin to skin as I struggle to breathe. I say it again, I call her all the names—harpy, shrew, sweetheart, domina, my heart, my Annie—as I turn her to her back and kiss her, move inside her, hardening again.

We make love again, my body never leaving hers. Over and over, with my hands and my lips and any words I can find, I tell her I love her, and she kisses my brow, my nose, my chin, my ear, she kisses me and whispers that she loves me. At last, maybe for the first time in my life, I'm not fighting anything. It is the deepest peace I've ever known, to lie in a tent under the rain with my body inside Annie's, with no fear and no limits.

"Everything, sweetheart." I watch her eyes. "Every heartbeat, every breath. I'm yours." I'm on the edge. I'm waiting for her, hardly moving, hardly breathing.

Holding my gaze, she whispers, "Mine."

Instantly, my body convulses and I come inside her, panting wildly, "Yours. Take me, don't let go."

Her arms and legs wrap close around me; her lips go to my ear. "I won't let go."

Even as the pulsing in my brain and body diminishes, I hold her close and beg, "Please, Annie, not yet not yet."

"No," she whispers.

"It can't be real," I croak. "I'm sure something will happen, something . . . awful but inevitable will tear you away from me."

"Let it try," she murmurs. "I'll kick its ass."

Chapter 25

One of Us Gets Hurt

The morning is damp but sunny, clear and crisp. Orange light filters into the tent with the birdsong and noises from the camp. I'm achy from climbing but bursting with happiness. Charles isn't awake yet; I want to wake him up, see his eyes again, hear him say it again. I bite my lips between my teeth and remember his face as he said the words—words I've suspected were true since his birthday. Words I've known were true since he kissed me in my kitchen and then looked at me like I was holding a gun to his head.

He wasn't afraid when he said it last night, though. That little smile appeared and I knew what he felt, and that was all I needed . . . and then he said the words. He said it. I watch him now, and I'm in awe. This beautiful man is in love with me. And this is it. He's it. This is the rest of my life, asleep on his back beside me, in a tent in Upstate New York. I wonder what he'll look like when he's seventy-seven and asleep.

I don't wake him up. Instead, I quietly leave the tent and walk to the bathhouse for a shower, letting the hot water ease the post-climb aches.

When I return, scrubbed clean of climbing grime, Charles is

awake, but dilatory and amorous. He pulls me down to lie with him again.

"'How is't, my soul? Let's talk. It is not day,'" he says, rolling me to my back and kissing my shoulder as he adds, "Let's stay in the tent."

"For how long?" I giggle.

"Oh . . ." he ponders, as he pulls off my shirt and leggings, leaving me in just my panties and socks, "just until . . . ," and kissing one breast, "forever?" His lips move to my other breast and I touch his head, put my arm around his shoulders.

"I love you," I tell him.

"Beyond breath," he says, but then he shakes his head and says, wonderingly, "Can't be real."

I nod—not agreeing, but understanding—and ask, "What would prove it?"

"Dunno." He rests his stubbly chin on my sternum and looks up at me. "Maybe if I . . . broke a bone or something. We haven't really settled a thing until one of us is bleeding or broken."

I laugh, and then he does, too, but then he kisses me and kisses me and kisses me.

Then he sits up suddenly.

"Have I ever told you," he says as he pulls off my socks, "of my fascination with your feet?"

"My feet?"

He kneels between my knees, my thighs draped over his. As I lie there in nothing but my panties, his hands caress my legs and feet. He says, "When you stand barefoot, it's as if your feet are already half lifted from the floor; I could fit almost the whole of my hand in the space between your plantar ligament and the floor. There is energy in that space, forward movement.

"And when they're all pink like this, after a shower . . ." He's kissing them now, and he matches action to word. "The abductor hallucis bulges from the side, firm, bitable. The joints of your first metatarsal protrude, bony, calloused. The rest of them are flat and sinewy, leading to long, bony toes. Your heels, the balls of your feet, and even your toes are calloused. Yet the whole of your foot is sensitive like nothing I've ever known. Sucking your toes is the next best thing to sucking your clit; you squirm and moan and go helpless with arousal. Yeah, just like that. My favorite thing, though, is to kiss the arch of your foot with my tongue, like it can kiss me back, while I hold your instep in my palm. You see? Your toes flex while I do it, and I can watch the tension sharpen through your whole body."

I'm heated and restless by now. He pauses . . . and very deliberately tickles my foot.

"Aaugh!" I shriek, and I yank my foot out of his hand, kicking at him—laughing, "Fuck you, buddy!"—but he grabs my ankle—I twist to get my limb back, but he won't let go.

"Oh yeah? Fuck me?" he taunts as I try to grab his wrist and he grabs mine instead. "Bet you can't. Bet I can pin you before you can pin me."

"Oh, you are *on*, asshole," I say.

For a while, the only sounds are the heavy slaps of our bodies against each other and our huffing, grunting laughter in the confined space of the tent. I learn quickly that his arms and shoulders are just too strong for me to pin him with my hands, and the only reason he hasn't got complete control is that I haven't stayed still long enough for him to catch me.

I switch tactics. I roll him onto his back, but this time I kneel on his shoulders, facing his feet, and before he can flip me, I lean down and put my mouth around his half-erect cock, my hands on his knees.

"Oh, Christ," he breathes.

I laugh with his cock in my mouth and his abdomen contracts hard under me. I feel his hands on my thighs, on my butt, on my back, all over me, not trying to force me off, but caressing me, trying to touch every part of me. I cooperate when he pulls off my panties—I figure I've won, at this point. Gradually my knees slide off his shoulders to lower my pussy closer to his mouth, and then his mouth is on me, a fingertip inside me, and I grunt and thrust in response. My hands slide up his thighs and I suck him enthusiastically, loving the taste of him and the feel of him in my mouth, as his mouth is on me, a finger of one hand inside me, his other hand caressing my foot and ankle above his head—and then he tickles my foot again!

"Gah!" I yank my foot away with a wild kick that bruises my instep.

"Gah!" he yelps, and his hands release me.

I turn, straddle him, and shove his cock into me with a celebratory "Ha!" only to realize that Charles has both his hands folded over his nose. He is laughing silently, even as his eyes tear.

My jaw drops. "What happened?"

"I think you broke my nose," he wheezes through his laughter.

My hands clasp over my mouth. "Oh my god!"

"Just a little," he gasps, helpless with laughter. And then he laughs out loud, his belly shaking under me, his cock beginning to soften inside me.

"Let me see," I say, leaning down on one hand and trying to pull his hands away with the other.

"Careful careful," he says. "It's not bad, don't worry about it."

It isn't bad. There's no bleeding, and no swelling yet . . . but it does make a troubling clicking noise when he prods it tentatively.

"The bone's intact—I think it just detached from the cartilage," he says, as if this is all the reassurance anyone could possibly need.

"There's got to be ice somewhere," I say, and I try to move away.

"Oh no you don't." He grabs me and in an instant he pins me

to the tent floor and slides his half-erect penis back into me, his fingers laced into mine.

He holds my gaze for an instant—and then he snorts with laughter and collapses over me in helpless giggles.

And now I can't help laughing, too, feeling how he moves inside me when he laughs. I pant through my giggles, "I'm sorry, Charles, I'm sorry," but he just whoops again, and I laugh all the louder.

"It's hopeless," he gasps, and he begins to move inside me, even as he laughs, even as tears of laughter leak from my eyes. "So much for romance." His face is against my neck and he's kissing me as his laughter fades, kissing my neck and biting it and sucking bruises, deep and stinging, into my skin, marking me. With his fingers still laced in mine, I wrap my legs around his hips, push his hips with my feet, urging him deeper. He bites at my breasts and my nipples, sucks bruises there, too, on the sensitive underside of my breast, as he pushes deeper and faster inside me, with rising urgency, with rough sounds in his throat.

The orgasm grows slowly inside me and, when it comes, it feels like an explosion somewhere low in my abdomen, or an earthquake, spreading and consuming my entire body. I roll my pelvis, making raw, scraping sounds in my throat. I hear his voice tangling with mine, feel the three sharp thrusts of him coming inside me as we come together, his teeth biting my lips, his fingers gripping painfully into mine and the sounds of our breathing tangling together in the air around us.

Laughter bubbles out of both of us like aftershocks. I kiss his hair and he kisses my breastbone and my legs gradually soften around him and slip down to the tangle of sleeping bag under us, and eventually his penis slips out of me, and still we lie together wordlessly, breathing and listening to each other breathe.

Finally, he shifts off me, lies beside me, and, with a hand on my face and in my hair, he breathes, "Can it be real? Can she love me?"

"She does."

"Annie, I—" He kisses my eyebrow and looks at me almost sadly. "I'll need your help."

I nod and raise my eyebrows a little, waiting.

"I'll need you to tell me how to do boyfriendy-girlfriendy. What you like. What you want."

"Okay," I tell him. "You mean, like, court me?"

"Sure. Flowers and chocolate?"

I shrug and make a face. "I like words a lot. And sex feels romantic to me, most of the time. And . . ." I look up at the ceiling and consider. "Actually, I really like it when you confront the dragon and the mountain. That shit is hot."

He chuckles. "You're sure you don't prefer flowers and chocolate? That would be a lot easier."

"And—I don't expect you to say yes, but I'm just putting it out there, since you asked. I'd really like it if you could say it every day." I look at him.

"Say . . ." He swallows.

"Say you love me. Yeah."

"Every day."

"Yeah."

"Okay."

"I mean," I say, backtracking, "don't say it just because I asked, but like, when you feel it. Just say it when you feel it."

Matter-of-factly, he says, "If I said it when I felt it, I'd never say anything else."

I stop and stare at him, floored. "That was . . . good. That was, like, mega-boyfriendy."

"It was never about not feeling it—I've felt it since . . ."—he shakes his head, looking dazed—"I don't know, always, I think. The first moment I saw you, I think part of me must have known even then."

"Dude, you do not need my help with boyfriendy," I tell

him, and I push him to his back and kiss him for a long, long time before I ask, "So how do I be girlfriendy to you? What feels romantic?"

He thinks about the question as he touches me. He says, "I like this. I like when your body is open to me." So I open my body more to him. He kisses me and says, "My favorite thing might be when I don't have to fight, when I can drop all the armor and just . . ."

"Yeah." I put my hands on his face and kiss the little bruise on his nose. I kiss his right temple.

"I begin to think . . . god, do I dare say it out loud?" he says as I kiss him more places. "I begin to wonder if the strength that has gotten me out of the pit and the swamp and onto this never-ending rage mountain might really be sufficient for me to be your partner."

I rest my chin on his chest and bite my lips between my teeth, remembering the feeling I had after I swung myself through the crux of the Money Pitch, the strength and confidence, the pride in myself, the sense of connection with Charles below me and the universe around me.

The move isn't the hard part; the decision is the hard part.

He draws my face to his and says, "I will falter, my harpy, as I move toward you. I only ask that you stand where I can see you. Be still for me, domina, and I'll find my way."

"I will."

He says, "Do you trust me?"

"Yes."

"And you know I'm on my knees, at your feet—"

"Don't be on your knees," I interrupt, "just stand at my side."

But he doesn't stop. He rolls me to my stomach, pins me down by my hair, and moves his lips to my neck as he whispers, "—mad for you, desperate, besotted, chained to you. I love you. There is nowhere I'm content, my Annie, but when I'm inside you, hold-

ing you, certain that in this moment we belong to each other. Do
you belong to me?"

"Yes," I rasp.

"You're mine?"

"Yes."

"Say it."

"I'm yours."

"And I'm yours. Never forget." He bites my earlobe. "Even
when I can't find my way to the words, my termagant, my shrew,
never forget that I'm chained to you."

"Charles." My voice is rough, cracked.

"Be really still for me, sweetheart."

It takes us a long time to leave the tent.

As we finish packing up our stuff, ready to head out, I inhale
deeply and sigh, "Petrichor."

"Mh?" Charles hoists on his pack.

"Petrichor. You taught me that, that last semester in Indiana.
The smell after the rain."

He takes my hand and kisses me. "The fundamental unrelia-
bility of the universe."

We hike out of the campground, hand in hand, silent, the couple miles to his car.

When he opens the trunk to load our stuff, we hear his phone
ringing from the glove compartment.

"That's a weird coincidence," I say.

But his face goes dark as he drops his stuff into the car. He re-
trieves his phone and wanders away from me as he answers it,
with "Hi, Mum."

He stands, listening, with his head down, eyes closed, jaw
tight. He stands there, alone in the middle of the gravel parking
lot, out here in the middle of nowhere Upstate New York. I
watch him grip a fist in his hair, then look up at the sky, listening more than he's talking. At last, he pulls off his sunglasses

and covers his eyes with his hand. He nods and says something, then moves his hand to his forehead as he begins walking back toward me.

His voice sounds totally calm as he says, "Yeah, and listen, I'll give you a bell tomorrow, okay, and we'll sort something for this week. Right. Okay. Bye, Mum. Bye."

Then he looks up at me with a face like death.

Chapter 26

Train to Failure

"What—"

"I've got to get back. We'll talk in the car."

"Okay. Sure."

We drive the first hour in silence. I don't know where to begin, how to explain, and at first she's patient with me, waiting for me to reassure her that everything is all right. I can't do that. The cold has already begun to take hold of me; nothing will be all right again. As time passes, I feel her getting frustrated, and then she crosses her arms and blows her hair off her forehead.

"So," I say, and then give a dark, ugly sort of laugh. "It's stage four rectal cancer that has spread to his liver."

"Oh god," she says, and all the frustration melts out of her, under the warmth of her sympathy. How does she do that? The emotion just releases from her body, like magic.

"Oh no," I say lightly, eyes on the road, "that's the good news."

Annie doesn't respond to that.

So I tell her the real news. "She asked me to come home. Or rather, she didn't ask, but she indicated the place where asking was and clarified that she wasn't there. Which, for Mum, is almost begging."

HOW NOT TO LET GO 225

"Of course you should go," Annie says instantly. "When? For how long?"

I grip the steering wheel. "A year or two."

"A year or two," she repeats, stunned.

"My contract with BU runs through June. I'll leave after that."

"That's four weeks."

"Yes."

"And then you'll be . . . where, London?"

"Cornwall, mostly."

"Cornwall," she repeats. "Which is in England?"

"Yes, Erosthenes, it's in England. About three thousand miles from here. On the far side of the Atlantic Ocean. You begin to see the difficulty."

She settles back in her seat, as if I've just broken the tension of the conversation.

"So the boyfriendy-girlfriendy thing to do now is to work out a plan—" she says, and I shake my head, but she continues, "Don't do that—a plan for talking on the phone and video chats and seeing each other periodically."

There is a long, long silence as I search for words to tell her what will happen to me when I get there. A decade ago, I left my mother and brother and sister so that I could stop being what I am with him, so that I could become someone I am, in general, not ashamed to be, someone who has tried to earn her love and respect and trust. But I couldn't be that man for even a single hour with him in the room last year. And she expects that everything will be the same? She was there, she saw, how can she not know?

And then I'm not looking for words anymore; I'm lost in rageful thoughts of him. Always, he has used them as bait, Simon and Biz and Mum, to get at me, and always my reaction is this frozen, hateful, violent thing, the armor and the flail and the insistent urge to grab the sword he has stabbed into my gut and push it deeper into me, even as I bash his head in.

She breaks the silence, saying, for no reason, "I'm sorry."

That brings me back to reality. I scrub a hand over my face. "Look, none of this is your fault."

"I know," she says, gentle.

I laugh bleakly, and stare wildly at the road. I say, "Of course you bloody know, because you're sane. You're rational. You're not the one thinking, 'I could go, and I could kill him. I could kill him and release all of us—Mum, Simon, Biz, all of us.' I know how. It would be easy." I feel a vicious sneer contort my face. "I think I might enjoy it. I think it might make me the fucking hero."

She doesn't answer. There is no answer.

After a long silence, she says, "I don't understand. You can't mean that you're just going to leave and it'll be over for us. You can't mean that, after everything it took for us to—" She stops, watching me, recognizing that that is indeed what I mean.

I take a deep breath, with a white-knuckle grip on the steering wheel. I'm suddenly very aware of my accelerated pulse and breathing. I'm aware that we're locked in a metal box traveling seventy miles an hour. "We've got time. We've got a few weeks. We'll spend that time together."

"You're serious."

I don't answer.

"Sure. We'll spend a few weeks together, and I'll just wave good-bye as you fly off to England. Have you *met me?*" She's beginning to yell. "Can we at least *try* to connect your internal world with reality?"

This isn't her fault. All my frustration and rage are directed at him, at my fucking father. But my fucking father is not locked in this car with me, yelling. I keep my hands gripped on the steering wheel.

She says, "We are *going* to argue about this, you know that, right? There is going to be a fight!"

"I don't want to hurt you," I say, keeping the defensive rage on a choke chain. "I've tried not to." We're in the city by now.

I'm counting seconds until I can get out of this car. I'll go for a
run, I think. I'll lift. Break myself. Train to failure.

She is dumbfounded. "I know. Because you fucking love me.
And if you get on a plane with the intention of leaving me, you
will definitely, *definitely* be hurting me."

"And that will definitely, definitely tear me to pieces," I say
bluntly. "But better it should be all at once, and unambiguous,
than slow, painful failure over months and years of trying to—"

"Why would it fail?" she presses as I turn onto Mass Ave. I've
been driving on automatic, I realize, heading to my flat instead of
hers. She's saying. "I don't understand why this is complicated!
We love each other plus your douche-bag dad is sick plus your
mom needs your help minus I'm in school so I can't go with,
equals . . . long-distance relationship for a while. That's how the
math works. What variables am I missing?"

"This is not about geography—"

And then I see Biz on my front steps.

"Oh god."

"Oh god," Annie echoes, spotting her too.

Annie and I look at each other. I see her frustration with me
drain out of her to make room for sympathy about Biz. How does
she do that?

But I look at my sister, skeletal and pale, sitting on my steps
with her bags, and my rage expands with this new reason to hate.
My fucking father is killing my sister.

I muzzle it, shove it into the closet, jam the door shut. If she
sees it, she'll feel it's her fault. It's not her fault. It's not Annie's
fault. It's no one's fault but mine . . . and his.

She doesn't smile as we emerge from the parked car and Annie
calls, "Hey, Biz."

She winces against the sun and says, "I'm on my way home.
Didn't want the next time I saw you to be in front of *him*." As always, no need to specify which "him."

"How long have you been waiting?" I ask, pulling our stuff
from the trunk.

She looks at her phone. "Half an hour."

"Is your semester over already?" I carry my gear and one of her bags up the steps, keys in hand.

"No."

"Uh, Charles, I have my thing," Annie interrupts.

"Er." I put a hand on my head. "Right. Sorry. Er . . . let me give you a lift—"

"I can walk."

"You should come back," Biz says.

"Okay," Annie says, and she looks to me, questioning.

"Yeah. Yeah, we'll . . . okay," I say.

"Okay," she repeats. She pulls on her pack and kisses me on the cheek. "I love you, dumbass. Bye, Biz, see you tonight."

Biz and I both watch her until she turns the corner.

Then I turn to Biz.

"Have you taken a leave of absence of something?" I ask, and I let her in, picking up her case.

"No!" Biz answers as we go up. "The school couldn't get their *shit* together *fast* enough, so I just left a note on my desk. They'll work it out."

"Christ, Biz."

She rolls her eyes. "The administration is so fucked up and *slow*."

"Being slow is what bureaucracies are for," I inform her as we rattle up the three flights. "The slower it is, the more it achieves the Platonic ideal of an administration."

"Well, it's *bullshit*," she declares, puffing from the climb.

"Be that as it may," I say. "I'll call them and mop up the mess, shall I?" I glance at Biz as I open the apartment door. "Go through."

"If you want," she says brusquely. "I don't care."

"Mum will have to cope with it otherwise. I'll do it."

"Fine." She goes into her room, slamming the door behind her.

I stare at her door for a moment. Then I stare at the photos Annie gave me. I've hung them by the door, so I see them every day when I leave and when I come home. Simon, Mum, Biz. And the person behind the camera.

I remember her at Christmas saying, "Every bit of strength you have, you paid for in loneliness." All my competence, all my capacity to cope with crises. It will allow me to protect these three people. And it will cost me the one I can't see.

Chapter 27

Necessary to Me

We sit up on the roof deck at sunset and get high because Biz can't take her stash on a plane. Well, they get high. I've got all this work to do.

She says, "Let's play the island game."

"Is this another of your tests?" Charles says amicably.

"It's not a *test*, it's a *game*."

"Right. Go on, then." Charles eases back on the deck chair and props his feet up, then folds his hands over his stomach and closes his eyes.

"You're on an island, and all you have with you is a *box*. It can be any kind of box, anything at all as long as it's a box. So the questions are, what is it like, how do you *feel* about it, and what do you and your box do on the island?

"And then one day you're going about your islandy business when you encounter a ladder. What is it like? How do you feel about it? How does it relate to your box? And what do you and the ladder do on the island?

"The next thing that happens is one day you find there is a *horse* here on the island with you. What is it like? How do you feel about it, what is the horse's relationship to you and your box and your ladder, and what do you and the horse do on the island?

"And finally, one day you spot that there are flowers on the island. Same questions: What are they like, how do you feel about them, what's their relationship to you and the box and the ladder and the horse, and what do you and the flowers do on the island? Right? Okay. So. Box."

Charles says, "Er, it's a wooden box about six foot cubed"—he holds out his arms—"full of wooden planks. I use the box as shelter and burn the planks on the beach as a signal to rescuers."

"What happens if you run out of wood?" I ask.

"I set fire to the box," he says instantly.

"It doesn't fill back up, like your cup?" Biz asks.

"No."

"Blimey," she says, then she turns to me inquiringly.

"My box is a treasure chest. It has everything I need—a tent, a water filter, first aid supplies, climbing gear . . ." I say.

"Oooh, that's lovely," says Biz.

"So what's yours?" Charles asks Biz.

"Mine's a tiny little jewelry box, like for a ring. It's red leather. Only it's empty."

"Where's the ring?" I ask.

"There never was one," she answers. "There was only ever an empty box." She pauses and I watch her battle tears just for an instant before she says, "*Ladder.*"

I start this one. "Mine's an aluminum ladder. It came out of the box. It's great because I can use it to climb trees and get fruit, I can use it to dry fish, and it never gets rusty even if I sometimes leave it out in the rain. But mostly I remember to put it back in the box. It's the only ladder I've got, so I take care of it."

Charles says, "I don't need the ladder to climb trees, I can climb them myself. The ladder is wood. I put it on the fire."

"And the horse?" Biz says, blinking.

I say, "Well, he's beautiful, he's got these pretty eyes and he's strong and fast and basically all I want to do is make friends with the horse. So I start spending a lot of time just sort of on the periphery of where the horse lives and gradually he starts to trust me and eventually he comes over and I feed him some coconut out of my hand and then we're friends. Eventually he lets me ride him and we go exploring all around the island."

"Charles?"

"Oh Christ, this is going to be embarrassing, isn't it?" He rubs his forehead. "How can there be only one horse? They're herd animals. Something must have gone wrong for this one horse to be separated from the rest and wind up alone on this island. So I'm worried about it, but there's nothing I can do, really, other than keep trying to be rescued and, if I can, take the horse with me."

"Humans are herd animals too," I object.

"And something has clearly gone wrong, that I'm on the island to begin with."

"So you want to rescue the horse," Biz says.

"In short," Charles agrees.

"And the way you rescue it is . . ."

"By setting fire to the box, in hopes of someone spotting the smoke."

She snorts a laugh. "And I'm afraid my horse is frightened of me and won't come near, no matter what I do. Right! *Flowers!*"

"I don't set fire to the flowers," Charles says. "They're native to the island. Most of what I do when I'm not trying to get off the island is study them. I learn to cultivate them and use them for things. I might even work out medicinal uses for them. The flowers I like a lot."

"I also work out medicinal uses for the flowers!" I say. "And I decorate my hut with them, and I feed them to the horse—and I can paint the ladder with them!"

We look at Biz.

"The flowers are what I eat," she says. "Okay, so the box is yourself, you see, the only thing you have with you." Instead of going through what we each said, she just continues. "The ladder is your friends. I'm sorry about this one, Charles: The horse is your *lover*. And the flowers are creativity. You see? Wasn't that a fun game? Well, I'm going to bed."

And, just like that, she gets up and goes inside. We hear her clatter down the spiral staircase.

And we're alone.

Charles leans back and covers his face in his hands, muttering, "God, oh god. Mum will be shattered when she sees her."

"What happened?" I ask.

"She went home at Christmas and saw how he was deteriorating, how he was treating Mum. And Mum's been talking to her about things and . . . when she feels out of control, food is something she can control. She made it sound like she just walked away from the semester, but I spoke to her dean, who said she had already arranged to turn things in electronically. She's done extremely well, academically."

"God, really?"

He shrugs. "Perfectionist."

"What does she mean, there was never a ring?"

"Empty. Worthless," he says. "Just a box, with nothing inside."

"Geez." And Charles set fire to his, to save the horse. "Geez."

He groans, with his head in his hands. "God, all the things I can't say. 'You are killing yourself. How do you think Mum will feel when she sees you? When is this going to stop? Why is my baby sister dying, and what can I do to make her well?' I just . . ." He looks up at me, his face bleak. "I look at my sister's starved body . . . and I see every kind of hunger I've felt. And I know that restricting isn't going to help either of us, and yet all the shit that's buggering up my relationship with you is buggering up my relationship with her as well. What a fuckshow I am."

I'm torn between sympathy for his struggle and frustration with, as he puts it, the shit that's buggering up our relationship. I aim for somewhere between the two feelings. "Neither of us needs you to set yourself on fire. I don't need to be saved."

Rubbing his eyebrows with one hand, he says, "Please, not now."

"I'm the sun," I persist.

"Termagant, please, I can't fight with you now. I'm too exhausted. I'm too high."

I frown at him, but then throw myself back in my chair and huff, "Okay."

A little silence passes before he looks at his watch and says, "Do you want to go home? Or . . . you could stay. Get some work done."

I think about going home and lying alone in bed, thinking about him. "I want to stay."

We go inside and downstairs. He sits beside me on the sofa as I pull books out of my bag.

"It's interesting," I say, with a pile of books in my lap.

"Hm?"

"Loving you feels really different now from how it felt a couple years ago." I say it quietly, mindful of Biz in her room.

He closes his eyes.

"It was fun, then. It was like a hot spot in my brain, you know? Just this hot, focused glow of dopamine and oxytocin, right? Just focused right in the ventral pallidum and nucleus accumbens."

The corners of his mouth lift and he takes my hand without looking at me. He says, "You do say the sweetest things."

I tell him, "Now it feels like the activation has spread outside the mesolimbic cortex and has begun integrating itself into my cortical functions. My language and decision-making and motor coordination. Do you know what I mean?"

He nods, his eyes on our hands entwined on the couch between us. "For me it feels like . . . I'm recovering from bodily integrity identity disorder."

We both laugh—quietly, still mindful of Biz.

"It was like I was convinced a part of my body wasn't a part of me. I was sure this thing couldn't belong to me. I didn't know why I was so attached to it, when I was sure my personhood, my soul, didn't extend into it. It wasn't mine, and yet it was always there with me. I was afraid of it. And then, over this last year, it has become a part of me. *You've* become a part of me. And now . . . when I leave . . . I will be leaving that part of myself behind."

I tip my head onto his shoulder. I want to tease him out of the darkness I feel inside him, so I nudge him and ask, "Hey, which part?"

But he answers in a choked voice, "My heart."

I can't say anything. I just turn my head and kiss his shoulder.

With a swift kiss on my forehead, he says. "We'll argue another time. Promise."

Charles is already out of bed when I wake up. I have my hand on the doorknob when I hear their voices.

She's saying, "Well, he wanted you, didn't he? Firstborn son. That bloody tree. Simon and me . . . we were redundant."

"Not to Mum you weren't. You're necessary to her."

"What's going on with you and Annie?" Biz asks out of nowhere. "Is she your girlfriend now?"

"She's . . . dunno," he says. "I love her, but I'm leaving."

There's a silence before Biz says, "Fucking Dad. Useless bastard."

More silence, and then she continues, "Will you come back after? Back here, I mean."

"Dunno" is Charles's answer, more abrupt now. He snaps, "Don't really want to talk about it."

"Sorry," and even from here I can tell she sounds like a whipped puppy.

"No, god, *I'm* sorry, I just don't know. I don't know how long I'll be there or what I'll find when I get there or what Mum will need or anything. I just don't know."

"How does she feel about it?"

"Annie? She's fed up with me."

"Does she know? How you feel, I mean."

"I just told her Saturday." And then Charles breaks my heart. He says, "I shouldn't have said anything, I s'pose."

"Yeah." Biz sounds like he's just announced business as usual.

There's a long silence. At last Charles says quietly, "He's not even worth the meat on his own bones. He's definitely not worth yours." Another silence, and then he says, "I love *you*, you know. You're my only sister. You're necessary to me. I know we haven't—" and then he stops.

There's another silence . . . and then one gusting sob from Biz.

More silence, broken only by the occasional shuddering breaths of her crying.

Very quietly, I open the door and peek out. I see her on the couch, folded over with her arms crossed over her stomach, and her head on her knees, and she's sobbing hard, but almost silently. Her hair is everywhere, spilling down her back and over her shoulders to the floor. Charles is sitting next to her with his knees crossed toward her and his hand resting on the center of her back. He looks calm. I recognize in his posture the same warmth and tenderness that I always felt from him in Indiana. The perpetual readiness to listen, the infinite capacity to be calm in the face of any storm. He looks like he sees this kind of thing every day—which he probably does.

I step quietly out of the room and Charles looks up. I point to the bathroom and make a silly face and he smiles at me with The Something—love—radiating in his face. I take my time showering, and by the time I go out into the living room, Biz is blotchy but calm and Charles is in the kitchen, pouring coffee. He hands me a cup and says, "There's turkey bacon, if you like."

"Yay," I say, and I kiss him—then I kiss him again because I can, and because I want him to know this isn't the last time. "I have to go to class. Can I take bacon with me?"

"Course."

As I roll some bacon in a paper towel, I say, "I'm going to class, Biz, will you be around tonight?"

"No, I'm leaving tonight." She stands and brings her cup to the kitchen. She holds it out to Charles for more coffee.

"Safe flight, then," I say.

"Bye," Biz says. "It was weird seeing you again."

"Weird seeing you, too!" I say, laughing, and I hug her, feeling her scapula under my hand. She doesn't hug me back, but she's smiling a little when I step away, and when I turn back to Charles after I pick up my backpack, he's watching me with a fierce look I can't interpret.

He follows me out, and in the hallway he holds my arm as if I'm about to run away and he needs to detain me.

"It's Monday," he says, like it's a challenge.

"So I'll see you at seven," I say back, baffled.

"I have to take my sister to the airport." He's glaring at me.

"I'll come with if you want me to, or I'll meet you at Butterfly whenever you get back."

His hand relaxes on my arm. "I'll meet you there."

"Okay."

"We'll argue Saturday, all right? Can it wait until Saturday?" he says, half defiance, half pleading.

Five days. I can hold on to this feeling for five days. I nod.

I step forward and put a kiss on his mouth, and another on the bruise at the bridge of his nose.

"I love you. We'll climb Saturday, and then we'll come here and have our fight. I gotta go. Bye. I love you." I start down the stairs, then turn around, remembering. I drop my bag to the floor, put my arms around his neck, and hug him hard. "Thank you for making me lead."

He puts his arms around my waist. "Oh god, Annie, what am I going to do?"

I let him hug me as long as wants. I have no idea what we're going to do, but I know that I will always let him hug me as long as he wants.

Chapter 28

The One Who Keeps Getting Hurt

As soon as I close the door behind her, she holds her fists up like a boxer and raises an eyebrow with a teasing smile.

"I'm ready," she says.

I try to smile back as we drop our stuff and kick off our shoes. I make coffee and keep breathing. Annie sits on her side of the sofa; I sit on mine.

"Okay," she begins, all business. "Want to start with desired outcomes? My desired outcome is: temporarily long-distance relationship. What's your desired outcome?"

"That I am never cruel to you," I say quietly.

She looks at me bewildered, her eyebrows knit together. She starts two sentences and tilts her head at me before she finally says, "Define 'cruel.'"

"Contemptuous. Violent. Manipulative. Deliberately hurtful."

"You're never any of those things," she says. "I wouldn't be here if you were."

I shake my head. "This is the missing variable in your equation. You saw what I am with him. When I go to that place, I will become that horrible thing for as long as it takes, to be a buffer between him and my mother. And I would rather . . ." I stop and lock my jaw against the blockage in my throat.

Silence. She stares at me in disbelief.

"That's it?" she says, eyebrows climbing to her hairline. She's already winding up. "Your dad is a douche bag who makes you act like a douche bag, too, and you don't want to treat me the way he treats your mom? You would just *never* do that."

"Think it through," I say as quietly as I can. I don't know if she hears the tension in my voice. I don't know if she even knows to listen for it. "I spend hours of each day locked in the armor that lets me do what little I can to shield them all, and then I go through the exhausting processing of stripping down to my skin so that I can be something like a human on the phone or on Skype with you, and then laboriously strap myself into the armor again."

"Wouldn't it be a relief, to be human for a while?"

I shake my head again. She's imagining herself in the situation, not me. "Imagine the feeling each day when I had to put the armor back on. It would kill me a little more and a little more. Better by far to stay locked in it."

"I think you're wrong, I think you're taking the easy way out by—"

"Easy?" I interrupt, my grip slipping a bit. "You think this is *easy* for me? All I've wanted for three years is to be as close to you as I can get, and the minute I—" I interrupt myself. I stand up and rub a hand on my forehead, pacing a little. "Life is not a Disney cartoon, Annie. I can't suddenly have a revelation that, surprise, the answer is love, and now everything is flowers and rainbows."

"But it's not *Lord of the* fucking *Rings*, either. You're not possessed by some evil magic that binds you to the . . . whatever! You get to make choices about how to treat people."

I turn toward her, reaching for patience, breathing through my self-contempt. "Yes. And those choices are constrained by my abilities. I've been nothing but honest with you. I said I wasn't where you need me to be, I said—"

"I know," she wheedles, "and I know I should be patient and understanding, but you're not even *trying*—"

"Not trying," I echo, stunned. "Not *trying?* Not trying is me shoving you out the door and never speaking to you again. But instead I'm standing here, letting you be angry with me—"

"So be angry back!"

"Sure. Fine. Let's be angry with each other." My face flushes hot. I feel the ugly snarl of my father's rage on my lip. I put my hands in my pockets. "I am much, *much* better at it than you."

"Good! Fine! You're better at a lot of things than I am! Gimmee all you've got. I'm not intimidated!"

"Then you're a lot stupider than I thought you were." I regret it as soon as I've said it, and I pace away from her into the kitchen.

She doesn't follow, but calls from the sofa, "Oh, awesome. Name-calling. I thought name-calling was against the rules, but let's go." I turn to snap an apology at her, but she's already launched herself into it. She chants, "Asshole, honeybunch, dickweed, lovebunny, buttmunch, snugglebucket, fuckstick, cuddlestuff, fuckball, fucknut, sweetheart, lambkins, beloved, beautiful . . . asshat!" she concludes with a dramatic gesture. "I fucking love you, you asshat! I love you! I was gonna be *so* reasonable today, I had this plan that we would make lists and calendars and shit, but how do I make a list if the problem is *feelings?* And now I'm so mad I can't even—"

She takes an enormous breath, like she's going to scream . . . but instead she puts her fists on either side of her head, puffs out her cheeks, squinches up her eyes, and make a voiceless "Pchrw!" noise in her throat as her fingers burst from her fists.

She's just made her head explode.

Then she flops her face into the pillow in her lap, saying, *"Why-did-I sleep-with-you-before-you-were-friends-with-your-dragon-I knew-it-was-a-bad-idea I love you so much* oh my god this is terrible I suck. So much. At fighting." This last she says while banging her head against the pillow. With her face still buried in the pillow, she says, "I don't want to yell at you. I'm sorry I yelled."

In any other state of mind, this precocious display, so thoroughly characteristic of Annie, would make me laugh. But now it only makes me disgusted with myself, even as my heart races.

"I don't know why you slept with me," I say, leaning against the wall, my hands still in my pockets, "but I won't importune you again."

She throws herself back on the couch. "That was, like, the least important thing I just said. Did you even hear what I said?"

"You're sorry you yelled," I reiterate dully through the thudding of my pulse. "You don't know how to fight. You love me. And you regret—" There I stop, remembering her body in the dark, trembling as I held her against me, under the patter of rain on the tent. I remember how it felt not to have to fight at all. How it felt when we surrendered to each other. In despair, I finish, "You regret it."

She flinches a little, eyes on the pillow she still holds in her lap. "I don't regret it. Last weekend was . . . the happiest I've ever been in my life."

"And I fought for that," I snarl, stepping toward her with my heart bleeding. "I fought my way to you. If you think I'd give you up easily, or for my own benefit, you have fundamentally misunderstood me. If I turn away from you, it is only to protect *you*."

She bursts out, "How come I don't get to decide what counts as protecting me?! How about you leave the fucking armor on with me? It didn't hurt me last year when you—"

"I've been telling you," I bite. "You're not *listening*." She doesn't understand, why can't she understand, even now, when it's right in front of her, sneering at her, breathing too fast? When I love her so much I can hardly breathe and yet my fists are jammed into my pockets, shaking with the urge to fight? Does she not see?

"I *am* listening," she insists. "You said you get all ragey when your dad's around and then you called me stupid for trusting you when you're all ragey—even though you're all ragey right now and it's fine, I trust you."

"It's fine?" I rake my hands in my hair. She has no idea. Have I done that good a job? Have I masked it so well that she believes she can push indefinitely and I'll never break? I turn away with a growl of "This is pointless. We'll start over on Monday. Go home, Annie."

"I can't go home, we haven't fixed anything. I don't even understand your desired outcome yet, because you keep—"

"Go home." I walk away from her.

I hear her behind me, "Charles, you can't—" then feel her grab the back of my shirt, tugging me backward.

My blood pulses with adrenaline and pure, raging attack, as I turn and yell, "*Go home!*" My hands are halfway to her throat before I see her face. She doesn't look angry. She looks baffled and sad.

I raise my hands over my head, eyes on the floor, and take two steps back until I hit the wall. I put my hands on my head.

Through my teeth, I beg her, "Get out, Annie, *please.*"

"You're faltering. You told me to stand where you can see me. So here I am." She grabs my shirt and twists it in her hand, and the urge to shove her away, slam her against the opposite wall, is nearly overwhelming. I close my eyes, breathing through my nose, and I focus on keeping my hands relaxed and still.

"Are you angry right now?" she demands.

"Yes," I grind out. My heart is beating much too fast. I try to slow my breath.

"Because I am a pain in the ass," she agrees, "and you're on Rage Mountain. And are you being cruel, genius? Are you hurting me?"

"I want to," I say as lightly as I can.

"And yet you're not. How come?"

With my eyes still closed, I snarl, "You're pushing me on purpose."

"No shit," she says. "Because tell me one thing I have to lose. You're leaving. You've already *left*. So, like, fucking hit me and make me glad you're gone. Isn't that what this is? Here's your chance. Contemptuous, violent, deliberately hurtful. Hurt me for real. If I shouldn't trust you," she persists, "punch me in my obnoxious mouth. Hit me one time, and I'll leave and never come back."

"Christ." I let my body slump down the wall and she descends with me. With my elbows on my knees, I clutch my hands in my hair to stop them from reaching out. I say, "Stop it."

But she grabs my wrist, pulling my arm to vertical.

In my mind, I twist my wrist out of her hand and I grab her throat. I pin her to the ground until she's red-faced and choking—anything to shut her up. The thought makes me hate myself.

"I could hurt you," I say, hardly able to find my voice.

"Go ahead!" she says, and she actually laughs as she says it.

I don't move.

"See?" she taunts. "You won't even put your hands on me when you're mad."

I grab at her hand with my free one, press her fingers tight around my wrist, and turn my face away.

We sit there like that. I hear her breath and my own. One of us is trembling—or both of us. I feel her fingers shift a little under the pressure of my grip. I can't think what to do next. I can't think. But the anger is ebbing. I feel my jaw relax incrementally.

I lean my head back against the wall, eyes still closed. I take a full breath and release it slowly through my nose.

"Charles," she says softly.

I don't answer.

"Charles, my hand aches a little."

Without looking at her, I release her hand. She relaxes it around my wrist . . . but doesn't move it.

"Look how I can't trust you," she says. "Look how I'm afraid."

And then I feel her lips on my hand. She presses her lips to the back of my palm, the surgical scar there—I feel her breath—and then her cheek, soft, warm. My eyes burn and I feel choked.

She stays there, perfectly still. She gives me time. I feel the tension in my muscles ebb as my heart rate slows. I blow out a slow breath, still not opening my eyes. That's when she shifts her body in front of mine and carries my hand . . . to lay my palm on her throat.

"Charles," she says, and I can feel the vibration of her voice against my palm.

I don't answer.

She presses her hand over mine, holds my palm to her larynx. She says, "When I say, 'I love you,' this is what I mean."

I want to slam her head into the floor and run. I want her to cut me open and let me bleed. I want to curl up in a ball and dissolve into nothing. I want the world to disappear so that I can lay my body down with hers and make love until we both collapse.

"You think it's easy," I whisper, and I brush my fingers against the skin of her throat. "You think it's normal, what you're doing."

I feel her lean toward me, moving slowly. I can feel where her breath brushes my skin. When her lips touch the healing bruise on my nose, I flinch a little. Then she kisses my temple, where I fell last summer. With her lips there, she says quietly, "How is it that you're so worried about protecting me, and yet you're the one who keeps getting hurt?"

We sit there on the floor in silence. I feel wrung out, wasted. The anger is gone, leaving a hangover of shame and despair. I can't think. I can't move.

"Oh no," she breathes, "oh god." The grief in her voice is more awful than her anger. She slumps down, resting her forehead on my shoulder. My hand slides around the back of her neck as she says, "I'm doing this all wrong. You've been telling me. I *wasn't* listening. 'Be really still for me, Annie. Stand where I can see you.' Your favorite thing is when you don't have to fight, and here I am saying that unless you're fighting, you're failing. Dude, I *am* stupid."

"You're not," I whisper.

"I forgot about little-kid-you. 'There's no one to help, because you're not worth helping.' I've been so mean, saying you're not trying, saying you need to be friends with your dragon. But I'm the one who has to try. *You* need *me* to be friends with your dragon." I hear her breathe shakily. I caress her neck, loving her, dreading what's coming, longing for it, knowing I'll be indebted to her for the rest of my life.

"I'm sorry it took me so long, but I get it now," she says. "You go be strong, be the superhero, and if you come to me with your hurts, I will kiss them better. And if you don't . . ." And now the pain comes, the cut. Her breath comes in shuddering gasps for a moment, and then she grips both her hands in my shirt, over my heart. Her shoulders are shaking and there are noises coming from her throat. "If you don't, then I will wait for you and I will love you all the same," she says through gritted teeth, and she shoves me a little, "with joy in my heart, because I am so." She shoves me again, lightly. "Fucking." Another shove, weaker. "Proud of you." Her arms move a little but don't generate enough force for me to feel it.

She presses her forehead against her hands, piled up over my heart. "You're stronger than anyone. You're the best man I know. But you don't have to do it alone. You're not alone, Charles. Not unless you want to be."

She sobs there, gasping tears that make her whole body shudder. I feel her spine weaken, so I disentangle my hands to brace her against me, hold her up against me. I won't let her crumple to the floor.

"Oh god, this girl," I say. "The breath of my body, the beat of my heart. I don't deserve you. I'm a fuckshow, Annie. I've tried—"

"I know you have."

"God, listen to me. 'I've tried.' I've fucking failed is what I've done. I'm not where you need me to be. I'm sorry."

"No, I'm sorry. I'll do better now."

We sit there together for a long time, waiting for one of us to see the next move, to find a way forward.

"Holy crap, this is scary," she says, and then she laughs. She laughs, and my body receives her laughter like a balm.

"How can you laugh?" I say.

"How can I not?" she sniffs. "Look at us. On the floor, in a puddle, just because we can't figure out how to love each other. Poor us."

"When you put it like that," I say, and I kiss her hair.

When she kisses my throat softly, and then my ear, I turn my mouth to hers and kiss her.

I'm a fool and a coward. I put my hand on her face and push my tongue into her mouth. I want inside her, this woman who holds my hand and looks into my eyes and says yes. The woman I would choose, if I got to choose. I take her to bed. I take off our clothes, kissing her the whole time, and when I'm inside her, she makes a tiny noise and wraps me in her body, arms, and legs. With her lips at my ear, she whispers to me as she comes, "You won't be alone."

I am a fool. I am a coward. But I will hold on to this girl for as long as I can, because when I let her go, it will tear me to pieces.

Chapter 29

Be Really Still for Me, Annie

I'm a pest. I'm a harpy. A shrew. A termagant. I am all the bothersome, irritating things Charles has ever called me. But for a month, I stay still. I stand where he can see me and trust him to find his way to me. We don't fight. I don't push.

We keep our Monday at seven and our Wednesday/Saturday climbing. We add a Friday night sleepover—always at his place. I don't have time for more; every Monday he asks me to spend the whole night, but usually I can't. I have to maintain my life, my work. He understands. He likes it. He needs me to live fully in my own life, to be the person I am and not just "his."

Do I want to grab his shirt and scream, "COME BACK!" over and over until I'm hoarse? Do I want to press my face to the cool floor and sob until I die? Do I want to?

Yes.

But he knows. He sees what I'm doing and knows what it costs me. He knows he couldn't do it. He knows I had to be the one to let go, and I know that fact is hurting him more than anything else. Because I know him. I know every part of him.

And I know, because he's done it before, that he will not stop until he has matched me. He will fight his way through the fear.

He hasn't said he loves me since we got back to Boston, and now he's stopped calling me the sun and his heart and all his other ways of saying it without saying it. Now he tells me only with his touch. With his gaze. With the hesitation in his body when he hugs me good-bye, as he lets me go, saying, "Monday at seven."

We climb together and eat together and press our bodies together in the dark. The more I let go, the closer he holds me. Nothing is out of bounds when we're in the dark together. It is very, very fucking educational:

- There's how you feel about someone, and there's the relationship you can have with them. Not the same thing. I thought I learned this two years ago, but sometimes you need a refresher course.

- To love someone is to love the *process* of them, not just the way they are but the way they grow. To witness a human's personal evolution is to worship at the altar of their true selfhood. And all you have to do is listen well. Listen to what they say, what they don't say, and the context in which they're saying it. Keep listening. And then listen some more.

- Not everything that feels good is right and healthy. And not everything that hurts is wrong and dangerous.

- The more you practice being aware of what's happening right now, the larger becomes your sense of "right now." At first it's just this second. Now. And now. And now. Then your sense of "now" expands out. Ten seconds in a row are all "now." A full minute, so that "now" includes thirty seconds in the past and thirty seconds in the future. And in moments of total clarity and peace—for me, it's usually during or after orgasm—"right now" fills up years of time, all of our past and all of our future, collapsed into "now."

On the last night, I come over to find—

"Oh god," I say.

"You don't have to take it," he says softly, standing behind me, playing with my hair. "But it's yours, whether it lives with me or you."

The first edition *On the Origin of Species* he gave me as a graduation present. He wanted it to be a tie between us, and so I left it behind when I left Indiana.

I sit on the couch in front of the book and put my hand on the green cover. I lift the front piece and see the first page, with its stamp, like a notarization, marking it as belonging to the Belhaven library. I touch the raised marks.

With my eyes on the page I say, "I'm afraid if I take it home, I'll get it wet or rip it or something, you know? I'll ruin it somehow."

"I know the feeling," he says, and I look up to find him watching me. He says, "I can hold it for safekeeping, if you like. Until you know where you want to keep it."

I go over to him and wrap my arms around his waist, and he puts his arms around me. With my face against his shirt, I say, "Thank you. Thank you for giving me a thing worth protecting, and for helping me protect it."

He just hugs me back.

All of his kitchen stuff is packed, so we order Chinese takeout. The movers will come to put his stuff into storage tomorrow morning. His bedroom is empty except for boxes and the bed. I carry my laptop to the bed and lie curled up beside Charles as I play Beck's "Everybody's Got to Learn Sometime."

"This is what I listened to, over and over again, that first month after I left Indiana," I say.

He listens to the song, watching my face, then sits up and types something into my computer. It plays the song Simon played when he pretended to be a trumpet—Coldplay. "The Scientist."

He says, "I must have run hundreds of miles that year after you left, listening to this song."

I listen, and I watch him listening with a thoughtful, sad frown.

"We are both. So. Corny," I say with a giggle when the song ends. "Ooh, but then I found this song." And I play "Turn the World Around."

He looks up at me. "I'm sorry, Annie. I can't tell you how much."

I shake my head. "Don't be sorry. I'm not."

We spend the night together, of course, this last night. We kiss as he takes off my clothes and I take off his, and we touch each other's bodies, as if for the last time. It's not erotic—it's too sad for that. We just hold our bodies together and touch and kiss, all silent, until I fall asleep.

I wake in the middle of the night to find myself spooned against him with my head pillowed on his arm. He's kissing my neck, slow, soft kisses, as his fingertips graze my rib cage and belly and breasts. With a voiced sigh of pleasure, I signal my wakefulness, and his touch grows more deliberate, but still so light, so light over my breast and nipple and belly and hip bone, waking pleasure and desire.

As he touches me, his lips move from my neck to my ear. He kisses my earlobe, and whispers to me. He talks to me about the first day he saw me, and the first night we spent together, and the day I said I loved him, all in a voice that tells me more of love and good-bye than any words could.

And then, slipping his hand down my abdomen, he tells me about waking up the morning I left. "I tried to just get on with things."—He bites my earlobe, tugs at it with his teeth, pulling a noise from my throat.—"I made coffee and tortured myself remembering that morning in the kitchen, the first time I kissed you."—His hand travels almost lazily from my collarbones to my clitoris, softly caressing my skin, so that I stretch like a cat, rubbing my back against his body.—"I showered and thought of your palms pressed to the tiles and your wet skin against mine and your tongue in my mouth."—With my head still pillowed on his biceps, his hand grasps my throat and jaw, and I moan.— "When I looked in the mirror to shave, I saw the bite mark on my shoulder."—His fingers approach my mons, and they stay there, making soft circles over my labia, and I push my pelvis into his hand, seeking more . . . which he does not give.—"I put my fingers on the bite mark, I felt where your teeth had been."—Again he bites my earlobe, and his fingertips continue their tormenting, light circles while the hand at my throat presses my face toward his, seeking my mouth.

He kisses me. I put my tongue in his mouth and kiss him back. He keeps my face toward his, looking into my eyes, as he says, "There was a bruise on my shoulder blade and swollen streaks of red where your fingernails raked me." And I remember doing those things to him, remember my fist against his scapula, my nails scraping so hard I found a little blood under them the next day. He lays his warm palm flat against my vulva and tugs firm circles over my clit.

With his lips against mine, his breath hot there, he says, "When I saw that you'd left the *Origin* behind, I thought selfishly, how can I feel forgiven, if she doesn't have the book? Don't forgive me, Annie. Never forgive me."

"Too late," I whisper, and I put my mouth on his.

He rolls to his back, pulling me with him until I'm lying on top of him, my back to his chest. I feel his hand moving between my legs. I feel his cock enter me, not deeply, just a connection, as he holds my body close to his. He wraps his arm around me, holding my arms down.

He kisses me with a groan and fucks me and holds me, his fingers lacing with mine. He presses my palm against my clit, each of us moving a hand there as he kisses me and wraps our other arms across my chest. My feet slide out as my knees tip together and I shift and rock my body over his, pressing into our hands.

"Tell me," he whispers. "Tell me our story."

So I do. I turn my lips to his ear and, through the gasps of my arousal, I tell him about seeing him for the first time, about the way I had to practice saying his name to myself, before I could bring myself to say it to him—"Charles. Charles. Charles." I tell him how scared I was the first time I took off my shirt in front of him, and his cock slides deeper into me.

Then I tell him how *not* scared I was when he tied me to the bed and made me come until I couldn't come anymore, how I felt like I had come home, discovering a way of making love with him that asked me to surrender my body completely, let my body be his, and now, with a groan, he grips my body hard against his, his arms like iron bands, and he pushes his cock deep, deep into me, over and over, while I gasp with my lips still at his ear. He's pressing our hands to my clit, and I think he's going to come, that he's going to make me come, but instead, suddenly, he turns us, our hands between my legs, his own legs straddling mine. His other arm is wrapped under me, bracing my shoulder.

"What else?" he says on a breath.

He fucks me deeply, fully, as I tell him, through broken gasps, how I felt on his birthday, when I realized I loved him—again, still, forever—but I knew he wasn't ready. I tell him how, when he said he loved me in the tent, in the rain, my heart became his heart. His heart, beating in my body. And it was permanent.

"Annie." He turns me to my back, slides back into me. He marks my skin with his mouth and teeth and hands and nails, and I mark his. He kisses me as I wrap my body around him. I lift my hips off the bed, push closer, wanting his body closer, deeper, more, and he kisses me hard as he moves in me. With all my limbs tangled around him, he puts an arm around my waist and he lifts me fully off the bed, into his lap, kissing me the whole time.

There's only the sound of his breath and mine, the sound of

our bodies moving together. My whole body is shaking. So is his. With a desperate sound, he rises onto his knees, still kissing me, still inside me, kneeling as he would at an altar—kneeling as he did that night so long ago when we made love for the very first time. With my arms and legs wrapped around him, with no other support but him, I come. He comes with me, with those three big thrusts and a hoarse, wild noise. I feel his pleasure in my body, the terrible intensity of it. I'm part of his body. He's part of mine.

He throws our bodies down to the bed, holding me close still, inside me still as he breathes hard, kissing me and kissing me and kissing me. I hold him just as close, until the trembling ache in my biceps forces me to relax my arms. I bend them, with my palms flat on his skin, caressing him as I release him.

But he grips me all the harder and says, "No."

So I put my arms around him again, hold him hard against me. Though my muscles burn and tremble, though I'm struggling to breathe under his weight, I don't loosen my grip, not one bit. I can be and do whatever he needs. When I feel his lungs contract, I kiss his hair and hold him closer. We lie together, wrapped around each other, as close as we can get, touching everywhere we can. I feel the wet of his tears on my throat. I feel the trembling in his arms and the shudder of his breath. He kisses my shoulder, bites gently, presses his face against it. I brush my fingers over his temple, over his hair, as I hold him close against me, as close as I can bring him. As close as he'll come.

"It'll tear me to pieces," he gasps.

"And then we'll put you back together," I whisper.

When I wake, he's gone. He's not in the bed.

I sit up. "Charles?"

Nothing.

Adrenaline rushes through my blood and I think, *No. No. He wouldn't just leave. He would say good-bye.* I go out and search his apartment—bathroom, guest room, kitchen—there's coffee made, and on the counter by the coffee machine is my *Origin*. There's a key beside it—his apartment key.

"Oh god," I whisper, and, trembling, in a last ditch, hopeless attempt to find him, I run up the spiral stairs and onto the roof—and he's there. Sitting on a deck chair with one foot on the chair, his fingers braced around his shin, his coffee cup balanced on his knee. He's watching the sunrise, but he turns to look at me when he hears me come out.

"Hey," he says softly. "You're up early."

"Hey," I say, breathless and weak with relief. I want to rush over to him, but I stay still.

"I couldn't sleep," he says. "So I've been sitting up here trying to figure out what to say to you today."

Say you love me. Say you'll come back. Say it doesn't matter where we are, I'm yours and you're mine until we die. Say it again, just one more time, that I'm the sun, I'm your heart, I'm—

I don't ask for any of these things. I sit in the chair next to his.

"Make a wish on the magic coffee cup," I say, waving my fingers mystically in the direction of his mug. "What would you wish for?"

"I'd wish . . ." He leans back and closes his eyes as the orange of the sunrise gilds his face and hair. "Dunno. I'd wish he would just die, so I could get on with my life, but I'd hate myself for wishing it. I'd wish I weren't such a fuckshow, so that I could say all the words that name this thing that happens inside me when I think of leaving here, leaving you." He turns his head toward me. "That'll do for a start."

I wave magic fingers around his cup and say, "Skadoosh. So may it be." I drink his cold coffee. He takes the cup back and stands up. I breathe deeply as he goes inside. He's only going to refill his cup and bring me one, too. He'll be back in two minutes. Less. He's not going anywhere.

Yet.

"A year ago," he says when he's back and sitting beside me with a steaming cup, "remember? You taught me to say good-bye. I'd been dreaming about you, kept waking up expecting to find you and then you weren't there. So when we were finally saying good-bye, I felt as if I'd been saying it for days. Do you remember the formula?"

"It was great seeing you," I recite.

"I really enjoyed . . . everything," he says. He shakes his head. "Every moment. Even this one."

"I'll see you again . . ." I grit my teeth against the sting in my nose and then finish, "Someday."

"Thanks for . . ." With a frustrated growl, he puts his coffee on the concrete ground and stalks to the railing, where he leans on his elbows, hands clasped. He says to his wrists, "Annie, I'm sorry."

"*Par la souffrance, la vertu,*" I say, staying where I am, because: space.

"I won't go," he says suddenly. "Why should I hurt you, to help him?"

"It's not to help him, it's to help your mother. And you absolutely should go and support her. Apart from that, I don't know. Something magical will happen, deus ex machina."

"*Machina,*" he corrects my pronunciation with a grin as he turns to face me, leaning back on the rail.

"*Machina,*" I repeat, and I smile. "I never heard anybody say it out loud before. I like it."

"So we're looking for some manufactured magic. God from the machine." He tilts his head and turns his eyes to the sky. "Only we don't believe in god."

"But we do believe in the machine," I say. "I believe in the creative intelligence of a tool-using ape."

"I believe in the healing power of compassion," he says crisply.

"I believe in the fundamental reliability of the universe—usually." I smile a little at my mug.

"I believe in Mondays at seven," he says, and his eyes are on me when I look up from my coffee.

"I believe in you," I say. And I say it again. And then I say, "I have to go into the lab soon."

"It's Saturday," he says, and he looks so crestfallen I almost say, "It's your last day. I'll skip it."

But I'm staying still. So I shrug, "It's Harvard."

Our actual, final good-bye that night is mostly focused on the pragmatics of leaving for a long time and on the timetables and paperwork involved in international travel.

I drive him to the airport—he's leaving his car with me—I park and help carry his stuff in. Once he's checked his bags and got his boarding pass and everything, we stand over to one side, near the security line to say good-bye. He drops his one remaining bag to the floor.

I stuff my hands in my jeans pockets and say, "Well."

He doesn't say anything, just looks at the floor and swallows.

"Okay," I say, like he's just stepping out for a coffee. "You're the best man I know. I love you no matter what. Send my love to Biz and Simon and Carol."

He stares at the floor some more and breathes harder.

"Okay," I say again, more shakily. "Well. I've got all this work to do, so . . ."

His hand flashes out and grabs my wrist. "Not yet," he says through his teeth. "Please."

So I stay where I am, though my nose stings and I have to bunch my lips over to one side to keep the tears back.

He says to the floor, "I can't—"

He looks up at me suddenly and his face scares me.

"Everything," he breathes, and then his throat closes and he swallows hard again, eyes wide. He battles to breathe and says,

"All of it. God!" He glances around him without seeing anything. "I said it would tear me to pieces if I hurt you again, and now I have done, and it will do. Ah, this isn't what I wanted to say." He makes a vicious noise of frustration and locks his jaw. Then his eyes come back to mine. He looks like there's something evil chasing him, something he knows is about to catch him, and this is the last time he'll see me before it drags him under.

He opens his mouth, breathes in—his nostrils flare and the corners of his lips go down. He grabs my shirt in his fist, right over my heart. With his eyes on mine, almost pleading, I don't know what to say or do. I don't know what he needs, but I put my hands over his fist and nod, understanding. I'm crying, but sad, quiet tears in contrast to his struggling panic.

"Annie," he says, like he asked a question and he's impatient for an answer. "The Thing—" His throat locks up again.

"Is a Love Thing," I say, wanting to spare him this struggle. "I know, Charles."

"You're the sun," he gasps.

"Yes, I am." I caress my thumb over his fist. I take one step forward so that he can hear me clearly when I say softly, "You know what that means, asshole? It means wherever you are, I will be there. I will be where you need me to be."

With one hand still fisted in my shirt, he takes my hand in his and presses my palm to his larynx, wrapping my fingers around his throat. I feel his battle for breath there. I watch his throat move under my hand as he swallows. When my eyes come back to his, he whispers, "I'm scared—"

I rise to my toes. I leave my hand on his throat as I put my parted lips against his, just brush them lightly, and he makes a quiet sound in his throat. I open my lips a little more and kiss him again.

He puts his hand on the back of my head, holds me there and kisses me as I move my hand to the back of his neck. I slip the tip of my tongue into his mouth and he gasps, opening his mouth wider. When he puts his hands on my face, it's too much. I pull away and take a step back, so that his hands fall away.

I meet his eyes. "Bye, Charles."

I turn and walk away.

"Monday at seven," he calls after me.

I don't let go of the sobs inside me until I'm in his car.

Chapter 30

Torn to Pieces

She doesn't look back. I watch her until she disappears in the crowd, and then I keep watching.

She's gone.

She's gone.

Right. Okay. TSA. Gate. Flight.

Go.

I go. And slowly, one by one, as if I've been disconnected from life support, my organ systems start to fail. The respiratory system goes first. I've stopped breathing before I get through security, and without oxygen the rest of my body begins to shut down. My heart stops. My gut stops. And then, once I'm on the plane, I begin to rot. At forty thousand feet, my body seems to deliquesce, my skin loosens and begins to peel away, like a corpse drifting for days in the river. My bones and muscles atrophy and lose all integrity. By the time Stig meets me at the airport, there's nothing left of me. I have disintegrated.

I know it's an illusion, this feeling that the boundaries of my own body have dissolved and there is no me left anymore, but the illusion is an intractable one. I am gone. There is no thinking. There is no me.

When we arrive at the house, I bypass the front door, heading instead for the coast road. I make my way down the rocky path to the beach, where I take off my shoes and socks and sit in the sand, staring back across the ocean.

This empty shell is supposed to take care of Mum. This . . . nothing.

This nothing, I realize, is what all those other layers were there to protect: this knowledge that ultimately I do not exist. There was no me at the core of it all.

There was no me, but there was Annie. Annie, who loves me.

She can't love me; there is no me, there was only the shame and rage and self-contempt . . . and now even those are gone. But she loved them.

"Where did the shame and rage and self-contempt come from?" asks the Clarissa in my head. "Who built all those defenses?"

Some little boy built them like a sand castle on the beach. The tide has washed it all away now.

And where is the boy?

I open my eyes. I'm lying flat on my back on the sand. I'm staring at the sky, where it's threatening rain. The wind smells of salt and rot.

Right.

Okay.

Who the fuck am I?

The answer comes: I'm the best man Annie Coffey knows; I'm the boy who built the castle.

I built it so that I could be safe in an unsafe world—safe both from being harmed and from doing harm.

Well, they're all gone now, the defenses, and I can't bring myself to miss them. They hadn't even worked. I hurt Annie and then I disintegrated into nothing.

No, the defenses disintegrated into nothing, leaving behind the boy who needs a way to feel safe, he needs a base camp. A home.

Annie.

It begins to rain. I close my eyes and lift my face up to it and recite to the sky, " 'Remember when you drank rain in the garden? That was for this.' " *Boil me some more*, I think. *Hit me with your skimming spoon. I can't do this alone.* Rumi loves a colloid.

I grip my fingers into the sand and say to the rain, " 'Ye though I walk through the valley of the shadow of death' "—my throat closes. The tears are hot against my skin as they mix with the rain. I think, *I will fear no evil for thou art with me. Thy rod and thy staff* . . .

" 'They comfort me,' " I whisper to the sky.

I will stand on my bare feet and walk across the sand into that ugly great house, without any of the old defenses. I will stand before my dragon without armor or sword.

"And it'll be like *Harry Potter*," says the Annie in my head. "Shit'll just bounce off you, because: love."

Surprise. The answer is always love.

It's raining hard now. I carry my shoes and socks into the house and follow the sound of the piano to the music room and my mother. She turns when she hears me.

"Charles, dear, how lovely," she says, as I put my hand on her shoulder and kiss her cheek. "You're all wet."

Biz is sitting on the sofa reading, so I go and kiss her cheek, too. She looks at me as if I've gone mad, and for all I know, I have.

"Annie sends her love," I say to them both. "I'll go and see him after I've dried off and had a cup of tea."

That's what I do.

And that's when things really go wrong.

Chapter 31

God from the Machine

The phone rings at 6:56 p.m.

I know this because I've been sitting on my bed, heart pounding, mouth dry, with my phone in my hands, staring at the clock, since 6:43.

I let it ring twice before I answer it.

"Hey," I say.

"Hey," he says back, and he sounds no farther away than his South End apartment. I close my eyes and take a deep breath.

"How's it going?" I ask, aiming for casual but sounding squeaky to my own ears.

"Er, unexpected. It's er . . . there's something I have to tell you and it's right out of bounds."

"Okay." My heart is thumping and scenarios are running through my head, based on nothing more than the tone of his voice. His mother is sick. Biz—

"So . . ." He clears his throat. "It's pretty bad. Like Mum said, the prognosis is a year or two, but he appears to be in a lot of pain a lot of the time." No need to specify which "him." "He hates it."

"I'm sorry," I say.

"Oh, this isn't the out-of-bounds part at all," he says. "This is just the preamble. God, I don't know if I'll be able to say it."

"Hey, I know what we should do," I say, responding less to his words than to the unsteadiness in his voice. "We should both turn off all the lights and lie down in our beds and then we're just talking to each other in the dark before we fall asleep. Let's try it. Wait, let me pull my curtains. Okay. I'm lying in the dark. Are you?"

"Yes. On my bed, in total darkness, except for the bit of light from my phone. I'll close my eyes. Total dark."

"And my voice."

"Hey," he says. I hear his grin and I grin back.

"Hey," I answer. "So now nothing is out of bounds."

"Yeah . . . Christ. I don't know if I can."

"Anything I can do to make it easier?" I ask gently.

"Just . . . listen and be calm, okay?"

"Okay." Stay still. Got it. I'm good at it now.

There's a silence, then I hear him take a breath, and he says, "He's asked me to help him die."

My face prickles as the blood drains away. "Whoa."

"Yeah."

"That is . . . unexpected."

"Yeah."

"When was this?"

"The morning I arrived. I'm the one he trusts, he said."

"That's . . . complicated."

"Slightly," he says, laughing. And then he adds, "It's why he pushed Mum so hard to get me to come home sooner rather than later."

"What did you say?"

"Nothing, I laughed. I laughed, and I walked out. It was the first time he'd . . . He touched my wrist. That alone, his hand on my skin, was . . . I can't remember the last time he touched my skin, and now he wants me to . . . ."

Just the fact that he's leaving so many sentences unfinished tells me how hard he's struggling.

His voice is vehement as he says, "I hate him, you know. I've wanted to beat him bloody for as long as I can remember. I've wished him dead for my mother's sake more times than I can count. I've even said . . . But now . . ."

"So the hero, filled with righteous anger at the dragon who's been terrorizing the villagers, laboriously climbs the mountain to its lair, and instead of confronting a snarling, fire-breathing monster, he finds it sick and in pain, and it actually says, 'Please kill me.'"

"In a nutshell," he says. "Jesus, Annie."

"Sorry."

"No, it's . . . If I were here as his doctor, and not the fucking hero, I'd want nothing else for him but a quiet, easy death."

"Sure."

"But how much of it is that he's in pain, and how much is that he wants to see how far he can push me? It's a power play. I left, I literally moved to a different continent, to avoid being manipulated by him."

I hear him take a few deep breaths, trying and failing to start the sentence before he says, "And I'm disturbed . . . by the pleasure I feel in watching him suffer. I reach for compassion and it's not there. I reach for basic human respect, and even that slips out of my grasp. Does he deserve the ordinary, mundane dignity of a human being? If it's possible for someone to lose that right, I believe he has lost it, and yet I can't quite convince myself that anyone can lose that right. Not anyone."

"He's not a good guy," I say as lightly as I can.

"He's not."

"And you *are* a good guy," I say.

I hear a little huff of laughter and then he says, "I'm the best man you know."

"You are," I tell him. "You're the best man I know."

"What do you think I ought to do?" he asks.

"I don't know," I say. "You'll do what your heart tells you is right."

"That's why I'm asking you," he whispers. And then he says

in a cracked voice, "A dog in the street. A stranger on the train, literally anyone, anyone else, I'd feel compassion for their suffering. Not pleasure."

"I know."

"You were right about the dark," Charles says. "I feel like you might be right next to me if I reach out my hand."

"I am right next to you. I'm right here."

We're silent for a long minute, long enough for me to have the unworthy thought, *The sooner he dies, the sooner Charles comes back.* But I don't say it. I'll never say it. I mean, "Yeah, do it, euthanize your dad so that you and I can date"? I almost laugh, it's so warped. Not even in the dark is that worth saying out loud.

"Would you do it?" he asks.

"I don't know," I say again. "I've never had someone in my life who treated me the way he's treated you and your family."

"What if it were your own father?"

"If my dad were dying painfully and he asked me to do it, I'd want to do it, as long as my mom agreed—though I'm sure she'd be the one to do it. But we love him. For both of us, it would be an act of love. You don't love your dad."

"I don't," he says, and then sighs heavily. "I think about ten years from now. I don't want to have done it with hate and anger. I know I'd regret that, I'd feel ashamed of it. If I do it, I want to do it with compassion. But . . ." He stops. When he speaks again, his voice is different, like he's talking through gritted teeth at first, and then gradually like he's snarling into the phone. "I'm not sure I *want* to have compassion for him. I might prefer to watch him struggle in agony. God, Annie, it feels *just*, it feels *fair*, to see him in pain, and it's easy to argue that letting nature take its own, unsparing time is the right thing to do, isn't it? Why not just . . . let him suffer? Not everyone gets a good death."

Silence. More silence. He asked me to listen and be calm, so that's what I do. I hear him take a deep breath and release it slowly.

He says, "Doesn't it disturb you, that part of me enjoys seeing my father in pain?"

"Nah," I say, like I'm turning down a drink. "Mostly it makes me want to hold you until you stop hurting."

"But you'd never feel this way."

"Are you kidding? When I think about how he's treated all of you, part of *me* wants to watch him die in pain, too," I contradict. "Part of me even wants you to do it with revenge in your heart, because fuck that douche bag for all the ways he hurt you and the people you love, right?"

"Right," he whispers with a dark chuckle. "Fuck that douche bag."

"But when I think about *you*, I know that if you did either of those things—if you watched him die slowly, knowing he wanted release and knowing you could give it, or if you ended it with revenge—you'd be left with a wound that would never, ever heal."

"I hadn't thought about it that way," he says.

A long silence, as we listen to each other breathe.

"Well," he says. "Er, I know we agreed on Mondays at seven, but it seems the parameters have changed a bit. Could we, er . . . ?"

"When do you want to talk again?"

". . . Is tomorrow too soon?"

"Tuesday at seven," I say.

"I wish I could just come home," he says.

"Aren't you home right now?"

"No." He sniffs. "You're my home."

I know that the way he and I communicate best is skin to skin, in silence, in the dark. I know, too, that I need the *words*, that there's something about putting it into language that makes it more than simply how he feels, that makes it an incantation or a promise or a prayer.

And I know that that's exactly what makes it so difficult for him. He understood all of this before I did. I only learned it after that naïve moment two years ago when I first blurted the words to him, just because I felt them and they were true. I thought it was just a feeling—and in a way it is. It's a statement of truth. "I love you."

But to say to someone, "I love you," is a different thing than simply feeling it without declaration.

I've learned since that day, two years ago. I've learned what his heart-twisting smile means. I've learned that I was right when I felt loved by him. I've learned that when he didn't say it, it was because the words would be like a curse, would make him run from me, or from what he feared in himself when he was with me.

I've learned.

I need the words . . . but I need *him*, more. Can I live without the words, so that I can live with him?

"You're my home, too," I tell him.

Chapter 32

The Bloody Tree

His oncologist is hilarious. We got on before we'd even met—I giggled my way through his notes, which treat my father with a facetious balance of condescension and obsequiousness. The fact that he's managed not to be sacked by my father, while not prescribing him drugs of abuse, tells me a great deal about his character.

When I greet him as "Dr. Dean," he replies, "God's balls, man, call me Stuart," and says he wants to talk about my research, which he'd been following for years. Obviously a man of great intelligence.

"He's had it up to here with surgeries and hospitals and chaps like me telling him what to do" is Stuart's summary of my father's state of mind. "He's an addict, as I'm sure you know—and I mean that in the general sense, not just that he smokes heavily and drinks heavily, but that he'll take pretty much any drug he can get his hands on, and he is very good at getting his hands on them—his heart failure is severe, his cancer is inoperable, his drug tolerance means there's only so much we can do to help his pain, and he feels he is losing his dignity. He's looking down a barrel, as far as he's concerned: a year or two of escalating pain and increasing dependence on machines and, worse, on other people, and there really is no way round that."

In short, he's a walking, talking cocktail of government drugs, medical drugs, narcissism, and disease. He's continued to drink, detoxing with every hospitalization and then taking it up as soon as he's discharged. And now he's drinking in combination with Stuart's prescriptions and, it turns out, additional benzos and narcotics he's wrangled from some hapless prescriber or hoarded from previous procedures—but mostly they can't touch his pain. Mum is worried that any morning she'll wake to find he's overdosed, and the only reassurance I might offer is that his capacity to metabolize the drugs probably outstrips the rate at which he can obtain them.

"If he has a skill," I acknowledge to Stuart, "it is that he brings out the ingenuity in other people—if only because they'll agree to anything that will get him to go away."

"Yerrrs," the doctor says with one raised eyebrow. "Whatever it takes to get him out of the office, you know. There is a certain, 'not my circus, not my monkey' attitude that many physicians will bring to a patient like Lord Belhaven."

"Alas," I sigh, "this is my circus, and that is my monkey."

It is very strange to sit with my father without any armor.

He uses all the same weapons—inappropriate stories and innuendo, belittlement and contempt for everyone but me, competition where there is no competition. I watch him cast his line . . . but I don't get hooked. When I do not retaliate, his first instinct is to escalate. Then, when I still don't play, an unexpected thing happens. He cracks open, just a bit.

"What's the matter with you?" he complains.

"What's the matter with me? Gosh." I scratch my ear and the corner of my bottom lip tugs down. "My father's dying slowly in hopeless pain. He's asked me to risk my medical license and also possibly my soul, so that he can have fewer months of that hopeless pain, which will grow steadily more and more unbearable. I left the woman I love, for the sake of that father—who, a year ago, called that woman a 'little bitch with no tits.' "

"Has she grown a rack since then?" He laughs silently, but it doesn't hide the pain in his face.

There is no cold, there is no rage that he can provoke in me. I don't need to imagine stabbing him in the heart or breaking his jaw, because he's already suffering. His body has shrunk by half. He is in visible pain all the time. In the arms race that is our relationship, I have laid down my weapons, only to find that he has taken them up and used them on himself.

Thus released from the rage, I can at last see that his nauseous misogyny is genuinely the best way he knows to connect with me—and I see, too, that he *wants* to connect with me.

But when I see his pain, I don't feel compassion. Instead, I remember the expression on my mother's face ten years ago when she told me that the baby she'd lost at twenty-two weeks was called Marianne, and he—this shrunken man in front of me— wouldn't allow a funeral.

I remember when I was six, watching him hitting her with the butt of his rifle, in the music room downstairs; I remember the way her body crumpled to the ground, unconscious. I was carrying Bits—she must have been just a few months old—because she had been crying. I turned and walked away as fast as I could, so that she wouldn't see Mum on the floor.

And I remember waking very early one morning when I was about five and wandering down to the kitchen in the London house. Mum was there in her dressing gown, putting quinoa in the slow cooker for breakfast. She was crying silently as she did it.

For thirty years, she has borne his contempt and his rage. For thirty years, he has inflicted it, physically and emotionally. I remember when I was angry with her for staying with him—wasn't it her own fault, if she wouldn't leave? And I remember the moment when I realized he would quite literally try to kill her if she left, and she knew we needed her, Bits and Simon and I. She had decided that staying was the safer choice, if she wanted her children to have their mother.

I'm the one who left. I left her here with him, to save myself. Well, I'm back now.

So as I sit with him, there is no cold and no hate—but there is the darker feeling, the satisfaction of seeing him suffer.

With another man, I would ask him to consider what made life worth living. Small pleasures. The love of his family. The opportunity to put things right. A time of spiritual engagement. Often, the last months of life are filled with profound beauty and humanity. End-of-life care is one of the most profound parts of my job, supporting families as they create meaning from their suffering.

I tried that with him yesterday. He told me not to be a stupid fucking cunt.

And so I remembered that not everyone finds meaning and forgiveness and beauty in death. Some people harness their approaching death and use it as a weapon against their families. Some collapse into hopeless despondence, disengaging from life even as they are still living. Some fight despairingly and feel they are failures when they realize that they too—like everything that ever has lived, like everything that ever will live—will die. And only rarely do cruel or critical people become less cruel or critical as they approach death. I've seen a grandmother, three days from death, greet her granddaughter with, "You're looking fat," and a grandfather, not twenty-four hours from death, revive a fifty-year-old conflict about money with his son.

"I won't be your instrument," I say now, without heat. "But if you want to go to Zurich, I'll help arrange it."

"That's *months*," he moans.

"And still shorter than your prognosis."

"This is not my life," he snarls, with exactly the expression I felt on my face when I fought with Annie. "This is not who I am. I don't want to live someone else's life."

"Are you considering harming yourself?" I ask. It's a standard question, but it strikes me as redundant, speaking with a man who is smoking and drinking his way through cancer and heart disease.

"Considering it? You think I haven't tried?"

"I beg your pardon?"

"Twice. Three times if you count trying to talk the quack into botching the whatsit."

"The gastroenterologist placing the stent?"

"She just smiled like I was a dotty old man and said it would ruin her record. Referred me for bloody psychiatric care, the bitch. Before that I tried pills. And then I tried drowning myself in the bloody sea, but . . . Aristotle says that drowning is a death where you can't distinguish between courage and cowardice."

I watch him as I try to absorb this. I imagine him waking up from a pill- and booze-induced coma, probably covered in his own vomit and feces. I imagine him walking, drunk, down the coast road, striding into the cold ocean, and the taste of seawater as he tries to contradict his body's native instinct to survive. I imagine him giving up. Walking back up the coast road and into the house, wet—without a towel, because he thought he wouldn't be coming back.

With anyone else, I would feel compassion. With him, I'm only relieved that these images don't cause me active pleasure. I understand them, without concern—a piece of news that doesn't interest me, a royal wedding, a celebrity baby . . . or a parade of statistics I'm already familiar with: two-thirds of those who harm themselves have no strong intent to die; the overwhelming majority of attempts do not end in the person's death.

It's all impersonal. Nothing to do with me.

"Have you spoken about this with Mum?"

"Your grandfather made it ambiguous. I can do at least that much."

For a moment I am knocked breathless by this—scattered, the way a flock of birds disperses when a gun fires. This is the first time anyone has acknowledged aloud that his death was any-thing other than an accident.

"What makes it important that it be ambiguous?" I dare to probe, tentatively hoping that he might want to spare Mum the horror of assisting him.

But he says, "I won't have my reputation tarnished by people saying I took the easy way out."

Never mind that he *is* looking for an easy way out. Get his boy, the doctor, to do it for him. The flock reassembles itself, and so does my awareness of where I am, and with whom, and why. Don't be a stupid fucking cunt.

"You could stop eating and drinking," I say.

"Have you seen people die that way?" he scoffs.

"A few," I acknowledge.

". . . What's it like?"

Three days later, I'm staring out a front window of the music room, thinking about this morning's conversation with my father, when I register the state of the tree.

"What's the matter with the bloody tree?" I ask Biz, who's curled up in a chair, reading with her chin on her knee.

"Some disease in the root system, Mum said. It looked exactly like that at Christmas."

"It's dead?" I turn to her in delighted surprise.

"As the dodo," she affirms.

"I've just had an idea," I say. "Don't go anywhere."

And I head for the shed.

When I get back to the front room, I show her my prize:

"An ax?" she says.

"Let's cut it down," I grin.

She just stares at me for a startled moment . . . then speed walks to the front door, saying, "Come on!"

I've never tried to cut down a tree before, and neither has Biz. We are crap at it. The blade seems either to bounce off the bark or get stuck in the trunk, so that we have to yank it out with a mighty heave. We have a lot of fun, but we only succeed in chopping a mess of scars into the bloody tree. Laughing and breathless in defeat, we leave the ax in the tree and go back inside.

I'm lying on the couch with my book and Biz is curled up in a chair with hers, and we only know of Simon's arrival when we hear him say from the door, "What you got there, then?"

Biz reads aloud, " 'It has been said,' " he began at length, withdrawing his eyes reluctantly from an unusually large insect upon the ceiling and addressing himself to the maiden, " 'that there are few situations in life that cannot be honorably settled, and without any loss of time, either by suicide, a bag of gold, or by thrusting a despised antagonist over the edge of a precipice on a dark night.' "

"Well, quite," Simon says affably.

And I read, " 'The courageous man then is he that endures or fears the right things and for the right purpose and in the right manner and at the right time.' "

Simon sits at the other end of the sofa and rolls his eyes. "What a nnnumpty."

"You're calling Aristotle a numpty?"

He quotes in a pompous voice, " 'For that which can foresee by the exercise of mind is by nature intended to be lord and master,' says the mmman who can foresee by e-exercise of mind, 'and that which can with its body give effect to such foresight is a subject, and by nature a slave.' Why on Earth are y-you reading Aristotle, brother mine? He is a *numpty*."

"We had a little problem with my bloody tree," I say obliquely.

"The ax wasn't sharp enough," Biz offers her diagnosis.

"You tried to cut it down?" he says. He turns and looks out the window.

"It's already dead," Biz protests. "We weren't hurting it."

"Come on." He's already putting on his sunglasses. He picks up his hat and gloves on the way out, and we all troop out to the tree. Simon puts his face very close the wound Biz and I inflicted on it and tsks at us.

"You have to g-go at it from an-an angle, not flat across, and you d-don't do it all on one side, you do one ssside and then the other."

"How do you know that?" Biz asks, incredulous.

"I know everything worth knowing about felling foes of all sorts." Then he takes the ax in both hands and moves to the side we haven't hacked at. "My depth p-perception, by contrast, is quite shhhocking, but we'll give it a go." He starts swinging, first with the blade angled down, then angled up, then down, and up, hacking an open wound into the tree. He's clumsy but effective.

"Let me try!" Biz says. He hands the ax over with a satisfied grin and Biz has a go, using the ax with more finesse this time.

She makes good progress, but tires readily. She holds out the ax to me, panting, "Go on."

I take it and have my go. I can't believe how much easier it is, not trying to go straight through. I chop until my shoulders burn, and then I pass the ax to Simon. He begins whacking at the other side, where Biz and I got it wrong. He opens up the wound, and we go around again several times, taking turns hacking our indirect way to the center of the tree, from both sides.

It's hard to believe it can still stand with so little holding it up, but it has to be nearly finished. Simon stops, breathing hard, and looks up at the bare branches, then he looks at us and holds out the ax.

"Who wants to bring it down?"

I step back and put my hands in my pockets. I want Biz to do it. So does she.

She takes the ax, looking serious, and starts whacking as hard as she can. She soon slows.

"It's really hard," she says.

"Help will always be given at Hogwarts to those who ask for it," I say.

"No," she says, wielding the ax. "I want to do it."

By the end, I can see the trembling exhaustion in her arms and shoulders, she's openly crying in frustration, and she's making high-pitched grunts with each swing. Even when she has to pause to breathe after each and every stroke, she does not stop. Simon and I watch her in awe. She does not look at us.

The tree stands on a thread of its trunk.

"I think," she pants, with her palm on the bark, looking up at the bare branches, "if we all just give it a push, it will go."

Simon and I step forward. We all put our hands on the trunk.

I say, "On three? One—"

"Two," says Simon.

"Three!" grunts Biz, and we push.

With a great cracking sound, it goes down. We watch it fall across the empty expanse of grass.

We stand there, the three of us, arms at our sides, eyes on the tree.

If Annie were here, she'd jump for joy—literally—and make noise and throw her arms around my neck. I don't know if I'd haul her over my shoulder and carry her home, or just hold her as close as I could until the blur in my eyes cleared and this tightness in my chest eased and I could breathe again.

I look at Simon and Biz. They're looking at the tree.

"Hey," I say, and they both look at me. With a cocky grin I say, "We did it. No more bloody tree."

And they both grin back. Biz's face is stained with sweat and tears and bits of wood. There are wood chips in her hair and her hands are red and blistered. Simon's sweating through his shirt.

"Let's drag it up to the shed and then sit in the kitchen," I say. "There's something I need to speak to you both about."

In the kitchen, I wash my hands and then instruct Biz to do the same.

"They hurt," she says, looking at her red palms. Several blisters have broken.

"That's why you have to wash them. Do it gently."

I get an ice pack out of the freezer, along with a bottle of vodka. I sit at the table with a tea towel.

"Come here."

I put her in the chair next to mine and, one at a time, I take her clean, wet hands in mine and dab them with a vodka-soaked corner of a tea towel, anywhere there's a blister or irritation. She winces and sucks in her breath.

"Left's a lot worse than the right," I say, holding them palm-up and looking at them consideringly. "But you'll mend. This will help with the hurt." I lay the ice pack, wrapped in the tea towel, over one of her hands, then sandwich her other hand over it, with my hands outside hers. "Just hold that for about ten minutes."

Her eyes on her hands, she says, "Doctor Scientist."

Simon is making a plate of something. He puts it on the table. Cheese and vegetables and olives and things.

I return the vodka to the freezer, then sit at the head of the table. "I suppose you're wondering why I've called you all here today," I begin.

And then I just tell them. "He's decided he's ready to die. He plans to stop eating and drinking."

Biz and Simon look at me, then at each other, then away.

There is a long, tense silence.

Biz speaks first.

"Well," she says, sounding impressed. "That is literally every single emotion at the same time."

Simon and I both laugh, the tension eased somewhat.

We sit in silence. I cross my knees and drape an arm over the back of my chair, content to wait as they process.

"Is it murder?" Biz asks. "If we don't stop him?"

"It's not illegal, if that's what you're asking," I say. "But that's not what you're asking, is it?"

She looks down and bites at her hangnails on her right hand, her left hand still holding the ice pack.

"You can ask any question," I tell her.

She says, "How long would it take?"

"Difficult to predict. Some weeks, probably."

"Won't he be unbearably hungry?"

"Bits," I say, and I wait until she meets my eyes. "How long does food appetite last once a person stops eating?"

Her chin tenses and her lips make a wobbly frown as she nods. "Not long."

"Leaving behind all the other hungers," Simon notes. "There's a reason fffasting is a spiritual practice."

Biz presses the back of her palm to her lips and a pair of tears slip down her face. "Won't it be awful?"

"Compared to what?" I say, then amend that: "We'll do all we can to make him comfortable, but he'll have to decide each day, each moment, to continue with it."

"What if he changes his mind?"

"Then we feed him."

"Giving up food and water I can imagine him doing," Simon says. "But booze and cigs?"

"We'll manage the alcohol detox with meds. He can smoke as long as wants, but he'll probably stop wanting to pretty early on."

There's another long silence, and at last Biz says, "But he's got at least a year. Doesn't he want to *do* something with it?"

"A year of pain and dependence and a life that he already can't recognize as his own? Of uncertainty about when or how it will end? He wants control, more than he wants that year."

She nods. We, all three of us, understand the craving for control. "And . . . what would he actually die of?"

"Unless he strokes out or has another heart attack or something else from the alcohol detox . . . dehydration, probably."

She laughs, a quiet sniff through her nose. "I had flu when I was little, maybe eleven, so I was lying in bed, miserable and ill and feeling sorry for myself. And he came up to my room that afternoon—I can't remember any other time that he came to my room like that—and he asked me if I had read *The Rime of the Ancient Mariner.* I said no, of course not, I was eleven, and he sat down, there in my room, and read it to me."

"Did he?" Simon asks, incredulous.

She nods at him.

"Mmme too. When I was eight."

They both look at me. I nod my head, eyebrows raised, remembering his voice as he read and the way he sat with the book in his lap, his glasses perched at the end of his nose. "I was maybe nine."

Biz presses a hand across her forehead and says, "I wrote a *paper* on it last year. 'Water, water, every where, /And all the boards did shrink; /Water, water, every where,/Nor any drop to drink.'" She rolls her eyes and sucks her teeth, mocking herself. "The water is a *symbol,* obviously."

Chapter 33

You'll Wear It

That night I tell Annie about the tree and *The Rime of the Ancient Mariner*. "And I realized . . . you remember the metaphor?"

"The—yes. I'm the sun," she says, "but also you're the sun."

"Yeah," I grin. "And Simon and Biz, they're the little birds—but they're not. They're grown-up people and they can take care of themselves. I'm not failing them now."

"But *you're* the little birds."

"Exactly. And I'm the dragon." In a choked whisper, I say, "He's not the dragon. He's just a miserable old man in terrible pain."

"Hey," she says in quiet celebration. "There's that compassion you were looking for."

"Yeah," I say. "And it's not just the cancer, it's the lifelong pain. It travels across generations, this kind of pain. He feels what his father felt, and his father before him. I don't know when it started, but I know that I can end it, because I had Mum, attuned to me and loving me. And . . . and I have you, Annie."

"Yeah, you do."

And then I say, "He wants to stop food and fluids."

She says, "How is that for you?" in a voice of such understanding that my chest expands and my eyelids drop.

"It feels . . . like I'm not selling my soul."

"No."

"And it feels like I won't be alone."

"You're not alone," she says.

"I've told him what it's like, I've explained what—" I press my lips together and wait until I can breathe again. "Anyway, that's how I'll be spending the next few weeks—unless he changes his mind, which he may do, if only to torment us all for as long as possible."

"Well, he is a douche bag," she says casually. "And you can complain to me every day, either way."

Every day. She'll be there every day.

He doesn't change his mind, he doesn't stop being a douche bag, and it takes most of a month.

The first ten days, we pull food and alcohol. This was only supposed to be a week, and the lack of food is no challenge for him, but he detoxes badly from the alcohol and his tolerance for the benzos means we have to keep him on an IV. Only when we can transition to topical, injection, and suppository pain meds and anxiolytics can we pull all fluids.

That's when the decline begins in earnest.

Once he's bedridden, Mum shares with the nurse the task of massaging lotion into his skin and moving his limbs to prevent sores. The nurse he merely sexually harasses with inappropriate comments, and she bears it with remarkable complaisance, reminding him that the morphine suppositories are also part of her duties. Mum, though, he actively belittles and criticizes. She bears it as she has always borne it: in silence and with a quiet, "Charles, dear," when she sees me.

He never looks up at Mum and sees her patience and beauty. He knows, surely, that he can't do this alone, but he never recognizes that we are helping him. There is no deathbed redemption—except that each day, at least twice a day, I ask if he'd like to continue, and each day, for as long as he's able to respond, he finds a new and profane way to say yes.

I talk to Annie every day, for at least a few minutes.

"Nothing is how I expected it to be," I tell her, trying to describe my disintegration on the plane. "I'm all rawness and vulnerability here. It'll take me ages to forgive him for failing to be the man he ought to have been, and yet there are moments now when it feels easy to be compassionate toward the man he is."

"He's doing his best," Annie says. "That doesn't make his best what you and your family deserved. But it was and is the best he can do. It's unjust to demand anything else from people."

"I hadn't thought about it that way."

"Really?" she says, surprised. "Because I learned that from you."

One morning past the three-week mark, he responds to my inquiry about continuing, most unusually, by saying my name. "Charles." His mouth is shiny with glycerin.

His muscles are weak, his coordination poor, but he brings his hands together and pulls the signet from his little finger—it comes easily from his shrunken hand. He holds it in his fist for a moment before he turns his fist and opens his palm.

"You'll wear it," he says. "It matters."

I take it from his papery hand. The gold is warm from his body, the engraved bezel worn to smoothness from two centuries' wear. I can't read the words, carved backward over the backward coat of arms, but I know what they say. *Par la souffrance, la vertu.*

I put it in my pocket.

"I've brought something," I say, brandishing *The Oxford Anthology of English Poetry.*

It takes approximately half an hour to read all of *The Rime of the Ancient Mariner* aloud.

That is the last day he's conscious. There follow five days of Mum and the nurse and me moisturizing his mouth, turning him and moving his limbs, and reading Coleridge and Aristotle to his unresponsive body.

Simon and Biz are downstairs, and Mum and I are sitting with him when he releases his last breath.

Chapter 34

Tender Shepherd

In the music room, Simon sits at the piano, noodling, while Biz lies on the couch, staring into the fireplace.

"He's got a theme song, you know, in my mind," Simon says quietly.

"Go on then," Biz invites.

Simon plays "Rage Over a Lost Penny," just as he did that night of the dinner with Charles.

Biz raises one eyebrow in appreciation. "Is he the only one who gets a theme song?"

"'Course not. Everyone's got one."

"What's Charles's?"

Simon plays "Brothers in Arms."

"That's quite sad, isn't it," Biz answers at the end, "that it's a war."

"Mum's isn't sad, though," and he plays "Mamma Mia."

"Too on the nose?" he asks with a grin.

"Never," Biz says, smiling. "And you? What's your theme song?"

Simon plays a disposable little novelty song from the sixties, Bonzo Dog Doo-Dah Band at their most bonkers. He toots like a horn as he plays.

Biz is giggling now. "All right, then, let's have it. What's mine?"

"Ah. Well, now. When you were at Downe House, it was this," and he begins playing the unmistakable thundering introduction to Boomtown Rats' "I Don't Like Mondays." She adds the claps.

"That's pretty bleak," she says, but she's wearing a cockeyed grin.

"After you got out of hospital, it changed."

"To what?"

And he begins the equally unmistakable, pensive introduction to the Tori Amos version of "I Don't Like Mondays."

As he plays, she begins to weep. By the end, she's sitting folded over, her face on her knees.

Very quietly, Simon plays the twenty-third psalm from *Chichester Psalms*. Gradually Biz sits up, her elbow on her knee, her cheek in her hand, crying softly now.

And then with one hand, rather slowly, he plays just the melody of a lullaby they had both memorized before they were four, the one from the *Peter Pan* record they had grown up listening to and acting out together. Silently, with just one little gasp as she blinks at the tears, Biz rises and walks to the piano. Simon slides down the bench to make room for her, and she sits beside him. She waits until he's played through the melody once and he's begun it a second time, and then, an octave up, she begins the second part of the round. Without missing a note, Simon switches to his left hand and moves to stand behind the bench. He continues the first part in his left hand, and with his right hand, an octave above Biz, he plays the third line.

They play through the round twice this way, with Simon embroidering with the left hand the second time through. He stands behind Biz, his arms on either side of her. And if either of them remembers a six-year-old boy, tall for his age and serious of temperament, sitting at the piano with his anxious, ginger-haired baby sister in his lap, to teach her this lullaby, or if either remembers an even younger boy standing over an infant's crib and singing to her softly as she cries, neither of them says so.

And when Simon finishes the third part with his right hand, he stands up straight and does a daring thing: He puts his hand on his sister's shoulder. She squeezes her eyes shut, her body shaking as it fights the tears. She swallows hard. Hesitatingly, she lifts her trembling hand and puts it over his.

Chapter 35

Who I Am Isn't Bad

"It's all right, isn't it?" she whispers. She's shaking.

"Yeah, Mum. Everything's all right." At the bottom of the stairs, I stop and put my arms around her thin, trembling shoulders. "You did everything. You were everything all of us needed."

I'm not sure Mum knows how to cry out loud anymore. When I step back, she's weeping silently and staring straight ahead, seeing nothing.

We find Biz and Simon in the kitchen, where he's made a plate of cheese and vegetables and things. Biz has a small plate in front of her, and she seems to have eaten something.

They both look up when we come in.

Mum sits delicately in the chair next to Biz, and I slump into the chair at the head of the table.

Silence. And then—

"I don't want to know anything," Biz bursts out, and she scrapes back her chair. After a glance at Simon, she takes her plate with her as she walks out.

We sit in silence. There's nothing I want to say to Simon that I can say in front of Mum. There's nothing I want to say to Mum that Simon needs to hear.

"You boys are both all right?" Mum asks.

"Sure, Mum," we both murmur, nodding.

"And is there anything I can help with?"

"No, Mum, it's fine."

"Well, I . . . I think I'll just go and lie down for an hour," Mum says. Simon and I both stand as she does, and she waves us away, "No, no. I'm all right. Just need to lie down. Charles, dear." She kisses my cheek.

And then there were two.

I rub my hand on my forehead as I sit down again.

Simon looks at me. "Ah-I'll do the rest. Mb-bureaucracy sssuits me."

"No, it doesn't," I frown.

"Lllet me do the rest," he says quietly. "Go talk to Annie."

I close my eyes for a few seconds. Thank god for Simon.

"Thanks," I say.

He stands as I do.

"Thanks," I say again, and I meet his eyes before I turn out of the kitchen.

I text Annie as I climb the stairs to my room.

Got time?

Give me 10 min

I lie on the bed, take off my glasses, and wait.

Six minutes later, my phone rings.

"Hey."

"Hey."

I don't say anything. There is nothing to say. But I know that she's with me as the grief pulls me under. I press a hand over my eyes and let it have me, even as a small part of me stands aside to observe. I watch it roll in and over me like a swollen tide. I breathe underwater. I feel Annie at a safe distance. I feel her confidence that I can withstand the storm. It takes a long time, wave after wave, each breaking rougher than the last, until gradually they soften and at last the storm passes into quiet.

After a long, peaceful silence, I say, "It's weird. He will never have been what a father should be. There is no hope that he will ever be what I wish he had been. What he should have been. But I wouldn't be who I am, if he hadn't been so wretched. And who I am isn't bad, eh?"

"Who you are is the best man I know," she says.

For the first time, there is a part of me that believes her.

"I wish I could have been there," she says.

"I'm glad you weren't," I say, my voice fried. "It was—I don't know how to tell you. In a way it was the most beautiful thing I've ever seen; it feels . . . he was so human. I don't know what to do with any of it. I'm glad you weren't here for it, Annie, I'm glad you weren't part of it." Then I suck in a painful breath and say in raw despair, "But god, oh god, I wish you were here now. Annie, I miss you so fucking much."

Chapter 36

Yes, My Lord

I call Margaret and try to explain, to ask for advice. I grip my hand in my hair and say, "What do I do?"

She repeats, "What do you do?" like I'm an idiot. "What do you *do?* You go to fucking England, woman, you get on a fucking plane and go to him!"

"But I'm staying still," I protest, even though every cell in my body is shouting *WHAT SHE SAID.* I've already worked it out in my head: The funeral is in two days, so if I get on a plane tomorrow night, I can be in Cornwall, I calculate, shortly after it ends. "I'm letting him come to me."

"Are you kidding? If Reshma—"

"That doesn't work, 'If it were me,' 'if it were so-and-so;' Charles is—"

"Oh, poodlepie. Oh, you insane straight girl. Listen to me: One, Momma Duck is desperately in love with you. Two, his dad just died. He just helped his dad die. Three, you are desperately in love with him. Four, *his dad just died.* Just *go.*"

I flop back on the bed. I want to go so badly, I don't trust the logic of it. "I'm staying still."

"All I can say is if you go there and he does anything but fall to his fucking knees, there is something irreversibly wrong with him. Think about that. Think about being in a relationship with somebody who, in their moment of deepest need, wishes you weren't there. Look, I'm totally the Charles in my relationship, right? I'm the one with the screwed-up family and the screwed-up fear of intimacy and all of the rest of it. If it were me, I'd tell Reshma to keep the hell away because I'd want to protect her from my family's insanity and I'd want to hide my pain from her because why would anyone love a person as wounded as me, and you know what she'd do? She'd come anyway. And I'd probably be mad at her at first, I'd probably push her away, and she would just stand there at my side, understanding and supportive and I'd be forced to realize that she really does love me no matter what. *No matter what*, Annie. Do you have any idea what that means to me? Is there anyone else in the world who has ever loved me no matter what?"

"There's me," I say.

"I know, but it's not the same. You know it's not the same. I love you, too, but it's not the same as the way Charles loves you. I need you, but not the way Charles needs you. He needs you, Annie. Just go."

Which is exactly what I needed to hear.

I ask my parents for the thousand dollars it costs to book tomorrow night's flight to London. I explain the situation and they agree that it's important that I be there if I can. I don't tell them that I haven't told Charles I'm coming—there's a risk he might tell me not to, and that's just . . . no. I get the address from him by saying my parents want to send flowers—which they really do.

The flight is the hard part, of course. Once I'm on the ground it's easy: A simple matter of three trains, a bus, and a one-mile walk, and then whiz-bang, a mere fifteen hours after I set out for Logan Airport, I find myself looking out at the Atlantic Ocean I just flew over.

The great ugly castle sits by itself at the top of a small, grassy hill overlooking that ocean. I can see it long before I get there—

the bus stop is at the edge of the town, so a few turns and there it is, at the edge of land. It's a hideous building, plopped rudely in the middle of a beautiful landscape. There are cars parked all around it, so I know the funeral crowd is still there.

As I approach the house, the sound and smell of the ocean fill my senses, and I watch the blue waves from across the grassy cliff. I'm bleary with travel and sleeplessness and longing for Charles.

When I'm within hail of the house, I pull out my phone and call him.

He answers on the first ring. "Hey, your timing is fantastic."

"Yeah?"

"Yeah, we've just moved to the house. I was about to call you. Wait a minute while I get away from people a bit. Okay. Hey."

"Hey," I grin into the phone. "Where are you?"

"Out on the terrace. There's no one about. I can't talk long, though—Mum looks as though she's about to drop and I want to make sure I can take over."

"How was it this morning?" I ask.

"Not too bad, the vicar's been a star. . . ."

As he talks, I walk along the side of the house. I poke my head around the corner and I see him, though he doesn't see me. He's leaning one shoulder against the stone wall of the house. Head down, his phone pressed to his ear, he is breathtaking in a black jacket that comes all the way down to his knees, its tails and his hair whipped by the sea-scented wind.

I climb the steps up the stone terrace and approach him quietly. I'm about to tell him to turn around when he says, "Annie, listen. I want to say something, and I want you to think carefully before you respond, okay?" he says into the phone, not moving.

"Okay," I say quietly. He's about fifteen feet away from me now. I set my bag silently on the stone flags and sneak up to him, closing the gap.

"I love you," he says. And he laughs. I can hear it in the phone and see it in his shoulders. My breath stops. My feet stop. He lifts his face to the sun and says, "That's all. God, Annie, I'm so in love with you."

I find my eyes drawn to the curve of his ear against his skull, where the pale light shines translucent. Sunlight catches on a gold ring on his little finger.

He's saying, "I watched Mum with Dad, and I imagined you sitting beside my hospital bed, or me sitting beside yours. Holding each other's hands. Medication decisions. Knowing what's coming. And then I imagined a future with you—not a hypothetical future, but a concrete future, with petty annoyances and arguments about laundry and the beautifully mundane details of a shared household. I've been a fool and a coward, domina. Forgive me for that. I love you."

I hang up my phone, taking another step forward.

"Annie?" he says into his phone. "You there?"

"I'm here," I say, as I take the last step and put my hand on his sleeve.

His head turns.

He opens his mouth but no words come.

And then he grabs me around the waist with both arms, pulls me off my feet, and holds me against him. My arms go around his neck.

"Is it okay that I'm here?" I ask, my voice constricted by his arms.

Still no words come. He just squeezes me and shakes his head once.

"I guess that means it's okay," I laugh.

He laughs too then, and his arms soften. He allows my body to slide down his until my feet touch the ground. He stuffs his phone in his pocket, then moves his hands to my face, cradles my face between his palms, searching my eyes with his. Then, pushing both his hands through my hair to the back of my head, he pulls me toward him and kisses me hard. I laugh again as he kisses me, and I feel a change in his kiss.

"Oh god, I'm undone," he says, half laughing, half groaning, his forehead against mine, eyes closed. "God, Annie." He puts his arms around my neck, tucks my head against his shoulder. My arms go around his waist, under his jacket. His breath shudders with emotion, laughing or crying, I don't know, and he rocks us back and forth. We stand there for long seconds—maybe minutes. Maybe days. I hold my body against his and just let him hold me until his breathing smooths and his arms stop trembling.

At last he releases me and steps back to look at my face. His eyes are red-rimmed. He looks so tired, but he's smiling. With a hand on my neck, he kisses my eyebrow. "Who else knows you're here?"

"Nobody, I literally just walked around the house."

"Walked? From where?"

"The bus stop."

"Good Christ, you took the bus?"

"I've been traveling since last night," I say, admitting, "I'm basically asleep right now."

"Right. Let's get you to bed." Then he grins at me sideways, "Not in the sexy way. Alas." He picks up my bag and puts a palm between my shoulders to guide me through the French windows into the house.

"Er . . ." He searches as he walks, until he spots a lady in a gray uniform that looks to me like hotel housekeeping. "Andrea, excellent. Could you take this to my room, please, just leave it anywhere?"

The lady takes my bag, with a curious glance at me, and says, "Yes, my lord."

"For the love of god," Charles mutters, rolling his eyes as she walks away. Then he says to me, "Come and say a quick hello and then have your kip. Mum!" He's leading me by the hand into what must be the front room of the house—the windows overlook the lawn, not the ocean. He brings me over to Carol, who's looking pale and shocked. I find myself wanting to take her pulse.

"Annie, my goodness!" she says, a tired smile finding its way to her face.

"Biz," Charles is calling. "Here's Annie. She's here!"

Biz and Simon come over. Simon is wearing a suit identical to Charles's, with gray pants and a black jacket that has only one button in front and goes down to his knees at the back. He doesn't say anything, just lets me hug him. Biz hugs me—hugs me! voluntarily!—and says, "I told him you'd come."

He leads me through the enormous entry hall to the stairs and up to his bedroom, about which I notice nothing, apart from the bed, whose more important feature is that it is a bed. I throw myself onto it with gusto and a groan of exhausted pleasure.

I feel Charles's weight on the bed near my feet, feel him tug my shoes off my feet. Then he crawls over my legs to lie beside me. I open my eyes to see him there in his vest and shirtsleeves. He says, "Come here." He wraps me up in his arms, my head on his shoulder, and I tuck my arm under his waist so I can hold him all the way. Horizontal at last, my body is swamped with fatigue and I feel sleep wrapping me up.

"I know it's not romantic, but I really am going to fall asleep," I mumble.

"And I really can't stay." He kisses the top of my head. "Later, though."

I grin against the soft wool of his vest. "How's your dragon?

"Rolling about in treasure like a puppy in a mud puddle."

"What's the treasure?"

"Can't you guess?" he says.

I shake my head. "Too sleepy to guess."

He just grins and kisses me on the cheek.

Chapter 37

Par la Souffrance, la Vertu

He wakes me up after two sleep cycles, by getting into the bed beside me and kissing my face sweetly.

"Hey," he says, smiling, and he kisses my mouth.

"Hey," I say.

"Guess what," he says.

"What?" I say, grinning sleepily.

"I love you."

My grin softens to a smile.

"Yay," I say. "But you know what?"

"What?"

"I love you, too."

Silly, childish exchange. His arms come around my waist and he rolls to his back, pulling me on top of him. He runs his hands over my body, not erotically, just feeling all of me. "I missed you," he murmurs. "How do poets do it? Just when I'm feeling all the most poem-y things, the entire English language vanishes from my brain and all I've got left are the most trivial ways of saying it. I love you. I missed you. I can't believe you're here. Thank you, my domina, my termagant, for flying across an ocean for me. I love you."

"I love you, too."

After he kisses me for a while, he says, "Come downstairs and see what Simon's doing."

"Okay."

I pull myself together a bit and he leads me downstairs and through to that front room, saying, "Most people have gone now. It's just the family, the vicar, and the solicitor now."

Charles leads me into a room full of books and heavy furniture and a big, pale piano, where everyone is gathered. We sit on the long leather sofa that has buttons all over it. Carol sits in a huge leather chair, with a cup of tea, and the priest, a vibrant forty-something woman with streaks of gray in her brown hair, sits on the arm of the same chair. The lawyer is eighty if he's a day. He calls Charles's father "his late lordship" and he calls Charles "Charles younger." As in, "Charles younger was telling me you're a medical student" and "It's down to Charles younger, what we do with it all."

"It all" is this giant, ugly house and the money and the stuff. Nobody wants anything but the money, it turns out, and the lawyer is worried about Charles trying to manage it all from America, which, he has made clear to them, is his plan. Or rather, his plan is to pay someone else to do it. The lawyer is directing his frazzled chatter at Simon, and Biz is talking over the lawyer, giving Simon affectionate shit about how slow he is, and all the while Simon is setting up an Apple TV on the television. This is the thing Simon is doing, that Charles brought me in to see.

At last he connects his MacBook and then searches for something on his hard drive.

Then Simon sits on Charles's other side on the couch and hits play, and everyone stops talking, their attention instantly tuned to the screen.

It's a video of a choral concert. I don't know anything about choral music, and I don't understand any of the words. It's impressive and intense and interesting, but what the hell do I know?

"*Chiiichester Psalms,*" Simon tells me over an instrumental section.

"It was pissing down with rain all that day," Biz says, sitting sideways on the other arm of Carol's chair. "He didn't come, because it was pissing down with rain."

"He didn't come because he couldn't be arsed," Charles says. "I came up from Cambridge, and he couldn't be bothered to leave the house."

There is a drumbeat and then a pause in the music, and the siblings' attention focuses sharply on the screen. Then I see a terrified little boy with white eyebrows and thick glasses, singing what sounds to me like a slow, high lullaby, to the accompaniment of a harp.

"It's Psssalm Twwwenty-three in Huh-hhhebrew," Simon says by way of explanation.

"Psalm Twenty-three?"

"The lord is my shepherd. I shall not want," Charles clarifies in a quiet voice, his eyes on the screen.

The music is heartbreaking. It's stunning. It brings tears to my eyes. When I glance at the others, Biz is weeping openly, her hand over her mouth and nose, as she watches her brother on the screen; Carol's lips are pursed primly, but tears are streaming steadily down her face; Simon's twisting his drink around and around in his hands. Charles's jaw is locked up tight and I see the tears unshed in his eyes.

And then the music changes suddenly, more aggressive, more percussive.

" 'Why do the nations rage,' sssing the b-basses," Simon translates for me.

Charles clears his throat and says, " 'He that sitteth in the heavens shall laugh, and the lord shall have them in derision.' "

"Well, quite," Simon editorializes.

And then the white-haired boy is back, with a trembling voice, but sweet and true, rising with the harp in a gentle celebration.

Simon translates for me, without stutter, as the white-haired boy sings in the video, " 'Surely goodness and mercy . . . shall follow me all the days of my life . . . and I will dwell in the house of the lord . . . forever.' "

The little boy in the video concludes the phrase with a confident blink. I recognize that expression: He nailed it, and he knows it. I laugh out loud at that, even with tears in my eyes.

"The treble part is called 'David' in the score. Do you know the story of David?" Charles asks me, over the music.

"As in, Goliath?"

"Charles," says Biz. She presses the back of her palm against her mouth and sniffs.

"Same David, different monster." He quotes, his eyes on the screen, " 'And it came to pass, when the evil spirit from God was upon Saul, that David took a harp, and played with his hand: so Saul was refreshed, and was well, and the evil spirit departed from him.' "

"B-but it was *puh*-per-pissing down with rain all day," Simon says. "And he d-didn't come."

I look at the three women as Biz slides into the chair with Carol and takes her mother's arm in hers. The vicar puts her hand on Carol's shoulder.

I look at the brothers, sitting on the couch with their knees crossed toward each other, staring at the video, pondering monsters and evil spirits and how they can be conquered. With a song. With a slingshot.

Elizabeth translates the next movement for me, not waiting for the words, but just reciting it like a poem. " 'Lord, my heart is not haughty, nor mine eyes lofty, neither do I exercise myself in great matters or in things too wonderful for me to understand.' "

And Simon translates the finale as the entire choir sings a cappella. " 'Behold how good and how pleasant it is, for brethren to dwell together in unity.' "

"Well, quite," adds Charles.

I reach for him, take his hand in mine. When he turns his face toward mine, he gives me a look of such love and happiness that my breath catches.

"Come outside with me," he says softly. "Will you?"

I nod and he leads me by the hand onto the terrace, and then down across the lawn to a path that leads onto the beach. Where the ground transitions from stones to sand, he stops and takes off his shoes—the patent leather dress shoes that go with his suit—and his socks, so I take off mine, too. Barefoot, in his shirtsleeves and vest, he takes my hand again and we walk to the center of the empty patch of sand. We stand side by side, hand in hand, in silence. I close my eyes and listen to the ocean. I lift my face to the breeze and the setting sun.

Charles says, " 'Yea though I walk through the valley of the shadow of death, I will fear no evil, for thou art with me.' "

I look at him. He's watching the waves as they crash in a slow, steady rhythm.

"*Par la souffrance, la vertu,*" he says at last, still without looking at me. The family motto. "Virtue through suffering." He clears his throat and says with a kind of wonder in his voice, "I think I may have worked out what it means."

"Yeah?"

"I think . . ." He pauses and swallows. "I think it's about the fact that healing hurts."

"Virtue through suffering," I repeat, considering. "Like . . . healing through suffering?"

"I can't stand it," Charles says with sudden vehemence, "when people talk about healing as if it's a peaceful experience, can you? Healing hurts. The only reason we bother with it is that the sole alternative is entropy, the degradation, bit by bit, of the body's integrity, until there is nothing to hold it together. We suffer so that we do not die. Only a living body can hurt, because only a living body can heal. It's only the dead ones that are really peaceful."

I nod, halfway getting it. Virtue through suffering, because to heal is to suffer.

"You remember the night you left Indiana? I asked you to hurt

me?" he says, eyes on the horizon, where the sun is nearly touching the ocean.

"Yeah."

"I think . . ." He sighs and his body softens a little beside
mine. "I think pleasures are transient—this, right now, you next
to me . . . this will be gone in all but memory tomorrow. But . . .
when you bruise my skin or bite me . . . I carry the marks for
days. I carry the pain for days. When you hurt me, I carry you
with me in my body in this physical way."

He turns his face and looks at me, finally. With his gaze holding mine, he says, "You were leaving. I wanted to keep you with
me. Pain was all I knew how to keep."

I nod.

We stand together and watch the ocean rolling onto the shore.
I think about that night and about the day that followed and
about the months without him, about how I felt a part of my
body had been torn from me, and how, at long last, it had healed.
How, when he came back, our hearts and our bodies fit together
in a new way. How we relearned each other. How the pleasure
was all the more intense for our having healed.

And I realize that until we have healed, pain is how we bear
loss in our bodies. Sometimes we mistake the pain for love, so we
hold on to it, we stay there in the darkness, in the valley. Or we
think that if it doesn't hurt, it isn't love.

But when we allow ourselves to move through it and out of
it . . . eventually we heal. And only when we experience the entire journey, through the suffering to wholeness, do we know the
full scope of love.

I rise onto my toes and kiss Charles on the cheek. "I love
you," I tell him.

"Annie."

His hand is shaking in mine.

All of him is shaking, I realize.

He says, "Sunset on a private beach is pretty boyfriendy, eh?"

I watch his hair ruffle in the breeze. "Yup, pretty boyfriendy."

He turns to face me. Then he drops to his knees, his golden head bowed.

"What—" I say.

"That's interesting," he says, half to himself. "I had wondered why it is men get down on their knees for this; it turns out it's because they can't actually stand up."

"What?" I say.

He looks up at me, holding both of my hands in both of his. "Marry me, my heart," he says in an unsteady voice. Just like that. Blunt, but clear.

"What," I say.

"Marry me." He brushes his thumb over mine as his eyes watch my face. "Please say yes."

"What?" I say. My heart is thrumming in my chest. I'm trembling as much as he is.

"Or not. Just let me stand beside you for the rest of our lives. That's all that matters, domina." His voice is shaking but his words are firm. "You're it for me, Annie. I love you."

"Are . . . are you sure?"

"Yes." The corners of his mouth won't stop going down. "I'm not ready, but I am absolutely sure. Remember the ducklings."

The ducklings, who jump out of the tree before they can fly, just because they can hear the ducks calling to them from the water.

"Yes," I say—in an unsteady voice. Just like that. Blunt, but clear.

He exhales hard and pulls me down to him, kisses me, and then kisses me more. Then he pulls away and, with hands on my face and his gaze holding mine, he says, "When I'm not afraid anymore, will you remind me, please, what a fool I was?"

"If I were half as brave as you, I'd consider myself a superhero," I answer softly. Then I laugh and say, "I mean, you know what you're taking on with me, right?"

"Oh yes, my termagant," he says, and he laughs, too, as he kisses across my cheeks and my jaw, murmuring, "Yes, my darling shrew, my beloved harpy. My heart." And he kisses my mouth, and I kiss him back. Then I pull away to see the love in his eyes . . . and then I kiss him again.

And then just once more.

And maybe one more.

And he laughs as he kisses me, and I laugh, too, until we can't even kiss anymore.

I kiss his cheek and whisper, "You're the best man I know."

"Well." He kisses my neck, then wraps his arm more tightly around me as he pulls me down into the sand with him. "I must be, to deserve you."

Charles and me, I'm pretty sure our hearts were built right from the start to fit together—not just to fit together, but to grow together, so that they adapt to each other, evolving, forming and reforming themselves with every beat. It's not that we won't have any more fights or any more hurts; it's that we'll always kiss the hurts better. We will learn and relearn, all our lives, how to love each other better.

How do we know—how can we *know*—that after a hurt, a heart will heal?

That's what hearts do, when you let them.

DON'T MISS

HOW NOT TO FALL

Emily Foster introduces a story of lust,
friendship, and other unpredictable experiments. . . .

Turn the page for an excerpt from *How Not to Fall*. . . .

Chapter 1

Go with Your Gut, Girl

My lips are dry and my heart is racing and he's not even here yet.

This guy. He's the postdoctoral fellow in my psychophysiology lab. Tall. Blond. English. A *rock climber*, for crying out loud. And he graduated from Cambridge University's MB/PhD program when he was only twenty-three. Translation for civilians: he's a *fucking genius*.

The man is a dreamboat. We're all kind of crazy for him, all us undergrads in the lab—even Margaret, and she's a lesbian. And I'm the craziest of us all. In fact, this is how crazy I've gotten: I've asked him to meet me for coffee.

The coffee isn't crazy. We've had coffee before, he and I, to talk through papers or data or research projects. And the dry lips and racing heart are nothing new either—pretty much every time I see him (or, in this case, fail to see him), I feel this way.

But . . . I *may* have slightly led him to believe I'm struggling with some data, and that's why I want to talk with him. (The data are fine. My senior thesis is practically done, and it has gone more smoothly than I ever expected.) In fact, what I'm going to tell him is—and see, I've got it all scripted in my head, so I don't screw it up—"Charles: you know this is my last semester in college, and then I'm leaving for grad school. I think you and I have

A Thing and so I would like to engage in a physical relationship with you before I leave Indiana. What do you say?"

This is as straightforward as it gets, right? I for one would love it if people approached me this unambiguously.

As I sit waiting for him, I consider including in my proposal a list of attributes I think make me a highly promising sex partner—the way you would in a cover letter for a job. Those attributes are, in descending order:

(1) My brain. An asset for every other complex task I've undertaken, and I see no reason why it won't come in handy for this one.
(2) My athleticism. I don't know exactly how this will help me either, but I'm sure I've heard the phrase "athletic sex," and I'm sure I would like to try some.
(3) My enthusiasm. I feel confident it's better to have sex with someone who's really, really glad to be there with you than with someone who isn't.
And possibly also (4), my unblinking willingness to look like an idiot in public.

Am I a beauty queen? I am not. My nose has a great deal of character. My hair has some interesting ideas about its place in the world. My body is built more along the lines of a wristwatch than an hourglass—flat yet bendy. It works for me—I am my body's biggest fangirl—but I recognize where it falls short of the culturally constructed ideal. Specifically, right around the place where my breasts aren't.

Still, having talked this through with Margaret, my labmate and roommate, we've concluded I should lead with my strengths.

I've just told you a slight lie. I said "we" concluded I should lead with my strengths. In fact, the conversation went more like this:

ME: I'm going to do it for real. I'm going to ask Charles to have sex with me.

MARGARET: *laughs uproariously.*

ME: *completely straight face.*

MARGARET: *abruptly stops laughing.* You're serious?

ME: As a hemorrhage. (NB: I didn't really say this. It's the kind of thing I *imagine* myself saying. I think I actually said something pithy, like, "Yes." Also, don't be fooled into thinking I actually know how to spell *hemorrhage.* That baby is all spell check.)

MARGARET: But why not just ask him on a *date?*

ME: I don't have time to date! I'm only here for three more months, and I've got a thesis to write!

MARGARET: *staring mutely, in stunned disbelief.* And . . . when are you going to do this?

ME: Right before spring break. I figure if it doesn't go well, we can avoid each other for two weeks and then come back and pretend it never happened.

MARGARET: Dude. What are you going to say?

ME: Dude, I have no fucking clue. (NB: This is word for word what I said.)

We tried Googling "how to ask a guy if he'd like to have sex with you," but we found little of value. There was a lot of "how to tell if he *likes* you," but I already know he likes me—he just thinks of me as his duckling. Professor Smith is the Poppa Duck, Charles is the Momma Duck, and all of us undergrads are the ducklings, quacking and waddling our way through the lab, with somewhere between a third and a half a clue what we're doing.

I did not attempt a search for "how to convince your academic Momma Duck that you're not a duckling after all—you're a sexytimes lady who wants sexytimes with him."

Margaret's conclusion, having thought it through, was that I should not say anything.

"I wouldn't do it," she said. "It'll be awkward."

"I'd rather be awkward than never try," I said. "I really think he and I have A Thing."

And she said, "But maybe trying will actually make it less likely to happen, you know?"

I didn't know. I don't know. All I know how to do is try and keep on trying until I succeed, and then I usually try some more until I get good at whatever it is. That's how it works, isn't it?

So here I am, complete with dry lips, racing heart, and a coffee going cold in front of me. Because I decided it's fine, either way. It's no big deal. If he says no, he says no. We finish the semester, we go our separate ways; no harm, no foul. It won't change anything. Whatever happens today, I'll still graduate in May, wrap up my dance classes, go to the World Congress on Psychophysiology conference, and then go home to New York City to accept free food and lodging from my parents for one blissful month.

And then I'm off to Boston, to begin what can only be described as the Harvard/MIT MD-PhD program.

(I know, right? I kind of impress me too.)

And nothing Charles might say or do will change any of that.

I just want to pause for a minute and say, for the record, I applied to the Harvard program basically *as a joke*. Like, doesn't everyone apply to Harvard? Isn't that just what you do? I applied for undergrad and didn't get in, but last year I was looking at graduate programs and I thought, *Do it*. It's not like you have to take a whole separate MCAT; it's just one extra program to apply to, one extra essay to write. And the program is *a-fucking-mazing*, which is why everyone applies. But nobody gets in. You get rejected by Harvard, you go wherever you're accepted, it's fine.

Besides which, I spent my entire life expecting to go to Columbia University for med school—apart from a few lost years when I thought I'd be a dancer, but let's not talk about that. My parents both got their medical degrees at Columbia. They met there. They fell in love there. I'm a Columbia baby. It was my destiny. Until I got the letter from Harvard.

It's an embarrassment of riches, I know, and I am genuinely

appreciative of all the opportunities I've had. It goes to show how little I have to lose right now. The day the letter came, I sat on my bed, surrounded by my various acceptance letters, and did the only thing I know to do under these circumstances: I Skyped my parents.

I pressed my palm into my forehead and told them, "It's Columbia . . . or Harvard. I don't know."

My dad was like, "You gotta make the choice that's right for you, Anniebellie." (My name is Annabelle. Dad calls me Anniebellie sometimes. He's been doing it since I was born. I have no expectation that he'll ever stop, no matter how often I roll my eyes at him.)

And Mom was like, "Go with your gut, girl."

In other words, they were no help. So I went for a run through Bryan Park, and when I got back to the apartment, all sweaty and panting, I Skyped them again.

"It's Harvard," I told them. And then for no apparent reason, I burst into tears.

My dad sighed and said, "We're so proud of you. But you know what?" And he stopped for a second and sniffed. "We'd be proud of you if you lived in the basement apartment and worked at Starbucks for the rest of your life, because *who you are* is what matters, and you are a kind, beautiful person, Anniebee. You deserve it."

This next part is embarrassing, but I want you to understand my state of mind. All I could say in that moment was, "Daddy," as I sobbed in the direction of my laptop.

And my mom said, "Oh, eHug, honey. Hugs on electrons." Which is the kind of thing she says. She's maybe a little awkward.

So I laughed through my sobs and said, "I love you too, Mom."

Right? I'm lucky. I'll need to grow up eventually, I know; one day when I have a tough decision to make, I'll have to call someone other than my parents. But you know what? That day isn't here yet, and I'm not in a hurry.

Anyway, that was last week. And now here I am, still in undergrad, still at Indiana University. And even though, just at the moment, the idea of living in my parents' basement and working at Starbucks is sounding pretty attractive, I know that in actual fact there are no consequences of rejection I can't cope with. I've been rejected plenty, and accepted plenty too, and I'll be fine.

And oh fuck. There he is.

Connect with U(s)

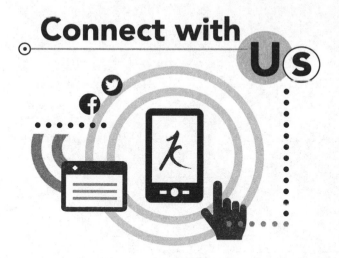

Visit us online at
KensingtonBooks.com
to read more from your favorite authors, see books
by series, view reading group guides, and more.

Join us on social media

for sneak peeks, chances to win books and prize packs,
and to share your thoughts with other readers.

facebook.com/kensingtonpublishing
twitter.com/kensingtonbooks

Tell us what you think!

To share your thoughts, submit a review,
or sign up for our eNewsletters, please visit:
KensingtonBooks.com/TellUs.